MICHAEL PRESCOTT

comes the dark

"A harrowing thriller of the first order."
—JEFFERY DEAVER

SIGNET

"With *Comes the Dark*, Michael Prescott delivers a harrowing thriller of the first order. His characters are flesh-and-blood real, the atmosphere's intense, and the plot races along unceasingly."—Jeffery Deaver, bestselling author of *The Coffin Dancer*

9 780451 192509

ISBN 0-451-19250-8

US $6.99 / CAN $8.99

50699

S EAN

INTO THE DARKNESS

Just inside the doorway Erica stopped, playing the yellow beam over the throne room in a widening series of slow spirals.

It was as she remembered it, the distant ceiling and the smooth floor and, carved like a high relief in the far wall, the limestone throne where she and Robert had taken turns seating themselves and playacting as monarchs of the underworld.

All the same, unchanged by time, except for one crucial, maddening addition.

A table stood in the center of the room. . . .

And there were straps.

One strap for the victim's feet; the other, to bind the arms.

A sudden awful thought made her dip the flashlight, splashing its glare on the floor, and she saw a tawny spatter of dried blood. . . .

This was not the throne room anymore, a place of childhood fantasy. This was a dungeon, a torture cell. . . .

COMES THE DARK

Michael Prescott

A SIGNET BOOK

SIGNET
Published by the Penguin Group
Penguin Putnam Inc., 375 Hudson Street,
New York, New York 10014, U.S.A.
Penguin Books Ltd, 27 Wrights Lane,
London W8 5TZ, England
Penguin Books Australia Ltd, Ringwood,
Victoria, Australia
Penguin Books Canada Ltd, 10 Alcorn Avenue,
Toronto, Ontario, Canada M4V 3B2
Penguin Books (N.Z.) Ltd, 182–190 Wairau Road,
Auckland 10, New Zealand

Penguin Books Ltd, Registered Offices:
Harmondsworth, Middlesex, England

First published by Signet, an imprint of Dutton NAL,
a member of Penguin Putnam Inc.

First Printing, February, 1999
10 9 8 7 6 5 4 3 2 1

ACKNOWLEDGMENTS

Many thanks to all the people who helped me in the writing and publishing of this novel, including Joseph Pittman, senior editor at Dutton NAL, whose detailed comments greatly improved the final draft; Michaela Hamilton, associate publisher, for her continuing support and feedback; Eben Weiss, editorial assistant, who provided helpful insights into the story and structure; Laurie Parkin, sales manager, who handled the difficult challenge of actually getting the book into the stores; Jane Dystel, my very capable and tenacious literary agent; and Seanna Beck, who reviewed the manuscript and offered many sensitive suggestions.

I found a number of books useful in fleshing out Robert Garrison's peculiar religion. Among the most valuable were two classics of historical scholarship, *The Greeks and the Irrational,* by E. R. Dodds, and *The Loom of History,* by Herbert J. Muller; two feminist interpretations of the ancient past, Riane Eisler's *The Chalice and the Blade,* and Marija Gimbutas's *The Goddesses and Gods of Old Europe;* the historical novels of Mary Renault, especially her highly entertaining *The King Must Die;* and, in a category by itself, Robert Graves's strange masterpiece of esoterica, *The White Goddess.*

Michael Prescott

The naked hulk alongside came,
And the twain were casting dice;
"The game is done! I've won! I've won!"
Quoth she, and whistles thrice.

The Sun's rim dips; the stars rush out:
At one stride comes the dark;
With far-heard whisper, o'er the sea,
Off shot the spectre-bark.

—Samuel Taylor Coleridge,
The Rime of the Ancient Mariner

PROLOGUE

Later, the children were what he would remember, not the bloodied bodies on the floor.

It had been a routine September night, chilly with a first taste of winter, and the black-and-white portable in the old Barrow P.D. station had been tuned to a baseball game out of Pittsburgh seventy miles away. Sixth inning, bases loaded, two out, batter with a full count, and the phone rang at the front desk.

"You're on duty, Claude," Paul Elder said from his swivel chair.

"Hell." Claude Wilke shambled over to take the call. "This had better be important."

The batter swung and missed, strike three, inning over, and above the disappointed hum of the crowd Wilke spoke up, a funny quaver in his throat.

"Lieutenant. You need to hear this."

That had been Paul Elder's rank then, in 1974, when he was fifty-two. Circumstances, not ambition, would carry him higher. He was content to be a patrol lieutenant in a small rural town.

Elder punched line one, lifted the phone, and heard a woman screaming.

In those days there was no instant trace on an incoming call. Elder had to coax the woman into coherent speech.

"Calm down, ma'am. It's all right. Just calm down." The TV went mute as somebody in the squad room dialed down the volume. "Calm down . . ."

She kept on screaming, or nearly screaming, her voice

breaking up like a weak radio signal. Through the clutter Elder could make out a single phrase, manically repeated: "It's *horrible*."

"Just tell me your name, ma'am."

He had to ask three times before she responded: "Mary Beth Squires."

Remotely familiar, but he couldn't place it. "Mary Beth, where are you calling from?"

"Great Hall."

Elder stiffened, and Wilke, listening on the desk phone, raised his head, eyes big.

Mary Beth Squires was calmer now, not screaming anymore, and though her breathing was fast and shallow she was able to form complete sentences.

"I'm the housekeeper here. I work for Lenore Garrison. She's dead. Lenore is dead. And Dr. Wyatt too—Keith Wyatt—her fiancé. They were supposed to be married next month. They're both dead. Mrs. Garrison and Dr. Wyatt, both of them, dead."

Wilke took over, keeping Mary Beth Squires on the line, while Lieutenant Elder led three patrol officers out the door.

Nineteen seventy-four was a bad year for Barrow and for the nation. A president had resigned in August, and the country still reeled, disoriented by his graceless fall. The ten-year deadlock in Vietnam had ended without victory. Many were dead, and few could explain what they had died for. People spoke of revolution. It was an edgy, harrowed time, dense with portents, Cassandras on street corners auguring the end.

These events had touched Barrow only glancingly. The larger world was mostly held at bay. Still, there was a strangeness lately, even here. It had begun with last year's tragedy, also at Great Hall. And now this.

Elder picked up two patrol units en route to the Garrison estate. By the time he reached the wrought-iron gate, he headed up a convoy.

Most of the mansion's windows were brightly lit. There were no unfamiliar vehicles in the driveway, and Elder found no sign of intrusion at the front door. The door, in fact, was locked, but because the police department did Mrs. Garrison the favor of checking up on her house whenever she was away, Elder had a spare key.

With guns drawn, he and five patrolmen entered the foyer, then paused on the threshold of the living room.

It had happened here, in the cavernous sweep of space that gave the estate its name. A fire blazed in the hearth, driving off the autumn chill. Its glow leaped and danced among the high rafters and the arrayed crystal chandeliers, and it cast a flickering sheen on two wide, ragged pools of blood.

The blood was visible only by its shine. In color it was indistinguishable from the royal purple of the carpet, dark and rich like a deep bruise. Elder spent a moment looking at the blood, bright as lacquer, settling slowly into the carpet's thick pile. Then he widened his focus to take in the two corpses in violent disarray.

They lay together—Lenore Garrison, chatelaine of Great Hall, and Dr. Wyatt, her fiancé. Where there had been elegance and refined conversation and staccato bursts of wit, now there was only a confusion of tangled limbs and blood-glazed hair. Lenore wore a nightgown and one slipper, the other lost like Cinderella's. It would be retrieved hours later, not by a handsome prince but by a bald, bespectacled evidence technician from the sheriff's department, who found it near the doorway to the library, ringed by a vivid spatter pattern of blood.

Keith wore absurd polyester slacks and a sweater. His feet were bare. Mary Beth Squires reported later that Keith liked to walk barefoot indoors even in cold weather. Somewhere, perhaps in medical school but more probably in one of the mimeographed counterculture magazines he liked to read, he had picked up the notion that shoes put an unnatural stress on the feet, stress that could lead to lower back pain as the body aged.

Aging, of course, was not a worry for him now.

Before that night, Lieutenant Paul Elder had seen only three homicides in his twenty-six-year tenure at Barrow P.D. One was a bank hold-up gone wrong, which had left a teller with a faceful of shotgun pellets. The other two were domestic quarrels. It was surprising, the things a woman could do with a kitchen knife when she got her back arched.

He sized up this one as a domestic quarrel also, but on a different order. No cutlery had been used here. Elder had done enough deer hunting to know a gunshot wound when he saw one, and so it was no surprise at all when the forensics team, gently disentangling the bodies, found a Colt .38 revolver locked in the death grip of Lenore Garrison's right hand.

By that time Elder had spoken with Mary Beth Squires after finding her in the kitchen, squatting on the floor with the telephone handset in her grip, oblivious to the long coiled cord twisting around her like a maypole ribbon.

Out for the evening, she'd returned at nine o'clock, letting herself in via the side door, which was used as a servant's entrance. The strange silence of the house had worried her. The place was rarely silent these days, she said. They fought all the time—Keith and Lenore—him criticizing her for drinking too much, and her telling him to shut up in front of the damn kids . . .

Then Mary Beth's face changed, and she looked at Elder in new horror and whispered, "Oh, God . . . the kids."

"My men are looking for them now," Elder said.

She started crying then, big noisy sobs that shook her large frame, and Elder just held her hand and asked no more questions.

Afterward the rest of her story came out. There wasn't much. Disturbed by the silence, Mary Beth had explored the house and found Lenore and Keith in the main hall. Panic had beaten her back into the kitchen, where she'd dialed Barrow P.D., reading the number off a list of emergency numbers chalked to a blackboard near the phone. The two kids had not crossed her mind at all.

They had been Elder's first concern, and he'd dispatched his men to conduct a search. For much too long a time the cops shouted for the children and got no answer.

Then from the second floor, at the rear of the house, a rookie named Blanchard yelled, "Found 'em!"

Elder mounted the grand staircase two steps at a time—he

could still do that in those years—and ran down a corridor to a back bedroom, joining the other cops.

In the far corner of a walk-in closet, huddled against hanging wardrobes and stacked cardboard cartons, were the two Garrison children, sister and brother, ages twelve and nine.

Like the pair downstairs they were wrapped tightly together, unmoving, silent. But these two were alive.

"I'll handle it," Elder said. He told Blanchard to go downstairs and wait for the damn ambulance, which still hadn't arrived. "Bring the medics up here fast."

As a very young man Paul Elder had seen action in the Pacific during the last furious months of the big war. He knew what shock looked like. The Garrison children had been badly traumatized, and the effects might be long lasting, even permanent.

He entered the closet, crouching to make himself smaller and less threatening. The overhead bulb was weak, and the looming wardrobes threw shadows everywhere. He advanced into the gloom.

"It's okay, you two. Nobody's gonna hurt you."

He expected no answer and got none.

The kids were in their p.j.'s. The girl's outfit was light blue, decorated in what looked like a floral pattern—carnations or something. Her baby brother had on a Superman suit, the stylized *S* standing out boldly in its dramatic triangular frame.

"Kids? You're all right now. Everything's all right."

The boy wouldn't look at him. His face was buried in his sister's arms. Perspiration soaked through his pajama top and pasted the fabric to his skin.

But his sister, at least, seemed to meet Elder's gaze. Her eyes were large, too large for her face, and she barely blinked. Yet she had not tuned out of reality altogether. He sensed an awareness, and something more: pain, harsh and raw like an open wound.

"Hey, little miss," Elder said with a lying smile that pained him, "it's okay."

She began to rock her baby brother.

"He shot her," the girl said in the toneless voice of a sleepwalker.

"It's okay. You don't need to talk about it."

"He shot her. Dr. Wyatt. Uncle Keith. He told us we should call him Uncle Keith."

Rocking the boy gently, gently in her arms.

"He shot her with a gun. Shot mommy with a gun. Shot her, and she screamed."

Elder hoped the girl hadn't actually seen it, hoped she'd only heard the shooting from a distance.

The girl fell silent. From outside rose an amplified wail. The ambulance, here at last.

Elder didn't think either child had sustained any physical injury, but he couldn't be sure. Tentatively he reached out to the girl.

"Are you hurt?" he asked, and touched her arm.

She flinched, and the rocking stopped.

Elder felt wetness, warmth.

Blood.

He saw it then—the red splatter soaked deep into her pajama top—the pattern he'd mistaken for a floral print.

And on Robert too, the same pattern, hard to see against the dark blue of the Superman suit.

Blood had doused them, gouts of blood. Not their own. Couldn't be. They couldn't have sustained such a blood loss and survived.

They had been in the same room with Lenore and Keith. And when the shooting started, they had been splashed with a hot red rain.

"Oh, kids," Elder whispered. "Oh, you poor damn kids."

"He would've shot us too," the girl whispered. "I know he would. But . . ."

Elder, remembering the .38 in Lenore's hand, supplied the rest of the thought. "She got the gun away from him."

A nod, the girl's eyes closing, remaining closed as if in sleep.

"She saved you," Elder said. "She loved you both. Don't forget that. It's something for you to hold on to. Your mother loved you both very, very much."

No response from either of them. Except one thing.

Down the boy's cheek ran a line of clear fluid, a single teardrop, glittering in the uncertain light.

* * *

The ambulance took them away, its siren crying in the night like a lost child, and Elder was left in the big old house with the patrol cops and the forensics crew and the bitter odor of blood.

"What is it with this place?" the crime-scene photographer wanted to know. "That business last year was bad enough. This is worse."

"People say it's the Garrisons," one of the cops said. "Too much money, too much power."

Somebody told him he was talking like a goddamned peacenik.

"I don't mean nothing political," he protested. "I mean it's, like, payback, you know. You got too much good luck, and you're due for some bad. Things gotta balance out."

"Those kids haven't had much luck," the photographer said. "What's balanced about their part of it?"

The cop shrugged, a fatalist. "Didn't say it was fair."

Another cop said he knew what folks in town would say. "They'll call it a curse, that's what."

Hoots greeted this prediction.

"I'm just telling you what folks'll say."

"So what's cursed?" asked a skeptic. "The house? Like, it's haunted? Or the whole Garrison clan?"

"Lenore's not a real Garrison," someone said. "She married into the family."

"Can you marry into a curse?" the photographer wondered, and there was laughter.

The cop who'd spoken of good luck and bad asked Elder for his opinion.

Elder stood at one of the high windows, his head raised to study the horned rim of the moon, its light clear and cold.

"I used to think there was a reason behind things," he said, and some quality of his tone drained the jocularity from the room and left it what it truly was, a place of death. "Used to believe if you could see what God sees, it'd all make sense. Now I don't know. Nothing's sensible these days."

But none of that was important. All this searching for some higher meaning, this philosophic disputation, was plainly irrelevant.

It was the children who counted. The children in their bloodied p.j.'s, with their pale shell-shocked faces.

Watching the moon, Elder wondered what would become of them, what kind of future they could expect. He couldn't guess. But one thing he knew.

Ill fortune, a jinx, blind chance—however anyone explained what had happened here tonight, those kids were the ones who would have to pay the price.

1

It was a myth, of course, merely a fairy tale, but a strangely beautiful one.

There was the queen, Leda, bathing in a pond when the amorous sky god Zeus visited her in the likeness of a swan. A grotesque union, the nude woman mounted by the huge, beaked, feathered thing, the bird's stiltlike legs entwined with hers, the long phallic curve of its neck lost in her tangled tresses.

An image bizarre and discomfiting, yet Erica Stafford found it oddly affecting also — a reminiscence perhaps of humanity's primal kinship with nature, a unity with things of shore and forest, lost now in the press and crush of the hurried world.

Or perhaps what moved her was simply the sculptor's skill that had brought the tableau to life as a polished bronze, eighteen inches high, on a ten-inch pedestal.

Whatever the reason, the piece exerted a compelling fascination. She'd sold nine copies so far, and this morning she would sell her tenth.

The sale would be easy. Erica knew her customer was hooked. He was a small round-faced man with round eyeglasses that made his round eyes look as tiny as ball bearings. He'd been circling her shop for twenty minutes, pecking with his gaze at every glittering bust and figurine, but returning, always returning, to the bronze Leda in the corner.

Erica had been fortunate to find the piece. It was the work of a talented young man in Naples whom she'd met on a recent tour of the Mediterranean. All his figures possessed a lightness, a streamlined grace.

In her poor, stumbling Italian she had told him so, and told him also that she owned a gallery in the United States. No doubt he pictured some elegant place on Fifth Avenue or Rodeo Drive, not two rooms in a converted warehouse in the partially renovated downtown district of Barrow, Pennsylvania, seventy miles from the nearest skyscraper.

She hadn't shattered his illusions. When he happily invited her to his workshop, she went along. He shaped and fired and cast his pieces in a shed at the rear of an apartment house on a twisting side street. The Leda had been there, the clay still wet and smudged with fingerprints. Even unfinished, it was unmistakably his best work yet, sensuous and strange, uncorrupted by cheap eroticism, a small masterpiece.

Her order of ten reproductions had been a huge sale for him. That night after dinner he had gently tried to cajole her back to his apartment, hoping to consummate the deal with a more intimate transaction. *I'm a married woman,* she said firmly, *and I'm too old for you.* He couldn't have been more than twenty-six, ten years her junior.

His declamations of her beauty and charm had moved her only to laughter, but it was laughter tinged with a dying note of sadness. When they parted, he took her hand and said she was not like most Americans he'd met.

Why is that? she asked, expecting another compliment, ready to find him safely amusing again.

Because, he said, *you have suffered. I see it. I see the deep hurt in you.*

Erica hadn't known how to answer, and so she'd said nothing at all.

"This is a marvelous piece," the small round man told her in the stillness of the shop.

She pressed her mind into active service in the here and now. "Isn't it? The artist is a young man in Italy who is, uh, unusually perceptive."

Her customer dared a look at the dangling price tag.

"Rather steep," he said, but only because he felt obligated to assert some control over the situation.

She smiled. "It's a limited edition. Only two hundred reproductions will be made. Each bronze is signed and dated by the
artist. I ordered ten. This is the last one."

"Selling like hot cakes, huh?"

"Maybe not quite that fast. I've been stocking them since
November. Now it's, what, March twenty-fifth? So roughly
two a month."

"I wouldn't have thought you'd get all that much business. I
mean, the store is very nice, but, well, rather out of the way. I'd
never have noticed it if I hadn't stopped off for a bite to eat."

"In the warmer months we do a fair business. People shopping for antiques, say. Winter's slow, but I get orders by mail."

"You've got a catalogue?" He sounded interested.

"Buy that piece, and you're guaranteed to be on my mailing
list."

The man gave in. "You can be persuasive, can't you?"

"I think you may have already persuaded yourself."

He put the purchase on his Visa Gold, and she boxed it for
him, her lean, strong arms showing tight lines of muscle as she
taped the carton lid.

"Run this place all by yourself, do you?" he asked.

"Just me. Five days a week."

"Sell a few more of these, and you can afford to hire an
assistant."

She merely shrugged, feeling no need to tell him that money
was not one of her concerns. The shop was for her soul, not her
purse. She loved the work for the sense of daily purpose it gave
her, and for the excuse to travel and explore and escape the
dangerous softness of her life into a larger world of risk.

After the man was gone and she was alone in the shop, she
resumed dusting and polishing her artworks. The clock read
one-fifteen. She had a lunch date with Rachel Kellerman at
one-thirty. Rachel was a gossip, a boor, assertively charming
in the most charmless way, but Erica had never acquired the
talent of forming close friendships. In her life she'd found no
soulmate, not even her husband.

She winced. Especially not her husband.

She polished harder, putting some angry muscle into the job.

It occurred to her that if she were as adept at choosing human companionship as she was in her aesthetic selections, she—

A noise.

Head tilted, she listened.

Softly, from the rear of the shop, a complaint of hinges.

She'd locked the back door, hadn't she?

Possibly not. When she'd arrived this morning, she'd been agitated, distracted. Things hadn't gone well at home. What Andrew had done to her . . . in the shower . . .

She pulled free of that spiral of thought. Andrew didn't matter now.

There was someone in her shop.

Either that, or the wind had pushed the back door ajar.

Outside, desultory traffic rattled past on Main. The blue sky gleamed, a limpid backdrop for the leafless trees and hunched brick buildings and the distant water tower.

It was one-twenty on a Wednesday afternoon in March, and she was in the center of town, surrounded by businesses and people. She couldn't be afraid.

Even so, she went to her office and found the sharp knife she used to cut packing tape before she entered the rear hall.

The door hung open, blue daylight limning the frame. The hall itself was in shadow, the side doorways dark. An intruder could be hiding in the storage room, the broom closet, the lavatory.

Erica paused on the threshold of the hall. "Hello? Who's there?"

The knife wavered in her hand. She asked herself if she had the nerve to use it.

Call the police—that was what she ought to do—but suppose it was only the wind, after all. She would look foolish.

Well . . . look foolish then. Play it safe.

She almost turned back. Instead, surprising herself with her courage, she took one forward step.

"Who's there?" she asked the stillness for a second time.

She stood directly alongside the storage room now. The door was shut. Did she dare open it?

There was no reason to take the risk. Except . . . she hated fear. Hated this numb paralysis, this frozen stasis between what-if and why-not. To be controlled by anything, by anyone, even by her own emotions—it felt shameful and weak and she couldn't stand it.

With a jerk of her left hand she threw open the door.

The storage room was cluttered with cartons, bubble-wrap, and unmailed catalogues, nothing more.

She tried the broom closet and the lavatory, finding nothing unusual, no bogeyman, no masked intruder.

So the wind really was the culprit, thank God.

Erica shut the outside door and locked it, then turned, and he was there.

A cry escaped her mouth, startling even to her.

For an instant the man was only a featureless shadowy form, tall and ragged and shaggy.

Then she knew him.

"Robert?" she breathed.

He came forward, a step, then another, until he was close and she could smell the mildew on his clothes. Distantly she understood that he'd hidden in her shop when she went into her office to get the knife, then had waited to sneak up from behind. Now she was trapped at the end of the hall against a locked door, a door she would never have time to open before he reached her.

But he wouldn't hurt her. Would he?

His eyes were gray like smoke, narrowed eyes in a windburned face that knew the sun too well. Through a nest of uncombed beard, his mouth was a bloodless line, and it barely moved as he said, "Damn you, bitch."

She drew back. The knife was still in her hand, but she knew she could never wound him.

Again: "Damn you."

"Robert. Why are you here? What did you—"

"Damn you, *call them off!*"

His sudden vehemence staggered her. She couldn't answer.

"Call them off!" He thrust his hands at her, fingers hooked into claws, and she was sure he would attack, go for her throat or her face, strangle or batter—but no, he sank his hands into the deep thicket of his own hair. "Call off your damned dogs, your bitches, send them away!"

Pain ravaged his face. In his eyes she saw bottomless anguish.

Against her own judgment, she instinctively reached out. "Robert, I want to help—"

"You want to kill me, slut. You want to drive me *insane*!"

But she knew he was already insane, had been insane for years.

"Now," he said between rough intakes of breath, "you listen to me. You call off your evil familiars, you make them stop, you cast them out. I can't stand it anymore, I can't, I *can't*!"

He pressed his hands to his ears, blocking out sounds only he could hear.

"You make them stop"—his voice plunged to a whisper—"or I won't be responsible. You understand me? I won't be held to blame for what they make me do."

Silence then, and she asked the question that hung between them. "To blame for what, Robert? What is it they make you do?"

Either he didn't hear or he wouldn't say. He merely brushed past her—reflexively she averted her face from the musky odor of old sweat—and in a burst of brilliance the door opened.

Blinking at daylight and at sudden tears, Erica watched him shamble down the steps into the rear alley. He was coatless, as if indifferent to the winter cold, and distantly she realized that she had not seen him wear a coat in years, no matter what the weather.

Past her parked Mercedes, his truck was visible, an aged Ford pickup, dented and dirtied, the tires nearly bald. He swung behind the wheel, and the engine started with a rattle and roar. The truck pulled away, trailing brown exhaust.

When it was gone, Erica shut the door and locked it and checked twice to be certain the lock was secure.

"God," she whispered. "Robert. Robert . . ."

Her muscles popped with tiny releases of pent-up strain. Erica walked back to the main room of the shop, then into her office to put the knife away. She was abnormally conscious of her every action, yet her mind was empty of thought. The inner monologues and dialogues of ordinary life had been silenced somehow, leaving a stillness, a sense of absence from herself.

Then the desk drawer slid shut, hiding the knife away, and a decision appeared in her mind, fully formed, without prelude.

I'll do it today. I'll do it right now.

She nodded, affirming her resolve, and collected her coat, gloves, and scarf from the office closet.

In the main room, locking the front door, she stopped abruptly and turned to look at herself in the mirror that occupied most of the gallery's far wall. What she saw was a tall woman of thirty-six, wearing boots and jeans and a striped oxford shirt with the sleeves rolled up. Her blonde hair was loose and full, and her eyes loomed big with fear at what she was about to do.

"You sure about this?" she inquired of the image in the mirror.

Her Doppelganger self considered the question, then answered with a nod.

She had to risk it. Had to know. After two months of doubt and worry—she had to *know*.

Erica threw on her coat and left the gallery at a run, forgetting even to switch off the lights.

The radio clipped to Ben Connor's belt crackled with occasional call signals, nothing serious. At this hour only two units were in the field, a pair of one-officer cars roving throughout the town limits of Barrow, Pennsylvania, population 7,321.

The town had been founded in colonial times and forgotten since. It was parked in the rural middle of the state, off Route 36, south of Interstate 80. Pittsburgh lay seventy miles to the southwest, Philadelphia about two hundred miles in the other direction. Right here, in this desolate spot, there was only rolling farmland, brown in the long winter, and woods and a few muddy lakes.

A far cry from Manhattan, Connor thought with a smile that touched his face but not his heart.

"Got any news?"

The question pulled him from his reverie. He looked across the table and nodded.

"Matter of fact," he said, "I do." A sense of the dramatic prompted him to take a bite of his turkey sandwich and wash it down with a swig of Pepsi before continuing. "Psychological profile came back from the FBI."

"Profile." His lunch companion snorted, as if Connor had

made allusion to a message from Mars. "You think any of that egghead yackety-yak is worth so much as a gob of spit?"

Connor smiled. "Your tax money at work, Chief."

"Don't call me that."

"Sorry."

"You're chief now, not me. You're the one man who answers to that title."

As always under these circumstances, Connor felt peculiarly chastened, like a child scolded for misbehaving. Well, the analogy wasn't too far wrong. He was forty-two, not a child by any means, but the man seated opposite him in a window booth of the Liberty Coffee Shop was nonetheless old enough to be his father.

Hell, at seventy-six—almost his grandfather.

"So what's this mumbo-jumbo amount to?" the older man asked with noticeable reluctance after Connor teased him with a short silence.

Ordinarily Connor would not have discussed details of a sensitive case in public. But no one could eavesdrop here, amid the bustle and clamor of busy people on the run, lunch orders given and hurriedly filled, trays clattering on Formica tabletops. Connor and his companion, ensconced in a corner, conversing quietly, were in no danger of being spied upon.

Not that the other customers wouldn't have liked to overhear. Connor caught more than his share of curious glances from other patrons. Twice he'd been pestered by folks stopping at the table for a casual hello that somehow segued into an inquiry about the Wilcott case. The questions had received his standard response: *We're working it hard; that's all I can tell you.*

He wondered how much longer that answer would suffice.

"They look at various factors," Connor said, dropping his voice just a bit. "The way she was taken. The way she died. The way the body was disposed of."

"From all that, they get inside a man's head and tell you who he is?"

"Not who he is. I wish they could. Just the sort of man we're dealing with."

"I can answer that. The evil sort."

"They try to narrow it down a little further."

"So tell it, will you?"

Connor could see he was intrigued despite his show of skepticism. No doubt this was the first FBI profile ever prepared for Barrow P.D. But then, the Wilcott case was the first such crime in the town's long memory.

Sherry Wilcott had been twenty years old, a limber, ash-blonde, pouty-faced thing who lived with her parents and excelled at getting fired from menial jobs. For fun she liked to thumb rides on Route 36, just to go places with strangers. It was not the safest pastime, and maybe it had gotten her killed. Or maybe not. Nobody knew just what had happened to Sherry.

All that was certain was that her parents last saw her on the evening of January 14. She had dinner, then went to her room to watch TV, but when her mom checked later she found the TV on and the room empty. Sherry was gone.

There were no signs of forced entry or a struggle. Her parents had heard nothing. Their first thought was that Sherry had left the house of her own volition, using the TV as a ruse. She'd done it before, sneaking out at night, and where she went and how she got there and what she did, neither her mom nor her dad could say or even wanted to know.

They figured she would show up in the morning, maybe hung over, maybe disheveled, and there would be a row, as always. But in the morning she was still gone, and as morning stretched into afternoon, her dad finally got scared enough to call the police.

The case was treated lightly at first, the assumption being that Sherry was a runaway, and after all the damn girl was over the age of eighteen. Still, it was odd that she hadn't packed a suitcase or even an overnight bag.

A week later, a retired utility linesman and his nine-year-old grandson were tramping alongside Barrow Creek with fishing poles on their shoulders when the boy stepped on something squishy and swollen, which was Sherry Wilcott's left hand.

Her nude body had washed up on the riverbank, facedown in the mud. Later it was determined that she had lain there for days while sun and insects worked her over. The autopsy was inconclusive in most respects: the multiple contusions and fractures could have been inflicted by her killer, either antemortem or postmortem, or by rocks in the streambed as the current rushed the corpse downriver. Signs of trauma in her genital area were consistent with both violent sexual assault and the sharp jaws of snapping turtles indigenous to Barrow Creek's oxbow lakes.

The only certainty was the cause of death. Sherry Wilcott's throat had been neatly sliced from one carotid artery to the other. No sharp rock or hungry turtle had done that. The fatal cut was the work of a knife.

This was, Connor had been told, the first homicide in Barrow County in five years. And the last one had been a stupid little crime, a dispute between neighbors that had turned deadly when one man fetched his shotgun. No mystery there. But Sherry Wilcott's death was unsolved, a who-done-it, and the locals, unaccustomed to any violence more serious than a bar fight, were both guiltily titillated and secretly scared.

Various theories had been advanced. Sherry was abducted from her room by an intruder who entered the house via an unlocked door. Sherry had sneaked out to go with some boyfriend, maybe one of those biker types she was sometimes seen with, who'd gotten high on meth or PCP and killed her in a crazy rage. Sherry had sneaked out and tried hitching into town, only to be picked up by the wrong man, perhaps some stranger just passing through, or somebody local—a psycho, anyway, who'd raped and killed her.

There was no end to the guessing game. In the first weeks after the body's discovery, everybody had spun a different scenario. The cops had their ideas, and the regular citizens had theirs, and the local paper printed all of them in one special edition after another. But the truth was, nobody knew a goddamned thing except that a young woman had disappeared and had turned up dead.

But now the experts at Quantico claimed to know more.

"All right," Connor said, leaning back slightly in the booth to convey an informal air. He'd found that people were less likely to eavesdrop if they imagined the conversation to be mundane. "First, her disappearance. Now she *could* have hitched a ride or gone out on her own, but you and I both know that's unlikely."

Unlikely because her purse had not been taken, and in the purse was her stash of birth control pills, which her friends swore she would never leave behind.

"If the killer gained access to the house, he either picked a lock or discovered an open door. In any case he was able to enter and explore the house, find the girl, and abduct her—all without making any noise. That would mean we're looking for a mature man, not a kid."

"How mature?"

"They estimate late twenties to late thirties."

"And they got that just because he walked on his tippie-toes?"

"That, and other reasons. What he did to her. It showed he was in control. You know about the ligatures."

Although it had been kept out of the press, Connor and his companion knew that Sherry had been bound at the wrists and ankles. The rope or straps had left deep bruises evident even after substantial decomposition had occurred.

"He tied her up," Connor said. "That means he felt he was in control of the situation. Calm, probably. Not frenzied, not flailing around, as you might expect from a teenager, say."

"Maybe he's killed before."

"They tell me it's possible."

"Then he might do it again."

"That's possible too."

The older man was silent, taking this in. Then he pushed back his plate, leaving his sandwich half eaten, and asked, "Any other pearls of wisdom from our friends in Virginia?"

"They could make a better guess if we knew whether or not she was tortured or raped. With what we've got, all they can say is that the neck wound is also consistent with a control-oriented personality. The way it was inflicted—one stroke, very deliberate, no hacking and slashing—is indicative of what they call an organized killer."

"Organized. Now there's one way to put it."

"He dumped the body where it wouldn't be found too soon. And he trusted the river to wash it clean. He's smart, they think. And he stripped off her clothes, took them or burned them. Could be another sign that he's smart, too smart to leave any evidence. Or it could indicate a fetish, some sick compulsion to hold on to her clothes as souvenirs."

"Souvenirs." The older man made a noise midway between a throat-clearing rasp and a bark of laughter. "This fellow's organized and collects souvenirs. Sounds like my Uncle Nate from long ago. Traveling salesman, kept his house neat as a pin, collected matchbooks from all the restaurants and hotels he visited. Organized, with souvenirs. No killer, though."

"Well," Connor said, "there is a little more. But it gets . . . speculative."

"Unlike the foregoing, eh?"

"*More* speculative. They think we're up against a loner. Someone with no intimate relationships. Lives alone, keeps to himself. An underachiever—above average in intelligence, but either unemployed or sporadically employed." He was nearly quoting from the profile, which he'd read just an hour earlier.

"What thin air did they pull that out of?"

"The way she was taken. He didn't pick her up, it looks like. He snuck in and snatched her. They say that shows a lack of social skills."

"Lack of social skills. They'll be grading his report card soon." But though his expression was sour, he didn't laugh, and Connor knew why.

"They say he could be the product of a broken home. Messy divorce when he was very young or . . . the loss of a parent. A thing like that can have a lasting effect on the ability to form intimate attachments."

Silence from across the table.

"Probably no women in his life, romantically, now or ever. He may have a distorted view of women in general. He may hate them or idealize them—or both, in some twisted way."

"How do they know that?" There was no irony in the question this time.

"The murder method. He killed her the way you'd kill a cow in a slaughterhouse. One knife stroke to open the neck. Now, it could mean that he saw the girl as no better than an animal, a dumb beast. Or the killing could be the opposite—a sort of ritual. So, you see? He could despise her, or almost worship her, or feel both ways at once."

"Like the way a child who's lost his mother might worship her memory—and hate her for leaving him."

Connor was startled by the insight. "You seem to know a little psychology yourself."

"Enough to see where this is leading. Where the finger of suspicion logically points."

Connor peeled the turkey off what was left of his sandwich and nibbled it, leaving the bread, which was dry.

When he was ready, he acknowledged the obvious. "The profile fits him. Yes. But it could fit other people."

"Not many locals."

"We don't know that the killer is local."

"We have no reason to assume he's not."

"Even so, we can't arrest a man without evidence. And a profile isn't evidence, just opinion. Speculation, as you said."

"But you do think it's him. Don't you, Chief?"

Connor had known the question was coming, but he had no ready evasion, so he decided on the straight truth.

"Yes," he said, "but I don't want it to be."

"Neither do I." Across the table, Paul Elder shook his gray head slowly. "I still see him as a boy, you know—a boy in Superman p.j.'s, his eyes so wide, his sister holding him tight. The Garrisons have been through enough. I don't want Robert to be guilty of this."

Connor had his private reasons for feeling the same way. "Maybe he isn't," he said without conviction.

Elder didn't hear. "It's not just for his sake. A thing like this would hurt *her* too. If he's arrested, she'll be dragged down by the gossip."

"There's gossip already."

"It would be worse."

"She can take it. She's strong."

Elder flicked a gaze at Connor. "Erica? Sure she's strong. She'd have to be, to survive what she and her baby brother went through. But there are some burdens even the strongest of us shouldn't be made to shoulder."

"It might not come to that. An arrest, I mean." Connor gave up his uneaten remnant of turkey and wiped his hand with a paper napkin. "We're not any closer to making an arrest than we were on the day when her body was found."

Elder's eyes gleamed with brief amusement. "May I quote you on that?"

"Oh, sure. That's just what I'd need. The town council would have you reinstalled as chief within an hour."

"I wouldn't take the job. Rather watch you suffer."

But Connor knew that Paul Elder, even at seventy-six, would gladly resume his old position, if he hadn't had matters at home that concerned him even more.

As it was, Elder kept his hand in the game. These lunchtime meetings, held once or twice a week, were of benefit to them both. Elder could keep up with events and learn unpublicized details of the investigation. Connor, the new kid in town, could learn the local lore and the lie of the land.

Besides, they liked each other. And there was that business which kept Elder at home. What he was enduring now was, in a way, not dissimilar from the hardship Connor had faced two years ago in New York.

Each of them knew about grief, about loss. Each of them knew how it felt to reach for a hand that wasn't there.

"Ben Connor—just the person I was hoping to find."

Connor looked up to see Rachel Kellerman leaning over him with an uncharacteristically forced smile.

"Rachel," he said, and Elder added, " 'Afternoon, Mrs. Kellerman."

She grimaced with operatic artificiality. "Twenty years he's known me, and I'm Mrs. Kellerman to him."

Connor smiled at that. Elder was known for his unbending formality, reflected in his upright bearing, his practiced courtesy, even the suits he wore, necktie and all, whenever he dined out. He was wearing one now, at a coffee shop crowded with people in denim pants and sweatshirts.

Then Connor remembered the first thing Rachel had said. "Why am I the one you're looking for?"

"Well, you aren't. Not exactly. Then again, you are. Good night"—a helpless giggle—"I'm all turned around. May I sit down?"

Elder stood. "Actually, I was just leaving. What do I owe you, Chief?"

Connor said he'd take care of it. He always did, and Elder always let him. It wasn't stinginess on Elder's part, Connor knew; medical bills were eating up the man's savings and his pension.

Elder said goodbye, and Rachel rushed out some words to the effect that she hoped he wasn't leaving on her account, a proposition Elder vehemently denied. Connor hid his amusement. He was well aware that Paul Elder could not abide phonies, gladhanders, hale-fellows-well-met of any variety and of either sex.

Then Elder was gone, and Rachel bustled into the leatherette bench opposite him, her purse swinging and her hands waving in a flurry of wasted motion. Connor knew her fairly well; everybody in town did. She was among Barrow's movers and shakers, if such a concept could be applicable here. Her husband, Leonard, was a big shot in real estate, and Rachel, as she rarely tired of explaining, was active in all the local charities.

Usually she was a nonstop torrent of gossip and chat, but not today. Even after seating herself she remained silent for a good half-minute.

"Something the matter?" Connor asked.

"Well, probably not. I mean, I can't imagine it's anything important. But I had a lunch date with Erica. Erica Stafford. And she stood me up."

Connor frowned. "So she's the person you'd most like to find."

"Well, yes. That's what I was getting at in my convoluted way. I know it seems trivial, missing lunch, but it's out of character for Erica. Of course *you* don't know her the way I do, but if you did, you'd know she's the most punctual and reliable person you'd ever want to meet."

"Maybe she got busy at the shop, and the appointment slipped her mind."

"Do you know, that was my first thought too. Trained minds think alike. Should I be a cop, you think? A detective like you?"

Connor wasn't a detective. He'd worked the patrol side his

whole life. In point of fact, Barrow P.D. had only a single plain-clothes detective on salary, who worked break-ins and rob-beries but never anything more serious. On the Sherry Wilcott case, detectives from the sheriff's department and the state po-lice were handling the major investigative duties, while Con-nor's patrol officers backed them up with legwork.

Even so, he didn't contradict her. "You'd make a first-class gumshoe," he answered easily. "Better than some of the layabouts I knew in New York. Did you call the shop?"

"Called twice. The machine answered. And she always picks up the phone when she's there. Doesn't want to lose any busi-ness, you know. God forbid somebody calls all hot to trot for some statue of Venus being raped by a centaur, or whatever it is, and she misses out. She's a dynamo, really. My Leonard says if he had a couple of brokers as hard driven as Erica Staf-ford, he could move every property on his sheet in a week."

Connor began to realize Rachel was upset. The woman was a talker, yes, but ordinarily her conversational efforts were considerably more polished than this loose associative stream.

"Rachel," he said gently, slipping into the calm tone he'd used with traumatized victims and witnesses in New York, "did you go over to the shop?"

The tone worked. She visibly got hold of herself. "Yes. I went. Rang the bell. No answer. The door was locked, but the lights were on. Then I called the house."

A small part of her anxiety was transferring itself, as by os-mosis, to Connor himself. He felt his heart beating faster.

"The house?" he prompted.

Nod. "Got the housekeeper, what's her name, Marie. She said Erica left for work as usual. Andrew's at the racquet club. Hadn't heard from either of them. So I didn't know what to do. Then I saw your car parked outside, and I thought . . . well . . . I thought you might know where she is."

"How would I?"

Briefly she hesitated, and then her face worked itself into a weak, helpless smile. "You're the police chief, aren't you?"

Connor wasn't entirely satisfied with this answer, but he let it pass. "What time was your lunch date?"

"One-thirty."

"Where?"

"The New Hope Inn."

"Any chance you might have left too soon, and just missed her? She might be there now."

"I'm not an idiot, Ben."

"I didn't say—"

"Look, I waited there until two-fifteen, for Christ's sake."

"Okay, okay." He checked his watch. The time was 2:28. "When you went to her shop, did you go out back to see if her car was there?"

She looked sheepish. "Never occurred to me. I guess I'm not cut out to be a detective after all."

"Well, neither am I. Failed the damn test twice." He got up and dumped some bills on the table. "Tell you what. I'll see if her car's there. Maybe talk to the proprietors of the other stores."

"I can come too."

"I think it's better for me to go alone."

Rachel stared up at him. "You . . . you don't suppose there's anything really wrong, do you?"

"I wouldn't worry about it," Connor answered smoothly, though he'd been a cop long enough to know the full range of possible tragedies attendant on an unanswered telephone. And in this town, a report of a missing woman was not to be taken lightly.

The thought quickened Connor's stride as he headed away from the table. Rachel's voice stopped him. "Oh, Ben. One more thing."

He turned, concealing his impatience. "Yes?"

"I ran into her brother. He hasn't seen her, either."

"You saw Robert? I thought he never came to town."

Rachel answered with a fluttery shrug. "He goes to Waldman's Grocery about once a month. To stock up on supplies. I happened to see him in the parking lot. That truck of his"—her nose wrinkled—"well, it does stand out."

"And you say he hasn't seen Erica today?"

"No. I only mention it because, well, he's so peculiar, you know. With Erica missing . . . and with all the talk about the Wilcott girl . . ."

She didn't have to finish. Connor understood the implication. If Erica really had disappeared, Robert Garrison would be the obvious suspect. But not if he had an alibi.

"Was he just arriving at the store?" Connor asked.

"Just leaving. Loading grocery sacks into his truck. Judging from the amount of stuff he bought, I'd say he was in Waldman's for at least an hour."

"What time was this?"

Another shrug. "Ten minutes ago. Two-twenty, maybe."

Then Robert probably could account for his whereabouts from roughly 1:15 to 2:20. Connor nodded, started to move away again, then remembered to ask one more question.

"How did he react?"

Concentration pinched Rachel's face. "You know, he seemed quite upset. Agitated, all of a sudden. Like it really bothered him that Erica would run off somewhere." She spread her hands. "I didn't think the two of them were all that close."

"She's his sister," Connor said. "It's natural for him to be worried."

"Guess he must be. You should have seen him, fidgeting and blinking. And he sure took off in a hurry. He left behind a sack of groceries. I called to him, but he didn't turn back. If you'd seen him, you would've flagged him down for a speeding ticket. He shot down Main Street like a bat out of hell."

2

Three miles out of town Erica turned off Route 36 and headed down the rutted dirt track of an old fire road, deep into the woods.

It was along here somewhere. She was sure of it.

Her gaze ticked to the rearview mirror, irrationally scanning the flicker of sunlight and shadow for a glimpse of pursuit. There was no way he could be after her, no way he could guess she would come here.

After all, nobody ever came here. The road was long abandoned, this section of woods an uninviting wilderness, with no nearby lakes or parks or high hills to tempt a visitor. Hunters might pass through, tracking deer; that was all.

In summer the trees would be full and green, but now they were ranks of skeletons, the branches raw and leafless, white as pickets in the thin March air.

Erica shivered. The heater was on, pumping hard, both vents canted in her direction, but there was a settled chill in her that would not dissipate.

She had not been so scared since childhood, had never imagined being this scared again.

The padded steering wheel turned under her gloved hands, following a curve in the track. Sun rays like icicles pierced her through a gap in the trees.

In an odd way she was outside herself. She saw Erica Stafford at the wheel, her face in profile, blonde hair swept back. High forehead, sharp cheekbones, proud jaw, her smooth skin windburnt and, near the eyes, dusted with pinpoint freckles. She saw the red scarf at her neck, the ermine-collar coat, the leather hand-bag on the passenger seat.

A woman in a white Mercedes sedan, stylishly attired, driving too fast down a dirt road to nowhere, through a Pennsylvania wood.

"What's wrong with this picture?" she said, then started, her own voice frightening her like a stranger's touch.

The jolt of fear released a laugh, and she calmed slightly.

But her eyes kept darting toward the mirror as she looked for a vehicle behind her. A truck . . . a blue pickup . . .

Then she took another curve, and by the roadside, to her left, a white oak swung into view. A hunched, splintered thing, mis-shapen and forked, the heavy branches sprawling lamely on the ground. A lightning strike had bisected it in 1970, and in the years since, decay had done its ugly work, rot hollowing out the tree and snapping the dry boughs. A gray paste of moss coated the trunk, reminding her of aged bronze.

The oak had changed with time. Even so, it was instantly recognizable as the landmark she remembered.

She braked the Mercedes. Dirt flew up from the rear tires, a slow-motion ripple white as flour in the pallid daylight.

Out of the car, into the bracing cold. It was forty degrees to-day, chillier with the wind factor, and chillier still in the bristling shadows of the sycamores and elms. Each breath was an ashen plumage, her scarf unwinding in stiff gusts.

From her purse she took the one item she needed, a tube of lipstick, then tossed the handbag on the driver's seat. She left the car unlocked, the key in the ignition. Somehow it seemed wise to prepare for a quick getaway.

The door swung shut with a heavy thud, shocking as a gun-shot. The noise made her abruptly conscious of the forest's si-lence and her isolation. She was far from town, miles outside city limits. No houses here, no phones—and she had stubbornly declined to install a cell phone in the Mercedes. The stillness was broken only by the wind, blowing in cold gusts, and a dis-tant thrum of traffic on Route 36, which paralleled the fire road. The knowledge that strangers were hurtling past this sec-tion of woods, just a half mile away yet utterly cut off from her, only made her feel more alone.

Alone, and beyond the reach of help.

She couldn't believe she was finally doing this. For two months she'd hesitated, afraid to take action. Two months since Sherry Wilcott washed up on a creek bank below Barrow Falls, her life taken by the blade of a knife.

She remembered reading the story in the Barrow *Register* at breakfast with Andrew in the sunroom. Amid the January sunbeams piercing the French doors, the caws of crows in the bare branches outside, she had heard a voice—her own voice—whisper a grim suspicion in her mind: *It could be him.*

Robert was insane. Everyone in town knew it, though euphemisms like *eccentric* and *peculiar* were commonly preferred to the stark truth. Perhaps some of the others believed he was merely a harmless oddball, wealthy enough—with his half of the Garrison fortune—to indulge in whatever unconventional lifestyle he pleased.

Erica knew better. She'd visited him often enough, listened to him talk. His was a mind that had spent too long in conversation with itself, until it had evolved a new language and a new way of thinking, nonlinear, phantasmagoric, metaphorical, perverse.

Her brother was probably a genius of a sort. But a deeply ill genius, whose point of intersection with reality lay on some other plane.

And he was capable of violence. Yes.

On her last visit to him, a year ago—her last attempt to reestablish contact—he had raged at her and finally had lashed out, wielding a knife that had appeared in his hand out of nowhere like a magician's prop. She'd escaped, fleeing without dignity, collapsing in tears when she was safe in her car. She had told no one except Andrew. And she had never gone back.

Sherry Wilcott had been killed with a knife. The newspaper had said so.

Had Robert murdered her? Erica didn't know. But it was possible. And the mere possibility had stalked her, remorseless in its tenacity, for two long restless months.

Today's confrontation had finally forced the issue. She could evade her own suspicions no longer.

I won't be responsible, he'd said. *I won't be held to blame for what they make me do.*

He was her brother, but some loyalties ran deeper than blood. And if he was the killer—*if*—then she would turn him in and face the consequences for both of them.

She left the fire road. Standing before the oak, she scanned the bark until she found two sets of initials scored in the tree. Inscribed so deeply that even after more than two decades, moss had not entirely filled them in.

E.G.

R.G.

Erica Garrison and Robert Garrison. Sister and brother, joined forever in the notched skin of the oak.

Erica trembled as raw emotion, too painful to identify, briefly squeezed her heart.

Please, she thought, please let this be a fool's errand, only a stupid and terrible delusion.

The alternative would be a hurt so deep that, like the carving in the tree, no passage of time would ever heal the wound.

Then with an unsteady hand she groped inside the hollow of the oak. She prayed that it was empty. It was not.

From the hollow she withdrew a soiled canvas bag, knotted shut. Her shaking fingers solved the puzzle of the knot, and the bag opened, revealing its contents.

A short coil of rope, knotted every few inches. A mallet. A package of metal stakes. And a big Eveready flash.

She tested the flashlight. Its beam wavered, a faint yellow cone in the shadows.

The rope, mallet, and stakes dated back decades, but the flash was new, and the batteries must have been recently installed.

So Robert did still come here, as she'd feared.

And perhaps on a night two months ago, he'd brought the Wilcott girl.

"No, Robert," she whispered, as her eyesight blurred, the notched initials shimmering like an uncertain memory. "No, you didn't do that. You couldn't."

But she knew he could.

Erica threw a last glance at the fire road, reassuring herself there was still no pursuit, then hurried into the woods.

The scarf beat against her face, a frayed, slapping hand, as she ran along a woodland path untaken since childhood.

No snow lay on the ground, and no ice, but the forest floor was stiff with winter rigor. Her boots crunched. They were designer boots, retanned and oiled leather with brass buckles, made for carpeted foyers and shoveled walkways, and she supposed they were all wrong here.

When selecting an outfit this morning, she had not expected to be outdoors for more than a minute or two. Her fur-collar coat was warm enough, but under it she had on just the lightweight cotton shirt and the beltless tapered-leg blue jeans.

Erica, she thought with a wry twist of her mouth, you simply are not dressed for this at all.

She threaded among pines and hemlocks, letting instinct and memory guide her, and then ahead she saw a low rocky slope rising like the gray back of a whale.

One end of the rope, trailing from the coil, nearly tripped her as she ran into the clearing. She knelt and dumped the sack beside a confusion of boulders, then searched among the rocks until she found the hole.

An opening in the hill's limestone face, the mouth of a narrow shaft that plunged down into the dark, just as she remembered.

The sinkhole was a secret known to her and Robert alone. She hadn't seen it in twenty-four years.

But when they were children, they'd visited here often, sometimes every day in summer. The rope and other gear, which they'd taken from the attic at Great Hall and never replaced, would be waiting in the oak tree's hidden niche.

They would climb down into an alien underworld, where adults never ventured because none of them knew the way in.

The Barrow Caves.

Once, there had been a main entrance to the caves, but in 1922 a rockslide sealed the cave mouth forever. In time, memories faded, and the caves took on a half-legendary quality. Today they were rarely thought of at all. Their very existence was scarcely remembered.

Erica and Robert had found the sinkhole by accident. They'd ridden their bicycles far into the woods on the fire road, then dismounted to go exploring on foot. At some point they'd split up, and Erica, entranced by springtime blooms of daffodils, had wandered well away from the road. Where the flowers ended, she'd glimpsed the cleft in the rock that led below.

Without ever discusing it, she and Robert had agreed that this place was theirs and theirs only.

If her brother had murdered Sherry Wilcott, then he had done it here, in secrecy and utter solitude. If evidence was to be found, the caves were the place to look.

Briskly, Erica spilled the contents of the sack onto the rocky ground, then picked up the mallet and a stake.

There were no trees within reach, nothing to serve as an anchor for the rope. To secure the line, she must hammer a stake into place near the lip of the hole.

She searched for a patch of soil amid the rocks, located a hard sandy square, and gouged it with the stake's steel point. Holding the stake with one hand, she swung the mallet down. Three blows, four. Thuds of impact burst like muted rifle shots.

She stopped pounding when she saw that the stake had bent in the middle, having made no downward progress. As children, she and Robert had come here only in warm weather. Now the soil was frozen, and she lacked the strength to drive the stake home.

So she couldn't do this after all. She'd have to give up. Leave.

The relief she felt shamed her into a second effort. Erica Stafford was not the type to make excuses.

She shook another stake free of the package, groped for looser soil, then held the stake rigidly upright in her left hand and attacked it with the mallet.

The wind kicked up, thrusting her scarf into her face again, blinding her. She tore it off with a curse. Caught by the wind, it fluttered away into the woods, a red streamer, incongruously festive. Gone.

"Hell," she whispered, "I never liked it anyway." Though in fact it had been her favorite, a gift from Andrew on their first Christmas together, in the best days of their marriage.

Frustration and anger and fear combined to make her strong, and suddenly she was hammering the stake with furious abandon, slamming it into the ground until it had sunk to the eyelet.

Done. She felt a savage vindication.

Next, the rope. A fifteen-foot coil knotted at eight-inch intervals. Her fumbling hands threaded it through the eyelet, secured it with a triple knot. She tested the knot to be sure it would take her weight without unraveling.

Crouching, she tossed the rope down the sinkhole. It uncoiled like a snake and vanished in the dark.

The flashlight, snapping on, sent a long tongue of light into the well. She saw the rope's end dangling at the bottom, casting a curled shadow on the chalky floor. An image from her childhood—yet she felt no sense of adventure now, no carefree exhilaration.

No one knew she was here. If the rope should break, trapping her below . . .

Or if Robert happened to come by while she was searching . . .

Or, perhaps worst of all, if she simply found the evidence that would mark Robert as Sherry Wilcott's killer and send him to prison or an asylum for the rest of his tortured life . . .

Squatting on her haunches, huddled against the cold, Erica allowed herself to consider, for the last time, the possibility of turning back. Then she remembered the bronze Persephone.

It stood on a wharf in a small Greek fishing village—a statue of the goddess, Demeter's child. Later she had been told it was a copy; the original long ago had been transferred to a museum. But even the reproduction, green with salt, gave the impression of antiquity.

Erica had never noticed the statue until the night she decided to end her life.

In her mind she heard it again: the distant squall of amplified music from the ouzo bar near the wharf. Somewhere in the smoke and darkness big Greek men were running their calloused hands over women's bodies, and mouths wet with liquor were meeting in convenient passion. There was music and laughter and lust—but not for Erica Garrison, eighteen years old, sitting alone at the far end of the wharf.

There at the water's edge, facing the smooth darkness of the

Aegean, she planned the last minutes of her existence, projecting them like a filmstrip on some inner movie screen. She would dive off the wharf and swim east toward a distant island, a jagged outline against a great wheel of stars. Swim and swim, her strong arms cutting the water, until she was too fatigued either to continue or to return. And then in an ecstasy of exhaustion let the black water pull her down.

Yes. It would be easy.

Rippling waves slopped against the hulls of the few fishing boats still moored to the wharf. Most were out to sea, not to return until morning. Would one of the fishermen find her, afloat in a skein of kelp, her face masked in a green caul?

She shivered, and the sea breeze, freshening the hot night, raised a rash of gooseflesh on her bare arms.

It was odd, what she was about to do. She had often imagined suicide, but she'd assumed the act would be triggered by some final, brutal affront—something specific, vivid, shattering. Yet this day had passed like any other, and the night as well. She had endured no torment but boredom, her old friend, and the steady background noise of sorrow, the motif of her life.

If she could endure it on a thousand other days and nights, then why not now? She didn't know. It seemed as if her reserves of strength had suddenly given out. After so many years, after anger and alienation and exile, she was all used up.

Now she was alone, and the sea beckoned.

Slowly she unbuttoned her blouse. She would swim naked to her death. Distantly she knew this was only a romantic gesture, embarrassingly mawkish, and when the authorities pieced together what had happened, they would smile sadly and say, *The girl was very young,* as if this explained it all.

Even so, she kicked off her shoes, laid her clothes aside. Nude, her hair streaming, her eyes dry, Erica Garrison took a last look at the world, and she saw the statue.

It was small, not quite life-size, no doubt an undistinguished piece of work. But in that moment, limned by starlight, it seemed curiously arresting, a vision from a dream.

Another naked woman like herself. And in her green face, the same despair and weariness . . . and something more.

In slow motion, unconscious of her own actions, Erica approached the statue. Words were engraved in the base, but in the dark she could not read them. She ran her fingertips over the incised letters, made out *pi* and *epsilon* and *rho,* and then she knew it was Persephone she saw.

Raising her hand, she touched the statue's face. Persephone was the most tragic of the goddesses, a girl—a young girl, eighteen perhaps—fated to spend a third of each year in the underworld as the bride of Hades, lord of death. Endlessly she would die and be reborn, and her every hour in sunlight was shadowed by the darkness she had known and would know again.

In her face, Erica read suffering and loss, but there was resolution also, captured in the slight lift of her chin and the level line of her brows.

Endurance, she thought for the first time, was itself a kind of victory. To hold on, to admit no surrender—perhaps in the end life was no more than this.

Or, if there was more, then it would be found in sunlight, not in the black water.

Abruptly she became aware of who she was and where she was and how she must look. A woman, unclothed, facing a bronze goddess who was her mirror, on a wharf at night under wheeling constellations named for other gods.

She retrieved her blouse, her shorts. Dressed herself hurriedly, afraid someone would come by and see her. Then left the wharf without looking again at the statue.

The next day, and for many days and nights afterward, she returned to the wharf and watched the bronze Persephone in different qualities of light. Not once did it recapture whatever illusion of life and soul had animated it. She was enough of a rationalist to concede that she might have seen only what she needed to see, that stress had triggered something akin to a hallucination.

But it hadn't felt that way, and she was not, after all, entirely a rationalist, was she? The way it felt, the way it *really* felt, was that she had been saved that night, saved by Persephone or by some prevenient grace.

Crouching by an open mouth in the rocky face of the earth, Erica Stafford remembered all this, and it gave her strength.

She wasn't sure if she believed in fate, in destiny, but if there was a purpose to things, then it was her purpose to be here now and to do what she had come to do.

She blew into her gloved hands, jammed the flashlight in a belt loop of her jeans, and climbed over the rim to begin her descent.

Fear lived in the town.

Connor could taste it as surely as he tasted the winter chill. Fear, he was sure, had been a stranger to Barrow before this year, but with the discovery of Sherry Wilcott's corpse, the town had changed.

Some unkind prank played by fate had delivered the case to him only two weeks after he'd assumed the office of police chief. It had not made his adjustment to a new job, a new town, and a new life any easier.

Though people were friendly, he knew what they were thinking: the man from New York was no Paul Elder. Elder would have solved the crime by now.

Never mind that Elder had faced nothing like the Wilcott homicide in his long tenure as chief. Never mind that the real investigative work was handled by detectives from the sheriff's department and the state police.

Fairly or not, Connor would be judged on this one matter, and so far he'd been found wanting. And the town, feeling leaderless, was afraid.

Well, so was he. Because where there was one murdered girl, there could be another. Soon.

He tooled down Main in his cruiser, a Chevy Caprice painted in Barrow P.D. colors, green and white. Downtown Barrow rolled past. It started with rows of century-old two-story cottages converted into offices and stores. Each residential side street was a gray line of similar cottages, with bare trees out front, the distant branches overlapping like smudged fingerprints. A water tower bearing the town's name loomed over the gabled roofs, beyond a snarl of utility lines cutting the pale sky.

Next came the brick firehouse with its proud sign: BARROW HOSE CO. #1. A playground, empty of children, all brown grass and rusty swing sets and dry leaves caught in a mesh-wire fence.

Then a row of marginal businesses: Harrigan Snowmobile Repair, Sandler's Tractor & Feed, and, bizarrely, Jose's Mexican Restaurant. Jose served hot tamales and Corona beer.

Ahead lay the converted warehouse that housed the only high-quality commercial establishments in Barrow, the ones that lured folks off the interstate or drew them here on Sunday back-road drives. A few more people were showing up as Barrow struggled to expand its getaway appeal with new bed and breakfasts on the lakefront, but so far the inns were busy mostly around Groundhog Day, when they handled the overspill of tourists from Punxsutawney, just down the road.

The warehouse, once a single vast room, had been divided into shops with generous floorplans and wide storefront windows. There was a hair salon, A Cut Above, which was reputed to do outstanding work, though Ben preferred the elderly slow-talking barber down the street. And a bookshop offering the best selection of titles within a hundred miles, and a gourmet food store, and a coffee bar, of all things. And finally there was Erica Stafford's gallery.

He cruised past the shop, noting the bright interior, then turned into the alley behind the warehouse, where the proprietors parked. There was only an empty parking space where Erica Stafford's white Mercedes ought to be.

She'd gone someplace, obviously. Not home, not to lunch. Where?

He parked, left his car, then checked the shop's rear door, expecting it to be locked.

The door opened under his hand, and he frowned.

"Erica?" he called into the darkness.

No reply.

He probed for a lightswitch and illuminated the rear foyer. Before entering, he unsnapped his holster flap and let his right hand dangle near his Smith's checkered handle. Eighteen years with the NYPD had taught him caution.

Quickly he went down the rear hall and into the front room. The overhead fluorescents mixed their glow with sunlight streaming through the wide front windows to wash the shop in cold white glare. He shouted her name again and heard the answer he expected: silence.

Slowly he circled the shop. Saving Grace, it was called. A peculiar name, but one Erica had explained to him at the welcoming party she'd hosted in his honor at Great Hall.

Art, she had said, was humanity's saving grace. As if embarrassed by this philosophical flourish, she'd added: *Or it's been mine, anyway.*

For some reason he had asked: *What did it save you from?*

He recalled her startled look—as if he'd touched her in an intimate place. Then she had smiled, dismissing the question as a harmless riposte, and drifted away without reply.

He had known women like her in New York, women with an unpracticed knack for striking an elegant pose. But with those women, it usually was only a pose, an image as smooth as lacquer and as shallow. In Erica Stafford he'd sensed substance, something raw and real but carefully guarded, hidden from the light.

He liked her from the start. At first he thought she reminded him of his late wife—but no, that wasn't it. Even after the miscarriage that had left her unable to conceive, Karen Connor had not lost her buoyancy, her fundamental uplift. But Erica Stafford carried a quality of hurt, of sorrow, of old pain and never-forgotten loss. Eventually he understood that he saw himself in her, himself as he'd been for the past two years.

And she was attractive. Funny how he'd stopped noticing women after Karen died, as if that part of him had been extinguished with her. But on the night of the welcoming party, he'd found himself studying Andrew Stafford's wife from across the wide, high-ceilinged hall. She was like one of the sculptures she prized, lean and angular, her body subtly stylized— lithe legs and trim waist, arms corded with lean muscle, her long neck and her delicate, ambiguous face.

An interesting woman. He'd found himself dropping by her shop from time to time, perhaps more frequently than courtesy demanded. Though he'd never been much for art, he found he appreciated her taste. Connor wouldn't have thought a shop catering to an affluent, selective clientele could prosper this far from any large city, but he had underestimated Erica Stafford's energies. She was a woman in constant motion, active in civic affairs, skilled as a hostess, yet finding time to run the gallery singlehandedly five days a week, Tuesday through Saturday, and to send out catalogues to distant customers who ordered by mail.

You're a shark, Connor had told her once, adding before she could take offense: *If you stop moving, you'll die.*

He reached the front door. Locked. But the sign she usually hung up when she left—the hand-lettered sign announcing OUT TO LUNCH, BE BACK SOON—rested on the windowsill, face down.

At the counter he checked the cash register, found more than two hundred dollars.

No robbery, then.

He went into her office, found a pile of opened mail on the desk. This morning's delivery, he would guess. First-class mail typically took three days to arrive, and nearly every postmark was three days old.

Connor knew the postman's route; the mail was delivered around 12:30. Erica must have had time to open and sort the letters. She must have been in her shop until at least 1:00.

He checked the answering machine. It had recorded only Rachel Kellerman's urgent inquiries, time-stamped at 1:45 and 1:57.

So that was the window he was looking at. One o'clock to 1:45. Erica had left the shop sometime during that time period.

Rachel had said she'd called Great Hall also. But there was another place Erica might go, a cottage on the outskirts of town which she rented as a hideaway.

No one would think of checking there. No one but him.

Connor dialed the number, let the phone at the other end of the line ring and ring.

She wasn't at the cottage. Or wasn't answering, anyway.

He put down the phone and stood motionless, trying to think. It was hard. Memories kept getting in the way, memories triggered by this room, the onyx lamps on the end tables, the leather sofa where she had reclined, her slender legs sprawling in elegant disarray.

An interesting woman. He hadn't expected her to care much about him. Why should she? She was beautiful and wealthy and married, and he was just some guy from New York with an extra inch on his waistline and a burden of guilt and sorrow he could never quite shake off.

But something kept drawing him back to this place, and one January evening he'd chanced to stop by at closing time. Just to say hi. Friendly visit. Nothing more, or so he'd told himself.

I've got coffee brewing in the office, she said.

They'd come in here together, and she poured two steaming cups. Outside, the wind screeched and hooted like a living thing. Connor talked about New York, the noises of the city, the blare of traffic, the craziness.

You miss it, don't you? she had asked.

He admitted he did, and she asked him why he'd left. So he told her about Karen. About the worst night of his life, and how he hadn't been himself since. He spoke of trauma and loss, and she understood.

Later he learned how well she understood, how much she knew of pain, upheaval—the hard lessons she'd learned as a child in Great Hall. She told him some of it, her account elliptical and oblique; local gossip filled in some gaps in the narrative; and Paul Elder, who'd been there, gave him the rest.

But on that evening in late January, he didn't know why his story had reached her, touched her. He only knew that she began to cry, and when he asked what was wrong, she said her marriage was a lie.

He used me, she whispered. *He's just a damn con artist, that's all. Married me for money, not love. And I fell for it. I believed him. Stupid, so stupid . . .*

Connor asked if Andrew had been unfaithful.

No, nothing like that, she said. *At least I don't think so. Who can say? He might be screwing the damn housekeeper for all I know. I don't care. I don't think I ever loved him, really.*

Then why had she married him?

Maybe because I didn't love him. It seemed . . . safer that way. If there's nothing at stake, there's nothing to lose. Does that make any sense?

You can't play it safe all the time, Connor said.

No? How about you? Have you taken any chances since Karen

died? Then she looked away, her face aflame with embarrass-ment. *I'm sorry, I shouldn't have asked you that.*

He said it was all right. And no, he'd taken no chances. *I'm better at delivering profundities than living by them,* he added.

This coaxed a smile from her. They talked some more, and he left, and that was that.

Except of course it wasn't. Because he came by the next night, and when she saw him at the door at closing time she said only, *I was hoping.*

He took her for the first time right here, in this office, on the sofa, by the gurgling coffee maker and the answering machine.

After that, they met more discreetly, using the cottage for their liaisons. It was secluded, and it had a two-car garage use-ful for concealing her Mercedes and whatever vehicle he was driving, a department cruiser or his off-duty coupe.

He had never been involved in an affair before. He would have expected it to feel cheap and hollow. But it was the best thing in his life, at least since Karen, and maybe even—sacrilege to think it—maybe even including her.

He loved Erica Stafford, another man's wife. He'd told her so and heard her answer. But in her voice and in her eyes there was always a disconcerting reserve, a coolness, a detachment. She was still playing it safe, he knew, afraid to lose herself in him and perhaps get lost completely. He had her, but not all of her, not all he wanted, but for now, enough.

And now she was gone, and he was scared, more scared than he had been since the night he said goodbye to Karen, knowing she couldn't hear.

He picked up the phone again and tried Great Hall, thinking Erica might have arrived there after Rachel's call. But the housekeeper, Marie, hadn't seen her.

"No, Chief Connor," she said over the babble of a daytime soap, the volume ridiculously high. "Mrs. Stafford left this morning, and she hasn't been back since. Is there something wrong? You're the second person who's called."

Connor calmed her. "I just needed to ask her a question," he lied smoothly. "Nothing important. Is Mr. Stafford at home?"

"He's at the racquet club. Should be back around three. Something really is the matter, I can tell."

"Just have Erica call me when she gets in, okay?"

"Is it about Robert? Is he being arrested? Oh, God, I shouldn't have said that."

"Nobody's being arrested. Have Mrs. Stafford call the police station. Or she can reach me on my cell phone. She has the number. All right?"

On the TV in the background, a woman was sobbing noisily, and Marie sounded close to tears herself. "All right, Chief Connor. And . . . what I said about Robert . . ."

"I've forgotten already," Connor said with a smile, which faded slowly as he cradled the phone.

Robert. Yes. Everyone in town regarded him as the prime suspect in the Sherry Wilcott case. People were expecting an arrest. They didn't understand that an arrest required evidence, something solid, tangible, and so far there was nothing at all.

He couldn't even be held as a suspect in Erica's disappearance. The timing was too tight. There was perhaps a small window of opportunity for Robert to have abducted Erica in her car, stashed her and the Mercedes somewhere, then returned to establish an alibi at the grocery store.

It was possible. But exceedingly unlikely.

And Rachel had said he showed genuine surprise at the news that his sister was missing. Left in a hurry. Agitated, upset.

For now, Connor would have to assume Robert had nothing to do with his sister's absence. He told himself he ought to be relieved about that.

But if Robert hadn't taken her, then where was she?

He had no answer. All he knew was that he couldn't lose her. He had lost Karen, and it had taken him this long to rebuild his life. He would not lose Erica now. He would not. He would not.

When he left the shop, he was running.

3

Erica slipped slowly down the knotted line, moving from hand-hold to handhold in a halting descent, her smooth leather gloves absorbing the friction. Knees together, she gripped the rope between her thighs to distribute her weight more evenly.

The exercise did not overly tax her. There was a small gym in Great Hall. It was Andrew's innovation, though he rarely used it. Erica, however, worked out daily on the Nautilus and the Stairmaster. And she took a morning run, four hard miles, much of it uphill, in every kind of weather.

The regimen had kept her fit; at thirty-six she was better conditioned than she'd been as a teenager.

Halfway down the twelve-foot shaft. Daylight dimming, the flashlight's downcast beam tracing crazy spirals on the limestone walls. The rope swaying as she slid down another few inches.

She hoped the rim of the hole was not too rough, hoped the taut span of rope anchored there was not fraying on the rock.

If the rope broke, she would survive the fall, but then her only way out would be to chimney up the shaft. For all her hours on the Nautilus, she wasn't sure she could manage it.

"Won't happen," she told herself, the promise whispered through gritted teeth.

Close now. Almost to the bottom.

Then a smile touched the corners of her mouth as she wondered what the people in town would think if they saw her now. Erica Stafford—the mistress of Great Hall, hostess of Barrow's most elegant receptions, local arbiter of taste—struggling into a subterranean hole.

Legs straightened, she probed below with her boots and touched something solid. When she had ascertained it was the cavern floor and not a ledge or stalagmite, she released the rope and balanced lightly on both feet.

Overhead, the entryway had shrunk to a disk of white sunlight, small as a coin. She stood in a splashback of glare from the Eveready, catching her breath.

It was warmer here than above. Her panting breath did not frost the air.

She slid the flash free of her belt loop and swept the beam in a full circle until its spotlight found a side passageway.

The space was tighter than she remembered. She had to turn sideways to squeeze through. The calcite outcrops caught at her coat collar like grasping hands.

Only a yard of this. Then she was in a wider passage, the main limestone corridor in the labyrinth.

A strange feeling rose in her, and she needed a moment to identify it as guilt. This was not her place any longer. She was an intruder here.

She took out the lipstick and traced a long red smear on the wall, with an arrow pointing toward the crevice that led to the sinkhole. Without markers to follow, she would be quickly lost in the maze.

Now, which way to go?

She had hoped to find a trail of some sort, but there was none. The labyrinth was pristine, unblemished. And the corridor, she knew, ran in two directions, branching off into numberless arteries. Long before she had searched even a tenth of them, she would run out of lipstick and strength.

But she didn't have to search them all, did she? There was one cavern in particular that he would have used. The one they liked best as children, the one with magic in it.

The throne room.

That was how they'd christened it, in honor of the artistry wrought by the slow seepage of water over time. The cavern itself boasted the majestic dimensions of a royal hall, with its high domed ceiling that cast back glorious echoes, its rounded corners hung with limestone draperies, its smoothly polished floor.

But the room's grandest feature was the throne that dominated one wall, a cascade of melted rock that had miraculously assumed the shape of a great regal chair, with high armrests, only slightly askew, and dripping folds of seat cushions, white as silk.

That was the place to find. And she thought she remembered the way.

She headed left, down the wide stone avenue.

There was no light anywhere except the cone of her flashlight's beam. The world around her was a glowing circle, a circle that shifted and danced as the flash moved in her hand.

Follow the bouncing ball.

Erica had read about a form of blindness in which sight narrowed to a pinhole. This was like that. The great darkness all around, and the single orb of light, smearing into an oval as it stretched across a slanted wall, shrinking and expanding as it fell upon surfaces far and near.

Progress was slow. After each cautious step she paused to whirl the flashlight in a full arc, first checking the floor for a sudden drop or a dangerous, foot-grabbing cleft, then sweeping the cavern roof for calcite overhangs.

In childhood it had been different. Over time she and Robert had distributed lanterns throughout the maze, antique glass-paned kerosene lanterns they'd found among a stash of storm supplies in a shed at the estate. Enough lanterns to light every one of the eighteen rooms in Great Hall. The lamps' absence was never discovered, and luckily no storm ever required their use.

The lanterns might still be here. Certainly Erica had not removed them. But she had brought along no matches, and besides, there wasn't time to seek out the lanterns now.

She kept going, step and pause, step and pause, lady in the dark. A scrap of textbook knowledge floated back to her from a long-ago college course at the University of Rome: the Eleusinian mysteries. Secret rites performed throughout antiquity, an initiation into arcane truths. The heart of the ritual was a slow progress through dark caves, the novice feeling his way, risking a fatal plunge as he negotiated narrow passages and fragile stone catwalks.

All ritual is metaphor, her professor had explained in his mellifluous Italian, *and the Eleusinian initiation is a metaphor for life itself. We search for meaning, wandering in the dark, and we may stumble, we may die, but if we reach our goal, our true and destined goal, then we will stand in glorious light. This is what the initiates learned. It is what we must all learn. For it is a search common to us all.*

Erica knew about that search. Her many trips to the Mediterranean had been part of it, as was her obsession with art and beauty. Her marriage to Andrew was part of it too, for better or worse. Even her relationship with Robert was tied into that quest, that longing for wholeness, for completion, for the almost mystical transcendence she had experienced on the wharf of a Greek fishing village, as she stood naked before a bronze goddess.

In that one moment she had glimpsed a purpose, a meaning, an order to things, but never since, not in eighteen years.

Perhaps she'd been too busy to find it—always running, running. Up at daybreak to sprint through the woods even in the gloom of winter. Managing her shop from nine to five, preparing her catalogues, sending out mail-order packages. Ever on the move, not cutting her pace, as if to stop, just stop, would somehow kill her.

Ben Connor was right, she thought suddenly. Funny she would think of him now.

But when he'd called her a shark—impelled to ceaseless motion, incapable of rest—he'd been more discerning than he knew.

She wondered what she was looking for . . . and what she was running from. In the end, it might be the same thing.

And if she ever found it . . . or if it found her . . .

With a shiver, she brushed that thought away.

The caves were warmer than outside, fifty degrees or so, a constant subterranean temperature, and under her winter coat and gloves and boots she was suddenly perspiring.

At a side passageway she hesitated, then decided yes, this intersecting route was the one to take. With her lipstick she marked the corner before continuing.

The new passage was narrower, the floor more uneven, the low ceiling studded with threatening stalactites. She groped with one hand, aiming the flash with the other. Bad thoughts harried her, thoughts of getting lost, wandering until the flashlight batteries gave out, then dying the slow death of a starving animal, entombed in the claustrophobic dark.

She was breathing fast but, funny thing, couldn't seem to get any air.

Another wary step, another. She had covered thirty paces since turning the corner. Was keeping count.

Despite fear, despite worry, she found something weirdly reassuring in the dreamlike familiarity of her environment. She had not thought of the caves in years, could not have described any detail of them beforehand, yet as soon as she saw each flowing curtain of rock, each broken pillar, she knew it intimately, with a pang of raw recognition, as if the memory had never left her.

Almost surely he would have felt the same way, would have been drawn to this part of the maze ahead of any other.

Wait.

Was that a noise?

Rigid, she listened, breath held, eyes wide. She could feel the itchy crawl of the short hairs on the back of her neck.

Just her imagination.

She went on. The corridor narrowed still further. Faintly she heard a low sibylline whisper, an aquifer coursing at the lowest level of the cave network, feeding into Barrow Falls.

The falls in turn fed Barrow Creek, where Sherry Wilcott's body had washed up on a muddy bank, to be found by a weekend fisherman and his nine-year-old grandson.

Her coat was a sweaty bundle, her heart racing.

Ahead, a looming aperture. The doorway to a grotto, large and deep.

The throne room. Their special hideaway.

She was here.

The offices of the Barrow Police Department were housed in a new civic plaza, an architect's dream of two-story concrete megaliths and concrete pathways lined in recently planted fir trees. The trees, shielded from the sun, were small and growing poorly, their lower branches drooping with brown needles, and the iron railings on the exterior staircases, similarly lost in shade, had been frozen since January.

Connor avoided using the railing as he took the steps two at a time. At his back a cold wind rattled the leafless elms distributed throughout the parking lot, their branches sharp and spiked, like TV aerials, against the bright sky.

He swung open the plate-glass door in a flash of sun and was enveloped in sudden electric warmth and fluorescent shine.

The desk officer, Tim Larkin, frowned at Connor's entrance. "What's the story, Chief? We got nobody on the street."

"Calm down, Sergeant. I'm doing a briefing right now. Squad room. You're invited."

Sergeant Larkin, all of twenty-eight and inclined to think he'd seen everything, wasn't mollified. "There was no need to call in both units. The radio—"

"The radio isn't secure. What I've got to say involves a sensitive matter. Who's on shift? Hart and Danvers?"

"Yeah. They're both here, and Woodall's hanging out too. He had some paperwork to finish up after the day watch. I told him to stay put."

"Good. We can use him. Lieutenant Maginnis around?"

"Her office."

"Have her join us. No, wait. I'll get her."

Connor had enough trouble with Maginnis as it was. Summoning her to a meeting as if she were a truant dispatched to the principal would only make things worse.

He was moving past the desk when he remembered to ask if Erica Stafford had called the station.

"Mrs. Stafford?" Bafflement showed on Larkin's wide, pockmarked face. "No."

Connor nodded, unsurprised. His cell phone, too, had been silent.

Walking away, he heard Larkin call out, "Hey, Chief— gimme a preview, will you? Just the coming attractions?"

"Patience is a virtue, Tim."

Connor was playing this one close to the vest. So far he'd

conducted the investigation into Erica Stafford's disappearance entirely on his own. He'd made a few seemingly casual inquiries of the neighboring proprietors, then had driven to the cottage she rented, the place where their trysts were held. Pain had riven him as he used a duplicate key, a gift from her, to enter.

The cottage had been empty, as he'd expected. He'd searched it quickly, finding nothing amiss.

And Erica still hadn't called.

There was nothing to do now but organize an all-out search. He checked his watch as he approached Maginnis's office. Nearly three o'clock. Erica had been missing since at least one-thirty. An hour and a half—not a long time under normal circumstances, but circumstances in Barrow would never be normal until Sherry Wilcott's killer was caught.

Connor found Marge Maginnis at her desk. She looked up sharply before he had a chance to speak.

"Heard you on the scanner. You called in both patrol units. Any particular reason?"

"Need to convey some information," he said. "In person. I'd like you with me." He didn't phrase it as an order.

"Oh, hell." Her chair scraped the floor as she stood up. She was five-ten, only an inch short of Connor's height. Redheaded and rawboned, forty-one, perpetually angry.

Well, she had her reasons, or thought she did. A twenty-year veteran of Barrow P.D., she'd expected a promotion to chief of police when Elder retired. The town council had exploded her hopes by bringing in Connor from outside. She blamed this injustice on the glass ceiling and the good old boys and, of course, Connor himself.

Which could be so, Connor reflected. But there was an alternative explanation. A police chief, even an appointee, had to be part politician, and a politician's prime skill was in making friends. This appeared to be a skill Lieutenant Maginnis lacked.

He hadn't expected problems of this nature in Barrow. It was different in the bureaucratic puzzle-palace of the NYPD, where backbiting and ass-covering had been honed to art forms. But Barrow P.D. was no bureaucracy. It boasted eighteen sworn officers and twelve civilian employees. Lieutenant Maginnis had the highest seniority and served as de facto Assistant Chief. Two other lieutenants supervised the post-midnight watches, and four sergeants—all about Larkin's age—would oversee less busy shifts. On the current watch, which ran from two P.M. to midnight, there were only two squad cars in circulation, each manned by a lone P.O. In emergencies the sheriff's department and the state police could be called on.

No empires could be built here, or so Connor had thought. But he had underestimated the human tendency to carve out territory and win prestige, whether in a royal court or a playground sandbox. Maginnis had wanted the job Connor now held, and she would not forgive him for having it.

To hell with her. He had a much more important matter to deal with at the moment.

He headed down the hall, the lieutenant trailing him at a sullen distance, no doubt wondering what was up but too proud to ask. As he approached the squad room, Connor unzipped his vinyl jacket and shrugged it off. Didn't want to appear flushed, convey panic. The situation had to be handled just right.

After all, it might be nothing. He had no facts, only an empty store and a missed appointment and the greasy dread boiling in his gut.

Hart and Woodall were at it again, and Vicki Danvers didn't know whether to be amused or annoyed.

"Gimme a break," she said mildly, and blew into her coffee to cool the steam.

Todd Hart grinned. "Officer, I'll give you anything you want."

"He would too," Ray Woodall said in a softer voice, "if he had anything to give."

"What's that s'posed to mean?" Hart puffed up, operatically offended. "I can give her just what she needs. I know how to treat a lady right."

"I'm no lady," Danvers countered, and sipped the coffee. Still too hot.

Hart was undeterred. "You're wrong there, Vicki. You got the stuff."

"I got a headache. And it has your name written all over it."

Woodall laughed, but Hart saw a new avenue to explore.

"Headaches are from tension," he said. "You need some relaxation, some quality time. A cop's life is stressful, you know? Now, if you were to hang with me—"

"She hangs with anybody," Woodall cut in, "it should be a guy who's hung." He showed Danvers a mischievous smile. "I've seen Todd in the locker room. You're missing absolutely nothing."

"Ray was looking in the mirror," Hart said. "You want to talk about hanging—"

Danvers turned away. "I don't. Really." She was irritated now. "You guys ever hear of sexual harassment?"

"Yeah, but that's only if your boss is after you." Hart spoke with professorial authority. "We don't outrank you, so it's okay."

Danvers didn't think Lieutenant Maginnis would say it was okay, or Chief Connor either. But she held that ammo in reserve. She didn't want to make too big a deal of it. These guys—they were all right, probably.

Truthfully, she sort of liked Woodall. Not especially good looking, true—his sallow face marred by persistent acne, his deep-set eyes underscored by purplish half-moons—but he was smarter than he acted.

She'd caught him reading books on his lunch break. Actual books—*Crime and Punishment* one time, a psychology text on another occasion. Rather sheepishly he'd explained that he wanted to understand the criminal mind. His shy embarrassment was more appealing than the self-conscious machismo he affected when in Hart's unstable orbit.

Hart was an asshole. Loud and bullheaded, he'd been hitting on her for months, ever since her training period ended and she stopped riding shotgun with Maginnis. Danvers had run out of ways to say no. And the sad part was that in repelling Hart's advances, she had to turn away Woodall too.

"In fact," Hart was saying, "this is the opposite of harassment, see? This is camaraderie. It builds morale. The buddy system, you know? Will you be my buddy, Officer Danvers?"

A hairy hand slipped around her waist, and her coffee spilled.

"Hey." She pulled free. "Look. I don't need this, all right?"

Woodall looked embarrassed, even guilty, though he hadn't touched her. For his sake Danvers softened her tone as she added, "Let's find something else to talk about."

For the first time she saw honest bewilderment in Hart's face. "What else is there?" Hart asked.

The door opened, Connor and Maginnis walking in, and Danvers was spared the necessity of an answer.

"Everybody take a seat," Connor said as he moved quickly up to the front.

The squad room wasn't much, just a scatter of folding chairs under banks of fluorescent lights. Maps of the county and the town were taped to the cinder-block walls. Framed in the lone window, a pine tree beat its needles against the glass.

Officers Hart, Woodall, and Danvers sat in a row, three pale faces, three blue uniforms. Not for the first time, Connor thought how young they looked, astonishingly young. He was only forty-two, hardly old, but these three—Christ, they were children. Woodall was the eldest at twenty-five, Hart and Danvers two years his junior.

"Problem, Chief?" That was Hart, a good kid, not so bright.

"Maybe."

"Don't give us the runaround, Ben." Maginnis chose a chair in the back row, keeping a defiant distance. "You dragged our butts in here, so let's have it. What the hell's going on?"

It was inappropriate to address her superior that way, especially in front of the troops, but Connor showed no reaction. He had tried various ways of dealing with Maginnis. None had worked, but staying calm at least allowed him the small satisfaction of a successful exercise in self-control.

"Just wait a moment," he said. "I asked Sergeant Larkin to join us."

On cue, Larkin hurried in and took a chair in the back row. Maginnis threw him a scornful glance for no evident reason, and Larkin frowned in return.

"All right." Connor took a breath. "Here it is. We may—I stress the word *may*—have another missing woman."

Sudden stillness in the room.

"So do we or don't we?" Maginnis asked.

"That's what we need to find out, and fast."

"Well, who is she?"

"Erica Stafford."

Woodall hissed an epithet, and the room was colder.

"Mrs. Stafford," Danvers said softly, as if speaking to herself. "She's nice. I mean . . . she was nice to me."

Her voice trailed off. Connor hated the way she'd put it: *was* nice. Past tense. As if Erica were already dead.

"You see why I had to bring you in," he told them, knowing they did. "This isn't the sort of thing we want to broadcast. Any disappearance is significant these days. But in this case, it's especially . . . sensitive."

Heads nodded. Erica Stafford, heiress to half the Garrison family fortune, chatelaine of the gray granite estate known since the age of industrial barons as Great Hall, was Barrow's most prominent resident.

Connor let them think about all of that for just a moment, and then he gave the details: the one-thirty lunch date, the shop with an unlocked rear door.

"She could have gone out on a whim," Maginnis said. "That art gallery is just a hobby anyway. Pastime of the idle rich."

Connor felt heat rise in his face. "As far as I know, no one's ever accused Mrs. Stafford of being idle."

"Well, maybe she's got a boyfriend on the side. Forgot about lunch with Rachel. Busy doing other things."

The words stung like wasps. Connor felt suddenly naked and exposed, as if Maginnis knew his secret—all of them did—and they were jeering at him and his pretensions of discretion.

No, she was just being a goddamned bitch, as usual. There was no subtext here.

Biting back anger, he asked her, "Have you got any grounds for that speculation?"

Maginnis backed off. "Me? Hell, no. I don't know her, really. I'm not sure anybody does."

"Everybody knows her," Vicki Danvers said, sounding indignant. "She's famous around here."

Maginnis was visibly perturbed at this dissent, especially since Danvers, the only other female cop in the department, was known to be the lieutenant's protégé.

"Folks know her," Maginnis said with a defensive shrug, "sure. The way you know a politician. But it's all surface. What's underneath nobody can tell."

Connor knew this was fair enough, but he wouldn't give Maginnis the pleasure of admitting it.

"Well," he said, cutting off the discussion, "let's hope Mrs. Stafford did go off somewhere and lose track of time. But until we know otherwise, we're treating this as a disappearance. And you know what a disappearance can mean in this town."

They knew.

"She's *his* sister," Hart said. "Maybe we should check him out first."

"He seems to have an alibi. Someone saw him at Waldman's."

"Son of a bitch is crafty, though." Hart's hostility was palpable. "Fucking hermit, living out there in the woods. I don't trust these loner types. They all got a screw loose somewhere. And when they're smart—like him—they can mess with you pretty bad."

"He wasn't in two places at once," Connor said impatiently.

Hart didn't answer, but the look on his face—part disgust, part superstitious dread—suggested that for Robert Garrison, a violation of fundamental laws of nature and logic might not be unthinkable.

Connor knew that many in town felt the same way. A kind of magical thinking seemed bound up in the subject of the Garrison family, as if, along with their millions, Erica and Robert had inherited some peculiar power or some unspeakable curse.

"Did you talk to her husband?" Tim Larkin asked, bringing the conversation back safely to the realm of reality.

Connor nodded. "Tried to reach him at home. The housekeeper, Marie, said he was at the racquet club. I called there a few minutes ago, but they said he'd just left. He probably has a car phone, but I don't know the number. Anyway, he left alone. Erica didn't meet him there."

"You said she closed the shop? Locked the front door?" This was Woodall, thinking aloud. Brighter than Hart and more analytical, he was hoping to transfer to the state police, make detective someday. "If she left voluntarily, it wouldn't fit the scenario of the Wilcott case."

"No one saw her leave. It could have been an abduction."

"In broad daylight?"

"Her car would have been parked behind the shop, in that little alley. There aren't any windows in the rear of the complex. If she was taken out the back way, no one would be the wiser."

"Car's gone too?" Danvers asked.

Connor nodded. "It's the car you've got to look for. You all know what she drives. White Mercedes sedan. It's a 400 SEL, 1997 model."

He recited the license number, then pointed to the map of Barrow.

"The search area is city limits plus a five-mile radius. We divide it into quadrants. Officer Hart, you take the southeast. Woodall, southwest. Danvers, northwest. Sergeant Larkin, northeast."

It wasn't much territory. Four units could cover the main roads and byways in an hour.

"Lieutenant Maginnis," he added, "I want you to initiate the standard missing-person procedure: Call the local hospitals, see if the highway patrol knows anything about a car wreck, even check the county jail. The works."

"What's *your* assignment?" Maginnis asked too sharply, challenging him for the sheer spiteful pleasure of it.

"I'm going over to Great Hall. I'll talk to Andrew once he gets home. And I'll pick up a photo of Erica too—in case we need to put out a wider APB. Any other questions?"

Larkin asked if they should bring in Harve Miller, the department's only detective. Connor had already decided against it. Miller was capable enough in limited areas, but he lacked experience with either missing persons or homicides.

"There's nothing for him to do," Connor said. "We'll have to dump this on the sheriff's people anyway, if Mrs. Stafford doesn't turn up."

"Or if she turns up dead," Maginnis added.

Connor's patience was worn raw. "Lieutenant . . ."

"Oh, keep your shirt on, Ben. She'll show herself. I still say she's got a boyfriend on the side."

She walked out without waiting to be dismissed. Connor sent the others away, warning them to be discreet on the radio.

When they were gone and he was alone in the room, he took

off his cap and ran a shaky hand through his thinning hair. He'd come close to losing it there.

If she turns up dead . . .

Maginnis's voice, taunting him, cold and harsh as the scraping of dry ice.

She wasn't dead. He wouldn't permit her to be dead. His world, which had begun to make sense again only recently, would lose all shape and order if Erica was dead.

Connor drew a tight breath, then squared his shoulders and left the station house, heading toward a rendezvous with Andrew Stafford, the lord of Great Hall—and the last man he wanted to face.

Just inside the doorway Erica stopped, playing the yellow beam over the throne room in a widening series of slow spirals.

It was as she remembered it, the distant ceiling and the smooth floor and, carved like a high relief in the far wall, the limestone throne where she and Robert had taken turns seating themselves and playacting as monarchs of the underworld.

All the same, unchanged by time, except for one crucial, maddening addition.

A table stood in the center of the room.

Four sturdy legs and a flat wooden slab, ruggedly bolted, the metal fixtures gleaming and new.

The flashlight shivered, her grip weakening. A pulse of lightheadedness staggered her, and she nearly fell.

Blinking, she recovered. This was no surprise, was it? She could not be really shocked.

Anyway, there could be another explanation. The table— perhaps it was a workbench. Perhaps Robert built things here, did carpentry jobs.

But a workbench would not be built at an angle, the legs at the base a foot shorter than those at the head.

And there were the straps.

Four narrow canvas bands, soiled, frayed at the edges, dangling from the sides of the table where they were secured with what looked like heavy staples. The ends were crumpled like tissue paper, where the straps had been knotted together, knotted tight.

One strap for the victim's feet; the other, to bind the arms.

A sudden awful thought made her dip the flashlight, splashing its glare on the floor, and she saw a tawny spatter of dried blood.

Over the beating terror in her ears she could almost hear Sherry Wilcott's cries rising to the ceiling to be cast back in waves of echo.

This was not the throne room anymore, a place of childhood fantasy. This was a dungeon, a torture cell—and she couldn't stand it, couldn't stay a moment longer.

Panic nearly hurled her into the dark in a headlong flight.

No.

If she tried to run, she would blunder into a wall or a stalactite or twist an ankle in a crevice. Or lose herself in the bafflement of passages and never find an exit.

Erica gathered herself, found strength. She had done it before in her life. There were wells of courage in her, courage tapped and tested when she'd most needed it. Now she needed it again.

Her heart slowed. She was calm, or almost calm. In control.

She could leave now. Retrace her steps, climb to daylight, drive into town, and tell what she'd found. Tell, though it was her brother's death sentence. Tell, so that no more girls would be brought here to perish in the dark.

"Do it, then," Erica whispered. "Go. Now."

She was turning toward the grotto doorway when she heard footsteps.

4

Erica covered the big Eveready flash with her hand, shielding its beam.

Sudden darkness everywhere, broken only by a trickle of light through her reddened fingers.

How could he be here? How could he *know*?

He must have driven along the fire road, seen her parked Mercedes. But why had he taken that route in the first place? It was far from his home. There was no reason for him to come here, no logic to it.

She had been afraid at other times in her life, but never like this.

If someone had asked her before this moment if she feared death, she would have said no. Would have said she'd seen death and contemplated it, learned even as a child to accept both its shocking arbitrariness and its ultimate inevitability.

But she would have been lying, lying even to herself. Because her search wasn't over. She'd wandered so long in the dark and had yet to find the light, and it wasn't fair for her to die with her quest unfulfilled, to die without even knowing exactly what she was looking for or how she would recognize it.

The footsteps continued. Closer.

On the wall outside the cavern doorway, a faint but brightening glow. A flashlight.

Where had he gotten it? She'd taken the flashlight from the oak hollow. He must carry a spare in his truck. He'd found the rope, shimmied down, and now he was coming this way. Advancing down the side corridor, moving cautiously, as she had, his steps slow, deliberate.

Had he seen the glow of her flashlight before she masked the lens? Possibly not. It took awhile for eyesight to adjust to darkness, and he could have been distracted by his own flash.

Even if he hadn't seen it, he must have noted the arrows marked in lipstick on the walls. He knew just where she was.

What to do, what to *do*?

She could simply stand her ground. Await his arrival. Talk to him.

No, come on, that was hopeless. She'd seen the table, the cave floor inlaid with a mosaic of dried blood. This was not a person she could reason with.

Could she run? If she tried to leave via the corridor, he would spot her instantly.

Hide, then. Or find another way out.

She crabbed away from the doorway. Her fingers, gripping the Eveready's lens, spread slightly to permit the escape of three narrow slits of light.

Feeble illumination, but enough to guide her as she circled the throne room.

To her left, a limestone wall, rippling like muscle, offering no hiding place, no escape route.

To her right, the table with the straps.

The awful chuffing noise was her own breath forced through gritted teeth. She could feel, actually *feel* a vein in her forehead pulsing.

Would he put her on the table? Would he kill her that way? Tied down, helpless—

Terror froze her, and for a moment she was twelve years old again, huddled in a closet with blood on her pajamas, paralyzed by shock.

She shook herself back to this moment. There had to be a way out. She couldn't go on the table, couldn't die that way, at Robert's hands.

Still exploring the room's perimeter, moving fast, adrenaline supercharging every sensory perception.

A detail arrested her attention momentarily—two columns of red chalk marks on the wall at different levels, and with that image came a memory—she and Robert measuring their heights, awaiting the day when he would be the taller.

Then I'll be big enough to beat you up, he said. Laughing.

The remembrance, sharp and clear as glass, nicked her in a tender place. She felt an absurd stab of guilt for trying to get away. To run from him—it seemed almost disloyal.

Then she saw him as he'd looked in the hallway of her shop, wild, raging, and she knew his childhood self was irrelevant. He was a different person now. A stranger, homicidal, psychotic.

And closing in.

Something hard banged her knee. Furniture—homemade like the table—a cabinet, which she hadn't noticed before. Unsanded wood, nails imbedded at irregular depths and angles, some bent in half, crude work. It was small, too small for her to hide in, and she only glanced at it as she moved on.

Now at the back of the room. The rear wall mocking her, the limestone throne like a vision from a movie set. At the base of the sculpted chair—a patch of black that was deeper than shadow. A crevice. A hole.

She didn't remember any opening there. In the years since her childhood ended, the drip of percolating rainwater must have dissolved more of the rock, exposing an aperture perhaps just large enough for her.

Quickly to her knees, shining the flash into the hole, and she found a tunnel, a crawlway. Where it led she couldn't guess, but it was at least a way out, a chance.

She thrust herself inside, but her shoulder jammed in the entryway. Stuck. The crevice was too narrow. She couldn't fit. Unless maybe, without the coat . . .

Fumbling at it, popping buttons, Erica on her knees, twisting like a madwoman. The Eveready on the floor beside her, balanced upright on its lens to screen its glow.

The coat came off, was flung aside, landing shapeless in a corner, a shaggy hibernating animal.

She picked up the flash. Clumsily she let the beam fan out, a bright spray of light.

He must have seen the glow this time.

The footsteps, very close. And faster.

Go.

Into the hole again, scrambling forward, and she made it,

cleared the entrance, then was crawling, covering distance on her belly and elbows.

It was a gun-barrel tube, coffin tight, extending in a straight line into some infinite distance beyond the flashlight's range.

Her best hope was that Robert wouldn't—couldn't—follow. He was big in the shoulders, maybe too big to get through.

Desperate terror competed with a tug of shame. Though it was ridiculous, she couldn't shake free of the thought that she was abandoning him. Again.

She sucked air, tasted dust. Grunting as she propelled herself over sharp ridges, past clutching projections of rock.

The flashlight shivered with each inchworm jerk of progress, its white dazzle gyrating around her, swirling pulsations of light. Like that ouzo bar—a smoky dive in Athens where she'd gone years ago—a band blaring, everybody drunk.

Backward glance into the dark.

No glow of a pursuing flashlight. Velvet blackness, pure and whole.

By now Robert must have reached the throne room. Must have seen the huddle of her coat, guessed where she'd gone. But he wasn't after her. Hadn't entered the crawlway. Maybe he really couldn't fit, as she'd thought.

It seemed too much to hope for, but there was no other explanation.

Erica kept going. Would continue until she reached a dead end. Or until her strength and will gave out.

She plunged forward, covering another yard, and that was when she felt her brother's hand close over her leg.

Paul Elder hesitated by the hothouse tomatoes. Two ninety-nine a pound. Pretty steep.

But his Lily loved tomatoes, not the waxy kind so common this time of year, but vine-ripened, juicy, like these.

He selected four tomatoes, added them to his shopping basket. He would deny Lily nothing now.

Elder made his way through the narrow aisles of Waldman's Grocery, a tall patrician man with thinning silver hair and a proud face deeply furrowed. Coatless, he wore a suit jacket, dress shirt, and necktie. The habit of sartorial formality died hard. There were mornings when he still found himself reaching for the starched blue uniform in its plastic wrap, before remembering that he was a civilian now.

After lunch with Connor, he'd run a few errands, stopping at the hardware store for a new shower curtain—he was using the guest bathroom now, to be near Lily on the ground floor—then at the bank and now, finally, the market. Each chore took longer than it needed to, because he found himself pausing for conversation with nearly everyone he passed.

Folks in this town knew him, sought his company—lately, it seemed, more than ever. It was as if the anxieties raised by the Wilcott case had stirred a need in people, a childlike yearning for reassurance from someone older and authoritative.

When the basket was full, each item on his short grocery list methodically checked off, plus a few extras like the tomatoes for his wife and a Sara Lee frozen cherry pie for himself, Elder headed for the checkout counter. On his way over, he picked up today's Barrow *Register,* glancing at the headline.

Another nonstory reporting no new leads in the only criminal investigation that mattered around here.

He joined the checkout line, saying hello to Mrs. Doyle, ahead of him. She was off her diet again, or so it appeared from the tubs of ice cream and boxes of frozen pies in her cart. She never used to eat like that, but then her Jimmy started getting into trouble, setting fires, vandalizing school property, and finally ended up in a reformatory, or whatever such places were called now . . .

Elder sighed, mildly astonished at the free run of his thoughts. Yes, he knew this town, all right, knew it inside and out.

Truth was, he knew more about it, and about one aspect in particular, than he truly cared to know.

But that sordid business had been over and done with for years. No need to think of it anymore.

Besides, cops always saw the dark corners, the hidden guilt. He recalled a visit to Philadelphia last year, where he got a guided tour from a Philly PD homicide detective of his acquaintance.

Behind that building there, the man would say, *is where we found a woman's torso one time. Just the torso. Couldn't ID her, so we named her Sheila, after this babe in Personnel, 'cause she was all tits and no brains. Never cleared that case . . .*

Next door, that hotel, that's where we nabbed a serial rapist. He used to dress up like a bellboy, get 'em to open the door. What you call room service, I guess . . .

Now over here . . .

A ghoulish travelogue, but Elder had enjoyed it, safe in the certainty that nothing so bad could afflict small, rural Barrow.

That was before Sherry Wilcott, of course. And the end of his conceit.

He reached the checker, unloaded his basket. Jennifer was on duty. "Hi, Chief."

They still called him that, everybody in town, though he did his best to discourage the practice.

"How's Mrs. Elder doing?" the girl added with a sympathetic smile.

"Better every day," Elder said with gruff joviality. "She'll be out and about in no time flat." He dropped his voice to a mock whisper. "Personally, I think she's faking it. She's gotten used to the easy life, with me as her errand boy."

The lies came without effort. He'd grown accustomed to fending off pity with humor.

Jennifer laughed. She was a chubby little thing with a round face and fat fingers, the type who'd make a good wife if she could find a grown-up man, one whose romantic fantasies had not been entirely molded by cover girls and centerfolds.

"Had some excitement here today," Jennifer said as she set to work scanning his purchases.

"Oh?"

"*He* came by. You know."

Robert, she meant. That was who they always meant when they said *he* with that certain emphasis.

"Did he?" Elder felt a twinge of misgiving, as he always did when this subject arose. "It's been a while."

"Oh, yeah. Like, over a month. We started to think maybe he was getting his groceries someplace else. Wouldn't've minded if he did. That guy is *so* creepy."

"Just different, Jen." Elder said it automatically. He had always felt a need to defend and protect the small, shocked boy in the Superman pajamas, even though that boy no longer existed.

"I had to ring him up," Jennifer went on as she searched for a price code on a cracker box. "He was, like, watching me the whole time."

"Maybe he's lonely."

"Yeah, probably. But he's so weird. Didn't say a word. Just sort of zoned out, and then I saw he was staring at the *Weekly World News*."

"Him and sixty million others. Did he buy it?"

"Nah."

"Well, he showed some good sense there."

"But the thing is, he was, like, *obsessed* with it."

Elder glanced at the tabloid, stuffed into a wire rack near the Snickers bars and the astrology guides. A headline in enormous black letters posted a lurid warning—SCIENTISTS SAY: DEADLY POLLUTION WILL END ALL LIFE IN TEN YEARS! Under this, an "artist's conception" of a terrified mob choking on black fumes, the Manhattan skyline dimly visible in the background. In small letters, a grim afterthought: *"Only Cockroaches Will Survive!"*

"They may have a point," Elder said, smiling. "Been to New York lately? I'd put my money on the roaches."

Audrey, the checker in the next lane, joined the conversation. "Tell the chief what happened when he left."

"Oh, yeah." Jennifer shivered with a thrill of dread. "You know Tommy? Tommy Stadson, we got him stacking boxes and rounding up the shopping carts?" Elder knew him, and knew his parents too, and his grandparents to boot. "Well, Tommy says the guy was just standing there in the parking lot, staring at me through the front window. Right *at* me, Tommy says."

Audrey shook her head. "We all got scared when we heard that."

The customer in line behind Elder, a portly man he didn't recognize, but who apparently knew him, spoke up. "Why in hell hasn't that new man Connor arrested that freak by now?"

Elder had heard the question many times in the past two months. "Being eccentric's not a crime."

"Killing a girl sure is. Using a knife to carve her up . . ."

"We don't know who did that."

"We can guess. I got a daughter. Same age as this girl here." The man fingered Jennifer, who shivered again. "It's getting so I can't let her out of the house."

"Everyone's real scared, Chief," Audrey said, as if this were a revelation. "They ought to do something."

"He was staring right at me," Jennifer repeated.

Elder put up his hands, requesting silence.

"Now, look." He kept his voice steady as he studied each of his interrogators in turn. "This poor fellow's been living near town for most of his life. Isn't that right? Grew up here, went off to boarding school, then came back."

The portly man started to interrupt. Elder hushed him with a gaze.

"And in nearly all that time," he went on calmly, "we never gave him a second thought, now, did we? Felt sorry for him, that's all. Now we're scared, just as you say, Audrey. We're scared and looking for a villain, and he does make a convenient one. But this isn't Salem, and we're not having any witch-hunts here."

"He ought to at least be investigated," the portly man said. "After all, who's to say he *didn't* kill her? It's more likely him than one of my buddies at the Lions Club."

Elder had an answer for that, but couldn't use it. The answer was that Robert Garrison already had been investigated rather thoroughly.

Connor had handled the matter with admirable discretion shortly after Sherry Wilcott washed up on the creek bank. Accompanied only by a close-mouthed forensics expert from the state police, Connor had visited Robert at the small, secluded cabin that had been his home for fifteen years. He'd requested permission to search the place. Robert could have refused, requiring Connor to obtain a warrant, if possible. But he'd proven surprisingly cooperative. As Connor told it, Robert had stood by idly, watching without expression as his house was professionally tossed.

Nothing had turned up. None of Sherry Wilcott's clothing, no incriminating photos or notes. There was one moment of muted excitement when the forensics man discovered a patch of freshly turned earth outside the cabin. Evidence could be stashed there, it was thought; but a half hour's spadework revealed only earthworms and rocks. If anything had been buried there, Robert had transplanted it.

The investigation had gone a step further. Connor was persistent. He persuaded Robert to take a polygraph test. It was administered at the cabin by an expert brought in from Philadelphia. Connor paid the travel expenses out of his own pocket and kept the visit a secret.

Again, Robert could have declined to cooperate; again, he had proven remarkably agreeable. He'd sat patiently as he was hooked up to the lie detector and put through his paces. The result? No trace of deception, even when he was asked direct questions about the Wilcott girl. If he was lying, he had fooled the machine.

So there was nothing Connor could do. This wasn't Red China, for God's sake, or Fidel's Cuba, where a man could be locked up just on somebody's say-so. Proof of guilt was needed. Facts. Something solid, not rumor and supposition and the lynch-mob murmurings of the people. Robert was innocent in the law's eyes. Might really be innocent, for all Elder knew. That profile fit him, sure, fit like a glove, but what did shrinks know?

So that was the full story, but Elder could tell none of it, because word of Connor's investigation would only boost the heat on Robert Garrison. Bad enough that folks whispered he might be a killer. Still worse for him, if they knew the cops had thought so too. Nobody would care that the investigation had proved fruitless. All that would matter was that it had been initiated.

Elder tried a different tack. "That's where you're wrong, Phil," he said, the portly man's name coming back to him out of some reservoir of memory. "About the Lions Club, I mean. I spent a few years in law enforcement, as you folks know. And I can tell you, a fellow who'd do this sort of thing is one who's good at keeping secrets. He may be the last person you'd expect. He may be the most popular man in town."

"That would be you, Chief," Audrey said, then giggled nervously, as if afraid he'd take it the wrong way.

Jennifer informed Elder of his total. "Well," she added, "whoever the bad guy is, I just hope they catch him. I heard he did more to Sherry than just cut her with a knife. I heard she was raped."

"Raped and tortured," Phil, the portly man, put in.

"I heard there was a five-pointed star carved on her chest." This was Audrey's contribution, submitted with a shudder. "A devil sign."

"None of that's so," Elder said patiently, not prevaricating this time. "That's just a lot of hooey. You know how this nonsense gets started."

Rumors were everywhere. He'd heard them all. Sherry had lived long enough to scrawl the name of her murderer on the muddy bank, but rain washed most of the letters away. Or she had been cut up in pieces, and only her head and torso had been found. Or the police had received an anonymous note promising that a girl would die every two months. Or every six months. Or, ugliest of all, Connor had found conclusive evidence of Robert's guilt, but Robert had paid him a million dollars to keep silent.

Elder did his best to squelch such gossip. It wasn't easy, though. Fear, it seemed, had a life and a mind of its own.

He paid in cash. "You folks take it easy," he said, hefting two plastic bags of groceries and passing a smile around.

"You too, Chief." Jennifer was already ringing up the portly man's purchases. "And say hi to Mrs. Elder for me."

Elder promised he would, though he knew Lily was mostly too far gone these days to even care.

At the door he was stopped by a fellow he knew slightly, George Hunnicut, loudmouthed and assertive, who accosted him with a clap on the shoulder, then leaned in conspiratorially.

"Overheard the conversation," George said. His breath smelled of onions. "I'll tell you what. You've got it wrong when you say it could be anybody."

"Do I now?" Elder was feeling tired. He wanted to go home.

"It's Robert, all right. Has to be. These things always happen in threes."

"What things?"

"First, the way their father died. Then their mother and that gigolo boyfriend of hers, back in seventy-four."

"Keith Wyatt was a doctor," Elder said mildly.

"Gigolo doctor boyfriend, then. Bad business. Now here we are, more than twenty years later, and again there's blood. It's all related, has to be. It's the Garrisons. It's Great Hall."

"I don't follow you, George."

"Whenever something bad happens in this town—something really bad—it's always the Garrisons who are at the heart of it."

"Interesting theory." The grocery bags were getting heavy.

"You know it's true."

Elder sighed. He remembered hearing similar talk on the night when Lenore and Keith were found dead. Talk of fate, a curse—childish nonsense, unworthy of even a curt dismissal.

"What I know," Elder said, breaking away, "is that the Middle Ages ended a long time ago, George. Everywhere but here."

He left the store and crossed the parking lot, walking fast in the cold. At his car he turned and looked back at the supermarket's front window. Yes, the interior was clearly visible, Jennifer in plain view.

For a moment Paul Elder just stood there, wind raking his face. He imagined Robert lingering on the asphalt, watching cute little Jennifer through the glass.

What had the man been thinking? What was he capable of?

And how could a boy in Superman p.j.'s grow into a monster— if indeed he had?

Shaking his head, Elder unlocked the car, stashed the grocery bags on the passenger seat, and slid behind the wheel. With age, they said, came wisdom. But he was seventy-six, and life was a mystery—a greater mystery now than when he was a young man of twenty-one.

Perhaps this was wisdom, only this, an acknowledgment of the strangeness of things, the fundamental enigma of existence.

Or perhaps he simply didn't want to understand.

He sighed again, his breath fogging the windshield, and drove home to his Lily with his gift of vine-ripened tomatoes, a taste of next summer, which she would not live to see.

* * *

Erica screamed.

A hand on her leg, her left leg, five fingers clamping hard on the thin fabric of her jeans, and it didn't make sense.

She had looked behind her, had seen only darkness. Robert was carrying a flashlight, she would have spotted its glow, so this couldn't be his hand on her calf.

But it was.

Erica heard an awful growl, an animal noise, a noise she had never imagined coming from her brother, never, not in the worst of her nightmares.

In a surge of blind terror she lashed out with one leg. Knee bent, she struck backward, her boot flailing in space, then making contact with something flat and fleshy, something that must be his face.

Howling now. A hurt dog. But still holding fast to her.

Fear competed with an awful bottomless guilt, guilt at inflicting harm on him, something she above all had no right to do.

She didn't believe she could hurt him again, even to save her own life, but her body disagreed, obeying the imperative of survival at any psychological cost.

She snapped her leg at him a second time, her boot heel driving into a soft padded mass that might be his neck or shoulder.

This time he let go, whimpering.

Panic propelled her forward. She dropped the flashlight, freeing her right hand to crawl faster, and as the Eveready rolled away she realized why she had seen no light behind her. Intent on pursuit, he had left his flash in the throne room. With the glow of her flashlight to guide him, it was an encumberance he didn't need.

Scrambling on all fours she kicked and clawed her way through the passage, but she had covered only a few blind yards when he caught her again.

He had her by the waist this time, was gripping her denim pants with one hand.

She slapped wildly at him, cut herself. The sliver of pain bisecting her palm brought her up short, and she understood.

He hadn't caught her. It was not his hand she felt. It was a projection of limestone, sharp and flinty, which had hooked one of her belt loops.

She struggled with the stubborn, stupid thing, fighting to tear free.

Behind her, movement.

The abandoned flash illuminated a few feet of the crawlway. Two hairless big-knuckled hands burst into its glare, trailing two pale scrawny forearms.

He'd recovered from the kick, was coming.

Erica screamed at the intransigent belt loop, the grasping rock.

Blood on her hand, slimy and warm, her fingers fumbling, uncoordinated, the goddamned rock resisting her attempts to work it loose.

He was past the cone of light from the Eveready, his shaggy head and wide shoulders traced in silhouette. Hirsute and savage, a caveman, meant for this place.

In final desperation she seized the belt loop, ripped it from its stitching.

Free.

He grabbed for her, missed, and she propelled herself forward, and there was a wall.

Dead end.

She was trapped, and he was closing in.

A scream bloomed in her, a fierce scream of two words—*Go away!*—but she had no voice. Her breath was caught in her throat, couldn't reach her lungs.

Tumbling out of darkness he came at her, draping her like a bearskin, bathing her in his stink of sweat. She tried to kick again—no use—her boots were useless at such intimate range.

She knew what this was. This was hell.

Her throat unlocked, and she gasped a plea. *"Let go!"*

He bent her arm behind her back.

Pops of pain. Shoulder, elbow, wrist.

Screaming from someone, somewhere.

Disconnected thoughts, images. Chalk marks on a wall. Child's laughter. *Look, Erica. Now I'm big enough to beat you up.*

Her left arm bending at a crazy angle, fingers lodged between her shoulder blades.

Numbness and agony, her neck craning, hips twisting under his hard, flat weight.

Then a final angry yank. Sizzle of agony in her shoulder, and a cry from deep inside her, a cry wrenched from her belly like the wail of a mother giving birth.

It came over her in a rush, a bright fog of pain. There was a hum, louder and louder, and it became a crowd's babble, indistinct and distant, many voices.

She was glad the crowd was here. This was her last thought before the babble rose to a beating roar. Glad, yes—glad she wouldn't have to die alone.

5

Andrew Stafford played hard on the tennis court. He drove home from the Barrow Racquet Club's indoor arena with his brown hair dripping, his lean face flushed, having passed two and a half hours in intense competition and won the match two sets to one.

Success he attributed not primarily to his whiplash serve or his pitiless volleys at the net, but to a manic, almost instinctual combativeness that drove him to exploit his opponent's vulnerabilities, to score points like a predator inflicting wounds. He had read of how the leopard would hook its claws into a quarry's belly and hang on until the stomach opened in a rush of guts, and this was the image he held focused in his mind as he tossed the green ball high and rifled another stinging ace into the service box.

Singles' play was his forte. Man on man. To size up the enemy, study his habits, map his weaknesses, then play them off against his own strengths. He was tall, an inch over six feet, and sinewy and quick. He could cover the court, stretch for nearly any ball. And he was a thinker, always changing tactics, keeping his opponent off guard.

He was a magnanimous winner, a disgruntled loser. Regardless of the outcome on the court, he never lingered in the clubhouse afterward, hoisting beers and watching ESPN with the other members. Tennis for him was not a social event. It was battle.

He steered his red Ferrari down Highway 322, exceeding the

posted limit for the sheer pleasure of speed and risk. Took the exit at Tall Pine Road, downshifting the manual transmission with unconscious skill, and under a canopy of high branches he rode to Great Hall.

Whenever he saw the large rambling house behind its brick walls and iron gate, he felt the same primal thrill that enticed him to the racquet club. The hot exhilaration of challenges met, of odds overcome. Of victory.

The house had gone up in 1889, raised by Hugh Garrison, a wildcatter in Pennsylvania's northwest corner who'd drilled a lot of dry holes before striking oil. The gush of crude had made him a millionaire. He'd acquired a wife half his age and built Great Hall as a rural retreat. Local legend pictured the aged Hugh as feudal overlord of Barrow, a monied, lecherous tyrant who, weary of his wife, had enforced his personal right of *prima nocte* on frightened virgin girls. How much of this was true, Andrew couldn't guess. But he admired crusty old Hugh. The man had been a son of a bitch, sure, but he'd known what he wanted. And he had taken it.

Upon Hugh Garrison's death in 1940, the family fortune had passed to his only legitimate heir, Duncan, then twenty years old, having been sired when his father was a robust sixty. The habit of late paternity persisted in the Garrison line; Duncan was forty-two when his daughter Erica was born; Robert came three years later, in 1965. Duncan's death at the age of fifty-three had made Lenore a rich widow; when she died a year later, the family fortune had been placed in trust for the two children. Upon reaching adulthood, they'd divided it. Erica's share of the millions had included Great Hall.

She hadn't resided at the house when Andrew met her. The estate was rented out at five thousand a month to a corporate CEO in Pittsburgh, who used it only on weekends. Erica herself was ensconced in a two-bedroom cottage on the outskirts of town. Money was not the reason; rental income from the estate barely covered the costs of maintenance, taxes, and staff. She simply did not choose to live there.

Andrew talked her into it. He was good at that. The game of persuasion was, to him, another blood sport. He had hooked his claws in her and had not let go until he'd won her complete capitulation.

Their courtship had followed the same pattern. He'd met her at an art auction in Philadelphia, introducing himself as a dealer in rare artworks, with galleries in town. Initially he viewed her strictly as a short-term project, an attractive woman, sure of herself yet curiously shy. He took her to dinner at the Ritz-Carlton, and then they went upstairs to her hotel room. She told him she never did this sort of thing, and he believed her. She conveyed an air of wariness, of tight self-control. But he said the right things, and she surrendered, as he'd known she would.

It might have ended there, except that some intuitive feeling prompted him to take his laptop into the bathroom while she slept in the hotel bed. There was a phone in the lavatory; he used the outlet to hook up his modem. Then he accessed the Internet and ran a database search on Erica Garrison.

She was mentioned sparingly—he'd guessed she was not the sort to seek or attract publicity—but even those few references were enough to establish a fact of fundamental importance. The woman was rich.

Heiress to the Garrison oil fortune. That was how it was stated in one write-up culled from *Art Collector* magazine.

Later, through more sophisticated research methods, he learned the precise value of her holdings. Eleven million dollars in invested assets, plus Great Hall.

He'd decided to make her a long-term project, with marriage as the goal. And no prenuptial agreement, either.

The task had proven easy enough, in one respect. She was open to his charm, flattered by attention—embarrassed by it, almost, a strange reaction to observe in a beautiful woman. He met her again in Philadelphia, then arranged a trip to the Adirondacks. After six months of courtship he proposed, and she said yes.

But even as she accepted the engagement ring, there was sorrow in her eyes. He had wanted to ask why she was sad, how he could help. He knew she wouldn't tell him. She kept her deepest feelings hidden, allowing him only glimpses, when he wanted much more.

And in that respect, his courtship of Erica Garrison had not been easy at all. Because during their time together, something in him had changed, some twist of perspective had altered his view of the world and of his image in a mirror. He sensed she had been hurt, and he didn't want to hurt her further, didn't want to use her and discard her as he'd planned—a short marriage, a quick divorce, a lucrative settlement.

The thought of it, of what he'd meant to do, would wake him at night, his heart racing. He took late showers to steam off his night sweats. At times he thought of severing the relationship, even as he neared his goal.

He didn't know quite what had come over him. Attack of conscience or some damn thing.

It wasn't until their wedding day that he understood. He lifted the veil and kissed her, and with a lurch of vertigo he realized that somehow, without meaning to, he'd fallen in love with this woman who was now his wife.

There was no way he could explain it. He'd had many women; seduction came as naturally to him as any other brand of deceit. He had never been in love, had half-disbelieved the whole idea of love, which might be just another scam, perhaps originated by an itinerant troubadour who needed to stir up business, or by somebody at Hallmark. Deep feelings of any kind were not his style.

Still, he'd grown to notice little things—the delicacy of Erica's hands, her slender fingers, the blue traceries of veins behind the warm Botticelli skin. The glow of her face in the light of the bedside alarm clock's dial, and the soft whisper of her breathing. The tilt of her head as she listened for distant thunder. Tunes she hummed. Her steps, light as a dancer's, as she crossed a span of tiled floor in a wash of Vermeer daylight. The slow throb of her pulse against his lips when he teased her neck with kisses.

This was love, he guessed. If it was a scam, then it had fleeced him, turned his pockets inside out.

Now he had Erica Garrison and Great Hall and the Garrison millions, and everything should have been fine, should have been perfect. Instead he was on the verge of losing it all—or nearly all.

The thought stirred petulant anger in him, and he was rough with the car as he manhandled it to a stop on Great Hall's long circular drive. He popped the trunk and slung a Wilson bag over his shoulder, then entered the house through the front door.

The foyer was marble, opening into the living room and the dining room beyond. Together the rooms formed a single cavernous expanse of gray granite, hung with a tapestry of sunbeams slanting through a tall bay window under the raftered ceiling and an array of chandeliers.

It was for this central sweep of space that Great Hall was named. Andrew paused to admire it, as he nearly always did. The dimensions of the hall and the museum quality of its fixtures gave him the feeling of a tourist at Versailles. But he was no tourist here. If this was Versailles, he was Louis XIV, at least for a short while longer.

Only one aspect of the decor failed to meet with his approval. The thick pile carpet was tinted a deep burgundy, purplish in shadow. He'd been told the house had always featured carpet of this shade, selected originally by Hugh Garrison's wife to set off the gray granite walls.

Andrew disliked the color. To him, it looked like old blood.

The rest of the house was dismayingly ordinary. Hugh Garrison, though eager to impress his guests at dinner parties, had been indifferent to everyday comforts. Most of the eighteen rooms were cramped, poorly ventilated, hot in summer and damp the rest of the year. The place looked immense from the outside, but much of the floor space was wasted by an inelegant architectural scheme.

If he'd had his way, he would have remodeled the house. Broken down some walls, consolidated the smaller rooms, added new ones. It had been a dream of his, a dream destined to be unrealized. Great Hall would not be his much longer. And neither would Erica.

Still, he played to win, and he would win this game. She could take back her house and her millions, but in a master stroke he had outmaneuvered her, though she didn't know it yet.

He ascended the high staircase, the bannister pulsing to the rhythm of Vivaldi, playing over Great Hall's sound system. Marie had put on the CD. Not for her sake; the girl's tastes ran to insipid country-western songs crooned by gravelly-voiced suburban cowboys who rhymed *break* and *sake* and *heartache*. *The Four Seasons* was for him; he'd instructed Marie to play it whenever he was due back from the club.

Halfway up the stairs, he heard her thin voice call to him over a surge of music. From a height he turned and saw her at the foot of the stairs, his housekeeper, Marie Stopani, a lean raven-haired girl of twenty-two whose chief interests were horoscopes and celebrity scandals. She was Great Hall's only live-in staff; cleaning women and gardeners visited two or three times a week to maintain the house and grounds.

"Yes, Marie?"

"Did he reach you? On the phone?"

"Did who reach me?"

"The police chief. Chief Connor."

Andrew felt a very small twinge at the base of his stomach. "Connor? No. What are you talking about?"

Marie spread her hands helplessly. She looked petite and helpless and flustered, but she always did.

"He called here. Twice. The first time, he asked for you."

"When was this?"

The question might have been a conundrum of particle physics, requiring deep and sustained thought.

"The first time was maybe two-thirty or a little later," Marie said finally. "Second time, I guess fifteen minutes ago."

"Did you tell him to try the club?" She nodded. "Well, he must have missed me." Casually he added, "What did he want?"

"I don't know, he didn't say."

"Are you sure it's me he asked for? Not Erica?"

"For both. First Mrs. Stafford, then you."

He began to understand. His fear receded, and guilt spilled in to fill the void.

"I see." His voice was calm. "Well, probably he was calling about some charity function he's involved in. Like that police benefit last Christmas."

He resumed climbing the stairs.

"Maybe," Marie said, plainly unconvinced. "He seemed worried, though. Mrs. Kellerman did, too."

This stopped him. "Mrs. Kellerman?"

"She called first. She was asking for Mrs. Stafford. She was upset. I could tell. She was talking really fast."

He nodded, still unconcerned. "Rachel always talks fast. Too much caffeine. Don't worry about it."

"Don't you want to call Chief Connor?"

"Later."

Upstairs, he shut the door to the master suite, then stripped out of his tennis whites. He knew what was going on. It was obvious.

Erica wasn't at her shop. If she had been, there would have been no need for Rachel and Connor to ask for her at Great Hall. So where could she be?

On one of her drives, of course.

It was something she did when she was upset. She climbed into that big white Mercedes of hers and piled up miles on the odometer, traveling the rural routes, going nowhere. She'd never taken off during business hours before, never abandoned her precious shop, but today she must have been unusually distressed.

Well, he knew the reason. It was his fault. What he'd done this morning—inexcusable.

He entered the lavatory and ran the shower hot, then stood under the cone of steaming spray, erasing sweat and fatigue. He wished he could as easily erase the memory of his behavior just hours ago.

It had been an act of impulse. Of instinct, almost. Needs could be denied only so long; then they would break out into action, heedless of scruples. But none of that was any excuse.

He had raped his wife.

Well, not rape, not quite, not exactly. But close enough.

He grabbed the bath sponge and scrubbed himself, still feeling dirty despite the rush of water. The shower could not make him clean. Certainly not today. It only reminded him . . . brought it back . . . every detail, incriminating as a police report.

He remembered.

Erica had risen at six for her daily run, four miles in the dark and cold, an obsession with her. Half asleep, Andrew had murmured that she ought to skip it today, just this once, as he reached for her with a needful hand.

But she pulled away. Donned her sweatsuit, her Nikes, and a down jacket for warmth. And left him without a word.

He heard her retreating footsteps as he drifted back to sleep.

At seven she returned, flushed and trembly, hair pasted to her forehead with sweat. He watched her strip in the master suite, studying her flat belly, her breasts in profile, then the deep cleavage between her shoulder blades as she walked away into the bathroom, still unspeaking. There had been no words of consequence between them for three months.

He loved her. But she didn't believe him when he told her so. Even when emotion brought him close to tears, she would turn scornfully aside. She would say, *You lied to me before,* and there was no need to add the obvious corollary: *How can I know you aren't lying now?*

Had she asked it, he wouldn't have known how to answer. In truth, there was no reason for her to trust him. But if she could have looked inside him, peered into his heart or soul or whatever poetic image one chose, she would have seen that he was not lying this time. He loved her, needed her, and again and again she walked away.

Abandoned, he lay in bed, his fist around his penis, counting the exact number of days since he'd made love to his wife. Then he heard the hiss of shower spray from behind the bathroom door, and suddenly he was out of bed, tugging off his Jockey shorts, walking naked into the lavatory, through warm mist to the shower door, sliding it wide, stepping in with her as she blinked in astonishment and something very much like indignation.

She resisted at first, not violently, but with curt demurrals, some nonsense about errands to do, a schedule to keep, but this only aroused him further—that she should deny herself to him, even then, after so long an abstinence.

He backed her against the wet tiles and in the cone of stinging water he entered her, pumping hard, and she said, *No, Andrew, no,* but he wouldn't listen; he fought her into submission until finally she let her head drop back, water streaming over her closed eyelids, her open mouth, rivulets of shampoo soaping her shoulders and breasts in a filmy gloss of bubbles, and as he reached a climax he pressed his lips to her ear and heard himself whisper, *You like to run, don't you? Well, don't run from me!*

When he was done, he left her in the shower, not bothering to close the sliding door.

She'd left the house, her face red with anger. Pride had stopped him from offering an apology or explanation. Besides, he'd known that the only true explanation was the one she would not accept.

He loved her. God damn it, he loved her so much, and she refused to believe it, refused to believe any words of tenderness from him. But it was the simple truth. He loved her.

"Well, asshole"—the hiss of his voice merged with the shower's sizzle—"you sure picked one *hell* of a way to prove it."

With a violent jerk of his wrist he twisted the faucet to the off position. He toweled himself dry and ran a comb through his hair, taking longer than necessary, not out of vanity but because the comb's rhythmic strokes soothed him. When he was calm, he dressed in long, loose trousers and a Madras shirt.

She would come back. She always did. But she wouldn't love him, ever.

A knock on his bedroom door. "Mr. Stafford?"

It was Marie, a peculiar piping urgency in her voice.

"What?" he snapped.

"Chief Connor is here. He says he needs to see you. Right away."

Andrew lowered his head, took a deep breath. He had hoped to avoid this conversation.

"All right, Marie. I'm coming down."

He found Ben Connor in the sunroom, his concern instantly evident in the strain on his face, the haunted intensity of his eyes.

"Andrew," Connor said evenly, his voice betraying no stress.

"Ben."

There was an awkward moment of hesitation, and then both men simultaneously extended their arms. The handshake was a single pump, impersonal and forced.

Connor, at forty-two, was five years Andrew's senior. With

his square, rough-hewn face and narrowed eyes, he had the look of an NYPD cop, a look that was both stolid and slightly cynical. His years in the city had worn him down; his close-cropped sandy hair was thinning on top, and his broad shoulders were slightly rounded in a perpetual slump. He was a couple of inches shorter than Andrew, maybe five-eleven, with big, thickly muscled arms and large, calloused, workman's hands.

All in all, Andrew had found Connor an odd choice to fill Chief Elder's position. He would have preferred someone more polished, someone with style, smart and slick and angular—someone more like Andrew himself. Yes. He always felt more comfortable around men he understood.

"I tried to get in touch with you," Connor said.

"Marie told me." A flicker of reaction shadowed Connor's face, and Andrew added, "I was just about to return the call." The lie was smooth enough to pass even a cop's inspection.

"I'd prefer to speak with you in person, anyway." Connor hesitated, as if reluctant to broach the topic, and Andrew jumped in.

"It's about Erica, isn't it? She can't be found."

This time Connor's reaction was more than a flicker. "How'd you know?"

"Simple deduction. You and Rachel Kellerman both calling the house, asking for her. Anyway, there's no cause for alarm. My wife is perfectly all right."

"Then you know where she is?" Connor took a step forward, and Andrew had the unsettling impression that the police chief was ready to seize him and shake the information out of him.

He held up a hand to ward off this attack. "Not exactly. But I know what she's up to. She has this habit of going off on long drives."

He explained it to Connor while the police chief stood listening. Distantly Andrew thought that it was odd they had both remained standing, like boxers challenging each other in a ring.

The room around them was bright in the crisp winter sun. A restful place, impeccably designed and decorated. Bare elms were framed in the high French doors. A bowl of apples and pears rested on a glass table like a still life.

"Long drives," Andrew was saying. "Into the mountains, sometimes. And there's no way to get in touch with her. I've told her she ought to get a phone installed in the Mercedes, in case she breaks down on some back road, but she said no, she wanted her privacy. She likes to get away from phones, voices."

Connor rubbed his chin. The energy that had animated him a few moments earlier seemed curiously dissipated now. "So you're saying she just takes off in her car and stays out for hours?"

"Right."

"Why?"

"It's her way of blowing off steam."

"You mean she only does this when she's worked up about something?"

"Yes." Andrew hated where this was leading.

"Did anything happen today that would have upset her?"

The Vivaldi was still playing, piped into this room and every other room on the ground floor. Andrew wished Marie would turn it off.

"We had a fight," he said quietly. "This morning. Before she left for her shop."

"A bad fight?"

"Bad enough. No words were exchanged. That's not the way she does things. She keeps it inside. Holds back. Anyway, she left, and I'm betting she never even went to the shop. Never opened for business at all. She's probably driven all the way to Philly by now."

"What did you fight about?"

Andrew wanted to say it was none of Connor's concern, but of course he couldn't. "Marital difficulties," he said curtly.

Connor looked at him, then looked away. "Has this been going on long?"

"Long enough." Every syllable was an effort. "Since December."

"And she's gone out for drives before?"

"Repeatedly. That's all this is. Domestic dispute. Sorry to have wasted your time."

"Did she say anything when she left?"

"I told you, she holds things in."

"So you don't really know—"

"I know *her*, God damn it. She's my wife. She'll come back."

Connor had to see that there was nothing worth investigating here. Yet he stood unmoving, as if the interview had barely begun. He must be enjoying himself. Watching rich Andrew Stafford confess the disintegration of his marriage. It was a show for him, a spectacle, and Andrew hated him for it, hated the smug, smiling son of a bitch . . .

Except Connor wasn't smiling, was he? His face was grim, his squinty eyes distracted by worry. And a new feeling crept over Andrew, an intimation that he was missing something, that his perspective had been dangerously skewed.

"What is it, Ben?" he asked in a softer tone. "I've told you what must have happened. How come you don't want to believe it?"

Connor stuffed his hands in the pockets of his vinyl jacket, hunching his shoulders like a shy schoolboy.

"Because," he said, "it doesn't exactly fit the facts. See, Mrs. Stafford did open up her shop this morning. She even got her mail, which means she was there probably as late as one o'clock. Then she disappeared."

Andrew blinked, trying to take this in. "After one o'clock?"

"That's how it looks. She failed to keep a one-thirty lunch date with Mrs. Kellerman. I went over to the gallery, and I found the rear door unlocked. The lights had been left on. It appeared to me she'd left in a hurry."

None of this made sense. By one o'clock Erica would have had time to collect her thoughts and contain her anger. She was good at that. And she wouldn't stand up a friend for lunch, not without a compelling reason. And she would never leave the shop unlocked . . . the shop, with its small fortune of merchandise gathered from around the Mediterranean . . .

"I've got four units looking for her," Connor added. "Or for her car."

"Four units . . ." Barrow had a small police force. Four units must be nearly every patrol car Connor had. That kind of full-court press would be applied only to a top-priority case.

But there was only one top priority in Barrow lately. The case that was on everybody's mind. The case . . .

"Oh, Christ," someone said in a week, reedy voice, and Andrew needed a moment to realize the words had come from him.

He got it now. He got it. What Connor was worried about. A missing woman. An unlocked door.

He took a step backward and sank into a low settee. "Christ," he said again as the room brightened and blurred. "It's like the Wilcott girl. That's what you think."

"I haven't said that." Connor leaned over the settee, his manner soothing, like a doctor's. "Just stay calm, Andrew. Help me out here. Okay? Help me out."

Andrew ought to be furious at being addressed in that patronizing tone, but oddly he found it comforting. "Okay," he said, feeling as small and helpless as a child.

"What time did she leave for work?"

"Eight. About eight."

"Did you hear from her at any time after that?"

"No. Of course not. I told you, we had a . . . rather bad morning."

He wondered if their encounter in the shower had been their last time together. The thought squeezed his heart.

"Did she say anything when she left? Anything at all?"

He shook his head.

"Can you think of anyplace she might go?"

"There's a cottage. She lived there before I convinced her to return to Great Hall. She still rents it."

Connor hesitated just long enough for Andrew to look up into his eyes.

"I know about the cottage," Connor said. "I already checked it out. She's not there. Anyplace else?"

He was about to say no, then stopped himself.

Because suddenly he had a very good idea of where his wife might have gone.

What would have prompted her to do it on this particular day, he couldn't guess. But it was possible. Definitely possible.

"Anyplace else?" Connor snapped, his veneer of patience cracking.

"A hundred places," Andrew said, the words coming easily, as his lies always did. "The copy shop to run off next month's catalogue, or Harlan's Nursery—she said she needed fresh flowers for the gallery—or the post office to send out some parcel . . . You know her, Ben. She's a dynamo. Always rushing around. I tell her to slow down, but . . ." He let his answer trail off with a shrug.

He thought it sounded okay, but to his discomfort he felt the police chief studying him with new intensity.

"I'm asking about someplace less obvious," Connor said. "Someplace no one would think of looking. You're sure you have no ideas along those lines?"

"God damn it, Ben." Fear of Connor, fear of what he might be on the verge of guessing, made Andrew abruptly angry, and he rose from the settee, strong in rage. "I told you so already. What is this, an interrogation? Am I under suspicion here?"

Connor seemed unfazed by the outburst. "I didn't say that."

"The husband is always a suspect, though. Isn't that right?"

"There's not even any evidence of a crime."

"Maybe you think I killed the Wilcott girl. I'm beginning to regret all the money we've raised for your department. That kid with leukemia, the sergeant's boy—you were pretty damn grateful for the bash we threw for him. I guess gratitude only lasts until you cash the fucking check."

Fury felt good. Like crushing a volley directly into his opponent's face. Intimidation at the net.

But Connor was not intimidated. He merely spread his hands in a sad, regretful gesture. "I'd better get going."

"Do that," Andrew said, then wished he hadn't. The words came out weak and spiteful.

Connor was leaving the room when he stopped by a framed photo of Erica on a rattan table.

"Hate to ask," he said, "but may I borrow this?"

"Her portrait? What the hell for?"

"We may have to fax it to other departments."

Other departments. If the search went statewide.

And if his wife had gone where Andrew suspected . . . if something had happened . . .

Then the photo could be used to identify the body, couldn't it? When she washed up on a river bank, cut and bloated?

His rage vanished, and with it his strength. Andrew let his head drop.

"Sure, take it. Shit."

He watched Connor fumble the glossy eight-by-ten out of its rosewood frame. It was a glamour shot of Erica, done by a local photographer to accompany newspaper ads for her shop. She hadn't wanted it in the house—"too vain"—but Andrew liked the shot and had insisted.

"I'm sorry," he said softly. "About what I said. Lost control there. It's not . . . not really like me."

"Understandable. I'm not much of a diplomat."

"Me neither." He gestured weakly at the photo. "I . . . I'd like that back. I mean . . . well, we must have the negative someplace, but . . ."

"You'll get it back. Don't worry." Connor touched him lightly on the arm, as if handling something fragile. "I know the way out."

Andrew stood in the sunroom and listened to the retreating tread of boots. Thinking. Thinking hard.

By the time he heard the front door close, he knew what he must do.

In his bedroom he kept a blue steel Colt .45, the Combat Commander model. It was hidden at the back of his closet, in a shoebox tucked away behind other boxes, where Marie never cleaned and Erica never looked.

He loaded the gun, then wedged it in his waistband, donning a loose-fitting travel coat for concealment. Extra cartridges went in the cargo pockets.

When he looked out the window, he saw the driveway empty except for his Ferrari. Connor was gone.

Marie caught him going down the stairs, his coat half buttoned. She asked what was happening, why the police chief had come. He brushed aside the questions.

"If you see Erica or hear from her," he said, "call my car phone. No answer, page me."

He strode to the door, turned.

"And shut off that fucking Vivaldi."

Then Andrew was outside, the door slamming behind him as he sprinted down the steps to the red coupe, the gun barrel cold against his hip.

6

In the frosty air Danvers slipped the gas-pump nozzle into the Chevy Caprice and pulled the trigger.

"Check your oil, Officer?"

Looking up, she saw the lone attendant, Charlie something, wave to her from the cashier's window.

"Hey, Charlie."

"Catch any bad guys lately?" He said this every time she pulled into the lonely filling station at the edge of the woods.

"Couple bank robbers. And an arsonist. Been a slow day."

He had to mull over her reply before registering it as a joke. "Well, you can arrest me anytime."

Danvers sighed, her breath crystallizing in a cold cloud. Exactly what combination of biological and psychological imperatives drove men to hit on any woman deemed even borderline attractive?

She could have understood the constant attention if she were a beauty. But she wasn't. She was short and stocky, with what her high school gym coach had called a swimmer's build. Her square, freckly face and close-trimmed brown hair fairly shouted *tomboy*.

Guys said she had a nice smile, and this was probably so, but she wouldn't have figured a smile would go very far. And, in fact, it never had, until she joined the force.

The nozzle clicked off, the squad car's tank full.

So maybe it's the uniform, she reflected as she wrestled the nozzle back into its frame. Maginnis had warned her about that.

Men wouldn't take her seriously. They'd tell her she looked cute in blue.

I went through it, Maginnis had said. *So will you.*

Danvers remembered being naively amazed that anyone ever had dared to call Lieutenant Maginnis cute.

At the cashier's window she paid with a twenty, getting change and a receipt.

"Sure you don't wanna frisk me?" Charlie asked with a vaguely hopeful smile, as if he thought she really might.

"Some other time." She blew on her raw hands. "Much business?"

"Nah. Real slow day." Chuckle. "Like yours."

She did him the favor of smiling at this witticism. In that moment she resolved to ask Woodall out. On a date.

The decision came first; then she had to sort through her reasons. It was Charlie, she realized, poor Charlie and his dullness and bad jokes. He had never read Dostoyevsky, had never given a moment's thought to understanding the criminal mind, had no ambitions beyond the safe monotony of his undemanding job.

Most guys she met were like that. Woodall was different, and she appreciated him by contrast.

"You wear that for luck?" Charlie asked.

She blinked, momentarily unsure what he was talking about, then realized he was looking at her crucifix. It was a small silver Jesus, only an inch and a half long, crudely molded, hooked to a chain around her neck.

Normally the crucifix was safely tucked inside her shirt collar, but sometimes, when she was alone or lost in thought, she pulled it out to run her fingertips over it. Nervous habit.

"Yeah," she said, "I guess it's for luck. I shouldn't wear it. I mean, it's against regulations to wear anything on a chain, because somebody could grab hold of it, you know. But, well, my mom wore it all the time when she was an Army nurse."

The silver Christ flashed in the sun. Self-consciously Danvers loosened her collar and hid the crucifix again.

"She see any action?" Charlie asked.

Danvers nodded. "In 'Nam."

"Wow." Charlie seemed at a loss, then recovered with a gamin smile. "Here's *my* good-luck charm."

From under the counter he pulled out a single-barrel twelve-gauge Marlin shotgun. Danvers stiffened.

"That thing loaded?" she asked, regarding it warily. She had learned a sensible respect for all firearms.

"Sure is. Two shells and a three-shot plug. Boss says if you can't take care of business with two shells, you won't need a third."

"Let's hope you never need it at all."

Charlie shrugged. "I don't know. It might be fun to be a hero."

Danvers doubted it, but she didn't argue, merely collected her change and nodded goodbye. "Gotta run."

She was walking away, stuffing the bills and receipt in her back pocket, when she remembered why she had asked Charlie about business in the first place.

She turned back. "Hey, you haven't had a white Mercedes in here, have you?"

He scratched a blackhead on his cheek. "Merc? Nah. Might've *seen* one, though."

"Seen one where?"

"On the road. That's what I do, you know? When there's no customers, I watch the cars go by. Count 'em. Identify 'em. It's sort of a game."

This sounded to Danvers like a pretty boring game, but she kept this opinion to herself. "So," she pressed, "you saw a white Mercedes?"

"I think it was."

"What time, about?"

"Gee, I don't know. At least an hour ago. Maybe longer. Like I said, slow day."

"Which way was it going?"

His face scrunched in concentration. "West."

"Could you tell who was in the car?"

"Nah. It just zoomed by. Swish."

She asked a few more questions, learning that the Mercedes had been a sedan, relatively new. "Okay, Charlie. Thanks."

"You ever need me riding shotgun," he called hopefully after her, "I'm ready."

"I'll keep it in mind."

In her car with the heater blowing hard, Danvers consulted a map. She was already outside Barrow's town limits, near the edge of the search area Connor had prescribed. To go west would take her farther into unincorporated county land. Technically the county sheriff had jurisdiction, but nobody was going to raise a fuss about that.

It wasn't the legalities that worried her. She just didn't know if Charlie had the least value as a witness. He might have seen Erica Stafford's white Mercedes, sure—or someone else's tan BMW or beige Cadillac. Or he might have seen nothing at all, and claimed otherwise just to pretend he was being helpful.

On the other hand, her search had yielded no results so far, and judging from the regular, carefully guarded updates from Hart, Woodall, and Sergeant Larkin that crackled over the radio, she wasn't the only one coming up empty.

Danvers set the map aside and pulled out of the gas station, hesitating only briefly before heading west.

She would go a mile or two. What was the harm?

Robert Garrison's cabin lay at the end of a dirt-and-rock road, on a low hill, leaning steeply against the sky. A fire some decades earlier had burned most of the timber on the hill, and only a few scraggly pines had dared a reemergence, forming a tangle of branches on the lower slope.

Where the cabin was sited, there was no foliage, no landscaping, just blistered brown grass, grown high but trampled down, and strings of creeping vines like varicose veins.

Andrew imagined that primroses would bloom here in spring, but spring had not yet come.

Crouching in a stand of pine beyond the fire line, he glassed the hill and the cabin, a pair of Tasco binoculars tipped against his aviator lenses. His gaze roved over the whole area but kept returning to the cabin's window, hot with reflected glare.

He wished the sun were lower. The angle of its rays masked anything or anyone waiting behind the window.

Still, he was fairly sure the cabin was unoccupied. Robert's truck, at least, was not in view. Ordinarily, as he recalled, it would be parked at the summit, fully exposed from this vantage point.

Erica's Mercedes wasn't anywhere to be seen, either. Andrew had expected to find it parked on the hill or the road.

He began to wonder if his wife had come here, after all.

It had seemed the obvious place to look. He knew Erica must suspect her brother of murdering the Wilcott girl; she'd told him last year—back when she was still confiding in her husband—that Robert had attacked her with a knife, right here, in the cabin, when she'd paid a visit to him and offered to arrange psychiatric help.

Andrew had wanted to press charges, but Erica had refused. Perhaps she'd been afraid of scandal or unwilling to subject Robert to public humiliation. Whatever her reason, the incident had remained secret. No one else knew of it, not even the police.

So when news of Sherry Wilcott's murder broke—the girl killed with a knife—Erica must have thought of Robert. And wondered.

To come here and confront her brother would be reckless, but a streak of recklessness ran through Erica, as it had through all the Garrisons. In her case it was usually hidden behind a facade of cool control. But Andrew had seen it. He knew she was capable of taking a large risk at the bidding of impulse.

But perhaps she hadn't. Perhaps he was wrong, and she had come nowhere near this place.

Or perhaps she'd come and faced Robert, demanding that he own up to the crime, and he'd lashed out . . . hurt her . . . even killed her. Then had hidden the Mercedes, the body—

The crazy son of a bitch had attacked her once before. Who was to say he wouldn't do it again?

Andrew considered the situation and decided he had to look inside the cabin. If such a scenario had in fact been played out, there would be evidence of a struggle, at least.

The gambit was dangerous, though. Truck or no truck, Robert could be in there.

Well, he was not unduly afraid of risk. On the tennis court he played a serve-and-volley game, charging the net, daring his opponent to pass him. In Philadelphia and, earlier, in New York, he had dared the police to catch him. On one occasion they'd succeeded, and he'd spent a few nights in lockup before raising bail. Nobody had messed with him, though he was more lightly built than the other prisoners. He had simply remembered the jaguar sinking its claws into a ripe belly and holding tight, and the cat's spirit had burned in his eyes and repelled any trouble.

People thought he was soft. He was not soft. He played hard. He played to win.

Unbuttoning his coat, he touched the Colt Combat Commander in his waistband. In a crisis he could thrust aside the flap and draw the gun instantly. He had practiced the maneuver often enough.

Breathing hard, he lowered the binoculars, letting them dangle from his neck. He stood, then left the grove, wading through dry brush that had grown over the fire-scarred land, an elfin forest rising to his knees.

At first he considered circling the hill and going up the back way. Then he shook his head. There was no cover anywhere. Subterfuge served no purpose.

He headed up the road, in plain view of the cabin and anyone within.

Built in the 1930s, the cabin had somehow survived the fire that denuded the hill. It was a squat one-story structure, smaller than even the guesthouse at Great Hall, stolid, unornamented. A brick chimney was the sole architectural flourish. Otherwise, it was a box, sturdy but crude, with a sloping roof but no rain gutters. A front door but no porch or steps, a single window but no sill.

Andrew crested the rise, his cheeks burning with cold. Close now, and at a better angle, he could see inside the shack, and what he saw was a heavy gloom that spoke of emptiness.

Against the windowless side wall crouched a large diesel generator, flanked by stacks of fuel drums. The generator was silent, inactive, a sleeping animal.

No lights burning, no motors running. Andrew relaxed a little, almost sure the place was deserted.

Even so, he drew the Colt before heading for the door.

It was locked. He planted a solid kick, splintering the frame, and the door swung inward, the dead bolt jutting free.

He went in fast, the Colt sweeping the claustrophobic dark.

A thousand movies and TV shows led him to expect a blaze of muzzle flashes from a corner, but there was nothing.

The sun blazed through the window at a steep angle, leaving half the cabin in murk. His hand groped for a lamp before he reminded himself that the generator was off.

For a moment he stood motionless, letting his vision adjust to the strange half-light.

He knew the cabin well enough from outside; he'd spent a night studying it not very long ago. But to be inside the place was a new experience, unsettling somehow.

The cabin consisted of a single room, the floor space limited to perhaps six hundred square feet. Its furnishings and appliances were an eclectic melange of modernity and primitivism. Robert had bought only what he could not build with his own hands.

Not an absolute ascetic, he had permitted himself a compact refrigerator and a full-size freezer, an indoor electric grill and hot plate, two mismatched table lamps, and a cot with an aluminum tubular frame. The cot's blankets and sheets were strewn in disarray, soiled with old sweat.

So much for the industrial age. In other respects the shack might have been a medieval woodsman's hideaway. No TV, no radio, no phone. A wood-burning hearth for light and heat. Hand-hewn tables and a desk and a single highback chair, the pieces large and crude and unfinished, like dollhouse furniture seen under a magnifying glass.

Wet laundry hung on a line stretched from one wall to another. In a corner lay a good-sized metal basin that must serve as both sink and washtub. The water was drawn from a well on the property, on the hill's south side, where there was a makeshift bucket shower for use on warmer days.

That was all. No lavatory; such needs were filled by an outhouse in the woods below the hill, safely away from the well. No mementoes, no artwork, no decorative items, no touch of a distinctive personality or an active mind.

With one exception. One detail Andrew had not seen from outside.

Bookshelves. A whole wall of them, handmade like the furniture, and crammed with volumes, pressed together spine-out, with still more books laid flat atop the others.

The books intrigued him, but he did not approach the shelves right away. First he scanned the room and the bare floor for indications of a fight. He saw no overturned or broken items, no blood, no scuff marks.

A ghoulish thought made him check the interior of the small closet near the bed, and of the freezer. The closet contained only Robert's meager wardrobe, dense with stitched repairs, and the large freezer was nearly empty of provisions. What he'd feared to find—Erica's folded body in a sack—was thankfully not there.

His anxieties, it appeared, were groundless. Erica had not been here today.

He ought to get out before Robert returned from wherever he'd gone. But the wall of books, row upon row, still exerted an odd fascination. They were a window into Robert's mind.

Know your adversary, Andrew thought as he crossed the room and stood before the books. He ran a fingertip lightly over a line of leather spines. Old binding, seamed with rivulets of age and wear.

Stooping, he made out titles. Shakespeare's *As You Like It, The Tempest, A Midsummer Night's Dream*—plays about exile and wilderness. Milton's *Paradise Lost,* a similar theme. Nietzsche's *Thus Spake Zarathustra,* the triumphant end of exile.

All right. He could see the pattern there. But what possessed Robert to own a slim volume by Plutarch titled *On Isis and Osiris*? Or Blake's *Four Zoas*? Or some damn thing called *Corpus Hermeticum*?

And there was more, so much more.

Chaucer, Gibbon, Swift. Seneca and Cicero, Sophocles and Aeschylus. Herodotus's *History,* Virgil's *Aeneid.* A bulging Bible flat against the *Iliad,* the *Odyssey.*

Andrew's lips pursed, then curled, forming a perfect O.

Had Robert read all these, and the dozens of other books?

The thought seemed shocking somehow. Andrew had not pictured this man as quite human. More like an animal or some cave dweller in a museum exhibit. Something primitive, exotic.

Reading Sophocles? Shakespeare?

Maybe not. Maybe he read nothing. Maybe the books were here for some obscure reason unrelated to their content. Talismans, totems.

He took comfort in the thought. Then his roaming gaze settled on a book on top of the shelf, lying open. He picked it up.

The Golden Bough, by Sir James Frazer. Andrew had read none of it, but vaguely he knew that it was a compendium of myth and folklore.

This book was volume nine. The pages were brittle and old.

And underlined. Marked in the margins with hectic scribbles. Pencil scratches everywhere, on page after page. Even the illustrations were bordered with intaglios of intensive commentary.

> *. . . see p. 184 . . . Artemis = Diana . . . observed by Callimachus . . . see Caesar,* Bell. Gall., *vi. 16 . . . compare w/Plotinus, II.3.15 . . .*

Scholarly notes, learned cross-references, suggestive of an erudition that would shame most Ph.D. candidates.

And this from a man who lived as a hermit, who was demonstrably psychotic, who had barely finished high school, for God's sake.

Andrew leafed through *The Golden Bough,* then let it fall open to a worn page, an illustration of the sacrifice of Artemis, smeared with thumb prints, annotated with marginal scribblings so dense as to be nearly opaque.

Incredible. He shut the book, lifting a plume of dust, white as talcum. In the stillness he let out a low, contemplative whistle.

"Robert," he said quietly, "you're just full of surprises."

But there appeared to be no further surprises here. He was about to leave when he noticed a scatter of loose papers on a pine desk by the window. He picked up the top sheet and froze.

Amid a scrawled chaos of helter-skelter gibberish, one word stood out.

Erica.

Andrew took a breath, then read the page slowly, struggling to find sense in it.

Call off the bitches Erica call off the hounds hags harridans harrying me filling my skull with noise Erica hear them scream beauty's sisters night's daughters Erica you whore for her you lie with her you lie for her Erica you lie Erica you die . . .

The last words ballooning into giant looped intaglios running off the page.

Andrew stared at the paper for a long time, comprehending only the simple fact of obsessive hatred—hatred of Erica, raw and explosive.

He riffled through the other sheets, found more of the same. A few pages bore crude thumbnail sketches of baffling subjects. Dogs' heads. The forked tongues of snakes. Animal claws.

Threaded through the words and pictures was Erica's name, compulsively repeated.

Robert must have written this just today. The pen he'd used, an old-fashioned fountain pen, had been left on the desk, its steel tip resting in a puddle of ink.

Erica you lie Erica you die . . .

He did have her. He must. Andrew was sure of it now.

How Robert had gotten to her, it was impossible to say. Where he'd taken her, whether she was alive or . . . or not . . .

No way to know. He might have kidnapped her from the shop, taking her in her own car. Or maybe she really had come here to talk with him, choosing the worst possible moment for the visit, when his paranoia and craziness had been heated to a fast boil.

However it had happened, he had her, all right. He had Erica.

And even if she was still alive, she surely would not survive the night.

Retreating slowly down the shaft, grunting with strain, enveloped in a cloud of rancid sweat, muttering as he dragged his burden inch by stubborn inch.

His cheek bleeding where she'd caught him with her boot heel. Well, he'd gotten even with her for that. Hurt her, yes. Her screaming had been good to hear, and her expiring moan.

Limp now, she was heavy, difficult to handle in the confined passageway. It had taken him long minutes to drag her just halfway along the gun-barrel tube. She'd imagined she could escape this way. No chance.

"Dead end, Erica," Robert Garrison breathed. "Dead end for you."

The darkness was nearly total. Her flashlight lay yards ahead in the shaft, abandoned, and his own flash was outside in the throne room.

Muttering, wheezing, straining with his load of limbs.

He pulled her sometimes by the ankles, sometimes by the belt loops in her jeans. Her blouse had come untucked, and when he grabbed for her, now and then he felt bare skin.

Her skin was smooth, and his was hairy. Jacob and Esau; which got the blessing, and which the curse? Or perhaps the more appropriate fable was *La Belle et le Bête,* Beauty and Beast, but even so the question remained: Which was which?

Robert knew what *they* thought, all of them, those others. He had caught them smirking in the grocery store, where he'd gone to replenish his supplies.

He hadn't meant to go there at all. It was Erica he'd gone into town to see. Erica who plagued him, who would not set him free.

Now the worm had turned. She was his.

"Mine," he said, and giggled.

Moira had arranged it. *Moira* had planted a thought in his mind, as he drove out of town in a rage—the thought of his empty freezer, his need for new provisions. *Moira* had turned his truck around and parked it at Waldman's Grocery, where all the good townsfolk did their shopping, the simple village burghers and their common wives.

They cast sidelong glances at him as he rolled his shopping cart down the aisles and filled it with frozen, canned, and freeze-dried foods, and bulk packages of paper towels and toilet tissue, and bottled water, a month's supplies for his sylvan retreat.

They stared, and no doubt behind his back they pointed, fingering the freak.

Robert Garrison, lunatic, pariah, outcast, scapegoat, accursed.

He had always sensed their hostility and disgust. But lately he sensed more. He sensed fear.

They were afraid of him, because of the Wilcott girl. They knew he'd done it. They all knew. They could prove nothing. But they knew, and they feared him, and their fear made him stronger.

For years he'd tried to gain their favor in his stumbling way. He would make small talk, or attempt it. He would smile, try to fit in, hope for acceptance, which never was granted.

Now he ignored them, disdainful as a king. Let them ogle and point. He didn't care.

At the checkout counter he was silent as the plump ponytailed girl scanned his long array of purchases.

He stood stiffly, feeling an itch in his palms, his gaze tracking warily from one customer to another, each of them turning away with practiced casualness, none of them willing to make eye contact.

Then his gaze drifted to a tabloid newspaper in a wire rack, and the headline caught him, held him breathless.

SCIENTISTS SAY: DEADLY POLLUTION WILL END ALL LIFE IN TEN YEARS!

Deadly pollution. *Miasma.*

Was it spreading, then? Was he not the only one? Were there others like him, and if so, how could he get in touch? Did they live like lepers also, and had they seen—

An abrupt silence jerked him out of his reverie, and he realized the checker had finished ringing up his order and was waiting for payment. And she was studying him, her fat eyes in her fat face popping big with fear.

She'd observed his fascination with the paper, and for some reason it had frightened her. Well, how could she expect him not to notice that headline? There was a good chance she had put the newspaper on display purely as a warning to him, or in mockery.

He felt their stares, sensed the churning of their thoughts. The checker in the next lane was sneaking glances at him from the corner of her eye. And the child on line behind him, a candy bar in his mittened hand—this child was gazing up at him in nervous fascination.

Hostility and suspicion on all sides.

How he despised them. Scum. Morons. Carrion birds feeding on his entrails while he lay chained to his rock of grief.

He remembered Sherry Wilcott's final scream, as the knife descended. Would the fat checkout girl scream so loud, or even louder? He would like to find out. Would like to cut her pale throat.

That's two-hundred twenty-one dollars and thirty-nine cents.

The checker, speaking.

He paid by check, as always. Signed his name in a large, careful hand. She did not ask for any ID. His checks were good. Had been for years.

When she offered the receipt, he declined. He wanted nothing from her, from any of them.

He loaded the groceries into the bed of his pickup. When he looked back across the parking lot, he could see the plump checker through the storefront glass.

She might do, he was thinking. He needed a second one. The Wilcott girl had not been accepted. A new sacrifice was required. Soon.

Yes, she might do . . .

But now—struggling, squirming, slithering in the crawl space—he wondered if she was in fact meant for him, or if his *moira* had brought him the victim he deserved.

He would find out.

Behind him, the glow of his discarded flashlight brightened, his slow backward progress finally bringing him close to the exit.

Not much farther to go.

He was surprised Erica had tried to flee. The whole exercise was so obviously futile. She must have known that it was not chance or choice that brought her here. It was another thing, larger than them both, a thing known only by an ancient word of layered meanings.

"*Moira,*" Robert murmured, sliding Erica Stafford along the rough limestone floor.

That word, which meant fate.

And justice.

And . . . death.

7

Before leaving the cabin, Andrew took the precaution of peering out the window to scan the terrain with his binoculars.

There was no one on the road or coming up the hillside, but in the brush below the hill, the same thicket where he had crouched, he saw a kneeling figure.

Robert? Must be.

Though he turned the focus ring, he couldn't make out the watcher's face. It was obscured by tall, dead weeds and by something more, a blur of joined circles . . .

Binoculars like his own.

He nearly drew back from the window before remembering that the wash of sunlight rendered the window opaque from outside. Whoever was glassing the cabin could not see its interior.

Still, he couldn't linger here.

He had knelt where the watcher was now. From that vantage point, he knew, the cabin door wasn't visible.

A plan formed in his mind, taking shape in images, not words.

His .45, tucked in his waistband again, received another reassuring pat as he slipped outside, hugging the side wall.

Fast around a corner to the rear of the shack. Then down the back slope of the hill. His shoes were smooth soled, all wrong for hiking, and twice he nearly slid to his knees when he lost his purchase on the loose soil.

At the bottom he headed into the woods and began to circle around, closing on his prey from behind.

The Colt was in his hand now. A hard, steady rhythm beat in

the bones of his skull. Was this fear or exhilaration? Perhaps equal parts of both.

He glanced up at the hilltop regularly, orienting himself with respect to the cabin. His steps were light and careful, and though he had no training or experience as a hunter, he moved without sound.

No twig snapped. No dry leaf crunched. Silence.

There.

A crouching masculine figure, huddled in a stand of withered shrubs, intent on the cabin.

His hatless head was exposed to view. Blond hair, sandy and short. And the nylon jacket—Andrew had seen it before—seen it at Great Hall in the sunroom within the hour.

It was not Robert. It was Connor.

Fear and exhilaration vanished together, and in their place was a quiet anger that built by slow degrees to rage.

Five yards behind Ben Connor, Andrew stopped. He stood gazing at the unsuspecting man.

Slowly he lifted the Colt

Took aim.

Connor's broad back floated into alignment with the front and rear sights. At this distance, an easy shot. Andrew—using not this gun, but a similar model—had nailed the X-ring in shooting-gallery targets at twice the range.

A cold swirl of wind hurried through the woods, shaking the trees in a clatter of branches.

Then the world was still and silent, and there was nothing but Connor's back and the Colt .45 and Andrew's forefinger squeezing the trigger slowly.

Two pounds of pressure. Three.

He lowered the gun and shook his head, smiling, amused at himself.

There was never any chance he would actually go through with it. He was no killer. Of course not.

Carefully he reset the hammer, then slipped the gun inside his waistband. He was pulling his coat flaps together when a shift of his footing dislodged a skitter of loose pebbles.

Connor heard.

He spun in a crouch, releasing the binoculars and snatching

at his holster, and then he recognized Andrew and, after a beat of hesitation, relaxed.

"Sneaking up on me?" Connor asked, not yet rising.

Andrew shrugged. "I thought you were him."

Connor picked up his binoculars without shifting his gaze from Andrew. "Was it you in the cabin?"

Nod. "He's not around."

Connor stood then, and stepped toward him. Andrew remembered his gun, barely concealed under his unbuttoned coat.

Of course he could justify bringing a gun along. Robert might be dangerous. But if Connor asked to see the Colt, there could be trouble. The gun was unlicensed, untraceable. Illegal.

He folded his arms across his chest in what he hoped was a natural motion.

"So why are you here?" Andrew asked.

"I could ask you the same question."

"But I asked first," Andrew said, then winced. He had expected this riposte to register as cool irony, but it had sounded merely childish. It occurred to him that he always felt weak and small around Ben Connor.

The wind stirred again, tugging at the flaps of his coat.

"I came here," Connor said, "thinking I might have a word with him." A nod at the cabin.

Andrew uncrossed his arms and tried to smooth the beating coat flaps without being too obvious about it.

"You must have known I was here," he said, watching Connor's eyes. "My car is parked down the road."

"I saw it. But I didn't know if you were inside the cabin or scoping it out, like me."

This made sense, but felt wrong somehow. Too pat.

"Well," Andrew said, "you can't be too careful. I wasn't taking any chances either."

The wind gusted, peeling back the flap on his right side, momentarily exposing the gun. Andrew thrust his hands in his coat pockets and jerked the flaps together.

Had Connor seen?

The police chief gave no indication of it. But Andrew was beginning to think Ben Connor was good at keeping secrets.

"Best not to," Connor said mildly. "Take chances, I mean. How'd you get in?"

The question, following so quickly on the laconic prelude, caught Andrew by surprise. "What?"

"The cabin. How'd you get in, if Robert's not home?"

"Oh." Andrew paused, calculating odds and risks, determining how much to reveal.

"Door was open," he answered evenly. "I guess he's not overly worried about his privacy."

"Any sign your wife might've been here?"

"No."

As if by mutual signal, they started walking together, down the road. Andrew flicked stray glances at Connor's face, trying to read the chief's expression, until he worried that Connor might sense the scrutiny.

"Is that why you came?" Connor asked. "Looking for her?"

"It occurred to me she might have come here."

"You could have told me."

"I didn't think of it till after you left. Anyway"—he shrugged—"it was a wild-goose chase."

In Andrew's back pocket, folded and refolded into a tight square, were the papers from Robert's desk. The telltale papers littered with Erica's name, smoking with rage.

He could show the papers to Connor, share his thoughts.

But when it came to Robert, Andrew preferred to handle things alone, despite the obvious risk.

There was, after all, a greater risk in openness.

Past a stand of hemlock, the Ferrari and Connor's green-and-white Caprice swung into view. Andrew unlocked his car on the driver's side.

"I take it there's no news from your patrol units," he said.

Connor sighed out a great balloon of frosted breath. "Nothing yet. They're still looking."

"They must have searched the whole town by now."

"Just about."

"I'm sorry to hear that. I mean . . ."

"I know what you mean."

Andrew climbed behind the wheel. "Looks like this was a waste of time for us both. Guess we should have known better."

"Should we? Why?"

"Because this is the last place Erica would go. She never talks to him. Never sees him. Not anymore."

He found his keys, started the engine. When he glanced at Connor again, he saw the police chief studying some far distance.

"Odd how they would drift apart so completely," Connor said. "Given what they went through as children."

"Perhaps *because* of what they went through."

"Could be."

"Or just because—well, he's crazy, you know."

"You'd think she would try to help him."

But she did, Andrew almost said. *She tried, and he rebuffed her, and finally he attacked her—came at her with a knife— maybe the same knife that killed Sherry Wilcott . . .*

He couldn't say any of that. Instead he glanced at Connor with a flash of anger. "Are you criticizing her?"

"Just rendering an observation."

Andrew didn't know how this man managed to rattle him. He had stood up to tougher and smarter adversaries.

He revved the engine, letting the Ferrari growl for him.

"Well," he said, "I'm sure she has her reasons. When we find her, we can ask."

He pulled the car door shut. It banged, a hollow sound, sharp in the still air, and he urged the Ferrari forward, cutting a tight U-turn, and left Connor behind in a biting spray of dirt.

"Sissy . . ."

The voice, familiar and yet strange, tugged at the edge of Erica's awareness.

"Sissy. You hear me? Hey, Sissy . . ."

He was calling to her. Robert, calling from some great distance.

She must go to him. Help him. His cry was a plea for help, it had to be.

Once before he had cried out to her, and she had done her best to respond. Her best . . . But not enough. Never enough.

Still, she had tried.

"Sissy . . ."

His voice fading, fading, as she sank deeper into dreams.

And remembered.

It was after the horror at Great Hall, Lenore and Keith dead, the children orphaned. Their mother's will had appointed the family lawyer, a stern, sallow man named Furnell, as their legal guardian.

This was a role for which cold Mr. Furnell was preposterously ill-suited. A busy man, he could not be bothered with two young charges. He found a child psychologist willing to assert that the posttraumatic effects of the tragedy could be assuaged only by a stable environment, such as that to be found in a well-run boarding school.

Mr. Furnell selected two fine schools, an academy in New Hampshire for girls, and a prep school in Maryland for boys. He was not a believer in coeducation.

On a January day, at the start of the second semester, Robert was driven to the Maryland shore by Mr. Furnell's personal assistant, while Mr. Furnell himself, in a rare act of parental responsibility, accompanied Erica on a plane flight from Philadelphia to Boston, then chauffeured her in a rented car to the bleak New Hampshire woods.

Even years later she could still feel the chalky press of his lips on her cheek as he wished her luck and said goodbye.

The cold months crawled past. Erica endured. She made no close friends. When not in class she wandered the wide fields where sports would be played in springtime, a lonely figure bent under the frigid wind. In the night darkness, wedged in her upper bunk, she heard the wind howl and thought it was her father's ghost, calling her name.

She read Shelley and Keats, poets who died young. The teachers and the headmistress knew enough of her background to feel a compassionate interest in the strange, remote young girl. They understood that trauma still held her in its clutch.

But she would get over it, they said. Time would heal.

Erica heard this formula often, and for their sake she pretended to believe it.

Then Robert telephoned her.

She took the call at the public phone in the dormitory lobby. He was not crying, but she heard the quaver of suppressed tears.

They won't leave me alone, he said. *They hate me.*

Only nine, small and scrawny, he had become the bullies' target. And somehow one of the older boys had read or heard about the events in Barrow. Now they all tormented Robert with questions about the fatal night, questions that brought back every detail of the ordeal.

And they had found he would not fight them. Terrified of violence, he would cower, he would run, he would cry . . . but he would not fight.

He was scared. He couldn't stand it anymore. He wanted to die. Just curl up and die . . .

Erica gripped the telephone handset and promised Robert that she would come to him, and soon.

And she did.

At suppertime she feigned illness and was excused to her room. Alone, she packed her one suitcase, stuffing her purse with two hundred dollars in cash. Her allowance, paid out of her trust fund, was fifty dollars a month; in four months she had spent none of it.

The dusky sky, gray with clouds, draped her in shadow as she fled across the fields.

She walked two miles to town and bought a train ticket to Boston. With her hair in a bun and her school uniform concealed under a heavy coat, she could pass for a girl of seventeen or so, just barely old enough to ride the train without raising suspicions.

In Boston she changed trains and headed south on a red-eye, sleeping fitfully on a soiled benchseat, her face resting on a windowpane so badly scratched it hid the night from view.

Penn Station scared her. It was a vast vault of echoes and shadows and strange hunched men with backpacks and bedrolls. She used the last of her money to buy a ticket from New York to Baltimore. The train did not leave until dawn, and she passed the intervening hours avoiding the furtive glances of strangers.

The third train ride delivered her to Baltimore in mid-morning. She knew the name of Robert's school and the suburb where it was located, but she had only a few dollars left, not enough for a cab ride, she was sure.

Near the train station was a pawn shop. She pawned her wristwatch for twenty dollars, then a gold ring for twenty-five more. She knew about pawn shops. She'd seen them on TV.

With the money she could afford a taxi. The driver, familiar with the school, dropped her at the driveway, not proceeding into the grounds at her request.

She remembered how he studied her as she counted out the fare and added a tip. He was from the Caribbean, and he had a fine musical voice and a nice face.

Don' you be a little young, missy, to be travelin' alone?

Erica lied bravely. *I'm eighteen.*

He smiled at that. *Well, mebbe. Mebbe not.* Then the smile widened. *Oh, I get it, mon. De mice, dey play, but dis cat too sharp for 'em, you bet.*

She was sure he would turn her in. After all her effort, at the threshold of success, she'd been found out.

But he simply accepted the fare and laughed. *De cat, he say dis chil' got a honey aroun' here. A boyfriend, what I mean. Dat so?*

Her flush of relief must have looked like embarrassment, because he waved off any answer.

She escaped from the cab and headed up the driveway. When the cab was gone, she retraced her steps and circled around the property's fenced perimeter. At the rear she saw boys playing soccer in a field turned newly green; spring came earlier in Maryland than in New Hampshire.

Robert wasn't there. Perhaps he was in his room. She knew the name of his dormitory building.

Unseen, she climbed the fence, first tossing her suitcase over. She explored the grounds, hiding from footsteps and voices. The school was small, the dorm not hard to find.

She crept down a deserted hall to the only room with an open door, and there he was, huddled in his cot.

Robert, she said.

She would never forget his comical walleyed surprise, and the abrupt grin that remade his face. *Sissy . . .*

Kneeling on the cot, she hugged him, feeling how small he was. God, he'd lost weight; he wasn't eating.

The reunion broke the dam of his reserve, and in his sister's arms Robert shook with explosive sobs.

It's been so bad here, he gasped when he could speak. *They're so mean, and they all hate me, and they call me things, they say things, they never stop, never, I hear them all the time, even when I'm asleep they don't shut up, I hear their voices in my head, in my head . . .*

She told him it was all right. She would get him out of this place. They would go away together. No more dormitories and detentions for either of them.

How she would manage this miracle, she couldn't guess. Her money was gone, though Robert might have some. Even if he did, two children unaccompanied by an adult could not get far. But they would find a way. They had to. For Robert's sake.

She could serve out her sentence in New Hampshire, but more time here would kill her brother, kill him, she knew it.

There she is, a stern voice said from the doorway.

Slowly she and Robert separated, and Erica turned to see three adults enter the room. They were, she later learned, the headmaster and his assistant and a groundskeeper who had seen Erica in the driveway.

I told Furnell she would come here, the headmaster said with evident satisfaction. His was the stern voice she had heard a moment earlier. *He's probably still got people looking for her in Boston, for Christ's sake.*

It was all clear to Erica then. Her disappearance had been reported sometime last evening. Somebody at the academy in New Hampshire had called Mr. Furnell, and Mr. Furnell had called this school, on the chance she was coming to see Robert.

And you knew, didn't you? the headmaster said, fixing Robert with a cold glare. *You lied when we asked you.*

Robert didn't answer. Erica felt his quiet trembling and knew he was crying again.

Don't make me go away, she said.

The headmaster told her she'd caused everybody a lot of trouble and concern, and was hardly in a position to ask for favors.

Robert needs me, she pleaded. *He . . . he gets afraid . . . when I'm not here.*

The headmaster's assistant said the boy would have to get used to it, that's all. Everybody had to grow up sometime.

This drew a vigorous assent from the headmaster, and another reprimand for Erica's incorrigible behavior and Robert's untruthfulness. The moral lines were drawn. Only the groundskeeper looked uncertain, and even at age twelve, Erica knew he was not in charge here.

Mr. Furnell arrived at noon to take her to the airport. He was cold with anger. Sharing the backseat of a cab with her, he spoke of cutting off her allowance.

Robert will die, Erica said, watching the smear of scenery in the window.

What?

She looked at Mr. Furnell. *He'll die.*

That's nonsense.

It's killing him—being there.

Nonsense, Mr. Furnell said again, adding that he had attended a quite similar school, and it had done him a world of good.

Then why did you turn out to be such an asshole? Erica asked.

It was the first really grown-up thing she'd said, and even at the bottom of her private abyss, she took satisfaction in it.

Mr. Furnell, stiffly furious, put her on a plane to Boston, telling her someone would meet her upon arrival. And there would be no more allowance.

She spent another six years in New Hampshire, seeing Robert only on rare holidays. School did not kill him. He survived. But something in him had died, the needful, hurting part that had cried out to her on a long-distance telephone line. That part was gone, excised—or buried deep.

She had not been there when he needed her, and so she could not save him. But it wasn't her fault. She'd done her best. She'd done everything she could.

But in the end it had been far too little.

And now he was calling to her again, using his childhood nickname for her, the name he hadn't uttered in years.

"Sissy . . ."

His voice reaching out to her like a desperate hand, a hand, his hand—

White, scaly in the flashlight's glow . . .

Closing over her leg, her arm. Twisting . . . hurting . . . until pain took her away into the dark, the dark—

Fear shuddered through her, vivid as a shock, and Erica opened her eyes.

She was on the table.

She knew it instantly, without confusion or doubt.

The table with the straps, in the throne room, which had become a dungeon.

Not naked as she might have feared. She was fully clothed. Only her gloves had been removed.

But tied down. Helpless.

One pair of straps—knotted tight to bind her legs to the cold hardwood plane. The other pair—pinning both arms above her head.

The ragged canvas bands had been wound around her ankles and forearms in double loops, anklets and bracelets of rough cloth, before being lashed together.

She was caught. Once on a long walk in the woods she'd come across a raccoon in a trap, dead of pain and fright. *How awful,* she had thought, *the poor thing must have suffered so.*

Now she was the raccoon.

She looked around for him, moving only her eyes, afraid of rolling her head and revealing that she was awake. She couldn't see him. He was lost somewhere in a fog of gloom.

She heard him, though. Muttering to himself, the source of his voice difficult to pinpoint.

"Silly Sissy," he was saying. "Sleepyhead, slugabed. She'll sleep her life away . . ."

He didn't know she had come to. But he would find out soon enough, and then . . .

Then it would be the knife for her, she was sure of it, the knife ripping her like a predator's fang, death flooding in as her blood rushed out.

In the chase she'd known terror, but then at least she had been able to move, take action. Immobilized, helpless as a paralytic, she understood what true fear was.

Her mouth pressed tight against a welling scream. She fought back a panicky surge, forced herself to think clearly.

The effort was hard. Harder than it should have been. Though she had shaken off unconsciousness, she could not seem to quite focus her eyes or her thoughts.

She cut her gaze first right, then left, probing the shadows.

The guttering light in the room was the glow of a kerosene lantern, one of those she and her baby brother had scattered throughout the tunnels and galleries, many years ago.

She didn't remember those lamps being so bright. This one seared her eyes like the sun at noon. It rested on a truncated limestone pillar, close to the table, near her feet. The kerosene crackled, and the light flared, pulsations of orange glare glazing the limestone walls and ceiling.

Her nose wrinkled. Smoke.

From the oil? She didn't think so. Something else was burning, or smoldering. Whatever it was, it filled the room with an acrid tang.

A curl of smoke invaded her mouth, and she coughed.

In a corner, movement.

Him.

With the cough she'd announced she was awake. He moved toward her, big in the flickering gloom. She saw it again: the shaggy outline of his head and shoulders, then the leprous whiteness of his hands.

Involuntarily she tried to draw back. The straps held her, but the slight shift in her position brought her left arm to life. It throbbed, raw with pain from wrist to shoulder. She didn't think any bones were broken, but the muscles had been savagely strained.

The arm must have been hurting all along, but this was the first time she'd felt it. Odd.

Then pain receded again, anesthetized by a new dose of fear as Robert's face eased into the light.

He bent over her. The table was slanted, her head higher than her legs, and his face drifted close to hers.

Erica stared up into two gray eyes. She glimpsed a pink flick of tongue along a bloodless lower lip.

She swallowed once. "Robert."

He watched her, the gray eyes steady and cold, his face half hidden behind a matted beard and a mass of brown hair, long and tangled, shot through with premature streaks of silver, flecked with bits of bark and limestone dust.

The lamp illuminated him from below. Unnatural shadows crosshatched his face, made his features somehow unreal. She thought of masks.

It is a mask, she told herself. *We both wear masks, don't we?* The thought was strange, alien to her, like a fragment of a stranger's dream. She pushed it away.

"Robert," she said again, hoping for an answer.

His lips worked. Beard rustled.

"Hello, Sissy."

There was a quality almost of tenderness in the greeting. She heard it, and abruptly she was riven by a feeling stronger than fear, an intense, debilitating sorrow, a loss that clanged inside her like the hollow tolling of a bell.

Brother and sister they had been, and still were. Playmates, partners, best friends, and more. Far more.

Now when she remembered the trapped raccoon, it was her brother she saw, his suffering she felt.

Oh, Robert, look what's happened to you. I should have done more for you. Somehow I should have found a way to help.

She wanted to cry, but then he touched her face with a calloused fingertip, and she went stiff with dread.

"Pretty Erica," he whispered. "Pretty Erica in a hole. In a whole lot of trouble."

He smiled at the odd play on words. The surprise of his yellow teeth, an animal's teeth, stained and diseased, hit her in time with a gust of sour breath.

"Robert," she said, "please let me go."

He didn't answer, simply retreated into the gloom.

She tried to follow him with her gaze, but it was difficult. The details of the room kept sliding away, as did the reality of her own body. At moments she was strapped to the table, and then she floated over it, weightless and free.

With an effort she forced herself to concentrate. What to do? Talk to him. Communication was her only hope.

"How did you know I was here?" she whispered.

"Oh, that? A friend of yours accosted me in town. You have

so many friends, and I have none. Who'll be the suppliant's friend, Sissy? Who'll light a hearth fire for the outcast?"

She ignored this, because it made no sense to her. "What friend of mine?" she asked, thinking it might have been Ben Connor. She hoped it was. She hoped—

"Rachel something," he said carelessly. "She was looking for you."

Rachel. Of course, their lunch date. Erica had forgotten it entirely.

She wondered if Rachel would report her disappearance to the police, or simply chalk up the missed appointment to a misunderstanding. The sooner the police started to look, the better were their chances of finding the Mercedes on the fire road.

If they thought of looking on the fire road. But why would they? No one used it, ever.

"When she said you hadn't shown up for lunch," Robert went on softly, "I knew. Just like that." Snap of his fingers, the noise sharp and startling, like a knot of wood popping in a fire. "I knew where you must have gone in such a hurry. What mischief you'd make."

"Not mischief," she breathed. "I . . . I was trying to help you. That's why I came here. I thought—"

"Help me. Yes. You've always been so helpful. You've been such a great big help."

At the edge of her vision he paced the room. She heard the last three words repeated several times under his breath.

"Robert." She stared at the high ceiling, struggled with the quaver in her voice. "You need to listen to what I'm saying."

No answer but muttered words she couldn't make out.

"I really was trying to help you. Honestly. And I still am."

The sound he made was a low oath or a stifled laugh. He circled around, crossing behind the kerosene lamp, and his shadow floated huge across the wall.

"I couldn't help unless I knew. All I had was a suspicion. I couldn't be sure."

Pacing behind the lantern, his shadow ticking back and forth in a pendulum's sweep.

"I was hoping it was someone else. I didn't want it to be you. Robert, you have to believe me."

"You lie. You're like a spider, always weaving, weaving your deceptions. And guess who's the fly."

"I'm not lying to you—"

He flew at her out of the dark, slamming down both palms on the table, craning his neck to bend over her. *"Guess who's the fly!"*

The answer stuck in her throat.

"You are," she croaked. "Is that right? You're the fly."

A smile lightened his expression. "Buzz buzz," he said softly.

She stared up at him. He was close to her, yet somehow far away. She didn't understand it. But this had been the case for years, hadn't it? Her brother—close, ever close, but so far out of reach.

Her mind seemed to be traveling down random tracks. Was it fear that had gotten her thoughts all scrambled? She shut her eyes, drew a long breath, tried to focus.

When her eyes opened, he was still bending over her, watching her intently, as if waiting for her to speak.

"Tell me why you killed her, Robert."

"You know."

"I don't. Tell me."

"All right, then. I'll tell. I led the victim to the sacrifice because *I won't live like this anymore*. You hear me? Not anymore. The scapegoat has grown restless in his quarantine. The exile yearns for home. For all the things you have, Sissy. Friends and conversation and comforts. I want to be part of society again."

She was trying to hold her full attention on his words, but inexplicably she was distracted by the orange flicker of lamplight. It made tiger stripes of color and shadow, the skein of lines shifting, transposing, in a patternless pattern, a meaningful chaos, fascinating.

Then she focused on his face again, his gray eyes studying her, and with effort she found the strength to question him.

"But . . . to kill somebody . . . to kill a girl . . . ? Robert, that's not the way."

"You know it is, Lying witch, woman of Endor, Medea's shadow—you know. *You know.*"

She shook her head, bewildered by this outburst, this abusive torrent.

"It's the way," he raged. "It's the only way. I am a pariah, unclean. I must be purified. Only blood will do it. I must bathe myself in ritual blood. Give an offering to the ones above. Win their favor. Earn their absolution of my sins."

"By murder?"

"Not murder. Sacrifice. You understand the difference, priestess of the dark."

"What are you talking about?"

"The girl was the ewe on the altar, the young ox whose throat is sliced for the god. She was Iphigenia in her glory, the maiden offered to eternity. I know what you're thinking," he added slyly.

How could he know, when she herself wasn't sure what to think? She waited.

"You're thinking I was wrong to perform the ceremony when I am still unclean. A priest should do it, and I should kneel as penitent to receive the blessing of the blood. And you're right. That is the ceremony's proper form. But who would serve as priest for me? You? Would *you* do it? Would you have cut the lamb's throat and filled the chalice with her hot essence?"

She moaned, terror and tears racking her together.

"No one would help me. So I must hold the office, unfit though I am. I grasped the knife, I filled the chalice, I washed my face and hands in her red ichor. I played the roles of both priest and penitent, and by the sacrifice I meant to lift pollution from my soul."

"Pollution . . ."

"*Miasma,* the ancients called it. Deadly pollution. Not mine alone. It will spread like a curse, like Oedipus's plague, and bring low this town and the whole world, end all life on earth within ten years—the newspaper said so, and the message was left in plain view for me to see."

"'No, Robert, there's no message, no . . . *miasma.* You've got it wrong, all of it. You've chosen the wrong way."

"I chose nothing. It was chosen for me by fate, by *moira,* and I am merely the fish in the net, carried where I am meant to go. I knew the others would never understand, so I performed the rite in secrecy, covering my trail. They suspect me, but can prove nothing. No one can find my sacred altar or my priestly tools. No one knows about this place."

"Except . . ."

"Except you, Sissy. And here are you, spying on me, *nosing around.*" His thumb and forefinger caught her nose, and he laughed. "Nosy Sissy. Gotcha now."

It was a childhood game of theirs—"got-your-nose."

She twisted free of his grip. "Robert, God damn it, *we're not children anymore!*" Anger thrust her forward, her head and shoulders leaving the table as she strained at her bonds, but then a spiral of wooziness slowly unwound in her brain, and she lowered her head, blinking. "This . . . this isn't a game," she added weakly, her strength spent.

"Well, of course it isn't." Robert frowned at her obtuseness. "*You* know the truth of that, better than anyone—you and the deity you serve. It's life and death. It's my soul, clean or corrupt. Redemption or damnation. No game at all."

"You don't need to be redeemed . . ."

"But I do. And they all know it, all the sheep in town. You get to walk among them, but as for me—I'm the fool on the hill. That's what they call me, the imbeciles, *your* friends, members of your *community.* Fool on the hill, I've heard them. Did you know that? Did you *know?*"

She felt a sting of tears, prompted by fear or pity or the biting smoke, she wasn't sure which. "No, Robert. I didn't."

"You *lie.* You *spy.* You spit in my evil *eye.*" He threw his head back and hawked a gob of phlegm at her face. She turned aside, and it struck her cheek, warm and gooey like semen. "How d'you like *that,* Sissy?"

"Please, Robert." Really crying now, and the room turning, turning around her like a room in a dream. "Please don't do this, please . . ."

"A little late for begging, I'd say. I told you to call them off—your devil dogs."

"I don't know what you mean by that."

"Of course you know. They're your bitches, yours and *hers*. I hear them bark at night. I feel their wet snouts on me, smell their rank musk. Now you say I'm wrong to seek absolution by a maiden's blood. Well, how else, then? How else, when I'm still unclean?"

Unclean. The word hung between them, prompting a question. She asked it slowly, her words coming like paste squeezed from a tube.

"If you killed her, if you performed your . . . sacrifice, then shouldn't you be purified already? Shouldn't you be clean?"

"Do I *look* clean? See these hands? See them?"

Thrust at her, long fingers, ragged bitten nails.

"Do they look clean, witch? *Do they?*"

She stared at the hands, watching as the fingers seemed to elongate, growing into claws, wicked and curved and brightly taloned.

Then she blinked, and his hands were normal again.

God, what was happening to her? Was she going insane?

"I'm *not* clean," he said, a snarl distorting the words. "I offered the girl, but it wasn't enough. It wasn't enough. Your whoring mistress said it wasn't enough!"

The hands withdrew. He backed away.

"There must be another. I thought it might be the pig-faced girl at the checkout stand. Maybe it will. Or maybe the next victim is even closer at hand."

She knew only too well what he meant by that.

"No," she whispered. "Not me. You don't want it to be me." Useless words, meaningless words, words uttered by someone else who still thought she had a chance to survive. "Please, you can't, you don't want to, please."

She tried to lift her head again, and immediately another spasm of vertigo clamped down, pinning her to the table.

The room blurred. Her vision was going fuzzy. Squinting to sharpen her sight, she studied the man before her. It took her a moment to understand that she was searching for the brother she remembered—a gangly boy, tall for his age, chestnut-haired, so shy he rarely met her gaze, never yelled, never swore.

That boy was still present, but only as a shadow. She saw hints of him in the long, pale forearms swinging restlessly, in the coltish shamble of ungainly legs, in the flickering gray eyes. A shadow, no more.

The hair had darkened with age, and so had the heavy brows. His shoulders had filled out, but the rest of him had thinned to an emaciated husk. He looked decades older than his thirty-three years.

Then the image fuzzed again, and he lost his individuality, becoming a stranger, the sort of man she sometimes saw on her visits to Philly and Pittsburgh and Manhattan, men clad as he was, in scuffed work shoes and loose trousers and an untucked corduroy shirt, the sleeves rolled up to the biceps. Those men pushed shopping carts laden with trash or begged belligerently for dollar bills.

She was scared of those men. Yet they were mostly harmless. While this man, once so close to her, had killed a woman here in the throne room . . . and soon might kill another.

Might. Was there any doubt? Yet he'd seemed uncertain, hadn't he? The way he'd phrased it: *Maybe the next victim is even closer* . . . Maybe. He wasn't sure.

"What are you going to do, Robert?"

The abject tonelessness of her own voice was frightening. It was the voice of someone already dead, a voice from the grave.

"You'll tell me," he whispered.

The words took time to register. They seemed to travel slowly down her mental pathways to the point of full awareness. And all the while the smoke deepened, the bitter fumes twisting around her like eels in water.

Then she blinked at him, bewildered. "I . . . I will?"

"You'll tell all I need to know."

Could this be true? Could he be waiting for instructions from her? It seemed unthinkable that her escape could be so easily arranged. But she had to try.

"All right, then." She heard her own words with peculiar detachment. "What you'll do is let me go. Untie me and—"

His laughter cut her off. "Not that part of you, Sissy. Not your lying mortality."

"My . . . mortality?" The word, redolent of death, frightened her, even as her false hope faded.

"You'll tell, Sissy. But a different you."

"Different me . . . ?" It was all so confusing, and she was tired, she was sleepy, she was fading away.

"Or maybe it's not you at all. Maybe it only uses your lips, your voice."

"I don't understand you, Robert. You're not . . . making sense."

Without reply, he turned from her. Wings of sweat lay folded on his back, darkening the plaid corduroy shirt, or were they really wings, bat wings, and were his hands claws after all, and was this a nightmare from which she would soon wake?

Fragments of music drifted through her mind. She heard her father's voice at bedtime, a voice she had not heard since she was a young girl, speaking to her of a princess in a castle, of a magic spell, of a long slumber . . .

Drowsy now. Eyelids drooping. Respiration slow.

But she couldn't sleep. Robert would kill her in her sleep.

She jerked alert, looked at him again. He was crouching, his back still turned, head lowered as if in meditation. Twisting her neck, she directed her gaze downward, and on the floor at his feet she saw a metal brazier, smoke rising from it, the smoke that filled the room like bitter incense.

She heard his rasping inhalation, saw his shoulders swell.

Something smoldered in the brazier, and he was bending over it, breathing the fumes . . .

A long-delayed connection lit up her brain, and she understood.

Whatever he was burning, its smoke had a narcotic effect. It was warping her perceptions, numbing her thoughts. It had even dulled the pain of her damaged arm and shoulder.

She rolled her head from side to side, fighting to clear her mind. "What's in the dish, Robert? What are you burning?"

"Do you like it?" He drew another long inhalation. "Does it make you dream awake?"

She struggled for alertness, clawing at hard facts—the cold smoothness of the table, the ache in her elbow and shoulder— as, drowning, she would have clutched at driftwood.

"What is it?" she gasped.

"Nothing harmful. Breathe deep."

He rose erect and spun in the same instant, the sudden

movement disorienting her, and his lips skinned back from his yellow teeth in a wolf's smile.

"The pythoness at Delphi breathed the smoke of burning laurel leaves. The laurel tree was sacred to Apollo. But the oak has always been the king of trees."

She didn't know what this meant, had no strength to think about it. Her temporary alertness, hard won, already was failing.

"I carved our initials in an oak." He began to pace again, circling the cave. "Remember?"

"Yes." Her voice a whisper.

"You must have seen them when you pilfered my climbing gear."

His steps quickened. He was making her dizzy, or perhaps it was the room itself that was disorienting her as it whirled in slow motion, a limestone carousel. She squeezed her eyes shut.

"I saw them," she answered.

Her heartbeat registered in her ears, weirdly sluggish, each thump distinct. Her pulse had slowed, possibly, or her perception of time was now so altered that each second stretched to a minute or more.

"The tree was mine when I cut it." His voice, echoing, seemed to come from all corners of the room at once. "The girl was mine when I cut her. She is sacred now, as the oak is sacred, and the laurel tree." He stopped suddenly. "I was telling you about the pythoness."

"Pythoness," she whispered, intrigued by the word. Pythons slithered, hissed, and the word itself was a slithery hiss, a hiss . . .

"She lost herself in the smoke, and another self emerged. They called it a god. There were many gods once, and they spoke to us, *through* us. But we stopped listening. They're still there, and they can still be heard, if we only listen. We learned all this as children, didn't we? Children reading in the library at Great Hall and playacting here?"

"Those are myths, Robert." Her words slurred, *myths* becoming *mists,* as her mind was a mist, the room a mist. "Myths from long ago. Old books and plays written by people long dead. That's all."

"Myth never happened, but always is. Sallust said that. No-ble Roman. Very wise. When you spend a great deal of time alone, you begin to feel the vibrations of the past. You see patterns that others overlook. You catch glimpses of a truth lost to the busy world."

"What truth?"

"You know already. You feign ignorance because you think it helps you. But it doesn't. Nothing can help you."

"Robert . . ."

"Breathe deep. You are my pythoness, my mistress of oracular wisdom. Virgin sister, breathe deep."

"I'm not a . . . virgin . . ." This was funny. She heard herself laughing as the room spun, spun.

"But you are. So was the Wilcott girl. She had known men; she told me so. But she was *parthenos*."

Erica knew this word. It was Greek. *Parthenos* . . . unmarried.

"But I'm not *parthenos*," she whispered as her mind flickered. "I have a husband."

"In name only. You've never given yourself to him. You couldn't."

"I . . . took a vow . . ."

"Words. You don't love him."

And she didn't, of course. But there was Ben Connor. He loved her, he'd said so, and she . . . she . . .

"You can't love anyone," Robert went on, almost as if he'd read her thoughts and dismissed them. "You're like the figures you display in your shop. A beautiful thing, shiny in sunlight, but at the core—poured metal, cold stone."

"That's . . . not true," she whispered, but part of her knew that it was, and wondered how Robert had seen it.

"You're as virginal as Mary, as Artemis, as the Mother in all her forms. You fit the mold. You are *parthenos*, and you will be my pythoness and perhaps something more. You'll tell me. You'll tell all."

"I've got nothing to tell you." She was crying. "Nothing."

"You do. *She* did. The Wilcott girl. She said she was meant for me. She asked for the knife."

"Asked . . . ?"

"I heard her."

Then Erica understood. She saw into the cloudy depths of

his insanity and knew what illusion his brain had conjured in the smoke.

A sound filled the cave, a moan like the anguished cry of a child, her moan. "No . . ."

"It was destiny. She said so."

"No, Robert . . ." She wanted to tell him that Sherry had said nothing, that he'd heard only what he felt the need to hear, that he had killed her in a fit of delusion.

But it was too hard to speak. Her mouth was painfully dry, her tongue a cotton wad.

"I didn't murder her, Sissy. I did only what she asked me to do. What the holy part of her requested."

Swallowing, Erica found moisture for her tongue, her lips. "She didn't ask for *that*." Was she even speaking aloud? Was she still awake? "She was only a girl, Robert, a young girl. She didn't want to die."

"You should have heard her. Her higher self spoke through her numb lips. The voice of *moira*. Of the god. Of eternity itself, overmastering the girl's human weakness to lead her to her fate, as the good shepherd leads the bleating ewe to the altar stone."

"Oh, Robert, damn it, Robert . . ." Slipping away, everything, and only the vast sadness was left like a chasm into which she would fall and fall. "You should have let me help you, shouldn't have turned me away . . ."

He wasn't listening. "In the sacred smoke she delivered oracles. She told me what I must do, and I obeyed."

"No . . ." A whisper, inaudible even to her ears.

"She told me. As will you, Erica. As will you."

8

Connor waited until Andrew Stafford had driven far down the forest road and out of sight, the red Ferrari flickering into invisibility behind a veil of trees. Then he turned and doubled back to the cabin.

He moved fast in a loping jog trot, keys and handcuffs jangling on his gun belt, his portable radio squawking softly with police-band chatter as it cycled among the frequencies used by Barrow P.D., the sheriff's department, and the state police.

Suddenly he had many questions, few answers.

He'd lied to Andrew, of course. It was not coincidence that they both arrived at the cabin at the same time. In the interview at Great Hall, Connor had sensed that Andrew was telling less than he knew. So he'd parked off the road near the estate and waited for the Ferrari to emerge, then tailed Andrew to his destination. When he scoped out the cabin from the brush, he'd known exactly who was inside.

His mistake was letting Andrew slip out unseen, sneak up behind him. He could have paid a high price for his carelessness. Because Andrew had been carrying a gun. Connor had seen the distinctive bulge of the handle even before a gust of breeze briefly exposed the weapon itself.

A Colt Combat Commander, it looked like. Seven-round capacity. Forty-five caliber.

Quickly he mounted the hill, made a circuit of the cabin's exterior, then paused at the door. Seeing the splintered frame, he nodded slowly, unsurprised.

Andrew had claimed he found the door open. Crap. Robert

Garrison, a recluse, a suspicious loner, was hardly the type to leave his home unlocked and open to all comers.

The broken door, direct evidence of the commission of a crime, at least gave Connor a legal basis for entering the cabin. He had always been a stickler for legalities. At times his less scrupulous fellow officers in New York had kidded him about it. *Yes, Your Honor,* they would tell him in mock chagrin when he reminded them of a fine point of law. The ribbing wasn't invariably good-natured; he'd drawn his share of resentment, especially from veteran cops who liked to make up their own rules.

Ridicule and hostility hadn't deterred him. He knew what happened when men with guns and badges started thinking they answered to no higher authority than their own will. There was a narrow line between a law enforcer and a lawbreaker. He'd seen men cross that line. Two men in particular . . .

But he didn't want to think about Cortez and Lomax now. He'd come to Barrow, in large part, to forget.

Connor stepped through the cabin doorway, surveying the single cramped room. He took in the shelves of books, the modern appliances and crude handmade furniture.

He had no intention of conducting a thorough search. He and a forensics expert had tossed the cabin once before—legally, with Robert's written permission—and had found nothing incriminating. Besides, he had no lawful justification for lingering here when there was no sign of vandalism or obvious indication of theft.

Still, he would like to find out what Andrew had been up to. The man had spent at least five minutes in the cabin. Doing what?

To have seen Connor in the brush, Andrew must have been standing by the window. Perhaps leaning over the large desk positioned there.

Connor went to the desk and found it empty save for a business card anchored by a rock paperweight.

One of Andrew's cards, listing various phone numbers.

Connor turned the card over and saw a line of hasty scribbles, incised in the impatient slanting strokes he remembered from Andrew's signature on a charity check.

We need to talk.

Below this, a telephone number—not one of those printed on the front.

So Andrew wanted Erica's brother to get in touch, and to use a private line. Why?

The explanation could be simple enough. Surely Andrew, if asked, would insist that honest familial concern had been his motive. Robert had a right to know that his sister was missing.

Yes, he would say that, or something close. As stories went, it was a pretty good one.

Still, Connor was sure it was a lie. There was more going on here. Tying in, maybe, with Philadelphia—though he couldn't see how.

Philadelphia. Where Andrew Stafford had made a comfortable living in the art market. Throughout most of the '90s he had operated two galleries in the city, both doing business mostly by mail order. In the early phase of his career he had specialized in lithographs and linocuts; later he'd switched to statuary. It was the latter preoccupation that must have brought him into contact with Erica Garrison, but Connor didn't know the details of their meeting.

Though that part of the story was blank, the greater part had been filled in easily enough. Connor had a friend in the Philadelphia PD, a detective working homicide now, who previously had been a member of the bunco squad. And though Erica hadn't spoken of her marriage or the reason for its collapse since their first, chaste night in the office of her shop, Connor had not forgotten her words: *He's just a damn con artist, that's all. Married me for money, not love.*

Literally a con artist? Or had it been only a figure of speech? The question had plagued Connor until finally he'd felt the need for an answer. Last month, in an hour-long phone call, his friend in Philadelphia had told him all the relevant facts pertaining to Mr. Andrew Stafford.

Andrew was indeed a con artist in the full, criminal sense of the term. His two galleries had been boiler-room scam operations, phone banks staffed by hustlers like himself. Their marks were novice collectors whose names and addresses were pulled from upscale mailing lists. Postcards and catalogues were sent out, then followed up by phone calls pitching incredible bargains. Signed Picasso linocuts for $1300. Original Dali lithographs for $1100. Limited-edition prints of Pollock and de Kooning for $2000 or less.

The linocuts and lithographs were unauthorized copies or plain forgeries. The limited-edition prints were photomechanical reproductions of illustrations in art books.

The bunco squad and the attorney general received enough complaints to be aware that Andrew Stafford was perpetrating a fraud, but no charges were ever filed. Most of his scams were small-time, and prosecution would have been difficult. He could always claim he didn't know the provenance of the pieces he acquired.

Andrew did have a record, though. He'd been convicted of real estate fraud in New York City, back in the late Eighties. No jail time, just five years of probation and a six-figure restitution to the folks he'd conned. After that, he'd relocated to Philly and learned the art trade. His new business was safer. Fraud was harder to prove, and most buyers either wouldn't know they'd been cheated or, learning, would quietly resell their acquisitions, tacitly perpetuating the scam. And Andrew would crank out more forgeries and knockoffs, and watch his modest fortune grow.

He's a real piece of work, this Mr. Stafford, Connor's friend had concluded. *So what's your interest in him, Ben?*

Connor hadn't responded, hadn't wanted to admit that his primary interest lay in Andrew's wife, and that his inquiry was a matter of personal curiosity rather than official business.

He running any scams now? his friend pressed.

No, Connor said. *He's retired.*

At the time he'd believed it. Now he wondered if Andrew Stafford was involved in a new kind of game, more dangerous than his earlier outings.

What game? Connor shook his head. He had no answer.

He left the business card on the desk, then quickly examined the rest of the room, touching nothing.

Besides the cot, on an upended apple crate serving as a nightstand, he noticed two lumps of wax. A moment of study was required to identify them as earplugs. Homemade, shaped by hand, still imbedded with the whorls of fingerprints.

In New York sometimes Connor had used earplugs—the

store-bought kind—to screen out traffic noise and sirens while he slept. But what use would Robert Garrison have for earplugs here? What would disturb his sleep in the vast silence of the woods?

What did he hear at night?

A bark of static cut into his thoughts, followed by a female voice.

"Central? A-three." Danvers, contacting the dispatcher, her voice weak and fluttery over his portable radio.

Connor dialed up the volume as the dispatcher acknowledged: "A-three, go."

"I may have found it. I'm not sure." Though the transmission was poor, Connor could hear the quaver of raw adrenaline in her voice. *"I may have found the car."*

Danvers had traveled well out of familiar territory, past apple orchards and farms, deep into the unincorporated part of the county.

She'd been stuck behind a tractor for a couple of miles, and had passed a rusted-out camper in someone's yard, but these were the most exotic vehicles she'd encountered.

She had seen no white Mercedes anywhere.

It was possible Erica Stafford had taken a side road, even one of the dirt lanes that led to greenhouses and private estates, but Danvers couldn't check every byway.

Still, she didn't want to turn back. She knew from radio reports that none of the other units had found anything either. Charlie's lead offered at best a slender hope, but it was something.

She decided to go one more mile along Route 36. There was a convenience mart at the Bristol Road turnoff; she could ask in there.

As she drove, her hand crept under her collar and touched the crucifix chained around her neck. She felt the small silver Jesus, no bigger than a toy.

The crucifix, having survived her mom's Vietnam tour, had been her companion since childhood. It had seen her through some tough math tests and an embarrassing prom night, when her date deserted her for another girl and she had to get a ride home with another couple. She remembered sitting slumped in the backseat, face aflame with humiliation, her fingers rubbing the tiny cruciform shape in the dark.

She rubbed it now and said a silent prayer to find Erica Stafford, please, God, please let her find that woman alive.

Because Mrs. Stafford was one of the good ones. This was the kernel of Vicki Danvers' philosophy, frowned on by sophisticates, mocked by the great big world that saw no good and bad, but only gray shadings everywhere.

There were good ones and bad ones, the decent people and the troublemakers. That was the whole of it for her. She didn't know why people better educated than herself had to make things so complicated. Doubtless they had their reasons. Maybe Woodall, after his forays into criminal psychology, could explain it to her sometime. She would have to ask.

What she knew was that Erica Stafford was the sort of person there ought to be more of. In the station house she'd said Mrs. Stafford had been nice to her, but this was not the whole story. The whole story was known only to them both.

Our secret, Mrs. Stafford had said, pressing a conspiratorial finger to her lips, *and let's keep it that way.*

Danvers had broken one of Mrs. Stafford's sculptures.

It was completely an accident. Just a few weeks ago she'd stopped by the store to ask Mrs. Stafford if she'd had any trouble with vandalism; another shop in the converted warehouse had suffered a broken window on a Friday night. There had been no problems at Saving Grace, and no need for Vicki to stay, but she'd lingered, entranced by the artworks. In the clean, classic lines of the sculptures she'd suddenly seen what got people excited about art, something she had never understood before—that art could open a window on a better world.

Then, disaster. She was not ordinarily clumsy, but the bulky gun belt was still new to her, and turning too fast she'd hooked the pedestal of a blown-glass figure with the handle of her baton.

She had a glimpse of the figure's otherworldly crystalline beauty, unreal as a dream, in the instant before it shattered on the floor.

Danvers had not cried since that awful prom night, after she was safely locked in her room, shut off from her parents' platitudes and her big brother's awkward sympathy. But she was crying when she stooped and made a senseless effort to gather up the shards and jigsaw them together.

I'll pay for it, she kept saying. *Whatever it costs, I'll pay.*

But Mrs. Stafford had not asked for payment. She had swept up the gleaming fragments and said there was no problem, and, remarkably, had meant it.

Their secret. Never told to anyone. Mrs. Stafford must have written off the loss without a word.

Not a trivial loss. The price tag had been taped to the pedestal, and Danvers had risked a look as Mrs. Stafford swept her dust pan into the trash.

Eight thousand dollars.

Vicki's heart had almost failed when she saw the amount. A fortune. And she, a probationer, earning fifteen hundred a month . . . It would have taken her years to pay off that sum. Years of even more desperate, hardscrabble economizing than she practiced now. And this was assuming she'd even kept her job, which she might not've, if Mrs. Stafford had made an issue of the incident.

She had apologized a dozen times, her voice catching. But Mrs. Stafford had shrugged it off, then said a funny thing.

If every mess could be cleaned up this easily, she'd remarked with what seemed like sadness, *we would all live different lives.*

Danvers had been too upset to ponder those words, but she considered them now, as she wondered if Mrs. Stafford was still alive.

Please, Lord.

The wooded roadside flickered past, dense forest now, farmland a memory. Only a half mile to the convenience mart, and still no sign of any—

Wait.

There. What was *that*?

She'd seen it only for an instant. On her right, deep in the tangle of leafless trees: a metallic flash of white.

Danvers hauled the squad car onto the dirt shoulder and cranked the gear selector into Park.

Twisting in her seat she peered back along the roadside, but from this angle she couldn't see what she'd just glimpsed.

Out of the car, into the startling cold. She ran on the shoulder, averting her face as a big diesel rig blew past in a clatter of gravel.

Ten yards from the squad car she saw the white patch again, stationary, half hidden by trees, perhaps a quarter mile from the road.

Had the trees been leafy and green, she wouldn't have spotted anything at all. As it was, the car—yes, definitely a car—was barely visible, and would have been lost to sight altogether, huddled in gloom, if the lowering sun hadn't caught a side panel full in its glare.

Was it a Mercedes? She couldn't tell. But it was white, and probably a sedan, and parked where no car should be.

She almost unclipped her portable radio from her belt, but the squad car's built-in radio sent a stronger signal.

Behind the wheel again, she switched the squawk box from simplex to the duplex mode so she could talk to the dispatcher on duty. "Central? A-three."

"A-three, go."

"I may have found it. I'm not sure." She heard her own voice rising with excitement. *"I may have found the car."*

"Say again, A-three."

Calm down, be cool, be a pro.

She steadied herself. "I've spotted what may be the vehicle. Request permission to take a closer look, try to confirm."

The dispatcher asked for her location.

"Parked on the side of Route 36, half mile east of Bristol."

The dispatcher said she was way beyond town limits.

"I know"—Danvers was getting impatient now—"but I received a report the car might have come this way. There's a white vehicle, a possible match, in the woods. I need to check it out."

The dispatcher asked her to hold on for instructions.

Danvers waited, one hand on the microphone, the other feeling the silver Jesus through the fabric of her shirt.

"A-three?" Central was back. "Meet Chief Connor on Tac One."

Connor. Damn. She'd been hoping for Lieutenant Maginnis.

Danvers took a breath and switched to the tactical frequency. "Chief?"

Connor's voice came through unexpectedly loud, his voice bursting from the cheap speaker. "How close are you to the car?"

Distantly it occurred to her that she'd never heard him so agitated.

"Hundred yards," she said, deliberately underestimating the range.

"Can't you get a make on it from there? Use your binoculars."

"It's screened by foliage."

Hesitation. "Then you'd better wait for backup. I'm closest to you. I can be there in ten minutes."

Danvers bit her lip, debating whether to argue. Reluctance to challenge her superior competed with concern for Mrs. Stafford's safety. Concern won.

"Chief, ten minutes could make all the difference. What if she's in the car? Hurt, maybe?" Danvers frowned at herself, astonished at her boldness. "Please, Chief. Let me check it out."

Brief silence, broken by beats of static. She waited, kicking her boots together like a child.

"All right," Connor said, and she heard something new in his voice, a kind of anguish. "Do a visual check, but don't linger, and watch your back. And give Central a callback in five. Acknowledge those orders."

"Visual check, be careful, callback five."

"Five minutes *max,* Officer Danvers. And I want you to go in with your weapon drawn. And no heroics."

"Roger, Chief. Out."

Danvers released a held breath. She was amazed Connor had yielded. She hadn't ever imagined that she could persuade him of anything.

Then again, maybe she hadn't. Maybe he had persuaded himself.

Danvers got out of the car, drawing her service revolver, then climbed over the guardrail and headed into the woods.

In the smoke he waited.
In the flickering glare.

Patient as a carrion bird.

Still as a corpse.

He watched his sister, listening to her groans. She had not spoken in some time. Her head rolled from side to side, and now and then she tugged feebly at the straps.

The Wilcott girl had struggled also. The squalling-infant part of her, the part that hungered always for more life, the part that fought its destiny, had held her body in thrall—until under the smoke's caress, the true self had surfaced to speak through borrowed lips.

Sherry Wilcott had told him what he must do, and Erica would, as well.

He watched her, thinking of the girl she had been. Well, she had grown up, hadn't she? The awkward child had become an elegant woman. Her hair, mussed now, had been stylishly coiffed when he confronted her in the shop. She wore casual clothes, not much different from his own—a striped shirt, a pair of jeans, boots—but on her slender figure even these mundane items took on a sheen of grace.

Her eyes were shut, and he wondered if she was asleep. The Wilcott girl had slept before possession had come over her.

Then Erica spoke.

"I'm scared."

This was still her own voice, but just barely. She spoke as if she were a child, and perhaps she had in fact reverted to childhood as the smoke took hold.

Her eyes opened, and she turned an unfocused stare in his direction.

"I love you, Robert. I'm sorry I couldn't do more for you. I would have, if you'd let me. I've always wanted to protect you, keep you safe. Always."

He knew this was just a final gambit by her living, lying self. Sherry had tried a similar feint to win his sympathy, babbling of the grief her parents would feel if she died. It had been a diversion, and so were the words he was hearing now.

"Breathe deep, Sissy," he whispered, turning aside.

Nothing further to say for either of them.

He waited, filling his lungs. The room hummed. He felt its energy. There were places that held the impress of the past, places stamped with primordial patterns. Places that were palimpsests, and when the surface markings were scratched off, older truths would stand revealed.

The throne room was such a place. It was a womb, smooth-walled, hissing with the susurrant heartbeat of a distant aquifer. A womb of Earth, humanity's true mother, and an echo of other sacred chambers where magic and miracles were done: the shamans' cells at Lascaux and Altamira, and the caves at Delphi, and the labyrinth where a line of Cretan kings donned the mask of the sacred bull, and the sepulchre where Jesus lay.

Here in the dizzying smoke he saw all things, he knew patience, he waited.

It was proper to think of the cave as a womb. The cave was a place of rebirth, his own renewal, his emergence into a larger world. Like a child in a birth canal he was drawn forward irresistibly into a new dimension of experience. He felt no fear or doubt. He was calm, as calm as he'd been on a night in mid-January when he'd gone to kill the Wilcott girl.

Days earlier he'd gotten her address from a telephone directory in a pay phone. Then he fasted, meditated, and whetted the blade of the knife.

When the moon rose, gibbous and white, over the bare trees, he drove to the Wilcott farm. He parked in the woods and approached the farmhouse from the rear. And there she was, framed in a ground-floor window, her face flickering in a television's blue glare. Her parents were home also—he heard Sherry's mother call to her from the front of house, asking if she wanted dessert. It would be better, safer, to abduct the girl when she was alone. But he was not to be denied.

The back door was unlocked—how convenient—and no one heard him as he crept down the hall and entered her room. Seeing him, she could have screamed and ruined everything, but shock sealed her mouth for a vital second, and a second was all he needed to club her unconscious with a swat of his forearm. She went down in a pile of disarranged limbs, and he hefted her on his shoulder and carried her to the truck.

A short drive brought him to the sinkhole, where he lowered her, still unconscious, on a harness of rope looped under her arms.

He burned incense that night, liberating her truest self, which spoke to him and verified her destiny. And then of course he did what he must do, his face masked, the sharpened knife at the ready, and the lustral water and the crown of leaves.

Afterward he waited for a sign of his redemption, but no sign came. His enemies still plagued him. The curse had not been lifted.

He hadn't understood until today. Now he began to suspect that the Wilcott girl had been only the staked goat that lured the greater prize.

It was Erica who might be truly meant for him. Or perhaps not. The decision was not his to reach. It belonged to fate. To the plan of his life, mapped before he was born. It belonged to . . .

"Moira," Erica said.

He heard the word distinctly, bubbling from her throat, rising in the heat of an alien will. But the voice was not quite hers—a hoarse baritone, a guttural whisper.

Again: *"Moira."*

Her lips were moving, or perhaps it was only a trick of the lamplight.

"Tell me the fate of this one," Robert said.

She shuddered once and endured a spate of stertorous breathing, and then came a rush of words in a rapid murmur, a sleepwalker's monotone.

"This one dies. Dies as a sin offering. Dies for catharsis. For purification through blood. Without blood there is no antidote to pollution, deadly pollution that will end all life in ten years. This one dies."

Her belly swelled with breath, and he felt himself exhale.

"This one dies," she said again, the words soft and insistent, like the whisper of his own thoughts.

Robert lowered his head, eyes burning with a threat of tears. Though he had expected as much, he'd hoped for a different message. Still, he could not disobey.

"Will this victim be accepted?" he asked tonelessly, his own voice now as husky as hers. "The first one wasn't. Or if she was, it wasn't enough."

A long span of silence. Then came the response, low and solemn.

"This one will win you favor," croaked the voice of the god.

"Favor enough?" he pressed.

The response came, slowly, unwillingly, as if dragged from the throat of the one who uttered it.

"This one will set you free . . ."

Robert touched his face and felt wetness. Freedom was what he had wanted, but not this way.

He waited for more, but there was only the aquifer's faint hum and the slow, regular breathing of the woman on the table, deep in sleep.

"I'm sorry, Sissy," he said, and coughed. His mouth was suddenly dry, his throat sore.

The smoke did that, sometimes. The smoke.

He approached the table, stood over her, touched her golden hair, shimmering with faint highlights in the kerosene's glow.

She had told him, as he'd known she would. He could not argue. Yet he was sad. Sad for them both.

But if this was fate, he would accept it. He would do as her highest self instructed. He would not fail his destiny or hers.

His hand stroking her long tresses, his voice a whisper: "As you wish."

A shiver, and she was briefly awake, eyelids fluttering like moth wings. "Robert?"

"As you wish," he said again, in benediction.

She blinked at him, a hint of the old animal fear widening her eyes, and then unconsciousness stole over her once more, and she let her head roll limply to one side.

"Rest now," he said. "Rest, Sissy. Tonight I'll cut you, claim you, dip my hands in your life essence and wash the sin away. Tonight, after moonrise, when the Mother watches. Tonight."

His voice broke on the last word, and he said no more, merely brushed her hair and watched her sleep.

After a time he retrieved his flashlight, then left the room, retracing his route along the side corridor. For a few yards a flicker of lamplight lapped his heels, then faded, until there was only the pale circle of his flashlight's beam ahead, smoke and darkness behind, and from the dark her voice calling, feeble, half-awake.

"Robert . . ."

He almost turned back, thinking vaguely that she was lost in the maze, his sister, crying for him, a little girl again.

Then he remembered that neither of them was a child anymore, and he kept going, hurrying now, as Erica's call died away in echoes and left him finally alone.

9

The white car was a sedan, was a Mercedes, was a Mercedes 400 SEL, was a Mercedes 400 SEL with Erica Stafford's license plate.

Danvers read the plate twice, standing thirty feet from the car, concealing herself behind a thick-boled sycamore, leafless in its upper branches but still bearing a fringe of dead rust-colored leaves on the lower boughs.

She scanned the fire road in both directions and saw no movement, no other vehicle in sight. The woods stretched on all sides, some trees wrapped in ivy shawls, others naked in the cold. The ivy and a stand of evergreen hollies were the only bright touches, the only reminders of life, in a scene drained of color, a grim sepia world.

Abandoning cover, she approached the car, first checking under the chassis, then surveying the interior.

A leather handbag lay on the front seat. Otherwise, the Mercedes was empty.

She tested the driver's door. Unlocked.

A noise startled her, and she whipped around, the revolver in both hands, but it was only a crow, black and shiny, darting through a drift of leaves.

"Mrs. Stafford?" Danvers said.

The words came out in a near whisper, useless. She tried again, louder.

No reply.

Okay, now what? Thing to do was call it in.

She kept the revolver in her right hand as she fumbled the radio free of the belt clip. Her heart was racing, her fingers unsteady, and she found it hard to switch to the duplex mode and thumb the transmit button.

"Central? A-three."

"A-three, go."

"Vehicle confirmed." The words were sweet in her mouth; she indulged in a second taste. "Repeat, vehicle is confirmed."

"Any sign of the occupant?"

"Negative. Car's empty. No one appears to be around."

"Copy that, A-three. Backup ETA five minutes. Sit and wait."

She disliked this instruction, which felt condescending. "Roger, out," she said curtly, and switched back to simplex, then reclipped the radio on her belt.

Perhaps because she resisted being ordered around by a damn dispatcher, she lingered near the Mercedes, her gaze panning the fire road again.

This time she caught sight of a faint horizontal line flickering behind a scrim of holly branches. Nothing in nature was so perfectly straight. It looked like the hood of a car.

Another vehicle? She approached, moving fast but pausing twice to check behind her.

Watch your back, Connor had said. She didn't mind taking orders from him.

The holly trees were bunched close together, branches intertwining in a dense skein of spiked leaves, glossy and green. She edged along the wall of trees until she found a narrow gap.

Peeling back a branch, peering through, she discovered a dented pickup truck with bald tires and sorry, spotted chrome.

The truck was a Ford, years old, blue but faded. If it belonged to someone local, then the owner didn't get out much. Danvers was fairly positive she'd never seen it in town or anywhere on the open road. Of course she'd been a Barrow cop for only a few months, having come here from Williamsport in late November after her application was approved. There was still a lot she didn't know.

Whoever it belonged to, the truck had been hidden here. The

driver had pulled off the dirt road into the concealment of the evergreens.

Danvers licked her lips and thought that right now would be a real good time to return to her cruiser.

But suppose Mrs. Stafford was in the truck. Trussed under the dashboard or covered by the tarpaulin in the open bed. Wounded, maybe. Dying even now.

She decided to risk a closer look.

The gap between the trees was wide enough to slip through. She stepped into the small clearing, then circled the truck quickly, knowing there was no value in stealth and a great advantage to speed.

When she was sure nobody was hiding under the chassis or behind the vehicle, she looked inside. Empty. She came to the bed and had to lift the tarp with one hand, pointing the revolver with the other.

There could have been anything underneath—Mrs. Stafford or her dead body or the kidnapper himself, grinning at her with a Smith Magnum in his deadly clutch—but in fact there was only a sprawl of brown paper grocery bags and their scattered contents: a month's worth of canned goods and frozen foods and sundries.

So whoever drove this heap did get into town, at least occasionally. He'd bought this stuff at Waldman's; the paper sacks bore the store's logo. It was where Vicki herself shopped.

Waldman's . . .

She'd heard something about Waldman's earlier today, she was sure she had, but she couldn't remember what.

The frozen items were thawing in cool puddles. The truck, if it had come straight from the store, must have been here for some time.

She let go of the tarp and stepped back, then pivoted in a full circle to scan the clearing in case somebody had crept up on her while she was preoccupied.

Nothing. Silence. Stillness.

Time to go, except for one task yet undone. She had to memorize the license plate. If by chance the truck was gone when she returned with backup, at least she could identify it.

The truck surely belonged to Erica Stafford's abductor—perhaps the same man who'd killed Sherry Wilcott. And *she* had found it. She would be a hero. The local paper would interview her. They might print her picture. She wondered what Hart would say about that, and Woodall, Maginnis, Connor—everyone.

The license number had to pass before her gaze three times before it stuck in her memory. She was excited and scared and buzzing with adrenaline, and she knew she'd better get going before she made a careless mistake.

Somewhere a branch snapped.

The sound riveted her. Abruptly any thought of heroism and acclaim had vanished, and she was looking everywhere around her, the gun shifting with each jerk of her gaze.

Nothing.

Maybe only another bird, or some small forest creature.

Anyway, it was definitely time to get the hell out of here.

She crabbed along the passenger side of the truck, using the vehicle as cover, just in case. At the hood she hesitated, casting another wide glance at her surroundings.

The ripple of motion across the windshield was so faint as to be ghostly, almost invisible, but on the margin of her sight it registered, and she focused on the glass in time to see the reflected blur of someone's shirt, a red shirt, plunging into cover ten yards away, on the opposite side of the truck.

Fear yanked her hard around, her arms extended over the hood, both hands aiming the revolver at the approximate spot where the shirt and the man wearing it had disappeared from view.

He was hiding in there, at the edge of the clearing, masked by high deadfalls of heavy branches, by nets of ivy creepers, by weeds grown knee-high, stiff and dead.

Her mom had told her of an ambush in 'Nam, a convoy under attack, the green jungle concealing snipers who picked off the Americans one by one, and how only the arrival of big Huey gunships, rotor blades chopping the steamy air, had saved them.

Jungle combat. Vicki had enjoyed the thrill of terror such stories had inspired. But not now.

Slowly she hunkered down behind the front end of the truck, using it as cover, and in her loudest voice called out: *"Police."*

She expected no response and got none.

"I see you there," she said, bluffing, as she peered over the hood. "I've got you covered. Other officers are en route to the scene. Raise your hands and come out *now*."

The radio at her hip crackled softly with police traffic, the noise a mere distraction. She ought to radio a code twenty, but somehow she couldn't get the fingers of her left hand to release their grip on the revolver's checkered handle.

"You won't be hurt. Show yourself right now!"

A rustle of weeds and grasses answered her, soft as a chuckle of malice.

He was crawling, shifting position, but the sound was too faint and diffuse to help her pinpoint where he lay.

She had to assume he was armed. If so, he might be circling the perimeter of the clearing, intent on getting a clear angle of fire. And while she waited here, thinking she was safe behind the truck, he would draw a bead on her from the brush.

But if she left cover, he could cut her down as she ran.

And what if there were more than one of them? Wouldn't there have to be at least two, if one had kidnapped Mrs. Stafford in her car and the other had driven the truck?

They could be closing in from two sides.

Her mouth was dry, and she couldn't seem to find any moisture with her tongue.

She didn't know what to do. The realization hit her suddenly and made her feel younger than she was. She had been trained well enough to carry out most duties, but in this situation she simply did not have a clue.

No more rustling now. He'd either stopped moving or learned stealth.

She looked behind her, at the wall of holly, then to her left, then right.

Yards past the truck's rear bumper, in a clump of winter-blasted foliage at the clearing's edge—a flicker of red.

Him.

She scrambled forward, past the Ford's left headlight, and took cover behind the grille at the front of the truck.

Her glimpse of his shirt had told her that he was still low to the ground, maybe leaning on his elbows, maybe sighting her along a gun barrel.

In her new position she was temporarily less vulnerable, but he could just sneak nearer, couldn't he? Get a better angle? Or aim underneath the chassis, take out her knees—cripple her, then finish her at closer range?

God, this was bad—she was very scared, she didn't want to be here at all.

Her heart was beating much too fast. The silver Christ was cold against her collarbone.

She decided to take a chance. If she left cover suddenly, running flat-out, probably she could get away. It was better than staying put, waiting for him to bring her down.

Rising to a half crouch, she tensed for a burst of speed. Her mind mapped the path she'd taken. Just go through the gap in the holly trees, then straight to the fire road and up the incline to the highway. No stopping, no backward looks.

As long as there was only one enemy and he was well behind her, she ought to be able to make it. Even an expert marksman would find it hard to nail a moving target in the woods.

No more delay. She had to do it before he got closer, before her legs started to cramp, before she lost her nerve.

She flung herself upright and hurtled forward, the holly rushing at her, a smooth green wall—where was the gap, where was it? There, found it, and she got through, bursting into the open woods, head spinning, lungs aflame, and the man reared up directly in her path.

She saw the red shirt and his bearded face. Confusion cost her a precious half second. He couldn't be here, he was behind her in the clearing, she'd *seen* him.

Then she remembered her revolver, too late.

His fist lashed out, cracking her cheekbone with astonishing force, and the world upended.

She hit the ground on her back, landing hard, all the wind

driven out of her, then groaned under a second impact as his knees plunged into her stomach.

He was straddling her, his hands on hers, fighting for the revolver, and she realized he was unarmed, he needed her gun, he was going to shoot her with her own goddamned gun.

Vicki was strong. She'd played soccer in high school and still had the muscular thighs to show for it, but pinned under him she couldn't kick, and her upper-body strength was no match for his.

He wrapped both hands around her right wrist. Teeth clenched, he forced the gun lower, toward her abdomen.

With trembling effort she held the gun at bay, the muzzle aimed at empty air, her arms straining.

"I know you," he said suddenly.

She glanced at his face, saw his eyes—not hectic and crazy as she would have thought—eyes that were intense and serious and probing.

"I know you"—his words were squeezed through his locked jaws—"and you can't stop me."

How could he know her? She had never seen him before. But his face, the thick beard, wild hair, the focused intensity of his stare—

Abruptly she knew who he must be. Robert Garrison. Mrs. Stafford's brother, the lunatic, the hermit, the fool on the hill.

And the truck loaded with groceries from Waldman's . . .

Connor had said Robert was seen shopping there today. It was his alibi. That was where she'd heard the store mentioned—yes, she remembered now—and it didn't matter because her gun inched lower, lower, and she knew she was losing the battle.

"Danvers," Robert barked, a kind of glee on his face. He said her name again, dividing it sharply in half. "Dan. Vers."

He'd read the nametag on her shirt. She didn't know why, or what it meant to him.

The gun barrel jerked downward another inch, almost brushing her belly.

"Huntress," he said. "Diana of the forest."

She put her full strength into a final effort to force the gun away, but all she could manage was a precarious stalemate.

"Hunting me. Bitch dog weaned on blood—hunting *me*!"

His right hand shifted its grip, and with a flash of terror she felt his forefinger curl over hers on the trigger.

When she glanced at his face again, she saw his huge malicious smile.

"Who's the hunter now?" he said, and wrenched the gun fully down, the muzzle diving into the blue folds of her shirt, inches from her navel, pressing deep, and he fired.

The revolver's report was muffled by the shirt and her undershirt and her own flesh, and for a blessed moment there was no pain, only an abrupt numbness and a lurch of vertigo.

Her head snapped back, and she felt her arms lose their power and drop away, surrendering the gun to him, not that it mattered now.

Then the pain reached her, a pain like fire, burning her midsection, parching her throat. It was bad, but distant, a report from some part of her body that was too remote to be of consequence anymore.

Something shook her—was it him?—no, only her own breath, stuttering out of her open mouth in a ragged wheeze.

Her stomach was wet all over, and she could feel the slippery runnels of blood tracing a skein of liquid warmth over her groin and thighs.

Above her was blue sky, the deep blue of late afternoon, pierced by leafless branches, jagged like cracks in plaster.

Then his face covered the blue, and he was watching her, and she felt the revolver's steel kiss on her chin.

Gonna finish me with a head shot, she thought with curious objectivity.

She waited, straining for breath, trying to remember the words of that psalm.

Though I walk through the . . . the shadow . . . shadow of death . . . Though I walk through the shadow of . . .

Couldn't get it. Couldn't think.

He leaned closer, staring into her eyes, and then he nodded. "I don't need to," he said. "You're done."

The gun withdrew.

She felt no relief, felt nothing.

The valley of the shadow of death, that was it.

Though I walk...

His hand, fumbling at her gun belt, extracting cartridges from the ammo pouch. Looting her body.

Though I walk through the valley...

Touching her collar now. "Won't help you," he muttered. "Not anymore."

He closed his fist over her crucifix, which must have slipped out from under her collar when she fell, or during the struggle, or sometime anyway.

She didn't want him to take it, but she had no voice to utter an objection. Almost gently he pulled the chain over her head, then slipped it around his own neck.

The silver Jesus flashed once in the sun.

Robert showed his yellow teeth. "Your totem won't help you anymore." The crucifix vanished under the red plaid shirt. "It's mine now. My power. Mine."

The blue sky returned as he stood and took a step backward.

I will fear no evil. The Lord is my shepherd, I shall not want.

Nausea rumbled in her, and she let her head roll to one side and spit up something viscid and hot.

Dry leaves crunched. Robert trudged away and disappeared through the gap in the holly.

He had left her. Left her for dead. But she wasn't dead. That seemed a good joke on him.

Vicki let her head fall back and thought of nothing, not even the psalm, aware only of the pain inside her and the fading brightness of the sky, while her left hand, of its own will, fumbled at her gun belt to unclip her radio.

Robert was shaking when he returned to his truck. That had been a close one. The huntress had nearly beaten him in this penultimate round. But he was sure he'd stopped her before she had a chance to call in his license plate.

She wore a police officer's uniform, but it was only a superficial disguise, no more significant than her facade of flesh. He knew who she really was.

Danvers, her nametag had said. Dan-vers. That was clever.

Vers, from Middle English *verte,* from Latin *viridis,* green. Verdure, verdant—green growing things—the forest. Dan, obviously a coded compression of Diana.

Diana of the forest. Green Diana, the huntress in the wood. Goddess of the hunt and of chastity. The Greeks knew her as Artemis. She had other names, older names, and newer ones.

Danvers was only the latest.

If he'd had time and opportunity, he would have dispatched her with proper ceremony. In the old rituals, said Frazer in *The Golden Bough,* Artemis was hanged by her arms from a high branch, then pierced with a spear. A spear between the ribs, like the Roman spear that in a similar rite pierced the crucified Jesus, whose image Danvers-of-the-forest had worn as her totem.

There was an illustration of the ritual on a page Robert had studied for many intent hours, scribbling notes. He had known her as one face of his enemy, the holy one who plagued him, the Earth Mother who was also Mistress of the Moon.

The Mother had many names, many faces. She had been revered and dreaded throughout history, in every land, by every people. She was Sekmet in Egypt, Kali in India, Astarte in the Levant. The Aztecs knew her as Coyolxuahqui, the Japanese as Amaterasu. To the Sumerians she was Inanna, to the Anatolians Cybele. Achilles and Agamemnon worshiped her as Artemis, and to her Agamemnon had sacrificed his daughter Iphigenia on an altar in a forest grove.

She had existed throughout time, ageless and omnipresent, showing sometimes a face of love and other times a countenance of death. She was nurturer and destroyer, bride and crone, sun and moon, life-in-death and death-in-life. Coleridge had seen her casting dice upon the deck of a ghost ship, and Shakespeare had heard her strange music on Caliban's isle. Dogs and madmen felt the thrill of her kiss when they raised their howls to the glowing moon.

At times she had ruled, and at times she had feigned subservience to a male master. But always she lived. Gods of storm and sky could usurp her throne but never kill her. Like the moon, which was her symbol and incarnation, she would wane, would seem to vanish, fading from sight, but her absence was only temporary, for she was forever renewing herself. She was the beginning and the end, the life force of nature, and Robert knew her well.

And hated her. Hated her.

But now he had her totem, and a sliver of her power. He had killed the Mother in one earthly incarnation. Killed Artemis the huntress, piercing her belly not with a spear but with a bullet.

"You can't stop me," he told the empty clearing, where she was sure to hear him, she who was called the Lady of the Wild Things, Mistress of the Animals, nature–spirit, earth goddess. "You *can't*."

For emphasis he hawked a silvery gob deep into the holly.

The one troubling question was why she had run almost directly into his arms. He was sure she hadn't done it deliberately.

At first, spotting her as she entered the clearing where he'd hidden the truck, he had thought of sneaking behind her. She had a gun, and he didn't; stealth was his only hope. If she reported finding the truck, he was finished.

But she had heard him as he crept through the brush on the far verge of the clearing. She'd taken cover, and he knew he couldn't get near. So he had doubled back, unsure of what to do.

And then she had appeared through a break in the holly trees, running blindly at him, seeing him only when it was too late.

He shook his head, baffled, and took a moment to scan the clearing. A few yards from the rear of the truck, something red glimmered in the foliage.

Not a forest color—certainly not at this time of year.

His gaze dropped to his plaid shirt, red also. If she had seen any part of him, it would have been the shirt, the only bright color he wore.

And having seen the shirt, she had been sure this other patch of red was him. And had fled in the opposite direction.

Robert crossed the clearing, parted the dead weeds, and saw a long ribbon of red fabric hooked on the thorns of a bush.

Someone's scarf. The wind must have carried it here.

He plucked it free of the brambles. It nearly got away from him as the breeze stirred briefly, but he held on.

The scarf was monogrammed. White cursive letters. *E.S.*

Erica Stafford.

It was his sister's scarf. Must be.

She'd lost her scarf, and the huntress had lost her life. That this was mere coincidence was not a possibility.

"Moira," he whispered, his voice hushed in reverence.

Fate had stitched the threads of this day's work, stitched them close. Fate had brought his sister to the caves. And when the huntress in her fleshly form dared to interfere, fate had delivered her into his arms, and he had put a bullet in her.

Even the Earth Mother could not resist the tug of fate. Fate was a riptide dragging both men and gods.

He rolled up the scarf and stuffed it in his back pocket. Perhaps tonight he would use it to gag his sister if, seeing the knife, she began to scream.

He didn't like to hear screams. The noise was too much like what he heard at night, in the haunted stillness of the woods. The voices—the awful gabbling voices, inhuman, frenzied with malice—sometimes barking like dogs or hissing in reptilian urgency or wailing, the notes incredibly high pitched, inharmonious, wild, rising to shake the roof of his skull and bring him to his knees in a fit of sobbing—

The same sound he heard now. Heard *here*.

With a flash of terror he was sure they were upon him, his tormentors, the Earth Mother's beasts who hounded him.

No.

Not them.

It was a siren he heard.

A police car, fast approaching on the highway.

Robert ran back to his truck, then took an additional few seconds to peer through the gap in the hedges at the fallen huntress.

He saw no movement, not even the rise and fall of breath. Well, that was no surprise. He'd known she was dead. In her eyes he'd seen the spirit fading, a look he'd seen also in the Wilcott girl as her blood filled the chalice.

The siren was close.

He slid behind the pickup's steering wheel, cranked the ignition key, and headed away over the low brush on the clearing's far side, charting a path between a brace of elms. Ignoring the fire road, he drove south, straight through the woods, skirting trees and deadfalls.

The ride was rough, the Ford's shocks shot. Robert bounced wildly in his seat, and under his red shirt the totem Jesus, the corn-king crucified, beat a cold tattoo against his chest.

Connor was three minutes from his expected rendezvous with Vicki Danvers when her voice, pale and whispery, sizzled over the cruiser's squawkbox.

"Code ninety-nine . . . A-three . . . code ninety-nine . . ."

Fear clamped down hard.

Code 99 was Barrow P.D.'s emergency call signal, shorthand for an officer in trouble, maybe ambushed, maybe hurt.

Danvers repeated the code once more, and then her voice faded in a rattling gasp.

Wounded. She had to be. Connor could hear blood in the wheezy whisper of her breathing.

The dispatcher was already transmitting the report to all units, a code-three high incident, officer-needs-help, even as Connor reached under the dash and flipped on the siren and lights.

Switching to duplex, fumbling for the radio mike, he heard himself scream over the siren's wail: *"A-five en route code three!"*

Accelerator on the floor, the big Chevy jumping forward, Route 36 smearing in a rush of speed.

Dispatch rogered him, and he switched back to simplex, monitoring all traffic, hoping to hear another transmission from Danvers, some indication she was still alive.

If she died . . .

Then it was his goddamned fault. He'd authorized her to go into the woods alone. She should have waited for backup—he knew that—but he'd been afraid, afraid for Erica, afraid of losing her.

Because of fear, he'd overridden his professional judgment and sent Danvers in alone—a rookie, hardly grown, barely older than the Wilcotts' daughter. She could be dead now or dying.

His fault. His guilt.

He urged the Chevy Caprice to seventy-five, whipping across a double yellow line to shoot past a slower car.

The dispatcher was calling for A-three, getting no response.

Connor switched to the duplex mode again, then to the frequency used by the state police. To the radio operator he explained the situation in a handful of words and code numbers. "Need extra backup, and my other units are too far. You got anyone?"

"Yes sir, one car in the area, he'll meet you at the scene."

There was no time for a thank-you. Connor could see Danvers's cruiser parked on the shoulder ahead.

He returned to simplex, dialing the volume to the max, but there was still no response from A-3 to Central's inquiries, only static and silence.

In a clatter of gravel he slammed the Chevy to a stop two yards behind the parked patrol car. Then he was out, gun drawn, running up to Danvers's unit.

He hadn't expected her to be inside, and she wasn't. She must be in the woods, using her portable.

Connor grabbed a first-aid kit from the trunk of his Chevy, wedging the small plastic box under his belt. He had given up on the trooper and was about to head into the forest alone when another siren wailed down Route 36.

A highway patrol car, eastbound at high speed. The car swerved across the opposing lane and braked in the shoulder, the driver exiting instantly.

Connor had seen him before, couldn't recall his name.

"What happened, Chief?"

"Officer down, somewhere in there." He nodded to the woods.

The trooper saw Connor's gun and unholstered his own. "How bad's he hurt?"

"Don't know. It's a she. Could be serious." Connor blew out a shuddering breath. "She was looking for a missing woman. Circumstances possibly similar to the Wilcott case."

"Shit."

"Let's go, Trooper."

They vaulted the guardrail together. Fast down a gentle slope through drifts of dry leaves, sidestepping fallen branches. Connor was looking for the white car Vicki had seen.

He didn't spot it until he reached the fire road. Then he looked to his right, and there it was, a Mercedes sedan, almost certainly Erica Stafford's, parked on the dirt road twenty yards away.

Connor ran for it, and the trooper followed. Their two walkie-talkies spluttered with incoherent chatter on rival frequencies. Connor caught enough of the state-police traffic to know that another trooper was on the way to help out. An R.A.—rescue ambulance—would be coming too; the Barrow dispatcher would have seen to that as soon as the code 99 came in.

Nearing the Mercedes, the two men slowed, Connor gesturing to the trooper for caution. He got close to the car, saw that it was empty, then scanned the rough terrain beyond the fire road and saw a swatch of blue.

A uniformed figure on the ground, half hidden behind a tangle of withered shrubbery.

Connor and the trooper cut a straight line through the brush, and found Vicki Danvers, twenty-three years old, supine and bloody, the radio loosely held in a nerveless hand, her eyes shut, bubbles of red frothing her mouth.

"God, she's been shot." That was the trooper.

Connor put the first-aid kit in the man's hand. "Stanch the blood. But don't move her."

He left the trooper with Danvers and hurried through the woods, aiming his revolver in every direction, looking for any sign of the man who had done this.

No luck. But in a small clearing bordered on one side by holly shrubs, he found parallel lines of flattened grass. Tire marks.

Someone had parked in this unlikely spot, and fled through the trees, traveling off-road. The trail vanished within yards.

Connor couldn't quite put together what had happened. Too many scenarios presented themselves. He would sort it all out later.

He left the clearing and ran to the Mercedes. On the driver's seat was a handbag—Erica's, he knew it on sight. Car keys dangled from the ignition.

He reached in and grabbed the keys, then forced himself to pop the trunk, afraid of what he might find.

Erica could fit in there.

But he found nothing in the trunk. Relief lifted him, but only briefly.

Then he was sprinting back to the clearing, harried by a new fear—that when he got back to Danvers, she would be dead.

The trooper, kneeling by her, read Connor's mind. "She's holding on," he said without being asked.

Connor let himself breathe again. "How does it look?"

"She took a round in the abdomen. I think I got the bleeding stopped." He was holding a wad of gauze on the wound, exerting firm pressure, his bare hand soaked red. "Her airway's clear now, but her pulse is way rapid, ninety at least, and pretty weak."

"Shock," Connor said, unzipping his jacket, shrugging it off.

The trooper nodded. "Think she's got a fractured cheekbone too, but that's the least of it. Gut-shot—that's bad news, Chief. I seen a guy gut-shot once."

"So have I." More than one guy, Connor added silently, his memory replaying old urban battles, the craziness of the city at night.

He knelt and draped Vicki with his jacket, taking care not to touch the wound or jostle her. If the bullet had nicked her spine or lodged there, the slightest movement could be fatal.

"Her sidearm's been taken," the trooper said. "Ammo pouch was cleaned out too."

Connor nodded. "But he didn't take her radio. That was a mistake."

"Was it the S.O.B. who nailed Sherry Wilcott, you think?"

"I don't know who the hell it was."

"You got the perp's car, anyway." The Mercedes, the trooper meant. "Probably stolen, but he might've left prints."

"That's not his, and I'm not sure he was even in it. Fact is"—he sighed—"I don't have anything. Except a cop who's shot and a woman who's missing . . . a woman who may be dead." Connor looked toward the glitter of moving traffic on the highway. "Where the hell is that R.A.?"

The trooper had no answer.

On the ground Vicki Danvers made a small noise like a whimper, then was quiet again save for her difficult breathing.

Not knowing what else to do, Connor gently clasped her right hand. The fingers were childishly small, and cold, too cold. He thought of his wife, Karen, the bloody bedclothes tangled around her like a winding sheet, and her red hand in his.

It had been his fault on that night two years ago. And this— this was his fault too.

"Hang on, Vicki," he whispered, but he knew she couldn't hear.

10

Robert was pleased with himself as he drove back to the cabin. Everything was working out quite nicely. The separate threads of his life and his sister's, always interwoven, had been stitched into a visible pattern. Fate had delivered Erica to him, and even the goddess of earth and moon had failed to cheat him of his destiny.

The sun was swinging low over the western treetops as he parked at the summit of the hill. He went first to the well and drew a bucket of cold water, then set to work washing his hands and forearms, spattered with Danvers's blood. He performed this chore outdoors, indifferent to the cold. Winter's chill rarely touched him. Sometimes at night he shivered, true, but it was not the cold that raised a stubble of gooseflesh on his neck and arms; it was the voices he heard, the cries of his tormentors.

Call them off, he'd begged his sister. But she had refused. And now she would pay the price, as *moira*—fate, justice— dictated she must.

He had only lately come to realize that it was Erica who was his nemesis. Inexplicably this simple fact had escaped his notice for years. Yet when the truth had finally awoken in him, he had seen instantly that it must be so.

Erica, he knew, had spent years in the Mediterranean. She was forever going back, ostensibly to collect new artworks. But he knew the real reason. She was paying homage to the Mother.

There were caves on the Attic seacoast and in the inland mountains, sacred caves, hidden and protected. In one of them, at a secret shrine, his sister had knelt in prayer before a triple-headed figure, the goddess herself, heavy with her many breasts, stern yet nurturing.

He knew it. Saw it. The image was as vivid as a memory.

She had given herself to the Mother. How else could she be what she was—the great lady of Great Hall, the belle of the town, regal as a princess, adored and honored by the commoners who spoke her name in whispers?

She was everything he could have been, should have been. There was no curse on her, no plague of *miasma*. The ill star that had hung for so long over the Garrison clan had not touched her with its corrupting light.

"Sold her soul," Robert murmured, nodding to himself. "Sold it to the devil."

That was a crude metaphor, of course, a holdover from medieval times, when the old earth-centered religion had been driven underground to be practiced in *wicca* cults by maidens and crones. Those caught in the act of witchcraft were said to have bartered their souls for strange powers. They'd been seen worshipping a horned figure, taken to be Satan.

But the horns were the Earth Mother's headdress, for the bull was one of many animals sacred to her. Or perhaps it was the Mother's consort they worshipped, bullheaded like the Minotaur. In either case their cult long predated Satan, and their rites, performed in hidden groves and dank cells and forest cottages, were the ancient orgiastic rituals that once had honored Astarte in the broiling Levant.

Erica was a witch of that sort. She was Medea. She was Sycorax. She served as priestess to the goddess who was snake and bat and dog and night and birth-blood and pain.

He would have been afraid to take her life, if she herself—or the immortal part of her—had not given her assent. The goddess might not want her acolyte to die, but *moira,* which bound all things living and divine, had required otherwise.

The Mother might try again to stop him before the fatal hour. Might visit him once more in some new persona, or might send one of her human minions to spar with Necessity. She had many tricks, that whore. She fought gamely, and didn't like to lose.

But she would lose. Robert could feel it. He would perform the sacrifice, redeem himself, lift the curse, and be set free.

Then he would laugh at the moon, which was her nightly dwelling place. He would laugh.

Chuckling now, he finished his ablutions at the well, then hurried to the cabin. He knew there was a good chance they would come by—Connor or some others—if only to inform him that his sister was missing. He had to be ready.

Then he stopped, and the smile clinging to his mouth vanished.

The cabin door was ajar. It had been forced open, the dead bolt splintered from the frame.

Had the police done this? Had Connor been here already, Connor with his suspicious, squinty eyes?

Drawing the huntress's gun, he entered the cabin, poised for another battle.

But the cabin was unoccupied and, except for the door, undisturbed.

He scanned the place, looking everywhere, until his gaze fell on the desk by the window, where the intruder had left a literal calling card.

Andrew Stafford's card, with his private phone number handwritten on the reverse.

And the papers that Robert had left scattered on the desk—they were gone.

It had been careless of him to leave those notes in the open. Even a man like Andrew, his mind sharp but narrow, could not fail to grasp the threat to Erica his jottings implied.

We need to talk, Andrew had written.

Surely he knew or guessed that Erica was in her brother's hands. And knowing, he was dangerous.

Was this another gambit of the Mother, or just a trick of chance? Robert couldn't tell, and really, it didn't matter.

Either way, he would have to deal with Andrew Stafford.

Soon.

Before the midnight hour, when Erica would die.

On his way back to Great Hall, Andrew detoured into downtown Barrow and stopped at the bank.

The bank manager knew him, of course. "Mr. *Staf*ford," the

heavyset bald man cooed with obsequious appreciation as Andrew approached his desk.

"Hello, Henry."

"We're offering an exceptional rate on our eighteen-month CD. You can't beat it anyplace."

"Not right now. I'm rather busy. Actually I just came by to check something in my safe-deposit box."

Henry was already on his feet, as eager to please as a dog sent to fetch its master's slippers. "I'll bring it out. How is Mrs. Stafford?"

It was Erica who really mattered to poor Henry, of course. Andrew was only an interloper from Philadelphia, but Erica was a Garrison, and the Garrisons had always been royalty here.

"She's fine," he said mildly, hoping it was true.

"Give her my regards."

"I will."

Andrew watched him retreat behind the tellers' counter to operate the controls that unlocked the vault. He wondered how Henry would think of this exchange—what suspicions would be raised in his mind—after he learned that Mrs. Stafford had been missing for hours when her husband had confidently asserted she was fine.

Surely it would occur to the bank manager that there was something odd about Mr. Stafford running an apparently routine errand when his wife might be in deadly jeopardy. And surely he would ask himself what Mr. Stafford kept in his safe-deposit box that was so critically important as to require his attention under such dire circumstances.

In due course these suspicions would be relayed to the police, and Chief Connor would come calling again at Great Hall, less friendly than before.

Andrew knew all this, and regarded the knowledge with disdainful indifference. By the time Connor paid him that visit, either Erica would have been safely returned, or she would be dead. If safe, she would lie for him; he was sure she would; and her lies would be persuasive enough to send Connor away with no proof of anything.

And if she were dead . . .

He shook his head. He refused to think of that.

The vault hissed open, and the bank manager disappeared inside, returning a few moments later with the rectangular steel box.

"Thanks, Henry."

"No trouble whatsoever, Mr. Stafford."

In a private booth, with the door closed and latched, Andrew unlocked the box. Within lay a miscellany of legal documents, scattered on top of a thick pile. Burrowing deeper, his hands found the envelope at the bottom.

A manila envelope, bulky and folded, elaborately sealed with tape. He smoothed it, ran his fingertips lightly along the edges, balanced it on an open palm to test its modest heft.

There was no point in letting Henry see that he'd actually removed something from the box. Andrew opened his coat and stuffed the envelope into an interior pocket, patting it down until it did not print too badly against the fabric.

He hoped it was better concealed than the damn gun had been—the gun now stowed in the Ferrari's glove compartment. Connor must have seen it, though he'd said nothing. Well, there was a lot Connor had left unsaid.

It hadn't occurred to Andrew until he was miles from the cabin, speeding east on a two-lane highway, but Ben Connor had scammed him—and in doing so, had exhibited a professional poise that Andrew, from his expert perspective, couldn't help but admire.

A con job was verbal sleight of hand, nothing more. The mark's attention had to be diverted from logical gaps or troubling inconsistencies in the sales pitch, his mental gaze refocused on distracting irrelevancies.

Replaying his dialogue with Connor, Andrew had identified the exact moment when the crucial substitution had been made, as neatly as a magician's skilled hands would slip a marked card into a shuffled deck.

So why are you here? he'd inquired of Connor.

And the chief had said, *I could ask you the same question.*

This was the move that had put him on the defensive, made him reluctant to pursue his original line of interrogation. And Connor's eventual answer had been weak and vague. He'd said he wanted to have a word with Robert. What did that mean, if it meant anything?

Connor had adroitly circumvented any real explanation of his appearance at the cabin—an explanation that was clearly required. After all, what were the odds that Connor would arrive only minutes after Andrew himself? And why show up at all? Andrew knew his reason for going, but what was Connor's?

Two answers had occurred to him. First, Connor might suspect Robert of kidnapping Erica. But if so, wouldn't he have checked out the cabin earlier, before stopping at Great Hall?

The second possibility was the only one that made sense.

Connor had tailed Andrew to the cabin.

Which meant the police chief already was suspicious of him. Perhaps he'd sensed Andrew's evasions during the interview in the sunroom. Or perhaps he knew more, much more, than Andrew had feared.

Buttoning his coat, Andrew wondered how scared he ought to be.

Very, he decided. Very goddamned scared.

At one time in his life he would have been scared, all right. When survival had been his only imperative, when nothing had moved him except the pursuit of comfort and the exercise of control, when he had been as conscienceless as any street thug—in those days, not so very long ago, he would have feared Ben Connor, would have run, yes, fled right now and not looked back.

If Connor figured it all out, the penalty would be jail time, lots of it—years.

Andrew shrugged. He didn't care. He felt no fear.

In his mind flashed an image: runnels of soapy water texturing the rounded smoothness of his wife's breasts. Eyes shut, he smelled the shampoo in her hair, tasted her hot mouth.

"Erica," he whispered.

Robert had her. He might have killed her already. If not, he surely would end her life soon enough—unless Andrew reached him first.

The risk was extreme, but he would take it. He would face any danger to save his wife. What happened afterward was of no consequence. She had to be alive, still part of the world. Nothing else mattered.

His hands were shaking as he shut the box and locked it.

Emerging from the booth, he found Henry loitering conveniently close by. He gave back the box.

"Always a pleasure to serve you, Mr. Stafford." The man gazed at him with puppy adoration. "I do look forward to seeing your wife again before long."

So do I, Andrew thought, but all he said was, "She'll be dropping by, I'm sure. Good day, Henry."

At the front door he paused to put on sunglasses for the drive home. Through the windows the sun was westering, low and orange, a swollen smear of glare.

Henry's voice, hushed but carrying, reached him faintly. "That's Mr. Andrew Stafford," the bank manager was telling a patron with evident pride. "Of Great Hall, you know. One of our very *special* customers."

Andrew pushed open the door and walked outside into the chill of sunset.

Poor Henry, he thought with a painfully tight smile. If only you knew just what I really am.

Marge Maginnis, on fire with rage, braked her Chevy on the shoulder of Route 36 and got out fast.

Spears of red sunlight, horizontal and supernaturally bright, stabbed her eyes as she hurried past a line of parked cruisers. Sergeant Larkin's, then Hart's, then Connor's, and at the front, Vicki Danvers's green-and-white.

The line of cars reminded her of a funeral procession. Maginnis blinked away the thought.

There was a highway patrol unit too, parked facing the other cars, and hastily slant-parked near it, a sheriff's department cruiser. More deputies were on the way; monitoring radio traffic, Maginnis had heard enough to know that the sheriff's substation had dispatched two more radio cars as well as a crime scene unit and Captain Hausen to supervise.

She knew Hausen. A good man. Better, she thought angrily, than the damn fool out of New York who was running the show in Barrow.

But he might not be running it for long.

Beyond the deputy's car was an ambulance, dome lights cycling. The rear doors hung open. The interior was empty.

"Mrs. Stafford . . . !"

"Erica Stafford . . . !"

Distant shouts yodeled through the twilight forest. Maginnis recognized Larkin's voice. The other man was presumably the trooper or the deputy. They were searching the woods.

It seemed like a pointless exercise. Surely Erica Stafford wasn't anywhere in the vicinity. Or if she was, she would be in no condition to answer a voice that hailed her.

Right now Maginnis didn't give a damn about Erica Stafford anyway. Her one concern was Vicki Danvers.

Scanning the woods, she caught a flicker of movement amid the deepening shadows—two paramedics marching quickly up the gentle incline to the highway, bearing a uniformed figure on a stretcher.

Maginnis must have stepped over the guardrail and descended the hillside, but she was unaware of it. From her perspective there was only a movie jump cut, instantaneous and silent. One moment she was watching the paramedics from a distance, and the next moment she was alongside the stretcher and looking down at Danvers—her wan face, her hair lank with sweat, her fingers slack and arms limp.

From somewhere close, the coppery smell of blood.

"How bad?" Maginnis asked.

"Gunshot wound in the abdomen," one paramedic said, chuffing as he ascended the hill. "She's lost blood, is in shock. Don't know the extent of internal injuries."

"We think she has some movement in her arms," the other added. "Not sure about the legs. Bullet could've nicked her spine."

"But we don't know," the first one said in a cautionary tone.

They crested the grade and lifted the stretcher over the guardrail. Maginnis thought about Vicki Danvers's first day on the job, four months ago. It had been late November, crisply glorious, bright with the last vermilion sprays of leaves. The girl tense but eager, straining in harness, her eyes so big.

Maginnis had never married. She was too tough for intimacy. She was like a battered old boot, serviceable and unglamorous, just doing her job. But Danvers was special to her. She'd all but adopted the goddamned girl. Trained her personally instead of handing the job to a sergeant. Shared Vicki's fears and aspirations and even her joys. They had laughed together, and for Marge Maginnis, how rare was that?

Now look at Vicki Danvers. Just look at her.

"There an exit wound?" Maginnis asked, the question forced past a clog in her throat.

The first paramedic shook his head. "One hole was all we found."

The cartridge had bounced around inside her, then. Torn her up like shredded meat.

God damn.

Maginnis reached out and touched Vicki's right hand, not squeezing it, just fingering the small cold knuckles and the slender wrist.

"You'll make it, Vick," she said, knowing the girl was unconscious and couldn't hear.

Then she let go as the stretcher was loaded aboard the R.A.

Barrow P.D. had not recruited a female officer for more than a decade until Maginnis insisted on bringing Danvers in. It was a fight she'd waged with Paul Elder, who for all his admirable qualities had proved resistant to the idea, stubbornly suspicious of change. But she'd worn him down, and Officer Vicki Danvers was the result. At the time Marge hadn't understood why it had mattered quite so much to her, but later she came to see that she wanted a legacy, another woman to carry on after she was gone.

Their month of training in the field had sewn a bond between them, an unspoken spirit of camaraderie. It was them against the world. Two women of different generations forming a stronghold against the young bucks like Hart and Woodall who would never take them seriously, who made lesbian jokes about Maginnis and used stupid pick-up lines on Vicki. A stronghold, too, against the older men, the ones with seniority, or outsiders whose mysterious male status always gave them an edge—the men who would always cheat them of advancement and recognition.

Men like Connor, damn him to hell.

Maginnis turned to look at him. He'd been present the whole time, flanking the stretcher on the left side, but she had refused to concede his existence before this moment.

"Where's Woodall?" she asked. "He should've gotten here by now."

Connor shrugged. "He did."

"Then he must've walked. I don't see his cruiser."

"I sent him on an errand. Hart went along, riding shotgun."

"What errand?"

"Some busywork," Connor answered vaguely. "They were both too shook up to be any good here. They know Vicki better than anyone."

Except me, Maginnis thought. "I'm surprised they didn't crack jokes about it."

"No jokes. It hit them hard. Woodall, especially. I think he cares about her. I mean . . ."

"I know what you mean." She felt a touch of jealousy. "He's a jackass."

"Just young," Connor said.

"You've got other men searching the woods. Why?"

"Whoever did this left Danvers hurt but alive. He may have done the same with Erica Stafford. She could be lying somewhere in the foliage, wounded."

"Long shot."

Connor ignored this. "I'm rounding up as many officers as we can find. Overtime for everybody, and the hell with the budget. We're going to comb every acre. Got some more deputies coming too. We'll have to coordinate with the sheriff's people under Captain Hausen." The woods lay in an unincorporated part of the county, and the sheriff had jurisdiction.

"It'll be dark soon," Maginnis said.

"They can use flashlights."

"It doesn't make sense. The Mercedes is here, right?" In response, Connor grunted an affirmative. "So how did the killer take off? On foot?"

"There was a second vehicle. It left tire tracks, but I don't know if they're clear enough to be worth anything."

"Second vehicle." Maginnis was trying to put it together. "So he kidnaps Stafford, transfers her to another car . . ."

"Or there might be two perps, one driving the Mercedes, the other behind the wheel of the second car. Or Erica Stafford might have come here on her own."

"Why the hell would she do that?"

"I'm not sure. Nothing's in focus right now. Let's just take it one step at a time."

The rear doors of the ambulance banged shut. Maginnis couldn't hold it back any longer.

"What in Christ's name were you thinking, Ben? You send her in without backup—after what happened to the Wilcott girl?"

The chief met her gaze frankly. She gave him credit for nerve, anyway. That was something.

"It was a judgment call," Connor said. "If she'd waited for backup—"

"Then she wouldn't be dying now."

"We don't know she's dying."

Maginnis looked away, the first to break eye contact, but only because she didn't want Connor to catch her sudden shimmer of tears.

"You fucked this up . . . Chief."

Connor didn't answer for a moment, and she glanced back at him and saw turmoil in his face. But his voice was steady when he said, "Yeah."

He'd admitted it. She wished she had witnesses. She meant to use this against him. She would force him out of the department.

The small sneaking thought in some back alley of her mind was that she was next in line to take over, and the town council couldn't deny her the promotion twice.

With a ululant blare the ambulance pulled away, the flashbar bright against the ashes of sunset.

"I'm going to the hospital," Maginnis said, not requesting permission, simply stating a fact. She started to turn away, and Connor stopped her.

"I can't let you do that. You're needed here."

"It's Vicki who needs me."

"She'll be in surgery for hours. You can't help her now. And I need someone from Barrow P.D. to take charge of our guys."

"How about you?" Maginnis bared a smile. "You're *so* good at taking charge."

"I have to be someplace."

"Got a dinner date?"

Connor didn't answer for a moment, and she knew that he was struggling for calm. It was a struggle he won. When he spoke again, his face was expressionless, his voice a flat line.

"I'm still your commanding officer, Lieutenant," Connor said. "Even if you don't want me to be. You're staying here. That's an order. Understood?"

He moved toward his car without waiting for her reply.

She couldn't let him have the last word. Every living part of her rebelled against it.

"Why did you leave New York?" she called out.

Connor stopped, then pivoted to face her. "What?"

"You put in eighteen years at NYPD. Nobody walks away from a full pension with only two years to go."

She saw him pull in a slow breath and release it. Limned in dusky light, shoulders hunched against the chill, he looked smaller than before.

"Maybe I got tired of the city," Connor said. "Wanted to breathe clean air."

"That's not enough of a reason."

"No, it's not." He expelled another breath. "But it's all you're going to get."

He walked away, and Maginnis stared after him, and far in the distance the ambulance cast its lonely, desperate wail.

The last time Erica ever saw Mr. Furnell, he drove her to Newark Airport to catch a Pan Am flight to Athens. She was eighteen, a graduate of the New Hampshire boarding school, old enough to own some kind of freedom, but not completely free; under the terms of the trust agreement, she would not obtain personal disposition over her half of the Garrison inheritance until she was twenty-one.

So with Mr. Furnell's assent she was going to travel in Europe on a Eurailpass. Greece had been her chosen starting point, though Mr. Furnell had recommended West Germany. *Might teach you a little discipline,* he'd said in a grim voice.

Still, he had permitted her to go. He seemed glad to be rid of her. No doubt he'd been afraid she would ask to live with him, like a real daughter.

At the flight gate they waited in awkward silence. The garbled voice on the PA system and the bustle of travelers laden with suitcases reminded Erica of Penn Station and the bad night she'd spent there as a much younger girl. How scared she'd been, and how alone. But she'd gotten through it, because she had felt compelled to reach Robert, reach him and rescue him, before it was too late.

And she'd failed. Her best efforts had been defeated by Mr. Furnell and the unholy ranks of like-minded adults who served under his stern command. Robert had not been rescued. He had remained at the Maryland school, and was still there, his prison sentence not to expire for another three years. And here she was, abandoning him on a jaunt to Europe.

The thought brushed her like a cold finger, raising a chill of guilt. But guilt was irrelevant. There was nothing she could do for Robert anymore. His time at school had changed him. On holidays he rarely spoke to her, would not open up, just sat alone. He was polite, capable of rudimentary conversation, but there was no spark in him, no personality, no life.

When she'd told him she was going to Europe, he'd merely shrugged. And though he could have accompanied her to the airport, he'd declined.

So it was just the two of them at the gate, herself and Mr. Furnell, with no hugs or loving sentiments to exchange even when the other first-class passengers began to board.

"Well," Erica said, gathering her two suitcases.

Mr. Furnell nodded. "Well."

She thought she should say something, but what? Bags in hand, she just stood there, expecting some gesture of affection, something that would redeem the cold futility of the last six years.

Mr. Furnell checked his watch. It was a Rolex, silver, and it flashed in the ambient light.

She knew he was thinking that if he left now, he could beat the turnpike's rush-hour traffic. And she knew this was all he was thinking.

"Goodbye," Erica said. "Don't wait for me to take off."

"I wasn't planning to."

"I know."

As she headed down the boarding ramp, she turned and

glanced back, feeling a need for a last look, though she couldn't say why. But he was already gone.

The first months of her exile were the hardest, the months when she traveled aimlessly along the Greek coastline, seeking a purpose in her life. And that one night, that terrible, mystical night when she had been sure she couldn't go on . . . when, stripping off her clothes, she had faced the smooth black waters of the Aegean and prepared for the long swim into oblivion . . .

Persephone had saved her on that night. The bronze Persephone on the wharf.

Redeemed, renewed, she ended her wandering and enrolled at the University of Rome, taking classes in art history and living in a one-room fourth-floor walk-up with no hot water. She was still there at the age of twenty-one when she was informed by telegram that Mr. Furnell had disappeared and was presumed dead. In his neat country-burgher house outside Barrow, a suicide note had been found, scrawled in a shaky hand, asking forgiveness for what he'd done.

What he'd done. Walking aimlessly past Rome's stone palazzos in the twilight, at the hour when a historian named Gibbon had once heard barefoot friars singing vespers and had conceived of writing the epic of an empire's fall, Erica tried to imagine what Mr. Furnell—that inflexibly upright, stiffly authoritarian man— could possibly have done that would have discredited him in his own sight.

A police investigation quickly turned up the answer. Mr. Furnell's stern moral impulses, it seemed, had extended mainly to other people, somehow bypassing himself. For years he had made a practice of embezzling from the various trust funds he administered. The sums were modest enough not to be noticed, but sufficient for the purchase of small, costly baubles, like that Rolex watch of his. He had not been above embezzling from the funds of his two young charges either, though in the vast ocean of money they each stood to inherit, the amounts their guardian had siphoned off would scarcely fill a teaspoon.

He'd been a cheat, their stern Mr. Furnell with his stoic exhortations to duty, his Spartan love of discipline. Erica had marveled at it, sometimes angry, sometimes merely baffled, as she watched the pigeons flock in a windblown piazza or climbed a hill for a view of the city's rooftops.

She had not attended the funeral. Neither, she was told, had Robert.

A year later she returned to Barrow. She had loved Rome well, and the Greek coast still more, but something had called her to the place of her childhood. She supposed it was Robert who had drawn her back. She'd heard of him living alone in a cabin, lost in solitude, and she had thought of helping him. But even after it was clear that he shunned her help, she had stayed, for no reason she could name.

Perhaps it was only a wordless sense that the answer to her life's mystery would not be found under Mediterranean skies. During her four-year exile she had studied history, art, religion, looking for patterns that might suggest a larger whole. She'd found them—the patterns of culture and thought—but the pattern of her own life remained obscure to her, a tapestry in darkness. And the sense of incompleteness lingered, the tantalizing awareness of a higher purpose, a deeper significance. Was this only an adolescent preoccupation, as she sometimes thought, or was it instead the great problem of modernity—to find meaning in a world where faith came hard and absolutes were easily toppled?

Whatever it was, it had the feel of a holy mission and a quest, and she could not let it go.

Once, after her return, she visited Mr. Furnell's grave—an empty grave; his body had never been found. She thought of him, of how he had faced the same smooth darkness she'd seen from the wharf. But in his hour of crisis there had been no Persephone to stay his hand. Perhaps if he'd asked for help, called out in the night . . .

Still, she couldn't criticize him for keeping silent. She had always done the same, hadn't she? Bottling her emotions tight, afraid to loosen the stopper and release a torrent that would sweep her away.

You can't love anyone. Robert's voice came back to her. *You're like the figures you display in your shop. A beautiful thing, shiny in sunlight, but at the core—poured metal, cold stone . . .*

No, Robert, it's not true. Or if it is, then it's your fault as much as mine. For pushing me away. For not letting me help you. Robert? I still want to help. Robert . . . ?

She was crying to him, crying across a void, and distantly she heard an answer.

"Mrs. Stafford . . ."

Not Robert's voice. Another's.

"Erica Stafford . . ."

Two voices, faint and faraway, like voices in a dream. But this was no dream. This was real.

Someone was looking for her.

A shock of hope jolted her awake. Head lifted, ears straining, Erica heard the cries again.

"Mrs. Stafford . . . !"

"Erica Stafford . . . !"

A pair of male voices reverberating through the caves.

The police. Must be.

"Down here," she answered, but her throat was raw with smoke, her voice raspy and low, and she knew they hadn't heard.

She blinked away the last confused shreds of whatever dream her sleeping mind had woven, then looked slowly around the limestone throne room. The high ceiling was painted in broad brush strokes of red and orange, the flickering glow of the kerosene lamp. Wisps of smoky incense curled prettily in the air.

Most of the smoke was gone. The smoldering leaves had finally burned out. The draft in the cave system was dissipating the fumes.

She could breathe again, breathe without a rush of vertigo or a new onset of lethargy and hallucination. She could think.

"Mrs. Stafford!"

"Erica Stafford!"

Were they in the caves? If so, they could follow the arrows she'd marked in lipstick, unless Robert had erased the signs.

No, not so near. They were above ground, searching the woods, close to the sinkhole but surely not seeing it. Hidden by rocks, the hole was almost impossible to find.

"Mrs. Stafford!"

The sinkhole and the maze of passages functioned as a vast echo chamber, passing shouts from one cavern and corridor to the next. She wasn't sure if it would work in reverse, if the peculiar acoustics of the labyrinth would carry her own voice to the outside world, but she had to try.

Gathering her strength, she shouted, *"Down here!"*

The cry raised a bright flurry of echoes, shrill as bat screeches, fading as they traveled through the nautilus chambers of the maze.

She waited for an answer.

"Mrs. Stafford!"

Had they heard? Were they acknowledging?

"Erica Stafford!"

No. Just continuing their search. And now their cries were dimming as the two men moved away.

Eyes shut, Erica swallowed a deep draft of breath, and then with all her strength she released a final cry.

"I'm down here, down here, help me, somebody help!"

The words flew away and broke apart and rushed back at her, slashing her ears like shards.

She was spent. Panting, she lay on the table, her throat scraped and burning, as the room spun and the kerosene lamp flared and dimmed, flared and dimmed.

They must have heard her that time. Must have.

The last echoes of her shout popped like soap bubbles and were gone. In the stillness wafted the pale ghost of a voice.

"Mrs. Stafford . . ."

Fading.

"Erica . . ."

Gone.

They had not heard.

Perhaps if she'd cried out sooner, when they were close to the sinkhole. If she hadn't been lost in dreams, memories. Perhaps.

Too late now.

She was alone again, and whoever had passed the sinkhole was unlikely to backtrack and provide her with a second chance.

No one would save her.

If she was to survive, if her long quest in darkness was ever to bring her to the light, then she would have to save herself.

In his car, running east, chasing the first stars on the far horizon, Ben Connor called the station house.

The desk sergeant was Dave McArthur, who'd been assigned the post-midnight watch but had been brought in early, along with every other sworn officer available.

McArthur's voice sizzled over the cheap cell phone. "Place is a damn madhouse, Chief."

"Can't be helped. How many men have we got?"

"Total of fifteen. Jeff Carvey's on vacation, and I can't reach Maddox or Gertz."

"Send most of them to the crime scene. We're running search patrols, and there's a lot of ground to cover."

"They're being briefed now. Lieutenant Jansen's handling it."

"How about Lieutenant Adamson? He there?"

"Just walked in."

"Transfer me to him, will you?"

The call was patched through to Adamson's desk. Chet Adamson was a fifteen-year Barrow P.D. veteran, beefy as a linebacker, but with the soft-spoken manner of a psychologist.

"Chet, I need you to go over to Great Hall and inform Andrew Stafford that we've found his wife's car." If anyone could deliver the news tactfully, it was Adamson.

"Okay, Chief." Adamson sounded dubious. "Thing is, he probably already knows."

"How could he? Has he been to the station?"

"No, but it's all over the radio. I was listening in my car when I drove here."

"The radio? My orders were to be discreet on the police bands."

"The AM radio, Chief. That's what I'm talking about. The local station broke the story about fifteen minutes ago."

"Shit." Connor felt sick at the thought of Andrew hearing some garbled version of the news from a radio DJ or from panicky friends calling to confirm the story or, worse still, from some goddamned reporter. "Well, get over there fast. And put McArthur on the line again, will you?"

The sergeant came back, his voice rising above a cacophony of ringing telephones. "Yeah, Chief?"

"Has anybody reached Danvers's folks yet?"

"Not so far. Got Harve Miller trying to find them. He tried

their home number in Williamsport—no answer. Now he's going through the Williamsport police."

"Tell him to keep at it. I don't want them hearing Vicki's name on some fucking talk-radio show." He rarely swore, but things were flying out of control. "And have Jansen beat the drums about news leaks. Our official motto is *No comment,* and that goes for everybody in or out of uniform."

"Got you, Chief. Will do."

Connor switched off, breathing hard. It was all too much—Erica missing and maybe dead, Danvers in surgery because of *his* stupid irresponsibility and recklessness, the AM radio spreading some combustible mix of facts and lies.

He needed help. Needed a steadying hand. And he knew who to call.

He punched in seven digits from memory. After a half dozen rings a gravelly voice answered, "Elder residence."

Connor pressed the cell phone closer to his ear. "Paul, it's Ben."

"Hey, Chief. Sounds like things are heating up."

"You heard?"

"I was relaxing to one of Debbie Reynolds's nicer songs when the DJ broke in with the news. Now he's taking phone calls from people who know absolutely nothing and feel the urge to share their ignorance."

"I need you, Paul. Can you get away for a while?"

"Don't see why not. The nurse and I just put Lily to bed. I was about to cook up some supper, but it can wait."

"You feel okay about leaving Lily?"

Elder sighed. "Chief, half the time she doesn't even know I'm here."

Lily Elder had Alzheimer's. It had come on fast and would kill her soon. Her husband had retired to spend more time with her, but his plans had been frustrated by the illness's rapid advance.

"So what do you need me for?" Elder added, and Connor heard both excitement and wariness in the older man's voice.

"Assistance in an interrogation."

There was a buzz of static on the line, and then Elder said slowly, "Interrogation."

"And maybe something more." Connor was thinking fast, outlining a plan. "Can you stay out late if you have to?"

"Nobody'll stop me. I'm a big boy. Even got a badge like yours, though mine's just a tin souvenir now."

The bantering tone barely masked an anxious appeal. Elder was desperate to escape the house.

Connor had been there. The Elders owned a modest cottage, tidy and trim, the air scented with potpourri to disguise medicinal smells. The sofa and easy chairs were draped with antimacassars, and on the mantel was a portrait of a vivacious bright-eyed girl with a scintillant smile, Lily in youth's bloom. Connor had sat with Paul and sipped beer straight from the can, while somewhere a TV rattled on. Several times the live-in nurse, washing Lily's hair in the guest bathroom on the ground floor, had interrupted their conversation to ask Paul for help. Lily didn't know the nurse, didn't want a stranger touching her hair.

Connor's mouth tightened at the memory. Yes, Paul Elder wouldn't mind a night away from home.

"You might want to bring a thermos of hot coffee," Connor said. "And a blanket, and something to eat."

"A stakeout." Elder's excitement was unmistakable now. "That what you've got in mind for me, Chief?"

"Possibly." Connor didn't want to reveal too much on a cellular transmission. "You up for it?"

"Hell, yes. Though I think a younger man might be a better choice."

"I can't spare anybody in uniform right now. Can you meet me in Barrow Woods in twenty minutes?"

The distance wasn't far. Elder's home was on the outskirts of town.

"If I break every speed limit and run every stoplight, sure. What part of the woods exactly?"

"The cabin," Connor said.

For a moment Elder didn't answer. There was no static, no sound at all.

"*His* cabin?" Elder asked finally.

"Yeah. I've got two men there now. They're detaining him for questioning."

"You think it's him?"

"I don't know. I was told he had an alibi, but I haven't confirmed it."

"Pray it's not him, Chief. Pray this all works out. Those children have suffered enough."

Elder clicked off, and Connor tromped hard on the gas pedal, charging into the newfallen dark.

11

Robert sat outside the cabin with the two cops, whose nametags read HART and WOODALL. Both names were redolent of the forest, binding the men in an oblique way to Artemis the huntress and to her emissary or her embodiment, Officer Danvers.

He nodded to himself, and one of the men, Hart, the slower and more pugnacious of the pair, said, "What?"

Robert just looked at him.

"What were you nodding about?" Hart pressed, sounding foolish, combative for no good reason.

"I was thinking," Robert said, "that it's a nice evening."

Hart stared around him at the twilight. The smoking remains of the sunset were just vanishing behind the farthest line of trees.

"Not so nice for you," Hart said.

Woodall told him to back off.

Hart snorted an obscenity, but he obeyed, turning away.

There was no more conversation for a few minutes. Robert watched the stars appear.

He knew what troubled the two men, of course. On one level—the superficial human level—Officer Danvers was their colleague, and they mourned for her. Surely they had been told of her death in the woods. Perhaps they had even seen the body.

And now they had been sent here to keep watch on Robert Garrison, the fool on the hill, and they had to suspect—even with such dim brains as theirs—that he was implicated in Danvers's murder. Yet they didn't know, couldn't ask, had been dispatched only to detain him and watch him until someone of higher rank arrived, and so anger and hate and frustration were all knotted up inside them. Hart seethed. Woodall, more stoic, merely suppressed it all and waited.

That was the obvious part. Then came the deeper truth. These two with their totemic names, one designating the roebuck and the other its thicket, were allied with Officer Danvers in some profound way that their human selves could never understand. *Moira* had bound them together, all three, and now one piece— the central piece—was lost, the pattern broken up. Naturally their psyches were ill at ease.

Robert almost nodded again, but prevented himself. He drummed his fingers on his thigh and lifted his head slowly to the dawning stars.

The universe, he knew, was not fundamentally matter or energy, but pure vibration. He was very sure of this. Consciousness was one frequency of the vibrating field, physical reality another. Two currents, out of phase, but intersecting at infinite points. And where they intersected was where myth and fate were born.

He had not worked it all out. There was much reading, much thinking, still undone. But he had made inroads. He had seen things. He knew so much, so very much more than anyone around him, so much more than Hart or Woodall or even Danvers could ever know. They were mere emanations of the immaterial essence of things, toys of fate, as was poor Erica.

"As are we all," Robert murmured, and this time he did nod.

Then he caught both Hart and Woodall studying him attentively, and he knew he must have spoken part of his thoughts aloud. He hoped he hadn't said too much.

They could trip him up that way, if he got careless and voiced what must remain unstated. It was his only real danger. Another lie detector test didn't scare him; he'd passed the first one easily, even when the operator had asked him the key series of questions.

Did you kill Sherry Wilcott?
No, he'd said.
Did you kidnap her?
No.
Did you strip her?

No.

Did you cut her throat?

No.

Even without being told, he'd known that the polygraph's needle had barely trembled at each lie.

The machine was not set to read his mind, only to detect galvanic responses and changes in heart rate, reactions triggered by guilt and fear. He had felt no guilt, no fear. He had felt nothing but the humming vibration at the secret heart of the universe, and so he had been safe.

This time he doubted they would even bother with a polygraph. They might ask to search his cabin again. That was all right. He had anticipated such an eventuality, and had taken all necessary precautions.

After finding Andrew Stafford's business card, he'd changed into fresh clothes, bundling his blood-spattered outfit into a sack. He put Danvers's gun and ammunition in the sack too, and her crucifix-totem, and Erica's scarf, and the card as well. Then he hid the sack under a loose floorboard beneath his bed.

Later he would bury the stuff. Later, when he was sure nobody was looking.

He'd forgotten entirely about the groceries until he gave the truck a once-over, checking for blood, and saw the array of spilled and leaking paper bags.

The police would wonder about that. It wasn't normal to buy two hundred dollars' worth of foodstuffs and leave them to thaw and spoil. Working fast, he unloaded the truck, stocking his freezer and fridge, then piling canned and freeze-dried goods and other household items against a wall.

He was just finishing when he heard an engine. He looked out the window and saw a Barrow squad car pulling up the road.

Robert had not invited Officers Woodall and Hart inside. This was, he supposed, a breach of hospitality. But they were the enemy, after all.

"Excuse me?" Woodall asked now.

Robert glanced at him and blinked.

"You said something about enemies."

He had done it again. Must control his tongue. Living alone, he'd grown accustomed to holding dialogues with air and water and sky.

"I didn't say anything," Robert told him.

The roebuck Hart spat on the ground. "You're a damn psycho. You know that, pal?"

"Todd," Woodall cautioned, but Hart waved him off.

"I don't give a crap how much money you got," Hart said. "You're a friggin' nut."

Robert smiled. "An acorn, maybe."

"Acorn. What are you talking about?"

"An acorn that fell from the tree. It was a long fall."

"This some kind of riddle?"

Robert shrugged.

He wanted to tell them that everything was a riddle, and nothing was. He wanted to tell them that the acorn was the fruit of the oak, and the oak was the sacred tree of many religions, kingly in its stature and massiveness and age, and that he was the son of a king, grandson of a king, product of a line of kings, so the oak was his tree, his and Erica's, and for this reason fate had made him notch their initials in the skin of an oak, to claim their mutual birthright, but then he had fallen, fallen, and only now had he seen the way to redemption, the way of sacrifice.

They would not understand a word of it. Imbeciles. He said nothing.

"This guy is really weirding me out," the roebuck said to Woodall softly, but not so softly Robert couldn't hear.

Woodall sighed. "Quiet, Todd."

The sun was gone now, even its memory lost, the sky deep blue shading to black, stars in their abundance waking to the night.

Robert shut his eyes and felt the tidal tug of fate, the ebb and flow of currents no science could detect, and he heard the hum of their energy, and he was at peace.

Out of sight of the cabin, at the same bend in the dirt road where Andrew Stafford's Ferrari had been parked earlier, Connor sat in his motionless squad car and waited for Paul Elder to arrive.

A dark masochistic curiosity had prompted him to turn on the car's AM radio and tune it to the local station.

The D.J. had stopped playing music in favor of taking phone calls, just as Elder had said. With few facts available, speculation ran uncurbed.

"I got a friend at the medical center who says two police officers were shot, and they were both DOA . . ."

"That last caller got it wrong. I know somebody who saw the ambulance come in, and they say it was a woman who got shot, just one woman, not a cop . . ."

"About the woman who was shot? It was Erica Stafford. Yeah, I'm telling you, I picked up a police call on my scanner and that's what they said. At least I think it was a police call . . ."

Connor was glad to hear the rumors. It meant that Vicki Danvers's identity so far had not been leaked. There was still a chance for Miller to reach her parents in Williamsport and break the news more gently.

The other comments over the airwaves were less welcome. When a family dominated a town as thoroughly as the Garrisons had held sway in Barrow, there would be resentment, suspicion, even fear. He heard all three emotions over the Chevy's speakers.

"They've caused nothing but trouble, and now it's their turn to get some trouble back . . ."

"That crazy brother of hers killed the Wilcott girl, everybody knows it, and now he probably went and killed Erica too, and I'm not shedding no tears for either one . . ."

"It all started with Duncan, back in seventy-three, and then Lenore a year later. Nothing's been right since, in Great Hall or in this town. They should tear down that house . . ."

"Should arrest Robert and fry him, fry him like an egg . . ."

"I think they were in it together, is what I think. Robert Garrison killed the girl, and Erica Stafford was covering for him. Blood's thick in that clan, always has been, and what do they care if a farmer's daughter gets killed . . . ?"

"She's always lording it over the rest of us, tooling around in that car that cost more than my Eddie makes in a year—don't gripe, Eddie, it's true . . ."

"They're both crazy, her and the hermit, and I say to hell with 'em both . . ."

Connor snapped the radio off.

Christ.

A town was like a rock, he supposed. Turn it over, and just look at what wriggled and crawled underneath.

He could understand the suspicion of Robert. But to suspect Erica . . . to broadcast such hatred and resentment . . .

He felt it again: the old corrosive anger that had been with him for most of the past two years. The anger that squeezed his hands into fists and made him want to lash out, draw blood.

But there was no one to fight. At least in New York he'd known who his enemies were. He could picture their faces. He could take action.

Here he was a stranger. After three months, still a man alone. He'd had Erica to comfort him, Erica to love and trust . . . and nobody else.

Except old Paul Elder, of course. He remembered this, smiled a little, and then headlights flared behind him in the dark.

Connor stuck an arm out the window and flagged the driver. Elder pulled his Buick alongside the squad car and rolled down the passenger window. "What's the plan, Chief?"

Chief. Elder always called him that.

"Park behind me," Connor said crisply, feeling better somehow. "You'll ride in my car."

The Buick reversed and swung into position at the rear of the Chevy, and a moment later the headlights went dark and the motor was stilled. Elder got out, closing the door quietly. Connor saw him in the rearview mirror, tall and patrician, clad in dark blue trousers and a matching windbreaker.

He must have changed clothes before leaving home. The outfit camouflaged him in the night. It was the first time Connor had seen him without a necktie. The thought raised another smile, warmer than the last.

Then the Chevy listed on its shocks as Elder climbed into the passenger seat.

"You don't want him seeing my jalopy," Elder said, "in case I've got to tail him."

"Right."

Elder nodded.

"You carrying a piece under that jacket?" Connor asked.

"Should I be?"

"Wouldn't hurt."

"Good thing I am, then."

It was Connor's turn to nod. He keyed the Chevy's ignition to run the heater, but didn't shift out of park. Some things needed explaining first.

"A lot's happened, Paul." Connor told him about Andrew Stafford's surreptitious visit to the cabin, then the discovery of the Mercedes in the woods, and the upshot: Vicki Danvers in surgery at the county medical center.

Elder listened, his stern face in profile, light from the dashboard limning a sharp cheekbone. He said nothing, showed no reaction, except when Connor got to the part about Danvers. Then he pulled his lower lip sharply inward, and a vein in his temple pulsed. That was all.

"I've got Maginnis working with Captain Hausen of the sheriff's department," Connor concluded. "They're supervising a search party for Erica Stafford near the fire road. Nothing's turned up yet. Woodall and Hart are holding Robert here."

"But you don't mean to take him in," Elder said. It was not a question. If Connor intended to hold Robert, even overnight, there would be no need for a stakeout or a possible tail.

"If he slips up, incriminates himself, or if we find anything, then I'll take him. If not, then I want him running loose, at least for the next few hours. He may lead us to Erica."

"So what's my role?"

"First, I want you there for the interrogation. I've thought about how to handle it. Not the standard good-cop, bad-cop routine. That's too obvious, and Robert's smart enough to see through it."

As an alternative, he'd worked out a variation on the theme. Elder nodded as the idea was explained.

"If he has any feelings for his sister," Connor concluded, "this might be the one way to bring them out. And if he's rattled, he may say too much."

"Maybe." Elder chewed on the idea. "But Robert Garrison's

a tight-lipped son of a bitch. Not sure anybody can reach too deep inside him."

Connor put the car in drive and eased it forward, advancing slowly over the deep ruts in the road.

After a moment Elder spoke again. "You said there were tire tracks. Could they be from a truck? His truck?"

"It was just a lot of mashed-down weeds. I couldn't see any tread marks. The sheriff's forensics guys might be able to gauge the width of the chassis, something like that."

Elder looked away. "I get the impression you're fairly certain Robert's your man."

"The thought occurred to me. But he *may* have an airtight alibi. And anyway, I can't quite see how it adds up. If Erica was abducted from the shop, then she was taken in her own car. In which case, she was transferred to another car—or truck—in the woods."

"Which could suggest two guilty parties," Elder said.

"And Robert's a loner, as far as anyone knows."

"Has been for years. Of course, maybe she wasn't abducted."

"I've been thinking that, too." The cabin swung into view, dim lamplight and a flicker of fireglow spilling from the single window. "She could've left the shop on her own. Could've gone to the cabin; maybe she's the one who broke in, not Andrew . . ."

Elder frowned. "Why would she do that?"

"I don't know," Connor said, but the words came out clumsily, and he felt Elder's gaze on him as the Chevy climbed the low hill.

In the windshield, Robert Garrison's cabin grew larger against the perfect darkness of the sky. Two vehicles were parked at the summit, Woodall's cruiser and Robert's pickup truck. Nearby stood two stiff masculine figures, crisp in their uniforms.

Robert himself was hard to see, a shadow among shadows, but Connor knew he was there.

"You know something you're not saying, Chief?" Elder asked.

Connor didn't answer for a moment. If he gave a truthful reply, then he would have to admit everything, and he wasn't sure he was ready for that.

But, hell, he had to tell someone, and Paul Elder—he was surprised to hear himself think it—Paul Elder was his best friend in Barrow, other than Erica herself.

"She may have suspected Robert of the Sherry Wilcott murder," Connor said.

They crested the rise. Connor could see Robert now. He sat cross-legged on the bare ground, wearing trousers and a long-sleeve shirt but no coat. With the sun gone, the mercury must have dropped to the freezing mark, and the stiff wind made it colder. Robert didn't seem to notice or care.

"Everyone suspected him," Elder said. "Why should she be any different?"

"I picked up vibes . . . nothing I could pinpoint. But it seemed as if she knew more than she was saying."

"Sounds as if you two were talking pretty often."

"Often enough."

Connor parked behind the pickup. His headlights burned briefly on the rear bumper, and he saw that it was dirt-spattered and flecked with chaff. The vehicle that left the crime scene had traveled off-road, and would have picked up mud and detritus. But so would any vehicle driving the dirt road to the cabin.

"Did she know we put her brother on a polygraph?" Elder asked.

"No."

"Did she ever come right out and voice her suspicions?"

Connor shook his head. "That's not her way. She's like Robert, you know—keeps things inside. Locked tight. She doesn't ask for help. I don't think she knows how."

The quaver in his voice gave him away, and Elder turned to him. "You seem awfully well acquainted with the lady," he remarked carefully.

"I am."

"So I see," Elder said, the words shaded with many meanings.

Connor switched off the headlights and engine. The car rocked briefly, rattled by a shiver of release, and then was still.

He and Elder were in shadows together, and somehow the dark made it easier to speak.

"Nobody knows about it," Connor said simply.

Elder grunted. "How long has this been going on?"

"Since late January."

"You took your oath on January seventh. Fast work."

"Come on, Paul."

"Just saying. I did notice you two talking up a storm at that party at Great Hall."

"I started visiting her shop after that. One thing led to . . . well, you know how it goes."

"Surprised a beautiful young creature like her would take up with a broken-down New York cop."

Connor smiled. "Same thought occurred to me." The smile faded. "She was lonely, I guess. Her husband—well, their marriage is in trouble."

"Sounds like."

"No, I mean it was already in trouble. I'm not sure why. She needed someone. I did too. I haven't—since Karen died, I—"

"I hear you, Chief. So how serious is it?"

"For me? Very." Connor heard a threat of raw emotion in his voice and worked hard to squelch it. "For her, too, I think."

"But you don't know?"

"I told you, she keeps things inside. She hides what really matters. Hides it from me—from everybody—maybe even from herself."

Connor saw Woodall and Hart looking his way, awaiting his next move. Robert stared dreamily at the high ceiling of the sky.

"And now she's missing," Elder said, his voice very quiet, very gentle, the voice of a man who understood about suffering and fear of loss. "Like the Wilcott girl."

"Yeah. And after what happened in New York . . . shit . . ." He tried a smile, but it felt crooked on his face. "I don't exactly bring good luck to women, do I?"

"It wasn't your fault. New York, I mean."

But Connor knew his wife would be alive if he'd reacted faster, thought more clearly, or if he'd never stirred up the whole hornets' nest of troubles to begin with.

"Sometimes, at night," he said, "I hear Karen calling to me. Calling my name. I . . . I wonder if I'll hear Erica too." He shook this thought away, moving his shoulders in a shuddering surge. "Let's go. Let's do this. Now."

He got out of the car and strode quickly toward the cabin, and Paul Elder followed, not saying a word.

"So that's all we know right now," the big man named Adamson was saying in his gentle voice.

Andrew sat on the armrest of an overstuffed chair in the living room at Great Hall, under an array of chandeliers and high rafters. He nodded slowly.

"They reported the Mercedes being found," Andrew heard himself say. "On the radio. But there was a lot more . . ."

"A lot of crap." Adamson spread his hands. "They're in the entertainment business, these guys."

"Entertainment." So that was what this was for most people. A show. A spectacle.

"I've got to get going." Adamson rose from the sofa, but Andrew remained seated. "Anything else happens, you'll be informed at once."

"Was there any blood?" Andrew asked abruptly.

"What?"

"In the car? Or near it? Blood?"

"No blood. No sign of a struggle."

Andrew nodded. He had nothing more to ask.

When Adamson was gone, Andrew got up slowly. He'd known Robert had snatched Erica—it was the only explanation that made sense—but a small part of him had cleaved to the secret hope that she really had gone for one of her long, aimless drives, and that he would hear her footsteps on the front stairs at any moment.

A baseless dream. She was gone—perhaps a captive, perhaps dead.

He left the living room and entered the kitchen, where Marie was preparing some sort of dinner in a mist of aromatic steam. Normally the countertop TV would be babbling, tuned to one of her infotainment programs—*Entertainment Tonight* or some such trash. Tonight it was the radio that chattered with the gossipy malice of telephone callers and the DJ's insouciant cleverness.

"Turn that damn thing off," he snapped.

The telephone rang for what must have been the twentieth

time in the past half hour. He ignored it, as did Marie. He'd instructed her to let the answering machine handle all calls, and to pick up the phone only if the police were on the line. He couldn't stand fielding any more inquiries from Erica's friends or, worse, from mere acquaintances who wanted an inside scoop.

Anyway, he had a far more important call to take. One he expected soon.

"I'll be in the guesthouse," he said crisply. "Don't disturb me unless it's an emergency."

"Yes, sir. Will you want supper?"

"I'm not hungry. Thanks."

He hurried across the cold windswept yard, past the swimming pool, covered by a tarpaulin in winter, and the leaf-strewn tennis court.

Night had dropped the temperature. His cheeks burned with cold; he cupped his bare hands and breathed into them to warm his fingers and his face. By the time he reached the guesthouse, he was wishing he'd worn his coat even for this short walk.

The guesthouse was Andrew's retreat, a small cottage, originally the servants' quarters, which he had converted into a den and office. It was equipped with a private phone line not listed on his business card. Only a few of his former associates in Philly had the number, and they never called except when they had a hot tip, something he could get in on with a minimum of personal involvement and exposure.

There was one other person who had the number: Robert Garrison. Andrew had given it to him months ago, and had provided it again today, in case the crazy son of a bitch had lost it somehow.

In their previous business dealings, Robert had never called him before nightfall. Andrew expected the pattern to continue. Now, with the raw blister of sunset finally patched by darkness, the phone could ring at any time.

He checked his watch. Six-thirty.

His gaze panned the office. Distantly it occurred to him that this small cottage—two rooms and a bath, merely an adjunct to Great Hall, neglected for years, rarely used even today—this wasted space was larger than Robert Garrison's entire cabin, and infinitely more comfortable.

Well, Robert could have had all this and more. He was a millionaire, after all. Upon reaching maturity he'd inherited half of Lenore Garrison's fortune. Erica, of course, had received the other half.

Eleven million apiece. Erica, the elder child, had gotten the house as well. According to an appraisal Andrew had surreptitiously obtained, Great Hall was worth at least two million dollars now.

Eleven million dollars was not a fantastic sum. In New York, in his salad days, when he was running real estate scams, Andrew routinely ran into men and women whose assets far exceeded that amount. Even quite ordinary people seemed to amass considerable fortunes in the most prosaic ways. There were millionaire carpenters and plumbers. In Philly he'd known a fellow who parlayed a single hot dog stand into a vending empire, and who was worth, conservatively, fifty million dollars.

Americans liked to complain about money, but to Andrew's ears their gripes were only the whining of spoiled children. Vast numbers of people in this country were swimming in luxury and comfort, spending what they had and charging what they didn't.

He lodged no objection to this frenzy of materialism. He was part of it, in fact. His life had been a desperate, harried quest for money, always more money, and somehow there was never enough.

He'd thought his quest was over when he married Erica, heiress to a fortune. But then Erica had learned the truth about his past and had retreated from him. She had not yet uttered the word divorce. But it was only a matter of time.

And though he loved his wife and couldn't bear to lose her, there was a part of him that could step back coolly and assess the situation with a banker's eye.

Purely from a financial standpoint, divorce would be catastrophic. It would mean an end to the fine living he'd grown to love. Great Hall, his circle of rich tennis-playing friends, his newfound respectability—all would disappear like smoke, and he would be left to hustle a living in the art racket or maybe in real estate swindles again.

Oh, yes, technically he would be entitled to a settlement. But Erica knew about his past. She would expose him. There was steel in her, behind the facade of fragility. Angry, exploited, she would take her cold revenge. She would allow him nothing. He knew it. Nothing at all.

A fever of urgency had heated his blood. If his marriage had to end, then he must salvage what he could. He'd needed money, money of his own that Erica couldn't touch, a cushion for his imminent fall. Then by pure serendipity he'd glimpsed the solution to his problem, a way to meet his financial needs for the rest of his life.

Andrew Stafford played to win. The thought had buoyed him during these difficult months.

Now the money didn't matter, nothing mattered except Erica's life. He might never get her back. But he would not let her die.

He stared at the phone, willing it to ring. Ring . . .

The sudden shock of sound nearly lifted him out of his armchair. He was halfway to the phone before he understood that it was the buzz of the intercom he'd heard.

Irritated, he stabbed the button. "Yes?"

"Mr. Stafford"—Marie's voice crackled over the speaker—"I'm sorry to buzz you when you said no disturbances . . ."

"What is it?"

"Mrs. Kellerman is here to see you."

Andrew frowned. Rachel. What the hell could she want? Then he remembered Connor telling him that Erica had missed a lunch date with Rachel.

She must have heard the news on the radio, and instead of calling, she'd chosen to drop by. Damn.

He didn't want to see her. He couldn't invite her to the guesthouse, couldn't risk taking Robert's call in her proximity. But if he went to the main house to chat with her, he might miss the call altogether, and Robert was a nut, unstable; no telling whether he would call again or give up after one try.

"Mr. Stafford?"

Andrew almost told Marie to send Rachel away, make some

excuse, but he decided he couldn't do that. It wouldn't be smart to raise any additional suspicions. His visit to the bank would be hard enough to explain later.

"Yes, Marie, I'll be there."

He clicked off. Before leaving the guesthouse, he hid the envelope from the safe-deposit box in the lower drawer of his desk, with the pistol underneath.

The cold assaulted him again as he sprinted to the mansion's back door. The rear hallway led to the kitchen. Marie was ladling some pasta concoction into a bowl.

"She's in the library," Marie said.

Andrew acknowledged this with a nod. Then for the first time he noticed the haunted hollows of his housekeeper's eyes.

Worried about Erica, he realized. He was slightly surprised to realize that Marie Stopani must feel genuine affection for his wife. For some reason he had never thought of Marie as part of the household except in a drably utilitarian sense.

He supposed he ought to stop and say something, offer some reassurance or comfort, but there was no time The task at hand was to dispatch Rachel as efficiently as possible and return to his vigil by the phone. He headed out of the kitchen and into the next doorway on the right.

The library of Great Hall was not large. The estate's builder, Hugh Garrison, had not been much of a reader by all accounts. But through the generations his heirs had acquired stacks of books, countless volumes crowding the bowed shelves almost from floor to ceiling.

Andrew recalled the bookshelves in Robert's cabin. Poor Robert must have spent more than his share of childhood hours in this room. Erica, too.

For a moment he could almost see them, the young girl and her smaller brother, one sprawled on the sofa and the other sitting on the floor, the two of them taking turns reading aloud from yellowed books, stumbling over difficult words.

Then he saw Rachel, standing at the far end of the room, and the strange vision fled.

She was backlit by a green-shaded table lamp, a cigarette smoldering between her thumb and forefinger, a white haze of smoke clinging to her outline.

He moved forward, and she turned to face him.

"Andrew."

"Hello, Rachel. I guess I ought to thank you." He stopped two yards away, uncomfortable in her presence, though unsure why.

"Thank me," she said, her tone curiously dulled. "Why?"

"Ben Connor told me you reported the . . . disappearance."

"Oh. Yes."

She was pulling hard on the cigarette, her face flushed. At parties and around town she was always self-possessed and sparkling, but charm had fled her now.

"Guess you heard the news on the radio," Andrew said, trying to move the conversation along, get this over with, return to the phone. "They found her car, but that's about it. They promised to tell me if anything else develops."

"I'm sure they will. You're her husband, after all."

This seemed a peculiar thing to say, but he only nodded.

"Actually," Rachel went on after another deep drag and a huge expulsion of smoke, "I haven't been listening to the radio."

"Haven't you? Oh. Well . . ." He couldn't understand where this was leading. "Well, it's not worth hearing—the garbage they're putting out over the air."

"Mmm," she murmured, and he knew she hadn't heard. She was waiting, marshaling some inner strength to explain her reason for this social call.

He watched her, obscurely worried. Then she pivoted sharply toward him.

"Maybe I shouldn't have told you," she said.

"What?"

She stared hard at him, repeating the words slowly, as if to a child. "Maybe . . . I shouldn't have . . . *told* you."

"Told me?"

"About them."

Then he understood. Part of it, at least.

In early February, Rachel Kellerman had run into him in town and insisted on lunch together at the New Hope Inn. And in the privacy of a corner booth, over bowls of Caesar salad, she had informed him that his wife and the new police chief, that nice

Ben Connor who'd been the guest of honor at a welcoming party in Great Hall, were having an affair.

That had been a month and a half ago. In all the time since, he'd known. He'd known as he and Erica passed each other silently in the master suite. He'd known as she rebuffed his advances. He'd known as she went for her daily runs, toning her body, her body that writhed under Ben Connor's caress.

What did Connor do with her, exactly? How did he do it? Was he slow or fast, gentle or rough, reserved or passionate? Did he do all the things Andrew had done? Had Erica told him what she liked, guided his hand to the special places most sensitive to a lover's touch? Or had he shown her new delights, things she'd never experienced in her marriage bed?

It tore at him—the images, the sounds. He could see Connor bending over her, see that man's mouth on Erica's perfect breasts, see him gliding lower, lower, and he could hear Erica's gasp, a shudder drawn from the deepest part of her, as she threw her head back and surrendered . . .

This filmstrip, unspooling ceaselessly in his mind, had driven him finally into the shower with her this morning, where against the tiled wall he'd given her what she'd had with Connor, whether she wanted it or not.

A tremor of recollection ran through him, revealing itself as a shrug. "Maybe you shouldn't have told me," he said with strained casualness. "But it's too late for regrets now."

"I felt just awful later. It was pure chance, you know. Leonard just happened to be in the right place at the right time. Or the wrong place. Or whatever."

Leonard, Rachel's husband, was a hotshot local realtor, shallow and garrulous like his wife. He'd been on his way to inspect a property when he saw Ben Connor's car pull into the driveway of the cottage Erica rented on the outskirts of town.

Andrew remembered his interlude with Connor in the sunroom earlier today. He'd mentioned the cottage to the police chief. Connor at least had shown the grace to hesitate before saying that he knew of it and had already checked it out.

He knew of it, all right. He'd fucked Erica there. It was their love nest, their romantic hideaway. Andrew had driven past it many times in the last six weeks, thinking of the secrets it contained, wishing he could steer his car into a skid and smash through the picket fence, the whitewashed wall.

And Connor had asked him about marital difficulties. *Marital difficulties*—the son of a bitch, the goddamned wife-stealing bastard.

"Anyway," Rachel was saying, "even though Leonard told me, I really shouldn't have passed on the bad news to you. It's not as if I'm the town gossip, you know." She tossed her head back, inhaling smoke. "I mind my *P*'s and *Q*'s, ordinarily. But I thought . . . if you knew . . . maybe you could patch things up with her before it was too late."

Andrew had run enough scams to recognize this line of argument for what it was. Anyway, it hadn't been hard to discern her actual motive. In the restaurant, while he sat stunned, the food tasteless in his mouth, Erica's good friend Rachel had reached across the silk tablecloth and gently clasped his hand. It was a gesture of comfort that lasted too long and felt too intimate. By letting him know that Erica was unfaithful, Rachel had given him permission to play around.

A workable plan in the abstract, but it had been defeated by a simple fact: He was not interested in Rachel Kellerman or in any other woman, because, despite everything, he still stubbornly loved his wife.

"We didn't patch things up," Andrew said curtly. "And I don't think you came here tonight to act as a marriage counselor."

He was tired of her. He wanted her out of here. The phone in the guesthouse might be ringing at this moment.

Rachel stiffened. "No. I just came here to ask one question. Did you have anything to do with it?"

The words hung in the room, drifting somewhere in the cloud of Rachel's cigarette smoke, turning in slow spirals as his mind processed them and finally decoded their meaning.

"Christ." It was an intake of breath more than a word.

"I need to know."

"For God's sake."

"Look at me and tell me you're not involved."

He closed the gap between them, stared directly into her face, and unblinking he told the truth.

"I'd do anything to find her, get her back. Anything at all."

She read his eyes, then answered with a slow, shaky nod. "All right."

He stepped back, exhausted by the effort at total sincerity. "Hell. Why would you even think I'd want to . . . hurt her?"

"I didn't, at first. Then it occurred to me . . . the way you looked when I told you, at the restaurant."

"The way I looked?"

"Like a crazy man. Like you could kill Ben Connor with your bare hands. Ben or . . . or maybe Erica." She shivered.

Andrew shook his head slowly. "You think I'd be capable of . . ."

"I don't know. It's possible. I think so." Head cocked, she studied him. "There's something hard in you, Andrew. Hard and . . . secretive. I suppose I found it an attractive quality. So different from Leonard, you know."

Different. Well, that was for sure. There was nothing hard about Leonard. He was all roundness and fleshy handshakes and too many chins.

"I noticed it right away," Rachel said. "It intrigued me. Scared me, too." She nodded. "You scare me. I think you could kill somebody. Yes. Not Erica, perhaps. I believe you about her. But . . . somebody. Ben Connor, for one."

Andrew said nothing, but he remembered the surge of pleasure and the brief temptation this afternoon when he'd had Connor, his wife's lover, in his pistol's sights.

Rachel stubbed out the cigarette in a bronze ashtray. "Anyway, I'm sorry. I shouldn't have come. But I had to know." She walked past him, pausing to say, "I hope Erica's all right."

Andrew's mouth barely moved. "So do I."

She left. He heard the fast retreating clack of her heels, then the slam of the front door.

When he emerged from the library into the kitchen, he found Marie eating listlessly in the breakfast nook.

"She took off in a hurry," Marie said.

Punctuating the statement, the roar of a motor outside, then a screech of tires as Rachel Kellerman pulled away.

"Yes, well." Andrew looked for something intelligent to say. He was usually so good at lying, but his mind seemed all knotted up right now. "She's upset. About Erica. We all are."

"Of course," Marie said, and went back to her fettucine.

He remembered the phone in the guesthouse, the urgency of returning. "If anybody else comes by—friends or neighbors, anybody like that—just say I can't see them now."

"Yes, Mr. Stafford."

He left the house and hurried across the rear yard. The air stung his face. He barely felt it. He was thinking of what Rachel had said.

I think you could kill somebody.

He blew plumes of frigid breath at the stark night. Well.

If he hadn't missed the call—if things could still be arranged—then within the next few hours Andrew Stafford might find out if he could kill a man.

12

"So why are you here?"

Robert's question hung in the frosty air, a substitute for a greeting, as he rose to confront Ben Connor.

Elder hung back, watching them, his gaze moving to Hart and Woodall just long enough to record the tension on their faces. He'd never seen a fellow officer go down, and he couldn't know exactly what the two young men were going through, but he could guess.

It was lucky they hadn't been left alone too long with Robert. Things could happen in a situation like that.

"Mr. Garrison," Connor said, "we've got some news for you." He expelled a ragged flume of breath. "Cold out here. Mind if we invite ourselves in?"

Robert stood in the cabin doorway, making no move to comply. The door, Elder saw, had been smashed open, the deadbolt torn from the frame. He remembered Connor saying Andrew Stafford had broken in.

After a brief silence Robert said, "I hadn't planned on hosting a dinner party."

Did Connor smile? Elder thought he did. "That's not on our agenda either," Connor answered. "Just a little talk, and we'll be on our way."

Robert considered the problem for another lengthy moment, while Elder's arthritis began to complain about the cold.

"You can come in, Chief," Robert decided finally. "You . . . and Mr. Elder there." He glanced at Hart and Woodall with cool indifference. "Not those two."

Connor frowned. "You have a complaint against these officers?"

"They seem hostile. Don't you think? That one, especially." A nod at Hart. "The roebuck."

Hart's hands closed into fists. Elder meant to caution him with a glance, but Woodall beat him to it. Good kid, Woodall.

Without turning to his men, Connor said, "You two wait out here."

"Chief"—that was Hart, explosive anger tearing at his self-control—"you can't let this asshole jerk us around."

"Stand post, Officer." Connor still didn't look back. "Mr. Garrison, let's go inside. Come on, Paul."

Robert led the way. Connor followed, Elder at the rear. Woodall caught his arm as he was entering.

"Sure this is safe?" Woodall whispered, his voice so low he nearly mouthed the words.

"Chief knows what he's doing," Elder breathed, hoping this was true. "Now how about if you boys give that truck a good looking-over. And take a peek in the outhouse too."

Woodall nodded, and Elder crossed the threshold.

The cabin was tidy enough, except for a line of laundry strung from one wall to another. A desk lamp, powered by the diesel generator outside, threw sixty watts of luminescence across the uneven floorboards. A log sputtered in the hearth, providing welcome heat and a secondary glow.

Robert sank into a chair by the desk and gestured vaguely at the cot. "Have a seat, Chief. Mr. Elder, shut the door."

Elder didn't want to. He hesitated, and outside the two patrol cops stiffened.

"Go on now," Robert said, a wispy smile floating at the edges of his mouth. "Wouldn't want to let in the night air, would we? You and the chief will catch your death."

Elder let his hand travel down the front of his jacket, confirming that the flaps were unbuttoned, the concealed snub-nose Smith within easy reach. Then he closed the door, wedging the splintered jam into the frame.

"Looks like you had an accident," Connor said mildly over the rasp of wood.

"Vandalism."

"Any idea who's responsible?"

A shrug. "Vandals. Or Huns, maybe. It might have been Huns." The ghost of Robert's smile finally materialized, a flash of canine brightness behind the matted mask of his beard. "Be seated, both of you. The bed will have to do. I'm not properly set up to entertain."

Connor accepted the offer. Elder lingered near the door.

"Prefer to stand," he said curtly. From this vantage point he had a better angle on the desk, just in case Robert happened to pull open a drawer and produce a weapon.

Robert seemed to grasp this strategy and nodded approval. "Fine, then. Fine. Well, isn't this nice? I've got company."

He let his head loll on his broad shoulders, his eyes unfocusing as they lifted toward the low ceiling, his hands slack in his lap.

Connor glanced at Elder, then shifted on the cot. "Mr. Garrison . . ."

"Robert." His voice was lazy, almost somnolent.

"Okay, Robert. There's something we need to tell you. Then I'd like to ask a few questions, and we'll be on our way."

"I hope they're riddles. I like riddles. The sphinx was a riddle. So was Jesus."

"Maybe we could hear your theological speculations later."

"Do you know why they nailed him to the cross?"

"Robert—"

"It's a tree. The cross—a symbolic tree. He was the corn king, your god. Slaughtered for the sake of a good harvest. His blood fertilized the growing maize, and he was resurrected in the tall stalks. Corn on the cob, that's your god."

"That's not why we're—"

"You think he's powerful, and he is, but there is one more powerful still. No, not the devil. This isn't Manichaeism I'm preaching, and I'm not Zoroaster, either. The Chinese speak of two principles at work in the universe, the feminine and the masculine, yin and yang, eternally opposed and yet bound together. Do you follow me?"

"Yes," Connor said. Impatient at first, he now seemed inclined to let Robert talk.

"I doubt you do, really. Or that you'd want to. The yin is primary and primordial. She is the ocean, the deep, the universal womb and maw, and she engulfs and swallows the male energy of the cosmos, as the black widow devours her mate. That's your corn king for you—bridegroom of the goddess, royal sacrifice, the harvest god hung from the sacred tree, whose blood will fertilize his wife-mother, Earth. Hers is the true power."

"No one worships goddesses anymore," Connor said evenly. "It's just a fable."

"That's where you're wrong. I knew you couldn't follow me. You see too little and too literally. You see only the outward forms, transient and meaningless—but not the essence."

"What essence?"

Robert didn't answer directly. "At Ephesus, in Turkey, there was a temple to the goddess in her various guises. She started as the Great Mother, and later the Ionian Greeks called her Artemis, and still later the Romans renamed her Diana. Paul wrote about her—not you, Mr. Elder. I mean the other Paul, the one struck down by epilepsy or epiphany on a Damascus road. He implored the Ephesians to give up the worship of their false deity for his true one, to dethrone the Mother and put the usurper in her place. Eventually Paul's side won. Or did it? The true power in the universe is not so easily defeated. She wins by stealth and subterfuge and seduction. There is an ancient legend that Mary, the carpenter's mother, settled in Ephesus. Around this legend a cult arose, active to this day. Do you see? In Ephesus they still worship a heavenly virgin. The forms change. Not the essence."

He stopped, breathing hard, worn out by his speech. Elder knew he was a man unaccustomed to conversation, yet desperate for an audience.

"Neither of you has any idea what I'm talking about," he said finally.

"We're willing to learn," Connor answered.

"Some things can't be taught. Anyway, you're here for quite a different reason. What was it you had to tell me?"

Connor leaned forward on the cot. "You may find it upsetting."

But nothing could upset the man who sat so loose-limbed in his chair. Robert didn't answer, merely waited.

"It's about your sister," Connor said. "I'm afraid she's disappeared."

"Has she?"

"It looks that way."

"Hmmm."

"There's a strong suspicion of foul play."

"Is that a baseball term?"

Connor blinked. "What?"

"Foul play. I've always wondered about the etymology. Baseball, you think?"

"I don't know."

"Huh." Robert pursed his lips. "Probably baseball. It's the national pastime, they say."

"Do you understand what I just told you?"

"Erica's missing. Foul play. Strong suspicion of. I understand."

"You don't seem overly concerned."

"We're not close. Besides, I already knew."

"How?"

"One of her friends—she has so many friends, you know—stopped me in town today to ask if I'd seen Erica. So I knew she must be hard to find."

"That didn't worry you?"

"Erica can take care of herself. She *always* takes care of herself."

"When was the last time you saw her?"

A beat of hesitation. "A year ago. She dropped by for a pleasant chat. Telling me I should see a psychiatrist, that sort of thing. I don't need a psychiatrist. Psychiatrists ought to be coming to me. I could show them what true insight is."

"She was trying to help you," Connor said.

"She's never helped me."

Elder spoke. "She did once. I remember. Don't you?"

Robert seemed almost to flinch, his composure disturbed for the first time. Good. According to the game plan Connor had worked out, it was Elder's job to shake up the suspect.

"I remember," Robert said slowly, and he turned in his seat and let his lolling head swivel toward Elder.

His eyes were not blank, as Elder might have expected. They were hard and bright and cold.

"You're not the police chief anymore," Robert went on softly. "What brings you out of retirement?"

"Chief Connor thought it would be better to have me here. After all, you know me. We're old acquaintances, aren't we?"

Robert said nothing.

"Sure we are. Known each other for years. But, funny thing, sometimes I still see you as a little boy. No offense. It's just an old man's mind playing tricks. I see you in those p.j.'s you had on that night. Batman, wasn't it?"

Reluctance made Robert's voice torpid. "Superman."

"That right?" Elder feigned surprise. "He was your favorite, huh? You used to play at being Superman, I'll bet. Maybe your sister was Lois Lane."

"No."

"You didn't play together?"

"Not like that."

"How, then?"

"We . . . acted out stories. Stories we found in books."

"Just the two of you? No neighborhood kids joined in?"

"We didn't need other kids. They wouldn't have understood. They would have laughed. They always laughed at me anyway, laughed and called me names, until Sissy . . . until Erica chased them away."

"Looking out for you, huh? Bet you were glad she was there." If Robert was innocent, then what Elder had to say next was cruel, irresponsibly cruel. But he and Connor had agreed on a general line of attack, which must be carried out. "And that night at Great Hall . . . you must've been glad for her company then, too."

Robert sat very still, no part of him moving except his hands, long-fingered hands resting in his lap and closing slowly, slowly into fists.

"Why would I be?" he whispered.

"She was there for you. Hugging you tight. Holding on for life. You loved her back then, didn't you, Robert? You cared about her then?"

"Never." The word a raw croak of pain.

"I think you did. And you still do. You still . . ."

Elder had more to say, but just then Robert lowered his head, and in the lamplight Elder saw the glimmering wetness on his cheeks.

Weeping.

And that boy in the Superman pajamas—he'd wept too. A single tear coursing down his pale young face.

Elder remembered that teardrop, and suddenly he couldn't go on. He knew what Connor wanted of him, but he lacked the will to push Robert any harder.

"Sorry, kid," he muttered, and turned away.

Connor stood. "Paul's told me all about it. You ought to be grateful to your sister."

Robert's head jerked up. "Grateful?"

"She got you through that night, Paul says. Without her, you might never have recovered."

Elder knew he'd never said any such thing. Connor was freelancing here. Must have realized old Paul had lost his nerve, so he was continuing the psychological assault on his own.

It took steel to do that. Steel—to face a weeping man and salt his open wound. Elder wondered if Ben Connor would be up to the job if Erica's life were not at stake.

"Without her? Without *her*?" Robert spat the words. "What makes you think I owe *her* any gratitude?"

"Paul says—"

"Fuck what he says. He doesn't know anything. Nobody knows anything!"

"He knows about that night." Connor took a step toward Robert. "He knows you—"

"That night, that night, *that night!*" It was a howl of rage, Robert half out of his chair, then remembering himself and sinking meekly down as the door groaned open and Woodall looked in.

"No problem," Elder said gruffly, and elbowed the door shut.

His heart was beating hard. Connor was pushing the kid's buttons, that was for damn sure.

"She did nothing for me on that night," Robert muttered, "or any other night."

"Of course she did." Connor moved closer to the chair. "When Paul found you—"

"She couldn't have helped me if she'd wanted to. She's not human. Suckle at her teat, and you're nursed on blood, black blood."

"You hate her that much?"

"She's a carrier. She's Typhoid Mary. She's the disease vector, she's the pollutant that leaves its stain on everything it touches, deadly pollution that will end all life on earth within ten years!"

The words were distantly familiar to Elder, but he couldn't recall just why.

"If she's that evil," Connor said, "she needs to be stopped."

"She'll be stopped." The agitated play of Robert's hands in his lap was awful to see. "She can't last. Things balance out. There's a cycle of seasons, and a cycle of reasons, and when you get to the heart of it, when you uproot the living stump, you see the plan and the purpose, you see what Tiresias saw."

"Who was Tiresias?"

"A blind man."

"What did he see?"

"Everything."

"What do *you* see?"

"Erica. I see Erica."

"Where is she?"

"In hell."

Elder could sense the effort it cost Connor to keep his tone steady as he asked, "You mean she's dead?"

Then Robert laughed.

It was the first time Elder had heard him laugh, at least since the good years of his childhood, before tragedy and trauma took his mirth away. The laugh was strong and rich, untouched by guilt or shame or even self-consciousness.

"You really are such hopeless literalists, both of you," Robert said gaily. "There are other kinds of hell."

Elder knew the game was lost, and in the sudden deflation of Connor's shoulders he saw that the chief knew it too.

"Is she dead?" Connor asked again, with stubborn insistence.

Robert let the laughter cling to his face in a wide, knowing smile. "How would I know?"

"Where is she?"

"How would I know?"

"Will she turn up like Sherry Wilcott?"

"How would I know?"

Connor stepped back, conceding the uselessness of this line of interrogation. "All right. Just tell me one thing. Where were you between the hours of one P.M. and two-thirty P.M. today?"

"Buying groceries."

"Got a receipt?"

"In the kindling."

"You burned it?"

"No. Not yet."

Robert left his chair and bent over a bucket near the fireplace, which served as a wastepaper receptacle.

"There are witnesses, you know," Robert said as he rummaged in the trash. "The cashier, for one. A young plump girl with a pig-snout face. And there was that friend of Erica's I mentioned. Rachel somebody. She was rather agitated. I asked her if she'd been crying for her lost children, like her namesake, Laban's daughter. She only stared at me, the way you all stare, all of you fools. Here it is."

He pulled out a long, crumpled strip of paper, then handed it to Connor and resumed his seat.

Connor studied the receipt. The time and date, Elder knew, would be printed in the upper corner.

"May I keep this?" Connor asked after a moment. He looked tired, and Elder knew Robert's alibi was confirmed.

Robert shrugged. "You can frame it, if you want."

Connor folded the receipt into his pocket. "Where did you go after you left the store?"

The question was asked by rote. Connor clearly had abandoned any expectation of a breakthrough.

"I drove around for a while," Robert said, "then came back here."

"Why drive around with a truckload of perishables?"

"Do I need a reason?"

"Rachel said you left in a hurry. As if you had to get someplace."

"She was wrong."

"The door was broken when you got back?"

"Yes."

"Was anything taken?"

"No."

"Was anything left? A note, say?"

Elder recalled Connor saying that Andrew Stafford had left his business card, but Robert, studying the police chief warily, merely shook his head.

"Mind if I look around?" Connor asked. "Just to see if there's something you overlooked?"

"Go ahead." Robert smiled. "But I don't overlook much."

Connor conducted a quick, efficient search of the cabin's nooks and corners. Robert watched him, serene as a cat.

The compact fridge, Elder noted when Connor opened it, was stocked nearly to bursting with groceries, as was the large freezer at its side. Additional confirmation of Robert's alibi, if any was needed.

Then Elder glanced at Robert and saw that the man's gaze had shifted to him.

"How's the wife, Paul?" Robert asked.

Elder met that heatless gaze. "Dandy."

"Is she? Thought I read something in the paper about a charity benefit on her behalf. My impression was, she'd dipped her Dixie cup in the River Lethe."

"She's not dead, if that's what you mean." Absurdly, Elder felt a threat of tears at the corners of his eyes.

"No, that would be the River Styx. The Lethe, well, it's another river of no return."

Elder had no idea what the son of a bitch was talking about, but now he regretted going easy on him earlier, airtight alibi or not.

Then a new thought occurred to him, and suddenly he knew why that babble about pollution had sounded familiar. "You read it in the paper," he said, expressing himself aloud.

"That's what I said."

"No, I mean that other thing. That pollution nonsense. It was the headline in the *Weekly World News*. The one you were staring at."

Robert took a long time to answer. Slow wheels of thought were turning in his brain. "How did you know?" he said finally, his voice muted with just the slightest hush of fear.

The answer could be easily given, but the pleasure of withholding it, of letting Robert imagine that his secret thoughts lay open to Elder's inspection like bones under an X-ray—well, it was just too much to pass up.

Elder chuckled. "I'm like your Tiresias, boy. Bet he was an old coot like me, now, wasn't he?" He watched Robert nod. "Well, there it is. Us old folks, we may be dumb as posts or blind as bats, but we know things, mister. We know things."

Robert slowly turned away, and Elder fought to keep his face clean of a smile.

By now Connor was finished with the search, having checked every obvious place without finding anything amiss. "Guess we'll be going," he said.

Robert, sunk in thought, didn't answer.

Elder opened the door. Connor stepped out, then turned.

"Funny about those earplugs," he said.

Blinking, Robert looked at him.

"The ones on that apple crate by the bed. I wouldn't have thought you'd need them out here."

Robert's voice was a whisper. "The mockingbirds can really get going. Usually start in the middle of the night. Just outside the window."

"I see. Noisy, are they? I thought maybe it was something else you heard. Your mother's screams, maybe. When Keith Wyatt's slug tore her open, and the arterial spray hit you in the chest—she screamed then, didn't she?"

Robert just stared.

"On the other hand," Connor added, "I guess earplugs wouldn't do much good when it comes to that kind of noise."

He left. Elder paused in the doorway.

"Pleasant dreams," he said to Robert, and walked out, gently shutting the door.

Connor was still on edge, riding a crest of adrenaline from the confrontation in the cabin, when he and Elder huddled with Woodall and Hart near the two cruisers.

"We taking him in, Chief?" Hart asked eagerly.

Connor shook his head. "We've got nothing on him. Besides, he's got an alibi."

He explained about the grocery store.

"The time printed on the receipt was two-fifteen," he concluded, "which fits what Rachel Kellerman told me. Robert purchased at least seventy items. Must have been in the store

for an hour or so. And Erica failed to make a one-thirty lunch
date."

"He could've kidnapped her first," Hart said.

Elder patted his arm. "Think again, son. Would he leave her
in his truck while he went on a shopping spree?"

"There's no evidence she was in the truck, anyway," Woodall
added.

In the truck.

Connor registered the words without allowing himself a visible reaction. But he felt his pulse accelerate, felt the familiar
outrage born and nurtured in New York.

"You took a look?" he inquired, keeping his tone even.

Woodall shrugged. "It was right in front of us. Parked in plain
sight."

"How about the interior?" He let a hint of humor slide into
his voice, encouraging an honest response. "You happen to check
that out, too?"

There was a moment's pause as the two patrol cops traded a
glance, then reached a silent agreement to speak.

"Hey, you know how it is, Chief." Hart flaunted a silly, boast-
ful grin. "The side door wasn't locked. Might've accidentally
come open."

"Same with the outhouse," Woodall said. "Man, does that shit-
hole stink to heaven. Nothing in there, though, except yesterday's
dinner, and a whole mess of yesterdays before that."

Connor let a moment pass, and in the sudden silence he conveyed disapproval for the first time.

"Inspecting the vehicle's exterior is one thing," he said finally, "but when you start opening doors, you're conducting a
warrantless search without cause."

"We weren't gonna get caught," Hart protested. "One of us
stood post—"

"I don't give a *damn* about that."

Abruptly it was back, the old anger, the furious indignation,
and for a moment the pair before him were not Woodall and
Hart, but Cortez and Lomax, and he was with Karen in the
bloody bier of their bed.

It's not about getting caught! He wanted to scream the

words. *We're not the ones who worry about getting caught! That's not who we are, don't you understand, don't you see?*

But he said none of this, because fury had choked off speech.

He knew he was shaking, shaking with rage. He groped inside himself and somehow found the eye of the storm, and in that calm place he recovered his voice.

"There are rules," he said, amazed to be speaking without rancor, in complete sentences that made sense. "Good cops respect the rules, always. Not just when it's convenient or when somebody's watching. All the time. It's that simple."

Hart was wounded. "Chief Elder said—"

"I'm the chief now." The flat finality of the statement silenced Hart at last.

Elder coughed and spoke up. "That's right. He's the chief, and I overstepped. But to be fair to these boys, Chief Connor, the whole thing was my idea, and I was wrong."

Connor barely glanced at him before returning his gaze to Woodall and Hart. "In the future you do it by the book. That's my way, it's our way, it's the only way."

"Yes, sir," Woodall said, chagrined.

Hart merely nodded, his face set in stubborn resistance.

Connor knew he hadn't really gotten through to them. They thought they'd played it smart, shown initiative, and here was this interloper from New York getting on his high horse over nothing at all.

Well, he'd have a longer talk with the pair later. He'd explain why the rules mattered, and what happened when cops started to think they were above the law.

Yes, he could relate a nice little story on that theme.

"Okay," he said crisply, dropping the subject for now. "I want you two to head back to the crime scene and join up with the search party. Lieutenant Maginnis is supervising, along with Captain Hausen of the sheriff's department. Get going."

Two muted affirmatives drifted in reply. Woodall and Hart began to walk away. Elder stopped them with a question.

"Either of you guys ever hear of a River Lethe?"

"It's from Greek mythology," Woodall said. "A river in hell. Drink from it and you lose your memory."

Elder just nodded slowly.

"Why?" Woodall asked.

"Never you mind."

Elder was silent as he climbed into the passenger seat of Connor's Chevy. Connor swung onto the grass to let Woodall execute a ragged U-turn. When Woodall had pulled away, down the hillside, Connor followed, driving more slowly than necessary.

Beside him, Elder said, "Sorry I led 'em astray, Chief. I should've known better."

"It's all right," Connor said, although it wasn't.

The other car's taillights shrank and vanished, and by the time Connor pulled alongside Elder's Buick, he and Elder were alone.

"Still want me on stakeout?" Elder asked.

"More than ever. His alibi's good, but all that means is he didn't kidnap her in town."

"But he's our man, anyway. That's what you're saying?"

Connor thought about it. "Yes," he said finally. "That's what I'm saying. In the movies it's never the most obvious suspect. In real life you play the percentages. He fits the profile. He hates his sister—Christ, how he hates her. And he's insane. Brilliant, in his way, but crazy . . . and capable of violence. Did you see him squirming in his chair?"

"I saw. Like a mean dog on a leash."

"He killed Sherry Wilcott. Cut her damn throat. Maybe it had something to do with that gibberish he was spouting. Some cult thing, ritual, whatever. He killed her, and now he's got Erica."

"If she's still alive," Elder said, then winced in immediate regret.

Connor waved off the remark. "She's alive. He laughed when I asked if she was dead. And when I said Erica should be stopped, did you hear his answer? *She'll be stopped,* he said. Will be. Future tense. And Hart and Woodall were with him since nightfall."

"So?"

"Night's the magic time for him. It's when he hears . . . whatever it is he hears." His mother, Connor still thought—screaming, perhaps, or simply calling to him, as he himself heard Karen call in nightmares. "His craziness is at its peak at night. If he's going to kill her, he'll do it in the night."

This was all clear to him, but he thought his companion would voice skepticism, even laugh. Instead Elder said quietly, "You ought to be writing up those profiles yourself, Chief."

Connor shrugged, embarrassed. "I'm no shrink. Just an old street cop."

"No, that's what I am, and I couldn't have come up with any of that." Some thought seemed to be taking form behind Elder's eyes, but all he said was, "Now what's the plan?"

"I don't expect him to spend a quiet night at home. Either he'll go out and lead us to Erica, or he'll be visited by Andrew Stafford. Now, I want you to drive as close to the cabin as possible, no headlights, and park in the tall brush—"

"I know that part of the drill, Chief."

"Right. Sorry. You got a two-way radio?"

"Not since I started wearing civvies."

"Take my portable." Connor fumbled it free of his belt and tuned it to the tactical frequency. "I'm setting it on Tac One. I'll monitor in my squad car. He goes anyplace, you tail him. He gets a visitor, you see who it is. Either way, call it in. Roger?"

"Wilco."

Elder got out of the car, then leaned in the window on the passenger side.

"Do me a favor, would you? Stop off at my place and tell Corinne—that's the nurse—tell her I won't be in? She was putting Lily to bed when I left, and I didn't want to interrupt. She'll worry if I don't get back."

"I'll do that. Sure."

"And while you're there"—Connor saw it again, that look of a newly formed thought in Elder's eyes—"you ought to take a peek in my file cabinet. In the den, next to the sofa. Bottom drawer. File labeled *Garrison*."

Garrison. "A file on Robert?"

"No. Not him. Look for yourself. It's . . . well, it's something I've kept hidden long enough. I didn't know quite what to make of it, or what it might mean. But you're a smart man, Chief. Smarter than I ever was, I reckon. You may see an angle I missed." A shrug. "Anyhow, it makes for interesting reading."

"If it's so interesting, why keep it hidden?"

"Up until now, I wanted to protect the Garrison kids from

any further scandal. Figured they'd been hurt enough, after what they went through that night. But now Erica's missing, and Robert, well . . ." Elder hesitated, and Connor knew he was thinking of the River Lethe and of his Lily, incontinent on rubber sheets. "As for Robert, I guess I don't feel quite so protective of him as I once did. Goodnight, Chief."

Elder straightened up and turned his back, retreating from the cruiser, and Connor had no chance to ask more questions.

13

Hopeless.

For some unmeasured stretch of time Erica had struggled with the straps that bound her wrists. Her neck ached from tilting her head to peer over her shoulder at the knotted canvas ends.

Each wrist had been wrapped separately; then the two straps had been tied together. To liberate herself, she would have to loosen the knot or rip one of the straps free of the table.

So far her desperate tugging and squirming had only tightened the knot. She could not work it loose.

"He wasn't a Boy Scout," she muttered, surprising herself with the hoarse rasp of her own voice. "Where'd he ever learn to tie a knot like that?"

Then with a groan she remembered that she had taught him. A lesson in woodcraft, big sister teaching baby brother to be a man. Well, he was a man now, a dangerous man.

And before long he would return to cut her throat.

Well, what if he does? she asked herself in a sudden access of bitter despair. What difference does it make? What have you got to live for, anyway?

The questions pained her, because she had no answers.

Her life had been largely empty for months. For years. She kept busy, always busy, but her desperate activity was only a ruse to distract her from the essential pointlessness of it all. She ran a shop to earn money she didn't need, and for an excuse to take Mediterranean trips that left her sad and drained. Her husband didn't love her, had never loved her, had married her for money—money, the Garrison fortune, her splendid inheritance, which so often felt like a burden and a curse.

She had no friends except chattering busybodies like Rachel Kellerman. People in town smiled at her, then whispered behind her back. The only meaningful relationship in her life, the only person she'd been really close to, was her brother.

And he was a psychopath who had tied her to a table and would kill her very soon.

There was nothing to fight for. Even if she survived, she would face a family scandal worse than any she'd weathered before. Robert would be jailed or hospitalized for life. She would be a freak on public display, an object of scornful pity. She could divorce Andrew and be alone, or stay with him in a sham marriage. She . . .

Alone. No, that wasn't quite right. Even without Andrew, without Robert, she would not be alone.

Ben Connor would be there.

Funny how she'd all but omitted him from the inventory of her life.

Well, she thought bitterly, it's only a fling for him. It's never meant anything.

He'd said otherwise, though. He'd said he loved her.

What did it matter, the things he said? It wasn't real. Andrew had claimed to love her, and it had been a lie. Robert had been her closest companion in childhood, her soulmate, a friend for life, it had seemed. Now look at him.

Love never lasted. It was an act, a role. You couldn't count on it. Her mother had pretended to love her, hadn't she? Until the pretense was unnecessary, and she had dropped the mask and revealed her contemptuous indifference toward the two children she had borne. *Get away from me*—that had been her mantra whenever Erica or Robert went to her for comfort. Those words, and the tinkle of ice cubes in a glass.

She'd abandoned them, as surely as if she'd left them by the side of some deserted highway. Her physical presence in the house remained, but there was no emotional connection, no warmth of understanding, no love, only the sour smell of alcohol on her breath and the cold, bloodshot malice in her eyes.

And Keith Wyatt . . . Uncle Keith, as he'd wanted to be called . . . he was worse. With him, love had never been even a pretense.

She'd known one love that was real—her father's—but it hadn't lasted, either. Death had taken him away. Death, which was the end of love, of hope. Death, coming soon to enshroud her in its chill.

Some combustive mix of emotions—part fear, part rage— shuddered through her body, and abruptly she was writhing on the table, pulling at the straps in furious desperation, aware of nothing except that she would not die here, in this dank gloom, she would not, *she would not.*

Her wrists twisted madly, fighting for release, and her legs flexed, and her left foot slipped just a little inside her boot.

She froze, gasping.

Her foot had slipped. Yes. She was sure it had.

But how could it? Wasn't her ankle bound?

For a moment she just lay there, afraid to move and jinx whatever opportunity had been presented to her.

Then very slowly she curved her spine, thrusting her shoulders forward, and she stared at her left foot in the lantern's harsh guttering glare.

"Oh," she whispered. And with the whisper came a smile, slow and uncertain, her first in hours.

He'd made a mistake, her Robert. Just a touch of carelessness, nothing very serious, but a mistake nonetheless.

In binding her legs, he'd wrapped one canvas strap around her right calf, pinning it to the table. But the other strap had been hastily looped around the top of her boot and tied in place.

Inside the boot, her left foot had some freedom of movement. Not much; the boot fit snugly to begin with, and the strap was pinching it tight.

Even so, she thought she could slip her foot free.

And if she did? What good would that small measure of freedom do her? She couldn't say. She knew only that any progress was better than none at all. If one leg was all she could liberate before Robert's return, so be it. She would do that much, at least. She would not die without a fight.

Erica worked on the problem for a long time, twisting her leg, flexing her knee, drawing her foot slowly up through the shaft of the boot. Her sock gave her trouble. It was a wool sock, fairly thick, and as her foot advanced, the sock began to wrinkle around her ankle and toes, forming a thick clump of folded fabric that impeded progress.

Finally she pulled free of the boot and lay there, panting.

She'd done it.

Now what?

Her gaze roved over the table and the three straps still pinning her down, then circled the room, the smooth limestone floor and the high ceiling and the kerosene lantern on its rock pedestal.

A crazy thought entered her mind. The lantern . . .

She recoiled from the idea. Too risky. Insane.

Half-heartedly she turned her attention to the straps on her wrists. She twisted her forearms, hoping irrationally that the straps would loosen by magic, but nothing happened, of course.

She found herself looking at the lantern again.

Yes, the idea was crazy. But it might be her only chance.

The lantern was one of many that she and Robert had taken from the storage shed at Great Hall. It dated back to the turn of the century, she would guess. The side panels were glass, and inside was a small tank of kerosene. A wick drew the fuel to the mantle, or upper chamber, where the flame burned.

Now suppose she were to reach out with her left leg and upset the lantern's balance, jostle it rudely from its limestone perch and send it crashing to the floor.

The fragile thing would shatter. Kerosene would spray the floor and ignite instantly in a fireball.

"And the table will catch fire," she finished in a whisper, "and you'll burn to death."

Yes. This was possible.

But . . .

The straps were bolted to the underside of the table. And the fire, blazing directly below her, might scorch and fray the straps, weakening them just enough to let her pull free.

Or the straps might not fail, and she would be roasted alive or asphyxiated by smoke.

"Forget it," she said sharply. "Think of something else."

There had to be another way. Something less dangerous, less unpredictable.

But no alternate plan occurred to her.

She didn't think the table would burn. It would smolder, that was all. And as for the smoke . . . well, there might not be enough kerosene left in the lamp to produce fumes in lethal quantity.

"No," she said. "It'll never work."

Even so, she straightened her leg experimentally and brushed the lamp.

She could reach it. All she had to do was hook her toes around the base and yank it forward . . .

Heart pounding, she withdrew her leg and lay stiffly on the table, afraid of her sudden obsession with this suicidal plan.

There must be some safer alternative. She couldn't think of it quite yet, but she would. She needed time.

But there might not be much time left. How long had she slept? Night must have fallen by now. Robert might be back at any moment. And then . . .

A stroke of the knife, slicing her carotid arteries, and she would bleed to death on the sacrificial table like a figure out of myth, or like Sherry Wilcott, washed up bloodless and nude on the bank of Barrow Creek.

The autopsy details had been withheld from the press, the Barrow *Register* reporting only that the murder weapon had been a knife. But Ben Connor had discussed the case freely with her. He'd told her about the incision in the throat, clean and wide, the semicircular path that had slit Sherry's tender flesh from ear to ear.

And Erica, listening, had remembered the books she and Robert had pored over in the library at Great Hall, the musty volumes of folklore and mythology, and the plays they'd read aloud to pass the long, lonely afternoons of their childhood, ancient plays by Aeschylus and Sophocles and Euripides, and the performances enacted here, in this warren of limestone dens, and even in this room, before the rust-streaked gour that looked so much like a throne of blood.

Ritual sacrifice had figured in so many of those myths and poems and plays. Often it was the sacrifice of an animal, but there were atavistic traces of human sacrifice as well. The most famous was the story of Iphigenia, Agamemnon's daughter, led to a stone altar in the woods, where her throat was cut by a priest to appease the angry goddess Artemis.

Had she and Robert rehearsed that scene as children, performing the ritual with a paper knife, perhaps? Had he played the priest and she the stoic virgin girl?

Erica couldn't remember. They might have. It was the sort of thing they would do here, in the lanterns' glow. Other kids played cops and robbers, cowboys and Indians, spacemen and Martians, but the Garrison kids were different. They played at myth, and they played alone.

Robert would be coming soon. And this time he would not be playacting, and the knife would not be paper.

The lantern. She was staring at the lantern, at the guttering flame.

It was the only way.

It *might* work.

She tugged at the straps. Useless.

"I don't want to do this," she murmured.

But already her leg was extending toward the lantern, and she could feel the flame's heat through the loose wool sock.

Slowly she curled her toes around the base of the lantern.

One jerk of her leg, and the lamp would plunge to the floor and detonate like a small bomb.

She could do it. She knew she could. Yet she hesitated, still afraid, much too afraid.

Afraid of what? Dying? When she'd already proven she had nothing to live for? Nothing but loneliness in a house that was too large and too empty, with a husband who had never loved her—and in a cottage in the woods, secret trysts with a man who must be lying when he said she mattered to him, a man who would betray her or abandon her, as Andrew had, and Robert, and even her father . . .

The lantern's heat singed the sock. Her toes were blistering.

Connor would leave her, or he would be taken from her, and either way she would be alone again, as alone as she'd been in the New Hampshire boarding school or on a wharf in a Greek fishing village or anywhere, everywhere, on every day of her life.

Tears blurred her sight. She shut her eyes. She wanted to go away. Just drop off into sleep, never wake. And in dreams she would run, run free through the woods and fields, run and never hear another lie or face another loss.

Run . . .

Then her eyes opened, and she knew what she had been running from—it was manifest and obvious for the first time—and in that instant of sudden clarity she knew she had to live, and why.

"Then do it," she breathed, her whole body tensing. "God damn it, no more fear, just *do* it, do it *now*."

Her knee flexed, dislodging the lantern, which teetered briefly, then swayed forward in a gentle downward arc.

Dropping to the floor. Dropping straight down.

Erica saw it fall—and in the instant before its crash, she knew she had made a terrible mistake.

Robert stood at the cabin window, shaking in an aftermath of fury, long after the two patrol cars had disappeared into the dark.

Scared. He was scared. The interview had gotten to him. His thinking, normally so lucid, so well organized, seemed scrambled and diffuse.

They had played with him—Connor and Elder. They had batted him between their paws like a mouse in the deadly orbit of a cat.

That talk about him and Erica, about their childhood, their games, the night at Great Hall when they became orphans—all of it had been a ploy designed to bait him into a fatal misstep. And he had nearly fallen victim to the scheme. Had nearly lost control and blurted the truth about Erica's whereabouts, or enough of the truth to bring out their hangmen's smiles.

Bastards.

He had underestimated Connor. The man was more than the dullard he appeared. And Elder—

A shudder moved through him like a twinge of nausea.

Elder had scared him. He had known about the newspaper headline. How?

An insight of that kind was a gift of the Mother. This was the only answer. She had enlisted those two as her allies. Whether they knew it or not, they served the goddess now.

Even so, there was no cause for him to be afraid. He could outmaneuver men like Connor and Elder, even if the Dark Mother had folded them under her protective shroud.

He must be careful, that's all. Must be—what was the modern term, the term used by all the nattering imbeciles with an ear for popular argot? Focused. Yes. He must be focused tonight, focused on nothing but Erica and her destiny and the intricate weave of fate that had united the patterns of their lives in a seam of closure.

He could afford no mistakes. He must think as his enemies would think, anticipate their strategy.

They had left him. He'd watched their taillights shrink until the splashback of their high beams vanished around a bend in the dirt road. They were gone.

But would Connor, or the Mother who played him like a lyre, really leave Robert unguarded on this night?

There had to be a watcher. Someone stationed on post, observing from some forest blind.

When he left the cabin, he would be followed. He would lead them straight to the sinkhole, and they would arrest him, save Erica, spoil everything.

That surely was their plan.

He nodded slowly, and turned to study the leaping play of fire in the hearth.

They were so very clever, all his enemies. At times he even wondered if they had deliberately placed the Wilcott girl in his path, so as to lure him into committing an act they defined as criminal. Perhaps they had watched him even then, when he first encountered the girl.

Was it possible? Had old Paul Elder or Erica herself been crouching in the bushes near the pond? Had they tricked poor Sherry into serving as a decoy to entrap him? Had they anticipated what would happen, where it all would lead?

He wouldn't put it past them, not any of them—not Erica the witch, nor Elder who had Tiresias's second sight, nor Connor, whose blunt, square face concealed a crafty mind.

Yes, they might indeed have done it, might have arranged the whole thing, although at the time, in his innocence, he had suspected nothing. He had known only that it was a summer day, bright and hot, a good day for a walk.

The month was June, named for Juno, Queen of Heaven, who was Hera, who was the primordial Mother, tireless in her fecundity. The woods were green and wild, every young shoot blossoming, nature rampant in a flood tide of verdure, and he drank in the sight and smell and sound of it—the insect buzz, the leafy rustle, the honeysuckle flavor in the air, and the walls and canopies of endless green.

His walk through the woods lasted for hours and seemed aimless, but fate guided him, or perhaps a witch-spell cast by his sister. He should ask her. Ask her tonight.

Whatever the cause, he'd ended his trek at a small pond near Great Hall, a place of blue water hemmed by tall hardwoods. Turtle Pond, it was called; he remembered the name from his childhood.

Normally the pond was deserted; there were other, better swimming holes. But on that day someone was there.

A girl, nineteen, her hair a fall of sunshine. She frighted, seeing him.

Hello, he said, wondering at this rare thing, the chance to greet another person. *Sorry if I startled you.*

She relaxed a little. But she studied him as he moved closer, and he caught the familiar wariness in her eyes. She knew him. They all did, everybody in town. They knew him as the recluse in the woods, the fool on the hill.

But they did not hate or fear him, not then. He was only the local eccentric. Harmless. Intriguing, even.

I'm Sherry, the girl said. *Sherry Wilcott.*

He nodded. *Robert.*

He sat beside her, and for a while they said nothing. They watched as a mallard skimmed the pond with a flutter of wings. They listened to the pull of the breeze on tree branches.

Something bad happened here once, Robert said. *A long time ago.*

What was it?

Someone died.

This talk of dying seemed to make her nervous. To reassure her, he asked why she had come to this spot.

Had a fight with my folks, she said, relaxing again.

His silence encouraged her to talk. She told him that her parents disapproved of the boys she hung out with, boys with tattoos and muscles who played pool in taverns. Bikers, she called them. Robert was unfamiliar with the term, but he nodded as if he understood.

In truth, he did understand everything that mattered. He knew about loneliness, about adults who held you prisoner and never let you go. He told her about the boarding school, the headmaster, the taunting children, and Mr. Furnell, his surrogate parent, who had separated him from Erica and banished him to that hell.

These were things he had not spoken of before. He felt a lightness, a giddiness almost, at putting them into words for other ears to hear.

You poor guy, Sherry said, pity written on her face. She asked him what it was like, to live all alone. He said a person could get used to it.

She was comfortable with him by then. From her purse she took out a hand-rolled cigarette wrapped carefully in a tissue. *It's pot,* she said. *Want to share it?*

They smoked the cigarette together. Robert knew something of narcotics and hallucinogens. He had made incense from forest gatherings, bark and leaves and gummy resin which, when burned in a brazier, produced heady, magic fumes. He'd never tried marijuana, though.

Strange feelings came over him. The sun brightened. The world accelerated its rotation. He and the girl laughed at a scurrying chipmunk for no reason at all.

He was hardly even surprised when Sherry took off her blouse and shorts, stripping to her underwear.

Getting hot, she said with a giggle. *Let's take a swim.*

She splashed into the pond before he could say anything. He watched her cavort in the shallow water, nearly naked, her blonde hair flying in wet tangled strands.

Come on in! She was waving to him.

He took off his boots and his pants but, after a moment's hesitation, left his shirt on. He waded into the water, and she laughed.

Your shirt'll get soaked. Take it off.

He only shrugged and sank under the surface, letting the cold water soak into his shirt and hair and beard, then emerged, face dripping, hair streaming behind him in a leonine mane.

She was watching him, and with a startling switch in perspective he saw himself as she saw him, a man of thirty-two, sun-bronzed, the cords of his muscles bursting through the clinging folds of his shirt. He had never once thought of himself in relation to the other sex, never imagined himself as an object of desire. Never until now.

Sherry swept her hair from her eyes, using both hands to do it, her breasts springing up under the wet brassiere that barely contained them.

You're an okay guy, she said, mischief lighting her face. *A little shy, but I don't mind. I like you.*

He couldn't think of what to say.

I'll take off mine, she whispered slyly, *if you take off yours.*

Her hands were behind her back now, fumbling with something, and then the brassiere came away and she was naked from the waist up. She tossed the bra onto the shore and stood with hands on hips, and he thought of Leda, Sparta's queen, bathing nude in a pond.

If she was Leda, then he was the sky god Zeus, who had visited Leda in the guise of a swan. Visited her and . . . covered her . . . coupled with her . . .

Robert had never done such things or conceived of doing them. But Leda—Sherry—was reaching out for him, her needy hands on his wide shoulders, her breasts rubbing smooth against the wrinkled denim of his shirt, her mouth meeting his in an electric shock of contact.

A sudden pounding frenzy filled his head. Sparks of sunlight dazzled him in all directions. He kissed her, tasting sweetness. Her hair was soft like young grass, like the first tender shoots that rise in a mist of green.

He shifted his position, instinct guiding him, and now his legs bracketed hers, and beneath the worn cotton of his underpants his phallus was hard and huge and insistent. He was kissing her face, her ear, her neck, a rain of new sensations driving him to a heady excitement unlike any he had known, and her hands moved over his back, his arms, and her fingers tugged at the buttons of his shirt.

There was a gasping from somewhere, from one of them or both, and he clamped his arms around her waist and wrenched her close, meaning to take her now, impale himself on her and put an end to this agony of pleasure. He couldn't think, he was beyond thought, but a wordless image flashed in his mind, an image of man and woman coupling in a pond, limbs entwined in a dance of mutual need, and then the image switched, and it was a swan and a woman he saw, sky-father and virgin, the swan grotesquely large, swollen by desire, and Leda surrendering with a cry.

His shirt came off.

She had unbuttoned it and parted the flaps, pushing the wet denim back over his biceps, and he felt her fingers spread across his pectorals and freeze.

Hey, she said, a strange note in her voice.

He tried to hold her, but she pulled away, staring at him, and her face changed.

Oh, Jesus. What . . . what happened to you?

She was looking at his scars.

A meshwork of scars, a skein that wrapped his torso as tightly as fate's net wrapped a human life. Parallel bands, thick and hard, binding him like rope. In other places, thin threads, densely interlaced, woven on the loom of his body.

The scars began at his navel and traveled upward in fantastic patterns and combinations and recombinations, elaborate as a tapestry. His abdomen and pectorals were ridged with matted tissue, white and lumpy and hairless. Everywhere from groin to shoulders he was a mass of healed pain and ravaged flesh.

What did they do to you? she was whispering as tears bloomed in her eyes. *What did they do?*

He thought he saw a way to reassure her. She imagined he was the victim of some horrible torture. If she knew the truth, she might understand.

No one did this to me, he said. *I did it to myself.*

You . . . ?

She began to back away, hands upraised, and he realized his

explanation had only made things worse. Still, perhaps he could make her see that there was nothing to fear.

He started to tell her about the temple of the body, and how this temple must be dedicated to the holy ones who abide in nature. There was more he could have said—about the bronze knife he used, an ancient knife he had purchased from a dealer in antiquities, a knife he'd purified in fire, and how the clever blade would catch the lamplight as he opened a score of red mouths in his own flesh . . .

But he had no chance to say it. She turned away suddenly and scrambled onto the bank, clutching at her bra and then her clothes, and she was screaming.

You're crazy—you're a freak, a goddamned freak—stay away, you just stay away!

Waist-deep in the pond, he stretched out his arms to her, wordlessly imploring for a hearing.

Fucking psycho! Stay away!

Her voice keening as she bundled her garments, and the ugly insults tossed at him like rocks at a cringing dog . . .

You're sick, you crazy freak, don't you come after me, don't you touch me!

Staggering away, and still screeching, screeching, then gone into the trees, hair swinging behind her, gold in the sun.

And Robert, the scarred man, dying inside as he stood alone in the pond where, many years ago, a different kind of death had taken place.

He stumbled onto the grass with some thought of pursuing her, but his knees betrayed him, and he sank down on all fours in a huddle of pain, shivers racking him like torture.

And in his brain—her voice, her shrieking voice.

Her voice, and other voices, voices he had not heard in years, rising together like disinterred spirits, blending in a furious medley.

You're sick . . .

Freak . . .

Fucking faggot, afraid to fight . . .

Look at him cry, the little queer . . .

Let's beat the shit out of him again, he asked for it . . .

We hate you, Robert, you stupid fairy . . .

Crying for his mommy, boo hoo hoo . . .

Those voices. The taunts and jeers that had pursued him in boarding school. Now they were back. He was a child again—a child, despite the initiation into manhood etched in white relief on the living canvas of his body. A child, weeping and alone.

And yet gradually, as the long weeks passed, he came to see that the voices that plagued him were something more than memories. And he began to understand what he must do.

That was when he took out the bronze knife and whetted its blade for a new use. A sacrifice.

In the hearth a knot of firewood popped like a gunshot, and Robert came back to himself.

He turned to the window again. Lifting his head, he scanned the sky. The moon had not yet risen but soon would. A horned moon tonight, a death moon.

When the moon was high, his tormentors would find him. He must take action quickly. No dawdling.

Think.

Eyes shut, he stood unmoving as he tuned into the frequency of the cosmic mind and the universal soul, the celestial harmony known to Pythagoras as the music of the spheres.

A plan took shape in his mind. A countermove that would turn his enemies' strategy against them.

Yes.

He could do it. He could win. He could beat them all.

Nodding, he knelt by his bed and retrieved the sack hidden under the loose floorboard, taking care to be sure that he was well away from the window.

The huntress's totem was what he most wanted. The miniature Jesus, corn king *in extremis*. It was his totem now, and with it came part of his adversary's power. He draped the chain around his neck, then concealed the figurine beneath his shirt.

He took Erica's scarf also, stuffing it in his pants pocket. He could feel his sister's spirit in the cloth, the impress of her personality.

And the gun. Robert disliked guns, as he disliked most modern things, products assembled on conveyor belts, stamped by the cold luster of the industrial age. Nevertheless, he wedged the gun inside his waistband behind his right hip, where it pressed against the small of his back like a cold, bony hand.

The extra cartridges, taken from Diana-of-the-forest's ammunition pouch, went into his shirt pocket. He buttoned the pocket to seal his treasures inside.

There was nothing else in the box but his soiled clothes, which he had no need of, and one other item, small and flat and rectangular.

Andrew Stafford's business card. He'd forgotten about it.

Robert picked up the card and studied the message on the back. *We need to talk.*

He didn't want to waste time on Andrew when destiny beckoned. He nearly crumpled the card and threw it away.

But . . .

Andrew could make trouble for him, if he wanted to. Serious trouble.

Dealing with the man might take an hour or two, but then Robert would be free of him and the threat he posed.

"Free," he whispered.

Free of Andrew. Free of Erica. Free of the voices that plagued him. Free, even, of Connor's suspicions, if his plan went as he expected.

Whatever risk he had to take, the reward justified it. If successful, he would be hounded no longer, neither by men nor by gods. He could rejoin society. The scapegoat, miraculously cleansed, would be welcomed through the village gate. The stain of pollution would be lifted from the suppliant, and there would be rejoicing.

He would do it, then. Call Andrew. Meet with him.

Kill him.

Then perform the ceremony in the caves, and dip his hands in a chalice of his sister's sacral blood.

A mistake—a stupid, unforgivable *mistake*.

The lantern hit the floor in a spray of shattered glass and a harsh flare-up of ignition. Reflexively Erica averted her face from the shrapnel and the burst of heat. Her cheek went numb. She'd been cut or something, but it didn't matter. Nothing mattered, except that she had screwed up, damn it, she'd done it wrong and wasted her one chance.

She hadn't kicked the lantern hard enough. She'd needed to sweep it forward, send it flying into space to crash under the table. Instead she'd merely jostled it off its perch, and it had dropped straight down, falling short of the table by a full yard.

Sudden smoke filled the cave with an acrid tang. The heat receded slightly, and she dared to open her eyes.

A puddle of kerosene was spreading across the limestone floor, burning vigorously, releasing thick fumes, but too far from the table to help her.

She squirmed, hoping that by some miracle the straps would have loosened anyway, but she was still held fast.

More smoke rose. She turned away and coughed weakly, wondering if she would suffocate before the kerosene was consumed.

Great plan, Erica, she thought bitterly. Just brilliant.

She tested her bonds again. Of course they remained secure. The fire hadn't even scorched the bottom of the table, hadn't frayed or weakened the straps at all.

When she looked at the fire again, she saw the smoke diminishing as the pool of kerosene rapidly dwindled. She wouldn't suffocate. Instead she would be left in darkness when the fire burned out, still tied down and now more helpless than before, because she was unable to see.

Stupid, she told herself. So stupid to try this.

Her cheek was stinging now. She felt something warm and wet trickle down the side of her face. Blood. She'd been cut by flying glass, but it didn't seem too serious . . .

Glass.

A new thought, and a sudden, desperate urgency.

Was there glass? Broken glass—within reach? A tool she could use, a way to cut herself free?

She craned her neck, surveying the inclined tabletop, and yes, there—she saw it—a long jagged shard glittering near her bound wrists, above her left shoulder.

It had nicked her cheek and landed close by, and she was almost sure she could reach it.

Wrists twisting, she groped for the shard with the fingers of her right hand.

Just out of range.

"Damn it, *no!*"

She jerked savagely at the straps, staining with her right hand, and between her index and middle fingers she snagged the precious fragment.

It trembled in her grasp. Carefully, so carefully, she lifted the shard, drawing it into her hand, closing her thumb and other fingers over it until her grip was secure.

The sharp edges inflicted paper-fine cuts on her fingers and palm. She didn't care. Pain was irrelevant. She had a chance. That was what mattered. She had a chance.

The cave went dark.

It happened in an instant. There was a fading fire glow, the dance of orange and red luster on the walls, then a fall of blackness, sudden and absolute.

The fire had burned out.

She couldn't see. For a panicky moment she was sure she'd dropped the glass shard in her surprise.

No, no, it was still in her hand.

All right, then. She didn't need eyesight to do this. She could work by feel.

Flexing her right wrist, she found the loop of canvas that secured her left arm. Gently she pressed the shard's leading edge to the strap, then began a slow sawing motion.

Back and forth, back and forth. The canvas had to yield. Just had to.

Without light she couldn't tell if she was making progress. Her shoulders ached. The air was acrid with lingering smoke. She found it hard to draw breath.

A sense of déjà vu crept over her. There was something uncannily familiar about it all—the tightness in her chest, her squirming body, and the tabletop itself, smooth and cold against her back, like the tiled shower stall . . .

That was it. The shower this morning, after her four-mile run at daybreak. In a cone of steaming spray she had lathered her hair and soaped down her skin, feeling energized and happy. Then the door slid wide and Andrew was there, bursting in, manhandling her with savage need, nearly raping his own wife against the tiled wall in the soapy stream.

She groaned, hating the memory.

The way he'd taken her—it had been as brutal as a crime, and different, so different, from what she'd had with Ben Connor. Ben, who never rushed her or forced her, Ben whose large hands moved with unself-conscious skill over the white hills of her breasts and the flat muscles of her belly, and who brought her to release in the instant before he emptied himself in her.

Something tore.

Erica heard it, the most welcome sound in the world, the soft protest of ripping canvas.

She tested the left strap. It was weaker, fraying, but it still held her.

"Come on," she whispered, going back to work, dragging the shard across the strap in rapid strokes, oblivious to the ache and exhaustion in her arms.

She thought about the two men in her life, one so cultured and refined, the other unpolished and streetwise—yet it was Andrew who knew how to hurt her, scare her, and Ben Connor who never had.

She could hurt him, though. She already had, without meaning to. She'd hurt him with her unexplained remoteness, her self-protective wariness, her unspoken expectation of abandonment, which he must have felt as rejection or, at best, reserve. She'd hurt him by running, always running. Running from him—from the past—from all the pain she'd found too hard to bear.

He might have understood some of this, but not enough. And she hadn't told him, because she hadn't known it herself.

Well, she knew it now, and she would tell him. No more running, not from him or from anyone. She'd spent her life running, searching, trying to find some meaning and purpose in an existence that seemed empty. But the meaning was not outside her, it lay within, and to set herself free she need only unlock the vault that sealed her heart.

She had learned vigilance, and had suffered for it. Now it was time to rediscover trust.

This was what she needed to say to Ben Connor, the man who most deserved to hear it. And this was why she could not die.

When she tugged again, the left strap gave way, and her hand was free.

"Oh, thank God." Her voice echoed in the dark. "Thank God."

She stretched her left arm, reveling in movement, in the pops of stiff muscles and the slow fire of soreness radiating from her shoulder to her wrist.

Then she raised her arm above her head and tried transferring the glass shard to her free hand.

The attempt failed. Her fingers were slick with sweat, and the shard dropped to the tabletop, sliding on the inclined surface.

She heard its distant tinkle as it hit the floor.

That didn't matter. She could untie herself.

With her left hand she attacked the knot that secured the other strap. The knot was tight, a Gordian puzzle, but she worked her fingers into it, prying at the bunched canvas with desperate urgency.

She would survive. She knew it now. She would escape from underground, find Connor, tell him everything he needed to hear, but her first three words would be: *I love you.*

He'd said those words to her often enough. Fear had stopped her from responding as she should have. Fear had kept her in her marriage bed, unwilling to be a wife to Andrew but afraid to make a clean break. Not anymore.

"I'll divorce him," she whispered, the resolution formed in the moment when she spoke the thought aloud. "Yes. I'll divorce the bastard."

And not discreetly either. She would make it public, show everyone just who and what he was. She would finish him.

He'd married her for money, but he would get none, not a cent. She would sweep him out of her life like so much dirt, and start again, and with Ben she would do it right this time.

The knot unraveled, the strap came loose, and miraculously both hands were free.

She lay gasping for a moment, the nerves of her shoulders and arms and neck lit up like a busy switchboard, transmitting signals of pain. Her exhaustion was more than physical, it was the bone-weariness that followed an emotional catharsis. She felt as if she had climbed a mountain and, at the summit, glimpsed a new horizon. She felt drained. She could have slept for years.

Instead she bent forward at the waist and reached for her right foot, secured by the remaining strap. She had to grope in darkness until she found the knot. Defeating it was as easy as untying a shoelace, so easy that she felt a curious sense of anticlimax when she finally swung her legs off the table and sat upright.

"You did it, Erica," she whispered, the tribute coming back to her in a feathery rain of echoes. "Good job."

Now what?

Return to the sinkhole, obviously. Climb up the shaft.

Almost certainly Robert had removed the rope, but the shaft was narrow, and there were handholds, footholds. She would have to chimney up. It would be a hard climb, but she was in good shape, and she had something to climb for now, a better future to win.

There was just one problem. She had no light.

The full significance of this fact became real to her for the first time.

No light. No lantern, no flashlight, not even a cigarette lighter because, damn it, she didn't smoke.

She slumped forward, sudden despair sapping her elation, leaving her empty of energy and will.

The darkness of the caves was absolute. Above ground, in any normal place, there would always be some light. Even in a sealed room, there would be a trickle of daylight or starlight through a crack under a door or an ambient glow of luminescent clock faces and nightlights. Something, anything. But not here.

Here was blackness as impenetrable and all-encompassing as death.

And the cave system was a labyrinth, a puzzle of blind alleys and circuitous detours. An obstacle course, too—the ceilings studded with stalactites, the walls thick with jutting outcrops, the floors uneven and treacherous, sometimes slimy with mold and brackish water, sometimes veined with fractures, sometimes sliding down into precipitous plunges.

Without light she could go no farther than ten yards before losing her way or trapping her foot in a crevice or fracturing an ankle in a fall.

Without light she was still trapped in this room. She was still Persephone, exiled in the underworld. She remained a prisoner in hell.

Without light she had liberated herself from the straps for nothing.

"Damn," Erica whispered, and hugged herself as she fought back tears.

She couldn't give in now. She'd gotten this far. She could figure something out, some way to defeat the dark. Some way to live.

But if so, she would have to do it soon—because time, she knew, was rapidly running out until her brother's return.

14

It was after eight o'clock, and Charlie Whittaker was about to close down the filling station for the night when a Barrow P.D. cruiser pulled up to the service island. He saw two cops inside, which was unusual, because ordinarily the local police rode solo. But under the circumstances, he guessed, maybe it wasn't so surprising after all.

Charlie had heard about it on the local radio station, first as a bulletin interrupting a stream of golden oldies, then as periodic updates throughout the evening. But even before the bulletin, he'd known something was up. The road had told him, the stretch of Route 36 that he watched during the long lonely hours of his shift, the way another man might sit and watch the sea.

The road had been busy with police cars—mostly Barrow P.D. and sheriff's department units, but an occasional state trooper too. Once an ambulance sped past, siren yodeling. He'd worried maybe there'd been a bad accident or some kind of hold-up, and then the radio had told him the real story.

But no details. And because the details were what he wanted and needed to know, he left his glass booth and sauntered across the tarmac to the two cops filling their Chevy with 87 octane.

In the wan wash of the service court floodlights he identified the pair as officers Woodall and Hart, who came in now and then. Hart always reminded him of the bullies who'd made his life unpleasant throughout his school years, but Woodall he liked.

They were talking quietly, tension in their voices and in their ragged chuffs of breath. Something about Chief Connor and what a hard-ass he was, and what the hell did he think he was running, a goddamned seminary?

Woodall said that. Hart didn't seem to know what a seminary was, and truth be told, Charlie didn't, either.

"Hey, guys," he said as he drew near.

Hart just grunted. Woodall showed him a preoccupied smile with no life in it. "Charlie."

"Lots of news on the radio." Charlie planted himself by the pump, hearing the steady click of the gauge counting tenths of a gallon, a sound he found reassuring somehow. "Something happened in Barrow Woods."

The upward lilt of his voice made it a question, but neither man responded. He tried a more direct approach.

"They, uh, they're saying an officer was shot. That true?"

Hart turned away, his shoulders bunched up. But Woodall nodded. " 'Fraid so."

"Barrow P.D. cop?"

"Yeah."

Charlie's heart kicked a little, and he knew he was scared to ask the next question, but damn if he didn't have to know.

"Who?" he whispered.

Woodall looked up at him, raw hurt stamped on his face. "It's Vicki," Woodall said. "Vicki Danvers."

The world tilted, and Charlie was suddenly glad he had the pump to lean on, the pump that was so firm and solid in a reality that had turned to Jell-O all around him.

"Oh," he whispered. "Oh, jeez."

This was what he had feared. The dread had been with him ever since the first coherent report on the radio, and the awful words about the possible shooting of a law enforcement officer.

"You okay, Charlie?" Woodall asked.

He realized both cops were staring at him.

"Yeah," he said through a curious thickness in his throat. "I'll be fine. It's just . . . I was afraid it was her. See, she stopped in here this afternoon, so I knew she was close by." He focused his thoughts. "She gonna make it? She gonna pull through?"

Hart and Woodall exchanged a glance. Hart answered this

time, his tone gentler than Charlie had ever heard it. "Sure she will. Vick's tough."

"Last we heard," Woodall added, "she was in surgery at the county medical center. They got good doctors there, the best around."

"Sure hope so." Charlie struggled to say more, though his throat was threatening to close up entirely. "Is there a suspect?"

"Yeah," Hart snarled, "there's a suspect, all right."

Woodall cautioned him to keep still. But Hart wasn't having any of it.

"If Connor wasn't such a pussy, we'd have that crazy son of a bitch in lockup right now."

Charlie knew of only one bona fide crazy person around, and that was Robert Garrison, the hermit in his cabin. But he couldn't picture Robert actually hurting anybody. He was harmless, or so Charlie had always thought.

The pump nozzle clicked off. Woodall replaced it in the cradle and took out his billfold, then glanced at Charlie. "You said she stopped in here?"

Charlie nodded.

"About what time?"

"Afternoon. Not sure exactly. I think it was about a half hour or forty-five minutes before the ambulance and the other police cars started coming by."

"She say anything to you? Give you any idea where she was headed, or why?"

"No, I . . ."

Then Charlie remembered. Funny how he'd forgotten until now. Worry about the news reports, the sick prescient fear that it might be Vicki who'd been shot—Vicki with her sweet smile and her square, honest face and the crucifix she wore for luck—had driven all other considerations from his mind.

He couldn't speak for a moment. Hart and Woodall both took a step closer. Hart asked what was the matter.

"I guess maybe I had . . ." Charlie paused to swallow the lump that was forming in back of his tongue. "Maybe I had something to do with it. I mean . . . she asked me if I'd seen a white Mercedes, and well, I had. I told her so."

"That's okay, Charlie." Woodall nudged his arm. "You did right."

"Yeah, but . . . she went after it. Went in that direction just because of what I said. Did she . . . did somebody shoot her because of the car? Was it finding the car that got her hurt?"

Neither cop spoke for a moment, but in their eyes he could read the answer.

"Shit," Charlie whispered, Charlie who never swore, because his folks had raised him better than that.

"It ain't your fault, man," Hart said with something like gruff sympathy.

"Look, she'll pull out of it." Woodall sounded as if he was working overtime to persuade himself. "She's tough, like we said. And the bullet didn't get her heart or anything."

"She'll be back on her feet in no time."

"Bet on it."

Charlie nodded, unable to speak, hating himself and his stupid game of watching the road. If he hadn't been watching, if he'd never seen the damn Mercedes, Vicki wouldn't be in surgery now.

"We might need a statement from you," Woodall said, breaking into the downward spiral of his thoughts. "Not tonight. Things are a little busy. Tomorrow maybe. Can we reach you here?"

Charlie summoned the strength to answer. "Sure thing. I work the afternoons, two to eight. Morning, I'll be home. Need my number?"

"You in the book?" Charlie nodded. "Then just your last name'll do."

"Whittaker. That's with two t's."

"Gotcha. Don't fret."

Woodall paid with a twenty, and Charlie made change out of his own pocket, unconscious of what he was doing, operating purely by habit.

The two cops were climbing back in their car when Hart paused. "Hey, Charlie. You know, we . . . well, we care about her too."

Then he ducked inside, and Woodall cranked the ignition hard, rousing a scream of complaint from the starter.

The squad car pulled away, and Charlie was left alone on the concrete island in the floodlights' glare, feeling scared and guilty and baffled by the monstrous unfairness of the world.

The slim manila folder was tucked away in Paul Elder's file cabinet, at the back of the bottom drawer. Even with the drawer fully opened, a wedge of shadow hid the folder from view, and Connor, kneeling, had to peer closely to read the hand-lettered label.

GARRISON.

He took out the folder. Its edges carried a thin coat of dust, fuzzy like felt. No one had opened the file in years. It was something old and forgotten, and as such it suited the Elder house, with its rows of knickknacks from long-ago vacations, its upholstered furnishings shiny with wear, its air stale with a musty nursing-home smell that lingered everywhere like the nearness of death.

Connor checked his watch. There was a great deal to do. He wanted another talk with Andrew Stafford, for one thing. Great Hall was only a ten-minute drive from here; he ought to get going.

And there was Vicki Danvers to check on. Last he'd heard, she was still in surgery, her prognosis uncertain. She had no family in town, and no Barrow P.D. personnel could be spared to stand watch at the hospital. But there must be someone, somewhere, who could go. Connor could stop at the station, ask around, and while he was there, he could pick up a portable radio to replace the one he'd given Elder. After that . . .

Return to Erica's shop, maybe. Give it a more thorough inspection. If necessary, bring in the sheriff's forensics team.

So much to do, and obviously there was no time to study a file that had languished unread in the bottom drawer of a dusty cabinet.

Still, as he got to his feet, Connor somehow let the folder fall open in a slant of lamplight, displaying the first item inside.

It was a letter, neatly typed on Barrow P.D. stationery. The date was March 4, 1983, and the signature at the bottom was Paul Elder's.

Connor scanned the letter. Elder had written to a certain Dr.

Lester Kondracke in Baltimore. No professional affiliation was listed; the letter had been sent to Kondracke's home address.

The letter itself was nearly empty of content, one of those enclosed-please-find cover notes, with a reference to "the material we discussed over the telephone." Elder thanked Kondracke for his kind assistance.

Assistance in what? And why should Barrow's chief of police—a promotion Elder had obtained in the early Eighties, as Connor recalled—require the assistance of a Baltimore doctor in a matter that presumably involved the Garrison family?

Connor turned the page and found an autopsy report.

He'd looked at a few in the course of his career, though not as many as a detective would see. This one was dated June 17, 1973, and its subject was Duncan Colin Garrison, a Caucasian male aged fifty-three.

Robert and Erica's father. Connor frowned.

He knew little about Duncan Garrison, except that the man had died suddenly when the two kids were still in grade school. He'd been late in marrying, and his wife Lenore had been many years younger—a trophy, people said.

In 1973, he calculated, Erica would have been eleven. She never spoke of her father's death, and Connor hadn't thought of raising the issue with Elder. Vaguely he'd understood that it had been sudden and shocking. He'd imagined a car wreck or a heart attack.

Connor flipped through the yellowed pages, a blurry photocopy of the original report, his practiced eye picking out key phrases.

Cyanosis . . . petechial hemorrhages . . . effusion of milky froth from mouth and nasal cavities . . . significant heart trauma . . . acute pulmonary edema . . . water in the lungs . . .

At the end, the coroner's summary. *All indications are that the subject, while swimming alone in Turtle Pond, suffered a massive coronary episode and drowned.*

So it had indeed been a heart attack, as Connor had half-guessed. Well, such things happened. Riding patrol, he'd seen plenty of examples in New York.

The name Turtle Pond was familiar. He thought for a moment, then realized he had been there once, on a chill January day. It lay just beyond the grounds of the Great Hall. He had sat for a while on a rock near the ice-flecked water, watching flights of ducks pass like check marks across the dull white sky.

In summer the pond, though small, would be pretty enough. It was the sort of place a man might go for a solitary swim.

Connor flipped back through the autopsy report and found a reference to the stomach contents. Sausage and eggs, partially digested. Breakfast. Duncan had died in the morning, then.

He thought of Erica's morning ritual, a vigorous jog through the woods. Perhaps her father had maintained a similar regimen, only in his case, weather permitting, he'd started his day with a swim in Turtle Pond. On this particular morning, he'd overtaxed his heart and paid the final price.

Stapled to the last page of the report was a contact sheet of autopsy photographs. Connor squinted at the tiny images long enough to see a nude, slightly bloated body on a steel table, the whitish skin vivid with patches of dark red lividity. The sequence of photos traced the disassembly of the corpse in clinical detail.

Connor was still studying the photos when a low shuddering moan drifted into the room like a cry from a grave.

For a disoriented moment he imagined it was Duncan he heard, Duncan who'd lain on the steel table under the fluorescent chill, Duncan crying for help or, like an Elizabethan ghost, for vengeance.

Ridiculous. Down the hall was the spare bedroom Lily Elder used, now that she could no longer climb the stairs to the second floor. The live-in nurse, Corinne, had put her to bed more than an hour ago, but she must have awoken. Confused in the dark, she was calling inarticulately for help. Corinne's fast footsteps answered the summons, and Connor heard snatches of gentle reassurance in a cooing tone. The small drama must be replayed endlessly throughout every day and night.

There were no ghosts. Yet something in the autopsy report had indeed cried out, in its own way—cried out to Paul Elder for further investigation.

It seemed Elder had kept his suspicions to himself until he was in a position to pursue the matter on his own, with no superiors to interfere. And when he had reopened the investigation, he'd done it unofficially. That was the only explanation for mailing the material to Kondracke's home address.

The next item in the file was the doctor's letter in reply. Dated two weeks after Elder's, it summarized a phone conversation in terse, carefully qualified language.

As per our discussion of March 10, Kondracke had written, *I am returning the enclosed items along with my findings. As I indicated, these findings are provisional and cannot be verified from the evidence at hand. Nevertheless it is my opinion that the cause of death in this case may have been cyanide poisoning.*

Connor released a slow, thoughtful breath.

Cyanide.

Nothing like this had ever come to light. He would surely have heard about it. Even the mere suspicion of foul play would have lingered as a local scandal for years.

Elder said he'd kept the file to himself. He'd meant it.

With effort Connor focused on the letter again.

Evidence for this hypothesis, Kondracke continued in his professorial tone, *includes the following:*

> *a) the distinctive, deep red or royal purple coloration of the lividity reported by the coroner and visible in the attached photographs*
>
> *b) the corroded condition of the stomach*
>
> *c) the unnaturally dark scarlet coloration of the blood*
>
> *In addition, both the obvious damage to the heart and the effusion of froth from the nasal passages, while consistent with the cardiac arrest/drowning hypothesis, are equally consistent with the recent cyanide-poisoning fatalities I have investigated.*

Connor paused on the last words. Recent fatalities Kondracke had investigated. He was a coroner himself, then. The name was vaguely familiar, wasn't it? Kondracke . . .

He pursued the smoky thread of a thought, standing absolutely still, only his eyes moving as his gaze wandered the den. It was a small room, comfortable but nondescript, with a patched-up couch facing a thirteen-inch TV on a wheeled cart,

and in the corner a potted fern, its large sprawling leaves darkened by dust. Lily would have done the cleaning; without her,
the Elder home was going slightly to seed. She'd done the
cooking, too, and . . .

Cooking.

He remembered now.

It had been a huge story at the time. A chef's assistant at a
restaurant in downtown Baltimore sprinkled cyanide in the fish
chowder. Thirty lunchtime patrons consumed the soup before
the poison's delayed reaction triggered dizziness, convulsions,
and collapse. Eight people died, including the chef, who had
sampled the soup before allowing it to be served. Food poisoning of a more conventional sort was suspected until Baltimore's
chief medical examiner found evidence of cyanide. Investigators linked the chef's assistant to a woman who worked in a
pharmacy lab. Both confessed. The assistant's motive was a
grudge against the restaurant. He had been turned down for
a raise.

The crime had taken place in the early Eighties, hadn't it?
Around 1983? The year Elder had sent his letter. And the alert
medical examiner had been Lester Kondracke, of course. The
man had been briefly famous. Later he'd authored a book about
the case.

So. Elder, suspecting cyanide in Duncan Garrison's death,
had chosen to contact a forensic pathologist superbly qualified
to test that diagnosis.

But not to prove it. Kondracke's letter concluded with an ad-
mission that proof was impossible.

*Because the Barrow County coroner did not perform the
necessary toxicological tests,* Kondracke had written, *there is
no direct evidence of cyanide in the body. Nor would exhumation of the remains yield such evidence at this late date, owing
to the chemical breakdown of cyanide into carbon and nitro-
gen over time.*

The letter concluded with a dry "Sincerely" above Kondracke's
illegible signature.

There was no proof. Was this why Elder had kept the new
findings to himself? The explanation seemed inadequate. At
the very least, the case could have been reopened. Duncan had

left two children, both grown to adulthood by 1983. Erica and Robert had a right to know the truth about their father's death.

Connor idly turned the page, not expecting to find anything else in the folder. But there was one last item.

A crinkled clipping from the Barrow *Register*, June 17, 1973. In oversized capitals the headline shouted: GARRISON SCION DIES IN DROWNING ACCIDENT.

Connor studied the news story and the grainy photo that accompanied it. Slowly he nodded.

He knew why Paul Elder had remained silent all these years. In Elder's place, he would have done the same.

He replaced the file but kept the *Register* page, which he tucked in the pocket of his jacket. When he left the den, Corinne was still comforting Lily down the hall, the nurse's voice a singsong whisper, her shadow large on the faded floral wallpaper.

Connor let himself out, and the night air, cold and clean, had never felt so good.

He slipped into his squad car and heard the squawkbox cackling his call number. Thumbing the transmit button on the handheld mike, he acknowledged. "This is A-one. Go."

"Chief, I've got Lieutenant Maginnis requesting a conference on Tac One."

Connor thought for a moment. With the news already leaked to the media, local reporters and miscellaneous curiosity-seekers were certain to be monitoring the police bands. The tactical frequency would afford no privacy.

"Has she got her cell phone with her?" he asked.

"I'll check . . . Yes, sir."

"Tell her I'm calling now."

He activated his own cell phone and punched in the lieutenant's number. She answered on the second ring.

"Maginnis here." Lingering irritation soured her voice, or maybe it was just a trick of the cell phone's cheap receiver.

"This is Connor. What's up?"

"Nothing's up. Hausen and I supervised a grid search of the whole area around the crime scene, a square mile, and nobody found a damn thing. I'm requesting permission to close down the search."

"Can you expand the perimeter?"

"Christ . . . She's not here, Ben. Get it? She's gone. She was taken in the second goddamned vehicle. You know it. I know it. This is a waste of time."

"I'll decide about that. See if Hausen will expand the perimeter."

"He won't. He's leaving, and taking his deputies with him. It's over."

Hell. Without the deputies, there wouldn't be enough personnel to cover a larger search area.

"Even the damn reporters are gone," Maginnis added. "Gaines from the radio station, Berghoff from the *Register*. They followed one of the squad cars out here and got in our way for a while. Then they"—her voice caught—"they got a hot tip that the shooting victim at County Medical died on the operating table. So they amscrayed over there."

Connor heard the question she was too proudly stubborn to ask. "It's got to be a false alarm," he said, praying this was true. "I would've been informed by now, if . . . if Vicki had . . ."

"That's the way I figured it." Her voice was not quite steady. "Another bullshit rumor."

"Last I heard, she was still in surgery."

"Right. Right . . ." He could feel her shake off emotion with an act of will. "Look, Ben, we're freezing our butts off, and we've been at this for about four and a half hours, and there's nothing more we can do here. So I repeat, I'm requesting permission to clear out."

Connor stalled, needing time to think. "How about forensics? They ever show?"

"Here and gone. They bagged and tagged some miscellaneous items and got a rough measurement of those tire tracks, but not a cast."

"Could it be a truck?"

"Wide enough, yeah, but like I said, the measurements are rough; we can't pinpoint it. The tracks weren't left by the Mercedes, though."

"Where's the Mercedes now?"

"Towed away after forensics was done. It's in the county impound lot."

"You're sure the patrols really covered the area?"

"Yeah, Ben, we covered it. I'm telling you, there's nothing."

"I still think she's there. Somewhere. Somewhere close."

"Why the hell would you say that?"

Connor had an answer. After the interrogation in the cabin, he was certain Robert Garrison was the perp. Yet there was no blood or other incriminating evidence in Robert's cabin—or in his truck, as Hart and Woodall had illegally determined. It was unlikely, then, that Robert had transported Erica from the crime scene. He must have left her in the woods, somewhere within walking distance of the fire road.

But he couldn't give voice to his reasoning, at least not on the phone. A cellular call was less likely to be monitored than a radio transmission, but it was hardly secure.

"Ben? You still there?"

"Give me a second," he snapped.

Had to think. The problem was, he wasn't the right man for this situation. He was a goddamned city cop, had been all his life. What did he know about tramping around in a forest? He was out of his element. In New York he would have known what to do. If a victim, alive or dead, was thought to be in a building, then you searched the damn building floor by floor, room by room, stairwell by stairwell. And if for some reason it was too dangerous to enter the building, or there were too many niches and crannies for a patrol to search?

Then it was a job for the K-9 unit. The dogs.

"Marge, you ever use bloodhounds around here?"

"Bloodhounds? Oh, Jesus."

"Just answer the question."

"We've used them. Not often. Not in a situation like this, where it's patently obvious—"

"Nothing is obvious. How long will it take to bring in some dogs?"

An angry pause. Then: "I can call Earl Cashew. He lives over near Punxsutawney, raises hounds."

"How long?" Connor pressed.

"Hour or two, maybe. Earl's not as young as he was."

"But he'll do it?"

"We pay his standard rate, yeah."

"Pay it. Get him A.S.A.P. And stay on site with the others

until he arrives. Continue searching. Check every place twice. She's there. She's close."

"We'll need something of hers for the dogs to sniff."

"I'll take care of that." He could get an article of Erica's clothing from Great Hall when he visited Andrew. It would be interesting to observe Andrew's reaction to that request. If he—

Maginnis was talking again, her voice harsh and angry in his ear. "I want to say, for the record, I think this is a waste of department resources. Money and manpower."

"Objection noted."

"I'll put it in writing. And the other situation too."

Danvers, she meant. Connor winced at a cold stab of guilt.

"Do whatever you have to do, Lieutenant," he said calmly. "Just get those dogs. That's an order. Out."

He switched off the phone and sat in the car for a long moment, hoping he knew what the hell he was doing.

Then he revved the engine and pulled away from the Elder house, heading south to Great Hall.

"God damn him."

Maginnis said it softly, not expecting to be overheard, as she pocketed the phone.

Then she felt someone's gaze and, turning, saw Captain Ron Hausen of the sheriff's department watching her from a yard away.

"Problem?" Hausen asked with a lift of his eyebrows.

He was a large man carrying thirty pounds he didn't need, a good deal of it having gathered under his jaw. She'd heard him joke that he'd done so much paperwork that even his chin was now filed in triplicate.

"No," she said with a shrug. "Nothing. It's just . . ."

Her voice trailed off. She wasn't sure she ought to talk about it. But hell, no one else was around. The Barrow cops were continuing their useless search along the perimeter, and Hausen's deputies had already cleared out. For the moment she was alone with him on the dark fire road.

"Just?" Hausen gently prompted.

"Connor. Just goddamned Chief Ben fucking Connor."

There. She'd said it, and with the words she felt a rush of relief at finally, after months of frustration, getting the resentment out into the open where, for once, it might stop eating her alive.

"He wants bloodhounds," she added before Hausen could respond. "Wants me to call in Earl, for Christ's sake."

Hausen chewed on this. "Might not be a bad idea."

"Oh, hell. She's not here. The suspect took her in the second vehicle. If he'd left her anywhere in the area, we would've found her by now. Between your guys and mine, we've eye-balled every inch of the vicinity."

"He's just being thorough," Hausen said.

"He's a fool."

"No, Marge. You're wrong there."

"How would you know?" she snapped, then regretted it. Damn, she had never been any good at talking to people.

But Hausen didn't appear to take offense. "Connor may be tenacious as hell, and he may be a pain in the ass, but he's no fool. At least, nobody in New York ever said so."

"You know about New York?"

"I have some friends there."

"Well, if Connor was so big in NYPD, what's he doing in Barrow? Only one answer. He screwed up, and the New York brass gave him the option of resigning or getting canned."

"No," Hausen said, "that's not it."

His tone, so quiet, almost pensive, caught her up short.

"It's not?" she asked. "Then what's the real story?"

"I'm not sure I should say. Might be better if he told you himself."

"I already asked him. He just walked away."

Hausen nodded, unsurprised. "He's not a talker."

"So you going to spill it, or what?"

The radio on Hausen's belt sputtered briefly, and he cocked his head to listen, then nodded as it became clear that he wasn't being called.

"Guess I've got a minute," he said. "And it's easy enough to tell. See, Connor was a watch commander in Harlem, and he started to think two of his patrol cops had gone bad. They were living a little too high. Lots of drug busts in that precinct, lots of opportunities for a bad cop to pocket part of a stash."

"So what? Tell it to Internal Affairs, let them handle it."

"He tried that approach. But, funny thing, I.A.D. didn't seem interested. Maybe because one of the two cops happened to be the police commissioner's son."

Maginnis grunted.

"So Connor, now, he gets mad. He doesn't give a crap about politics. A rogue cop is a rogue cop, period, no matter whose kid he is. When I.A.D. won't move, Connor confronts the two, says he's on to them and they better cut it out."

"But they didn't."

"No, they were in deep. Came out later that the commish's kid—Cortez was his name—had run up a bunch of gambling debts. He couldn't get out if he wanted to. And the other one, Lomax . . . well, he was just a dumb fuck who liked the action and didn't like being told what to do."

Hausen hooked his thumbs in his belt, and his paunch slipped out another inch or two.

"I guess maybe most guys would let it go after that. I mean, what are you gonna do, right? Save the world? But Connor's not the type to give up. He can't stand knowing there are these two bad apples under his command. I.A.D. won't help, nobody will help, so he'll do it alone. He calls in sick, then stakes out the station house in his personal car. When Cortez and Lomax leave on patrol, he tails them. Nothing happens the first night, so he calls in sick again. Bad case of the flu. He's out for a week, uses up his sick leave. But every night he's out there shadowing that cruiser."

"They didn't catch on?" Maginnis asked, intrigued despite herself.

A shake of Hausen's head. "Connor's smart. Could've been a detective, except he wanted to stay on the patrol side. He knows they'll notice the same car two nights in a row, so he borrows a friend's wheels, or he gets a rental, or he hires a cab for the whole shift. Sometimes he goes ahead of the guys and watches them in his rearview. Sometimes he's on a parallel street. He does whatever it takes, night after night, and those two schmucks never even know their own lieutenant is right on their ass."

"Okay. What's the payoff?"

"After five, six, seven nights—whatever—Connor finally

gets lucky. Cortez and Lomax make a drug bust, book a dealer. Next coffee break, they cruise out of the precinct, drive down an alley. There's this closed-down store, I don't know what it was, dry cleaner or something. Out of business anyway. Somehow these guys have a key to the back door. They go in, come out. Connor videos all this with a night-filtered camcorder loaded with low-light tape. Now he knows the score."

"They ripped off part of the dealer's stash," Maginnis said, putting it together. "But they didn't want to stow it in one of their lockers because they knew Connor was on to them. The shit was too hot to keep at home. So they were using this empty shop as a warehouse."

"Right."

"Why not just sell the stash right away?"

"Probably they wanted to minimize their risk. Accumulate a larger quantity, sell in bulk. Fewer transactions, less chance of getting caught."

"But they were caught anyway. Okay, Connor did a good job. More power to him." Maginnis was still unimpressed.

"That's not all of it," Hausen said. "I told you, this Cortez was the commish's kid."

"So?"

"Connor calls a buddy at I.A.D. that night. Tells him about the tape. Wants a warranted search of the store where Cortez and Lomax are building their stash. His pal says he needs to see the tape first, arranges a meeting for next afternoon, won't do it sooner. That morning Connor locks the tape in his desk. He's out of his office maybe five minutes, and when he gets back, guess what?"

"No tape," Maginnis said.

Nod. "The office was tossed. The locked drawer was pried open. They did this right in the station house in broad daylight, can you believe it?"

"Connor's friend at I.A.D. leaked to Cortez."

"Only explanation. Friendship takes you just so far, you know. Getting in good with the commissioner's brat could take you further."

Maginnis had thought she knew something about office politics, bureaucracy, the craziness of it. But she was wrong. There was nothing like this in Barrow.

"All right," she said slowly. "I'm guessing it didn't end there."

"No way. Connor won't let it end. Sure, he's been screwed. He's got no tape, no proof, no grounds for a warrant, and even if he had a warrant, you know Cortez and Lomax must've cleaned out that store and sold the stash, or flushed it. And I.A.D. won't help him. They can't even be trusted anymore. But he still wants to nail those two bastards, so he starts talking to the last dealer they collared."

"In lockup?"

Hausen nodded. "Naturally the guy won't cooperate. Cortez and Lomax did him a favor by taking most of his stash. Because he was found with less than five hundred grams, he doesn't get the mandatory five years. His lawyer has told him he can plea down to a possession charge. But it being coke, even simple possession is a felony, and with this guy's sheet, he'll do time. So Connor offers a deal. If the guy tells the truth in a sworn statement, Connor will work on the D.A. to drop all charges. The dealer wants to think about it overnight. Connor goes home."

Hausen paused, aware that he had Maginnis's complete attention and quite obviously savoring his hold on her.

"Connor goes home," Marge prompted. "And . . . ?"

"Well, Connor's latest tactic involved a certain risk. You can't talk to a guy in the holding pen without somebody hearing about it. If Cortez and Lomax got clued in to what was going on, they could panic, try something rash. And that's what happened."

"Tell me."

"By now they know Connor will find a way to nail them sooner or later. And they know he's the only one who will. Nobody else is stubborn enough or maybe stupid enough to keep picking at this particular scab. The way Cortez has it figured, no more Connor, no more problems. So that night they decide to hit him."

"Jesus."

"They slip the lock on Connor's apartment door, real professional, and come in loaded for bear. But Connor wakes up—hears them enter, or maybe just senses them, I don't know. He leaves his wife in bed, tells her to get down low, and then he leaves the bedroom with his off-duty weapon cocked and locked. The scroats open up on full automatic, and he shoots back, and wham! he's engaged in an all-out firefight right there in his god-damned living room."

Maginnis was silent for a long moment. She had never been in a gun battle. Couldn't even imagine one, except as a high-light reel of movie action scenes, and the movies never got any-thing right.

"Connor take them out?" she asked finally.

"He wounds one. The two scroats panic and flee. Connor's not hit, he's okay, and he finds a blood trail leading to the stair-well. He knows the lab will match the blood to either Cortez or Lomax."

"So it's over."

"Yeah. Except when he goes back into the bedroom, he finds that a stray bullet went through the wall and nailed his wife."

Maginnis turned away. She felt as if she had been slapped.

"His wife," she echoed.

"Name was Karen. She didn't get down low, like he told her. She was trying to grab the phone, call nine-one-one, when the slug caught her in the throat." A tired shrug. "You know how these apartments are built. Walls are plasterboard and spit. A damn BB could penetrate."

"How long were they married?" Maginnis asked for no reason.

Another shrug. "Years. No kids, but it was solid. Everybody said so."

She just nodded.

"That's not even the worst of it," Hausen said. "The worst was the ballistics report."

Maginnis felt a cold crawl of nausea in her stomach.

"See, the bullet that killed Mrs. Connor—it came out of her husband's 38."

"Shit . . ."

"He wasn't firing toward the bedroom, but you know how a hot round can bounce. Catch a bad deflection, and it flies like a pinball. It wasn't Connor's fault. He was popping caps in self-defense. No one could blame him."

But he blamed himself, Maginnis thought. She was no great student of human nature, but even she could glimpse what Connor had gone through—the pointless guilt, the unremitting self-hate.

After a moment she asked, "Did they nab Cortez and Lomax, at least?"

"Well, yes—and no." Hausen grimaced. "The blood was Lomax's. He was winged, had a broken arm. Bastard knew he was made, so he drove to Philly and tried to hop a jet out of the country, but the airport police picked him up. He couldn't deny involvement, not with his blood at the crime scene and a patched-up bullethole in his left biceps. Still, he refused to finger his accomplice. Cortez was brought in, but he held up under questioning. Refused to take a polygraph on the advice of counsel. Nobody could pin anything on him."

"There was the dealer—the one they busted."

"No luck. He heard about the dust-up in Connor's apartment and decided he'd rather do a little time than get Cortez and Lomax mad at him. Cortez might still be on the force, Mr. Clean, except for those gambling debts of his. Illegal gambling, natch. The investigation uncovered it, and that was how Cortez got bounced. Conduct unbecoming, and all that." He paused. "And a couple days later, Ben Connor turned in his badge."

"Why? He won, didn't he? I mean, he didn't put Cortez away, but even so, he *won*."

"He might not have seen it that way. Take his buddy at I.A.D., for one thing. The guy clearly talked to Cortez, but nobody could prove it, so he was just reassigned to Burglary, where he went right on drawing a paycheck. Connor wouldn't have felt too triumphant about that. But I think the real reason was something else."

High on the far ridge where the woods yielded to the shoulder of Route 36, headlights appeared. A car rolled to a stop, and Maginnis read the markings of a Barrow P.D. cruiser.

"Something else," she said quietly, wondering what other indignity Connor had been made to suffer.

"I told you Cortez and Lomax panicked. Lomax never was

very bright, but Cortez had a brain. But when you're scared, you get sloppy."

"I don't follow you," Maginnis said.

The cruiser's doors slammed, and two figures appeared in the dark, tramping quickly down the hillside. By their walk Maginnis knew them as Woodall and Hart.

"Well, there was this rumor." Hausen talked faster now, aware that he had to finish the story before the patrol cops arrived. "Never confirmed. Might not be true. But, see, there were cartridge cases scattered all over Connor's apartment, dozens of the damn things. Rumor was, the forensics guys found fingerprints on some of the cases. And some of those prints belonged to Cortez."

Maginnis nodded, taking it in. A careful perp would wear gloves when loading his piece. But a man in a panic might make the crucial, obvious mistake.

"His prints," Hausen said. "Pretty damning. But somehow this particular fact never made it into the report. Officially there was nothing to tie Cortez to the crime scene."

Maginnis grunted. "Officially. I see."

She did too, and for the first time in her life she felt dirty— dirty just to be a cop.

"Anyway," Hausen went on, "you got to figure the brass wasn't too disappointed with the way things turned out. Lomax took most of the heat, and he's a nobody, expendable. The scandal was contained. The case is cleared. And the commish owes the department a favor. Everybody's happy."

"Except Connor."

"Yeah. Except him."

Woodall and Hart were close now, almost within earshot.

"Only thing I wonder about," Hausen said, dropping his voice to a whisper, "is why he ended up here. All this stuff is on the grapevine. He could've gotten into any big-city department— Boston, Philly, Baltimore. Why does he come to central Pennsylvania, the middle of nowhere, U.S.A.?"

But Maginnis knew the answer to that. Connor had told her, though she hadn't believed him.

"Maybe he needed to get away from cities," she said quietly. "Needed to breathe some fresh air."

Hausen shrugged. "As good a reason as any, I guess. Good night, Marge."

" 'Night, Ron. And thanks."

Hausen tipped his cap at her, and with ponderous dignity he plodded away, passing Woodall and Hart as they reached the fire road.

Maginnis studied the treetops, then the sky. She felt very small.

"Lieutenant?" Woodall's voice. He and Hart had stopped before her. "We're supposed to join the search party."

It took her a moment to realize that some response was called for. "There's been a change of plans. We're bringing in bloodhounds."

"Hounds?" Woodall glanced at Hart, who made a soft noise like a snicker. "That the chief's idea?"

"It is," Maginnis said, and then she smiled, a sudden tight smile that pained her. "Damn good idea, too. Tell you the truth, I wish I'd thought of it myself."

15

Something was wrong.

Paul Elder felt it deep in his bones, a chill of intuition. He sat bolt upright in the front seat of his old Buick, parked in the brush, the distant cabin framed in his windshield.

The lamp in the cabin remained lit. Elder had seen Robert pass in front of the window some minutes earlier, then had seen the man's looming shadow on the interior wall.

The shadow had drifted out of sight, and since then nothing had stirred.

Well, Robert must be lying down on that cot of his. Taking a catnap, or lost in a mystic trance, dreaming of the River Lethe or of his mother's screams.

This was possible. But Elder wasn't sure he believed it.

He was beginning to think Robert had cleared out. Exited from the cabin unseen, leaving it empty.

"Now, Chief," he said reasonably. In private he still referred to himself by his former title. "You see that Ford truck parked up there, Chief? That's Robert's truck. He couldn't leave without it. If the truck's there, so is he."

Maybe.

On the other hand, maybe Robert had left on foot. Having lived in these woods for years, he must know them intimately. Even in the dark he could follow a deer trail, say, or a trail of his own making, and reach Route 36 or one of the back roads in fifteen minutes or so.

"Why would he, Chief? Easier to take the truck."

Easier, yeah. Unless he suspected he was being watched. He might have guessed Connor's plan. Besides, crazy people were paranoid, weren't they? Robert might imagine he was being watched all the time.

Or he might be asleep in bed, or knotted up in a yoga position on the floor, or reading one of those musty books that crowded his shelves.

"How am I supposed to know?" he asked irritably.

Hell. Stupid question. He would need to have a look-see, that was how.

And if Robert had guessed there was a stakeout, and was hoping by his stillness to lure the watcher to the cabin, lure him into a trap?

"Not likely," Elder said.

Even so, he loosened his belt a couple of notches and wedged the walkie-talkie under it, then removed the handgun from his coat pocket. It was his duty weapon, his old Smith .38, which he'd bought from the department upon retirement. He could have taken the gun for free, but he was a man who paid his way.

He checked the Smith to be sure it was loaded. The check was superfluous; he knew he'd tamped six rounds into the charge holes before leaving home, but damn, he was an old man now, and old men made mistakes.

There was no mistake. Six cartridges, sleek and cold.

He held the gun firmly in his right hand as he got out of the car and crept through the tall brush.

It was nearly nine o'clock, and Andrew, rigid with tension on the sofa in the guesthouse, had just about given up hope that the phone would ever ring.

Then, shocking as a gunshot, it did.

He sprang up and reached for the handset, then hesitated for a fraction of a second to compose himself. With an almost steady hand he lifted the phone on the second ring.

"Stafford."

"Hello, Andrew."

The voice was Robert's, thank God.

"Robert." Andrew fought hard against anxiety, maintaining a state of unreal calm. "I'm glad you called."

"I like to stay in touch."

The cool irony of the tone raised Andrew's blood pressure. He suppressed his anger.

"You have her," he asked quietly, "don't you?"

"How do I know there isn't some police detective recording this conversation?"

"Come on now. Do you really think I would do that? Do you think I *could*?"

A thoughtful pause. "I suppose not. You value your freedom too much—even if it is an illusion. We have no freedom, any of us. We're playthings of fate. Flies in a spider web, struggling."

"I asked if you have her."

"Of course I do."

"Is she . . ." Suddenly Andrew couldn't ask it—the most important question. His head pounded. His lips were so very dry. With effort he forced out the words. "Is she alive?"

"Yes."

The phone began to shake in Andrew's hand, and absurdly he thought there was some kind of earthquake or something, and then he realized it was only a spasm of relief.

"That's good, Robert," he managed to say. "It's good she's alive. You haven't, uh, hurt her?"

"She's very comfortable. She'll die soon, of course. Later tonight. She'll die like the other one, with a stroke of the knife. But don't worry. She'll be the last. She's the one who's been meant for me all along. It's not my choice. It's destiny. Her destiny—and mine."

"Now, wait, Robert. Just wait. Listen to me." He was ordinarily so good at selling, persuading, but at the moment he couldn't seem to get his thoughts together. There was tightness in his throat, and he kept tugging at his shirt collar to unbutton it, but it was already open. "Listen, okay?"

"You sound nervous, Andrew."

"I am nervous. I'm scared. I don't want you to hurt her. I want her back."

"Not likely."

"Hear me out, please. You have what I want. All right? We both understand that. But I have what *you* want, Robert."

A beat of silence on the line. "Do you?"

"I got it out of the safe-deposit box today. It's yours for the taking. Just give me Erica, alive."

"You mean to say you would surrender your advantage over me—for love?"

"Call it what you want," Andrew said stiffly.

"No, I want to hear you say it. You love her, don't you? You love my sister."

"I love her. Yes, damn it. I do." The words were like a second marriage vow, more binding than the first.

"You surprise me. I thought you loved nothing but money."

That's what she thinks too, Andrew almost said. But he kept quiet.

"Even so," Robert went on, "you know I can't agree to the deal."

"Why not?"

"Because she'll talk. Set free, she'll run straight to the police and tattle on me."

"No, she won't."

"Nonsense. She'll point the finger. I'll go to jail."

Frustration made Andrew reckless. "If she dies, *I'll* tell the police, God damn you."

"Threats." A chuckle. "You're in this, as well."

"Then we'll go down together, both of us."

"You're much too weak for such heroic gestures."

"Don't count on it. I can play hardball. You ought to know."

Another thoughtful pause. "Yes," Robert said slowly. "I guess you can."

It had been a while since Elder had crept up on a suspect. He tried to figure the best way to do it. Up the driveway was no good—he'd be a clean target from thirty yards away.

All right, then. The cabin had only one window. If he circled around and approached from behind, there was little chance Robert could get the drop on him.

Hunched low, Elder hurried through the brush at the base of

the hill, keeping an eye on the cabin. When it had turned its back to him, showing only the blind rear wall, he decided to make his move.

Fast up the hillside, breathing hard, memories pounding through him with every lurching footfall. He was running in a scatter of bodies on an island in the Pacific, Jap sniper fire falling in a hard sleet all around him, and everywhere the groans of men hit and the pleas of the fallen. He was chasing Hector Davis down a dirt lane after Hector beat the crap out of his old lady and fled from the law, and then Hector was on his knees sobbing that he loved her, and Officer Paul Elder was slapping on the cuffs and saying, *I know*. He was sprinting down Barrow's twilight streets in a jacket and tie, a bouquet flapping in his fist, because his damn car had broken down and he was late for what was only his second date with the beautiful Lily Everson, whom he already meant to marry.

Memories, good and bad, pieces of a life, and then he was at the cabin, hugging the blank wall and hoping goddamned Robert wasn't smart enough to anticipate this maneuver and take him out while he was winded.

Dangerous seconds passed while he caught his breath. When he'd quit sucking air like a landed trout, he checked to see that the gun was still in his hand—yep, right where he'd left it—and then he moved around the side of the cabin, past the throbbing diesel generator and the stacked fuel drums, toward the front door.

"You've been playing rough with me for the past two months," Robert said in his dreamy philosopher's voice, "haven't you?"

"Not as rough as you played with Sherry Wilcott."

"Maybe you would have liked a chance to have her for yourself. Is that really what this is all about? Are you jealous, Andrew?"

"You're insane."

"A predictable reply. Still, I wonder. Did you get a thrill out of handling her clothes? When you dug them up from where I buried them, did you have a—what's the vulgar term?—a hard-on?"

"It was just business."

"I'll bet if you breathe deep, you can smell her in the blouse. It was soaked in perspiration by the end. Translucent with her cold sweat. Then red with her bright arterial blood."

"I'm not the psycho, Robert. You are. I'm in this for the money, not for kicks."

"Is that why you think I took the Wilcott girl's life? For kicks? Is that why you think I'm holding Erica now?"

"I don't care about your motives. I only want her back. Do you get it, Robert? You've got leverage, if you're smart enough to use it."

"Leverage. A term of high finance, by way of physics. Two closely related endeavors, you know. Great bundles of numbers and formulae, and at the root of it all—no physical reality, only a collective will to believe."

Andrew was lost. "I'd love to continue this philosophical discussion, but—"

"No, you wouldn't. You're too shallow and pragmatic to concern yourself with the higher mysteries. Like the whelp Alexander, you'd hack with your broadsword at the Gordian knot, lacking the patience to tease out its secrets. When you suspected me in the Wilcott girl's death, you didn't think to ask why I would do it or what you might learn from me. You thought only of money. Of blackmail."

This was true, of course.

Sherry Wilcott had been found dead on January 21. Andrew had heard the news in town on the day the body was found. What kind of crazy monster, people asked in frightened anger, would take a knife to a young girl?

Andrew knew one answer to that question. Months earlier, when he and Erica were still on speaking terms, she had told him of her visit to Robert's cabin—and how he had attacked her.

Attacked her . . . with a knife.

The Chinese saw opportunity in every crisis. Andrew, facing the imminent termination of his marriage, and the end of his lifestyle of ease and indolence, had seized the opportunity that Sherry Wilcott's death had offered him.

On the night of January 22, he'd gone to Robert's cabin, watching with binoculars until Robert was asleep. Past midnight he'd examined the yard and found a plot of freshly turned earth. With a collapsible shovel from the trunk of his car, he'd exhumed a cache of women's clothes: shoes, underwear, skirt, blouse.

From the news stories published after Sherry Wilcott's disappearance, he'd known the outfit was hers.

Contrary to Robert's charge, he had felt no sexual thrill. The clothes were merely an asset, as unexciting as a sound mutual fund. Robert had handled them while the blood was wet. His bloody fingerprints were stamped on the items in a dozen places, irrefutable proof of his guilt.

Andrew reminded himself of that guilt now. "I don't think you're in a position to pass moral judgments," he said coolly.

"But I am. What I did was only what I was meant to do. Fate dictated, and I obeyed. The girl offered herself to me. Her soul begged for release from its bodily imprisonment. What I did was an act of love and faith."

"If you believe that, you're crazier than I thought."

"You, on the other hand, perceived only an opportunity to enrich yourself. Though I've never understood why such a course of action was necessary. Isn't Erica's fortune enough? Do you really need my half of the inheritance as well?"

"I never intended to take all your money," Andrew said, then regretted it. The lie was transparent, but worse, it put him on the defensive.

"No, of course not." Rare sarcasm bled through Robert's tone. "Only two million, and then another two million, and how much after that?"

Well, all of it, of course. Andrew had meant to bleed Robert dry.

The blackmail scheme had been carefully orchestrated. First, Andrew had placed the apparel in his safe-deposit box, with instructions to his attorney that the box was to be opened in the event of his death.

Then he took a trip. He told Erica he was going to New York, and he did; but at JFK he caught a flight to the Cayman Islands, where he set up a bank account under one of several aliases he'd developed in his earlier career. The bank was known for its discretion, and the assets were hard for U.S. investigators to touch.

Back home, he pinned a note to the door of Robert's cabin, telling him to call a certain number if he wanted to know the whereabouts of the items he'd buried.

Robert had phoned the guesthouse. Andrew had instructed him on what to do. Two million dollars must be transferred from Robert's holdings to the Cayman Islands account. When the transaction had been verified, Andrew would leave the evidence at a drop site near Barrow Falls.

Robert had agreed to go along. Despite his evident mental instability, he retained direct control over his assets. Erica, his only close living relative, had never challenged his competence. Once, early in their marriage, Andrew had asked her why. Her answer had been strange.

I couldn't do that, she'd said. *I could never hurt him again.*

By mid-February two million dollars had been ladled into the account of one Alex Stratford, whose address was a post office box in the Caymans. Then Robert had called again, distraught.

He had visited the drop site. The package Andrew had left contained only the girl's shoes, nothing more.

Where were the other items?

You know, Andrew had said, *two million doesn't go as far as it used to. What do you say we double it? Then I'll give you the rest of her things. Otherwise, I'll send them to the police.*

Another two million by late February, then another phone call from Robert on Andrew's private line. The second package at the drop site had contained Sherry Wilcott's undergarments. Skirt and blouse were still missing.

You'll get them, Robert. Eventually. But that darn cost of living just keeps going up.

When the total reached six million in the first week of March, Robert got the girl's skirt. But not the blouse. It was the final item, and the most incriminating. His bloody fingerprints were all over the thing, plainly visible, crying out in guilt.

Andrew let Robert think the blouse was coming. *Just another half million,* he would say. Then a half million more, and more.

He had the crazy homicidal bastard on a hook, and he enjoyed watching him wriggle and squirm.

Things would have gone on that way until Robert was penniless. Then, when Erica filed for divorce, Andrew would have left the country, losing himself in his smoke screen of aliases, funneling his new millions into a dozen untraceable accounts.

And the blouse? It would never have gone to Robert. The police would receive it in a package mailed from the airport. Andrew did have a conscience, after all. He wouldn't let a murderer roam free indefinitely.

This, at least, had been his game plan. But now the game was up.

"The money," Andrew countered lamely, "isn't the issue anymore."

Robert surprised him by agreeing. "The money never was the issue, not with me. I'm no materialist—in any sense of the word. Look at how I choose to live. Do you imagine wealth matters to me? I could have given it all away without regret. I don't begrudge you the money or even your treacherous route to obtaining it. But I do hate you, Andrew. Do you know why?"

Andrew was severely uncomfortable. The conversation had gone off track. "We don't have time for this."

"I hate you," Robert went on as if there had been no response, "because you are *her* pawn, *her* paramour."

"Whose? Erica's?"

Robert laughed. "Don't you even know the one you serve?"

"Look, it's getting late—"

"I suppose I can't judge you too harshly. She's crafty, that bitch. She can bend any will to her own, make any man her puppet, even a better man than you. Old Will Shakespeare knew her when he wrote his Dark Lady of the sonnets and his Cleopatra, the universal harlot, conquering her conquerors. The romantics wooed her. She was Hugo's Esmeralda and Coleridge's Death-in-Life. She's a trickster, gambler, slut, Lady Fortune, whore-mistress general, and you, Andrew Stafford, are only her latest one-night stand."

This was pure rant, and Andrew wouldn't listen anymore. "Damn it, stop babbling. We've got business to do."

"Business." Sigh. "Yes, with you, always business."

"Just listen to me. I'm offering you an option to get out of this mess. Get out clean, with no trace of suspicion, and be rid of me, to boot. No more money to pay, no more worries about the police. It can be done. Tonight."

"Is your name Merlin? And if not, then how exactly will you manage this particular feat of sorcery?"

"You'll get the package from me. I'll get Erica from you. A straight trade. Then she'll go to the police with some story. We can make up something. She had a blackout episode, perhaps, and found herself wandering by the roadside with no memory of the past few hours. The details don't matter. Her story doesn't even have to make sense, as long as she swears to it. You can't have a crime without a victim."

"And how, pray tell, will you persuade your wife to play along in this little drama?"

Andrew took a breath. "I'll tell her what I've done. How I blackmailed you. It makes me an accessory in the Wilcott girl's murder. I'll tell her that if you're arrested, I'll be next."

"You think she'll lie to protect you?"

"Absolutely," Andrew said, putting all his false conviction into the word.

"Well. That *is* interesting."

Andrew shut his eyes. It was working. The bait had been taken.

The cabin door, its deadbolt still detached from the splintered frame, swung slowly back and forth in a cold breath of breeze. Elder approached it with care, crabbing along the front wall.

He held the Smith in both hands, the nickel-plated barrel glinting in the light of the newly risen moon. The weapon seemed strangely heavy, hard to lift, like something in a dream.

He could use it, though. Whatever pity he might feel for Robert Garrison would not mean a thing when it came to shooting in self-defense.

The door was near. Only a yard away.

"I knew you could be reasonable," Andrew said. "You're smart, Robert. Smarter than I am." That's right, stroke the bastard, massage his ego. "You can see this is best for everybody."

"Yes. Yes, perhaps it is. Where would we make the exchange?"

"The drop site."

"Awfully secluded there. You wouldn't be planning an ambush, would you, clever Andrew?"

"You'll bring Erica. She's your protection. You think I would risk anything with her in the line of fire?"

"Probably not. Then again, suppose I decide to lie in wait for you. How can you be sure I won't?"

"I'll have to trust you," Andrew said.

Robert laughed. "First love, now faith. It's remarkable, this spiritual awakening of yours. Keep it up and you'll be a candidate for beatification before long."

"How soon can you get to the drop site?"

"An hour."

"I'll meet you there. And Robert—God help you if anything happens to my wife."

"God?" Rich mockery flavored the word. "Oh, I made an enemy of her a long time ago. I look up in the night sky, and she's glaring down at me with her cold white eye. She hates me, God does."

Andrew understood little of this, but he thought it was possible Robert felt guilty for old sins. He applied a dose of psychology. "Get Erica back to me unharmed, and it'll make up for anything in your past. You'll be forgiven."

"No, Andrew, there's no forgiveness, not from that bitch you serve. I can only pay her price, if she'll let me. She's a whore at heart. I can buy her, but not with money. Only with blood."

Blood. Not what Andrew wanted to hear. "We do have an agreement, right, Robert? Erica won't be hurt. Right?"

Hesitation. Then: "I'll be there. You'll get your precious wife. Though personally I think you'd do better to buy a dog. Dogs are loyal. They don't . . ."

His voice trailed away.

"Robert?"

"Someone's coming," Robert said softly.

"What?"

"I hear him. He's close. But don't worry. I can deal with it."

"Robert, what the *hell*—"

The line went dead.

Andrew stared at the handset, then slowly replaced it on the cradle. His hand was shaking again, but this time not with relief. With fear.

Because in the instant before the connection was broken, he

was sure he'd heard the cold snick of a revolver's hammer snapping down.

Thing to do was go in fast. No peeking in the doorway. That kind of nonsense was what got cops killed. You went in quick and low and ready for action.

Elder nodded to himself, hugging the door frame.

Robert might be doing something perfectly innocent inside, and Elder might look like a damn fool barging through the doorway with his gun arm extended, but it was better to look like the occasional fool than to be served up on a steel platter in the morgue.

Besides, he couldn't die, because then what would Lily do? She hardly recognized the live-in nurse. Without her husband she would be utterly lost, and Paul couldn't allow that.

So do it the right way. Ready, set . . .

Go.

The door smacked softly in its frame, then swung lazily inward on a new current of air, and Elder followed its motion, throwing it wide, and in a single stride he was through the doorway and into the cabin, his gaze panning the interior over the blur of his gun sight.

Nobody was there.

Robert's cabin was not equipped with a telephone, of course. A phone was one of those modern conveniences he was pleased to do without. To call Andrew Stafford, he'd had to leave the cabin and find a public phone.

And, conscious of being watched, he'd been careful to leave unobserved.

It had been easy enough. He'd simply dropped down on his hands and knees, below the window, then slithered out the front door. Concealed in shadows, he had belly-crawled in the tall grass down the back slope.

Once safely at the bottom of the hill, he had no further need for stealth. He broke into a run, agile and tireless as a wolf, covering ground in long loping strides. And as he ran, the moon rose low over the treetops, a horned crescent, its cold light bathing his face.

A waning moon. Death moon.

In a clearing, immersed in the leprous white glare, he had fumbled the crucifix out from under his shirt collar and raised the silver Jesus to the sky.

"See, moon goddess?" he'd whispered. "See, he's mine now, your totem. You can't hurt me now. Your devil dogs had best keep their distance now."

It had occurred to him that people would say he was crazy, talking to the moon. But people didn't understand.

With the crucifix flapping at his throat, catching spangles of stray moonlight, he had made his way to Route 36 and the gas station on the roadside. The place was dark and quiet, closed for the night, and he'd been certain he could find privacy here, as he had on all previous occasions when he'd called Andrew.

But on this night, it appeared he'd been mistaken.

Slowly he turned away from the pay phone, the revolver down at his side in the shadows.

From the dark a hoarse male voice ordered, "Hold it, mister."

Robert stared across yards of tarmac at a tall, scrawny kid in a ridiculously bulky overcoat, facing him over the barrel of a shotgun.

"Just hold it right there," the kid said, baring his teeth, trying hard to look mean. "Just don't you move, okay?"

Robert knew this kid. Having pulled in here a few times to tank up his truck, he remembered the pimpled, chinless clerk who worked the afternoon shift. What was his name? Oh, yes.

"Hey, Charlie," Robert said, keeping the revolver low and out of sight.

Elder swept the room once again with his eyes, a rapid survey, then lunged into a corner, afraid Robert was outside and would shoot him in the back while he stood on the threshold. But no shot came.

Gone. The son of a bitch was really gone.

Though Elder was sure of it, he took the precaution of searching the cabin and the immediate grounds. Robert's truck was still there, but there was no Robert in the truck or under it or hiding beneath the tarp, and there was no Robert playing hide-and-seek in the shadows of the cabin, either, as far as Elder could tell.

Somehow the man had crept away unseen, though Elder had watched the cabin steadily the whole time. Was there a secret exit, some kind of sliding wall panel or hidden tunnel? No, that was nonsense.

Well, maybe Robert had spent so much time communing with woodland spirits, he'd become a sort of spirit himself. Maybe he could make himself into smoke and just drift on the wind, to be reconstituted in his corporeal form somewhere far away.

The idea, preposterous though it was, raised a welter of gooseflesh on Elder's arms, and under his coat he shivered with a chill.

"Oh, hell," he said too loudly, and launched a wad of spit into the dark. "No magic about it. Bastard snookered me, is all. Him and his River Lethe got the goddamned last laugh."

The sound of his own voice was reassuring. He felt better.

Even so, he walked quickly away from the cabin, down the dirt driveway toward his hidden car, and around him the forest lay dark and quiet under a spray of stars and the crescent moon.

"It's just me," Robert said with a slow, false smile. "Robert Garrison. I drive a Ford truck. You know."

"Oh." The shotgun lowered, but only slightly. "Hey, Mr. Garrison. Aren't you cold, without a coat?"

The question seemed innocent enough, the gambit of a friendly conversation—but Robert noticed that the gun was still aimed at him, and Charlie was no less nervous than before. He wondered if the kid had overheard part of the phone conversation.

"I never notice the cold," Robert said. "I could go naked in weather like this."

"Hope you got on your flannel undies, at any rate."

"Nope." He wore only a denim shirt, long pants, and boots.

"Well, you must have ice water running in you. 'Cause it's freezing out here." Charlie's teeth chattered briefly, punctuating the statement. "Cold as a witch's tit, don't you think?"

"I don't know any witches." This was a lie, of course. He knew Erica. "So, Charlie . . . what's with the gun?"

"I heard somebody here, and no car had pulled in. That's kind of unusual."

"Well, my truck wouldn't start, and I had to make a phone call. My cabin's not far from here. I figured I could make it on foot."

"Guess so." The shotgun still had not dipped, and Charlie was frowning in fierce concentration.

Robert slipped the cocked revolver carefully into his waistband, behind his back, then took a casual step forward. "Thought you were closed," he said. "Everything's dark."

"Well, I did close up, but I stayed here, out back, kind of thinking."

"Thinking?" This seemed an unusual occupation for Charlie.

"Yeah, well, this hasn't been such a good day."

"Why not?"

"Because this cop I know, sort of a friend, who stops in here sometimes—well, anyway, this cop got shot." He directed a sudden probing gaze of raw intensity directly at Robert's face. "Hear about it?"

Robert shrugged. "Afraid not. I don't own a radio or a television. I prefer to keep the world at bay."

"The police—they, uh, didn't happen to stop by?"

So that was it.

Some cops—undoubtedly the huntress's allies, Woodall and Hart—must have told Charlie about the interrogation. That was why Charlie was studying him so fiercely, and why the shotgun had barely moved.

"A couple of patrolmen did come around," Robert allowed, "and asked if I'd heard any gunshots in the woods." He stepped closer to Charlie and spread his empty hands. "I couldn't help them, and they went away. But they never mentioned that a fellow officer had been killed. How awful."

The performance seemed to win over its audience. Charlie let the nose of the shotgun drift downward a few degrees.

"Actually," Charlie said, relaxing slightly, "she wasn't killed."

Robert blinked. His face, he was sure, betrayed no reaction. Yet inwardly he was suddenly drained, hollowed out. He had left the huntress for dead, but she had not died.

"She," he echoed, seizing on the first safe thing to say. "So it's a female officer?"

His evident surprise appeared to relieve the last of Charlie's doubts. The shotgun hung vertically, no longer a barrier between them.

"Yeah." Charlie showed a slightly goofy smile. "Her name's Vicki. She's real nice. Vicki Danvers."

Distantly it occurred to Robert that the name Vicki was all wrong for the huntress or even her human emissary. The girl should have been named Cynthia or Diana—other names for the goddess Artemis, who was *the* goddess, the one and only, the virgin-mother-crone.

"Do you know if Vicki will be all right?" Robert asked, sincere concern in every syllable of the question.

"Can't say. Last I heard, she was still in surgery."

The kid's voice cracked on the last word, and Robert understood that he was lovesick for his Vicki. He was in her thrall, another of the strumpet's paramours—and for this reason he was dangerous.

"I see," Robert said, and took another step. He was six feet from Charlie now.

"She'll make it, though. She's got to."

"Yes." Robert nodded. "She'll make it."

She would, of course. He had missed his opportunity to kill the huntress in her human form, and so he had not stolen her power, and her totem, which he had been so proud to wear, was useless to him, a bauble, a mockery.

Involuntarily his hand rose to the crucifix, wanting to jerk it from his neck, then drew back.

Too late.

Charlie had seen it.

There was something in his eyes. A sudden sharpness. A narrowing. Recognition.

Charlie had identified the totem, knew it was hers.

The clerk's gaze flicked to Robert's face, and for an instant their eyes met.

The shotgun swung up.

But Robert was faster. He plucked the huntress's revolver from the small of his back and fired one shot at a distance of six feet.

Charlie's face puckered, the bullet shattering the bridge of his nose in a wet explosion, and he went down in a flapping pile of limbs.

Robert shot him again, then a third time, and the clerk lay still. A black seepage of blood blossomed around him, glossy as the petals of a flower.

Dead. Where there had been life, there was only its raw materials, deprived of their mystic animating essence.

Robert felt himself shaking, shaking not with cold, despite the weather, nor with delayed fear after a close call. What shook him was a kind of passion—yes, passion, a word that signified both joy and suffering. He exulted in the blood he'd drawn, breathed in its copper scent, dizzy with triumph. Yet he sorrowed too, because Charlie had been only a toy of the one he served, a plaything capriciously selected, indifferently discarded. His unimportant life had been tossed away like scraps from the dinner table to feed the maw of fate.

Standing over his victim, breathing fast, Robert replaced the revolver in his waistband and said a prayer for Charlie, to speed his soul to Hades, where he might drink of forgetfulness and lose all memories of this life.

Then a bad thought struck him. He had left the huntress for dead, and she was not dead.

Could this one, too, be playing possum?

He knelt by Charlie and hauled him half upright, groping his neck for a pulse. There was none.

All right, then. All right.

The clerk was dead, really dead, not a faux corpse like Vicki Danvers.

And no one would suspect him of the crime. How could they? If he was right about Connor, then somebody was watching the cabin right now, perhaps at this very moment reporting into a police radio or a cellular phone: *He's still in there. I haven't seen anybody come out, and his truck hasn't moved.*

The police themselves would vouch that he had spent the night in the cabin. How, then, could he be held responsible for Charlie's death—or for Andrew's, which would follow soon— or for Erica's, when she washed up on a creek with a second mouth smiling below her chin?

By grace of fate, he already had an alibi for the time of his sister's disappearance. Now he would have an alibi, supplied by his own enemies, for the night of her death.

He released Charlie, who thumped on the ground. Something fell from a side pocket of his coat, clattering on the tarmac. Another totem? Robert retrieved the item.

Only a key ring, disappointingly mundane.

He was about to discard the keys when it occurred to him that Charlie must have a car. Though the drop site was within walking distance, driving there would be faster, and time, normally not a concern of Robert's, was critical now.

He had to get to the rendezvous, and quickly.

At the rear of the filling station he found an old but spotless Honda Civic, unlocked. One of Charlie's keys turned in the ignition slot, and the little hatchback throbbed to life, quivering like a puppy, eager to serve its new master.

Robert threw the car into gear and drove slowly around the side of the building, into the service court. His headlights illuminated the dead man like roadkill.

He pulled to a stop, thinking it was a mistake to leave the body here, where perhaps it would be found. He might move it, hide it, or . . .

The idea came to him fully formed, like Athena launched from the forehead of Zeus, and he knew what he must do.

He got out of the car and opened the hatch, then lifted his head to the sky.

"I haven't beaten you, bitch. Not yet. But you haven't beaten me, either. And you won't."

He closed his fist over the crucifix and with one yank of his arm he snapped the chain and flung the useless thing into the dark woods beyond the filling station.

"You won't!"

The scream echoed like a screech owl's cry, anguished and desperate and full of rage—but the horned moon, that whore, only winked at him behind a wispy veil of cloud.

Vicki Danvers lay naked on sterile sheets, an oxygen mask cupping her face, an endotracheal tube feeding nitrous oxide and penthrane to her lungs. One I.V. administered curare, and another provided plasma. There was a ventilator to assist her in breathing and, linked to the blood pressure cuff on her arm, a heart monitor that brightened the room with its reassuring blip.

Winslow had cut her open almost five hours ago, after a cursory inspection of the entry wound. The gun had been discharged at point-blank range; he could see gunpowder stippling around the bullet hole. When he made the incision, he found the bullet track contaminated with debris that had been sucked into the wound in the projectile's wake. Debridement, cleaning the cavity, had taken nearly the last two hours, but he was nearly done now.

He'd had higher priorities at first. The bullet that had eaten through Officer Vicki Danvers had done extensive damage. Entering her abdomen on the left side, it had fractured her sixth rib before traveling upward through the left lung, puncturing both lobes. Its trajectory would have carried it into the spine, inflicting irreparable if not fatal injury, had the fourth rib not intervened, sacrificing itself to deflect the bullet. After that, the bullet had tumbled briefly in the chest cavity, missing the heart and the major vessels, lodging finally in the muscles of the lower back.

When Winslow had peeled Vicki Danvers open, he found a sink of blood—an exsanguinating hemorrhage, draining her life away.

He'd tackled that crisis first, then addressed the deflated lung and the broken ribs. Retrieving the bullet had proven easy enough, and, thank God, the damn thing hadn't fragmented. He wasn't sure Officer Danvers could have survived fragmentation; a bullet that shattered inside the body was like a cloud of shotgun pellets flying every which way in a lethal swarm.

"You know ammo," he'd said to the assisting surgeon, Gander, a hunter on weekends. "What kind is this?"

The slug had been knocked around pretty badly by the two ribs. It was mashed and shapeless, but Gander identified it anyway. "That's a .38 semijacketed hollowpoint. Standard for the police around here."

"One of hers," Winslow said.

Gander thought so. "Perp got the gun away from her."

Perp. The word clanged hollowly in Winslow's mind. He rarely heard it here, in rural Pennsylvania. Gunshot victims were not un-known to him, but in the past they had been hunters injured acci-dentally or gun collectors who'd made the mistake of cleaning a loaded weapon. Once there had been a twelve-year-old who got hold of his dad's .45 and shot himself in the leg. That had been bad, but this was worse. This was an attempted homicide, and Winslow hadn't seen many of those.

He finished cleaning the wound channel. "How's she do-ing?" he asked the anesthesiologist.

"Vital signs holding steady."

"She'll make it," Gander said.

Winslow told him not to jinx it. He didn't like predictions of suc-cess until the incision was closed and the anesthesia withdrawn.

There was a lot of suturing. Despite fatigue, Winslow did the job with care, trying to minimize the scar. Vicki Danvers would have enough to deal with.

She would recover, though. He was sure of it. If she'd been found ten minutes later, or if the rescue ambulance had been slower, or if that butcher Cottman had been on duty tonight—if any of those eventualities had come to pass, then she might well be dead now, and the flag at the Barrow civic center would be flying at half mast in the morning.

But she'd been lucky, in her way. And she would survive.

Closed up, off the anesthesia, she was transferred to a recov-ery room cart, the plasma I.V. line swinging on its wheeled stand. Under the oxygen mask, her mouth moved, and Win-slow caught a low murmur.

"She's saying something."

This was unusual. She was still deeply sedated.

The murmur continued, soft and insistent. Winslow bent over her. "I can't make it out."

The scrub nurse asked why it mattered.

"Because they don't know who shot her. She might be say-ing his name."

The mask muffled her speech. Carefully Winslow peeled back a corner of it and leaned close. He listened for a long mo-ment, then replaced the mask.

"Okay," he told the nurses. "You can take her. It's nothing."

The cart and the I.V. stand were wheeled away. Winslow watched it go.

"What's she saying?" Gander asked.

Winslow looked at the latex gloves on his long-fingered hands, gloves that had been white and now were deep red.

"Blood," Winslow said. "Too much blood. She's saying it over and over, just those three words: *Too much blood.*"

16

Alone in the utter dark.

Erica hugged herself and tried to think. There had to be something she could do, some way to bring light into her world. She couldn't give up now.

But she was tired. Fear and adrenaline had worn her out, and her earlier euphoria had died with a shattering crash.

She didn't want to struggle anymore. She wanted an easy escape. Irrationally she found herself hoping Ben Connor would barge into the cavern with a flashlight and a gun. *I knew you were here,* he would say as he took her in his arms. *The search party reported finding the sinkhole, and I put it all together.*

A nice fantasy, nothing more. The searchers hadn't seen the sinkhole. Nobody knew about it. And Ben, wherever he was and whatever he was doing, would not arrive to rescue her.

"You have to do it on your own," she said, her voice floating in the darkness, disembodied and eerie.

On her own, yes. But she had no strength.

It would be easier, so much easier, just to sit here and await Robert's return. She wouldn't even fight him. She would simply recline on the table and let her head fall back, and as he raised the knife, she would think of the black waters of the Aegean Sea, the tidal pull summoning her to death. The knife would fall, the blade would kiss her throat, and in the spurt of blood, warm and salty, she would drown. Drown like her father, drown as she should have drowned years ago. A hallucination had saved her then, but nothing would save her now.

You need light.

The words appeared in her mind, spoken by a voice that might—or might not—be her own.

"Of course I need light," she said aloud, her tone argumentative and harsh. "There isn't any."

You haven't looked.

"I can't look. I can't *see*. That's the whole point."

There are other ways to see.

Erica nearly snapped a retort, and then realized it was crazy to be debating with herself.

If that was what she had been doing. If it had been herself. Or was it another's voice she'd heard?

Down here in the dark there were no bronze statues, but perhaps—just perhaps—a similar kind of epiphany was possible.

More likely, she was just losing her mind. Even so, she had sensed a kind of logic in the last words.

Other ways to see . . .

You could see with your imagination or with your memory or—

Memory.

She remembered the cave and its furnishings, didn't she? She knew the layout. She could visualize it now, the table in the center of the room, the kerosene lantern on its rocky perch, the cabinet against the far wall, and clouds of incense rising from the brazier on the floor . . .

A thought struck her, a thought so obvious and so important that it stopped her breath.

Robert had lit the brazier.

And to do so, he needed matches—carried perhaps in his pocket, but more likely stored here, in this cave.

Matches or a butane lighter. But intuitively she was certain he would not use a lighter, would eschew technology whenever possible.

If matches were kept here, they would be found in the cabinet. There was no other place to put them.

She lifted her head. She wasn't tired anymore. She had a plan, a chance.

And a purpose. If Ben Connor could not come to her, then she would go to him.

Carefully she slipped off the table, then reached behind her and found her left boot, still secured by the strap. She eased it free, then pulled up her sock and got the boot on. Using the table as a reference, she oriented herself toward the opposite wall.

Walk there? Couldn't risk it. If she caught a boot heel in some niche in the floor, she might go down with a sprained or fractured ankle, and that would be the end for her.

She sank to hands and knees, then crawled.

There was nothing but darkness, an ocean of dark, and no sound but her shallow breathing and the rasp of her progress across the yards of polished stone.

She thought it was amazing, really—what a person would do for survival. But then she remembered Ben and knew that she wanted more than merely to survive. She wanted to live.

How long had it been since she'd felt that urge, that passionate hunger—not to sleepwalk through the motions of living, but to seize hold of life and wring it dry? Perhaps not since her father had died, and she found herself in the care of a mother who was suddenly a stranger, in a house that echoed with drunken laughter that sounded too much like sobs.

Cold metal brushed her hand. The brazier.

She groped for the cabinet and touched its rough-hewn edge, then found a crude handle on the front door. Locked? No, it swung open easily.

A pine plank divided the interior into an upper and lower shelf. She searched the lower shelf first.

In a corner rested a clay jar barely larger than her fist. Liquid sloshed in it. Water? Abruptly she became aware of an intense thirst. She yearned to drink, didn't dare. It might not be water at all. It might be some strange intoxicant or narcotic.

Searching further, she found a dry, leafy thing—a wreath, the dead leaves woven with stiff, flaxen cord.

Beside the wreath rested a metal bowl on three stubby legs. A chalice, tripod-mounted. To collect the victim's blood, she realized with a shiver.

Her hands were trembling now, but she forced herself to continue the search.

There was nothing else on the lower shelf. She groped

higher, and on the upper shelf she discovered a woven basket. Gently she shook it. Something heavy shifted inside.

Too heavy to be a lighter? Probably. But she had to know.

She reached in, finding a drift of small kernels, like seeds or . . . grain. The ancient Greeks had used barley grain in their rituals, hadn't they? Grain symbolized Demeter, the harvest goddess, Persephone's mother.

Pushing through the grain, she touched something wickedly sharp.

Not a lighter. A knife.

But this was no kitchen knife. It was more primitive—heavy, bulky, the blade flat and tapered, sharp on both sides. The texture was one she recognized—not steel, but a metal her knowing hands had felt many times before.

Bronze. Like the castings in her shop, like Persephone on the wharf.

A bronze dagger.

"Oh, God," she whispered, as delayed understanding reached her like an electric shock.

The sacrificial knife. The knife that had opened Sherry Wilcott's throat in this very room.

The knife he meant to use tonight, on her.

For a moment she just knelt there. Then with an effort of will she closed her fingers over the handle and removed the knife from the basket. It leaned forward, top-heavy, the long blade bending like a divining rod toward the cave floor and the humming aquifer somewhere below.

She didn't want the knife, hated even to touch the damned thing, but she needed every possible advantage.

Clumsily she slid the blade through a belt loop of her jeans, angling it away from her body. It hung there, bizarrely medieval—no, older than that. Dorian. Achaean. Achilles might have worn a blade like this, and old Nestor, and olive-eyed Athena.

Erica felt her composure slipping. It was too crazy. She couldn't process any of it. This morning she had been a shopkeeper and an unfaithful wife and the lady of Great Hall. Now she had fallen through a time warp into a world of Delphic vapors and Bronze

Age weaponry, and in a dark cave, near a blood-stained altar, she was searching for light.

And not finding any. She had a weapon she probably couldn't use, but she still had no way out of this room.

There was nothing else inside the basket. She explored behind it, then ran her hands farther along the upper shelf.

What she found was something of carved wood—a box? No, this item was oddly shaped, with irregular ridges on top and matching indentations on the concave side, and twin projections, like horns, curving from one end. Some sort of leather strap was secured to the thing, and there were two holes cut in the wood. Slots? Or . . .

Eye holes.

It was a mask. A carved mask like the ones used in Attic theater.

Her mind fled back to history books she'd studied at the University of Rome. Masks were common in ancient Greece. Not only actors wore them. Priests did, as well, during sacrificial rites. And Robert saw himself as a priest at the altar.

Before cutting Sherry's throat, he had put on the mask. A horned mask—the face of a beast. A ram, a bull, something grotesque and inhuman. And the last thing the girl had seen in her life was this face hovering over her in the smoky dark, and the bronze blade diving down . . .

The mask clattered on the floor. Erica plunged both hands deeper into the cabinet, hunting in corners, desperate now.

In the farthest corner, the last place left to look, she discovered a cache of sticks, indifferently scattered, long and thin like straws, but with rough square heads.

"Matches," she breathed, the word a benediction.

Yes. They were matches, the extra-long variety used to light kindling in a fireplace.

She counted them, losing her place in her excitement and having to start over.

There were eleven in all, each precious. Ten went into the front pocket of her blouse, and with a shaking hand she struck the eleventh against the sole of her boot.

Flare of brightness, a wavering flame, and the dark receded

around her. To be in the light again was wonderful, exhilarating, like being reborn.

Well, she *had* been reborn, hadn't she? Rescued from despair, energized with a mission and purpose. She felt her whole being vibrate with new life.

Quickly she scanned the cave in the uncertain glow. Was there another lantern or flashlight? None was in view. Could she make a torch? The cabinet and the table were both too solidly built to be broken into pieces.

There was nothing else. She—

The match burned out.

Darkness.

She had ten matches left. She wasn't sure they would last long enough to get her to the sinkhole. But she would have to try.

Standing, she struck a second match on her upraised boot. The flame shivered before her, slender and exotic, a fluid, stylized thing, like one of the sculptures she loved.

Erica followed its wan flickering light as she left the throne room, heading into the labyrinth.

Past a row of spiked fence posts, the roof of Great Hall solidified against the sky, slouching under the stars like a great humped beast. Connor cut his speed as the driveway approached.

He wished he'd had time to prepare for this second interview with Andrew. Winging it wasn't his style.

A flick of the steering wheel, and the house filled his windshield, large and rambling, the ground floor dotted with glowing windows, the upstairs dark.

Connor looked for Andrew's Ferrari, but it wasn't parked outside as it had been before. Garaged, probably, for the night.

He pulled to a stop, got out of the car, and climbed the wide stone steps to the front door. His thumb held down the buzzer to release a long, sustained cry.

Then he just waited, his breathing a little too fast and shallow. Too many thoughts filled his mind, too many memories, nearly all of them images of Erica. Erica with her hair fanned on the pillow of the cottage's double bed. Erica polishing some bronze god in her gallery, sharp winter sunlight etching the planes of her face. Erica lifting her hand to catch a snowflake on a winter night, under a looming sky.

The door opened, and the housekeeper was there. "Hello, Chief Connor."

" 'Evening, Marie. I'm here to speak with Mr. Stafford."

"He isn't home."

Damn.

"When did he leave?" Connor asked.

"Just a few minutes ago. He, uh, he was in kind of a hurry."

"He take the Ferrari?"

She nodded. Something in her silence reached him, and he took a closer look at her. She was a petite, slender woman, dark-haired, pale-complexioned, with eyes that seemed somehow too large, out of proportion to her face.

Then he realized her eyes were open wide, watching him in what might have been mute animal fear.

"I just wanted to update him," Connor said slowly. "You know, on the case."

"Did you find Mrs. Stafford?" Tense eagerness in her voice.

"Not yet, no."

She sagged a little. "I hope you do. I hope . . . she's all right."

He met her gaze, and she averted her face.

"She will be," Connor said easily. "Anyway, there's something else I need. May I come in?"

She seemed to have forgotten he was standing in the bitter chill. "Of course."

He followed her into the foyer. They stood on the verge of the central sweep of space that had given Great Hall its name. Somewhere beneath the high raftered ceiling, Lenore Garrison and Keith Wyatt had died in mutual slaughter, but Connor couldn't think about that now.

"I need to pick up something of Mrs. Stafford's. An article of clothing. Something she wore recently."

"Something she wore?" Then Marie understood. "For dogs, is that it? You're using dogs?"

"We're going to try."

"Oh, God, I saw a thing like that on TV. One of those for-real shows. You know, where it's not fake, where it's really real? They had dogs, and they were looking for . . . a body."

"It works just as well when you're trying to find someone who's still alive. Can you show me to her wardrobe?"

A shaky nod. She started to lead him to the grand staircase, then paused. "There's nothing upstairs that hasn't been washed. The washing—it takes the scent out, doesn't it?"

"Right."

"I did the laundry just this morning. Everything's clean. Unless . . . Well, there might be a load I forgot to do. I hope so."

She turned away from the stairs and led him through the house. Somewhere the phone was ringing.

"It's been like that all night," she said without turning. "People calling. Sometimes the same reporter, over and over. And there were these two reporters who came by." She paused to glance back at him, distress on her face. "From the paper and the radio station. They made a big fuss, wanted an interview."

Connor grimaced. The media were the same everywhere. Manhattan or Barrow—it made no difference. "What did you do?"

"Told them if they didn't leave, I'd call the police. I meant it too." Her flare-up of wrath seemed to embarrass her, and she finished more softly, "They went away."

"Good for you. If they give you any more trouble, call Sergeant McArthur at the station. He'll handle it."

"I'll remember that."

The laundry room was in an alcove near the rear door. Connor saw a scatter of gossip magazines on a card table, movie actors grinning on the glossy covers. He waited as Marie lifted the lid of the wicker hamper.

"Empty," she breathed. "Damn."

"It's all right. There's probably something we can use. A sweater, maybe—something that doesn't get washed every time she wears it. Or . . . wait a minute."

A glimmer of red had caught his gaze. He reached behind the hamper and picked up a damp terry-cloth headband.

"Is this hers?" he asked.

"Oh, yes. Yes, it is." Marie broke into a wide smile. "She wears it when she goes running. Wore it just this morning. It must've slipped out, and I didn't see it. It wasn't washed, thank God. That'll work for you, won't it?"

The headband was limp with Erica's sweat. Connor nodded. "It's perfect. I'll need a plastic bag, one of those little sandwich bags, to put it in."

Marie hustled into the kitchen, where a radio was tuned to the local station. Connor heard a caller insisting that Erica Stafford had been found dead on a creek bank, raped and mutilated. "Got a friend in the sheriff's department," the crank was saying. "Well, he don't actually work there . . ."

Marie, rummaging in a drawer, grimaced at the words. "Mr. Stafford said not to listen to that stuff."

"He was right. It's all crap."

"I guess. But once he left, I turned it on anyway. Couldn't help myself. I mean, even if most of what they say is trash, there might be some truth in it . . . some real news . . ."

She found a Ziploc bag, and he sealed the headband inside, then slipped the bag into the side pocket of his jacket.

"You care about Mrs. Stafford," Connor said, "don't you?"

"She's always been real good to me."

"Has she?"

"Oh, sure. I've worked for two others, and she's the best employer I ever had." A grimace pinched her mouth. "Guess it sounds cold, saying it that way. What I mean is, not just the best boss, but the best person. She's decent. Doesn't treat you like . . . like you're just a piece of furniture or something."

"How about Mr. Stafford?"

She bit her lip. "He's okay. He's great, I mean. He's a fine man."

But he could see she was trembling. Her fear was back, the fear he'd first noticed when she told him that Andrew had left in his Ferrari.

He spent an instant sizing her up. She was young, unsophisticated. She read movie magazines. Watched reality-based TV shows, the ones featuring shaky handheld camera footage and tough-sounding voiceovers.

Connor took a shot. "Listen to me, Maria," he said, filling his voice with the cool authority of a television cop. "Mrs.

Stafford may be in danger. Her life may be at stake. Every minute counts. If there's any way you can help me find her, now is the time to tell me."

His little speech was a tissue of cliches; but, hackneyed or not, it seemed to reach her. In her darting eyes he read an inner struggle, then a tentative resolution.

"I'm scared," Marie whispered.

"You don't have to be. Just tell the truth."

"That's what scares me. The truth. Or what might be the truth."

He waited. He knew she would talk, and after a moment's delay, she did.

"I think maybe Mr. Stafford might be mixed up in this. I mean . . . he might know something."

"Why do you say that?"

She didn't answer directly. "Rachel Kellerman came by. Just about an hour ago."

"And?"

"Her and Mr. Stafford had a talk in the library." Her head inclined briefly in the direction of the east wing. "I wasn't supposed to hear, but . . . well, I eavesdropped a little. Mrs. Kellerman said . . . she said . . ."

"What, Marie?"

"That Mr. Stafford might have had his wife killed."

The words spilled out in a rush, to be followed by a shaky intake of breath and a new spate of trembling.

Connor didn't buy it. Andrew was a white-collar crook, not the type for murder plots. And in the sunroom, when he learned that Erica was missing, his grief and fear almost certainly had been genuine.

But just suppose Rachel was right. Then Robert was a red herring, and it was Andrew who should have been watched, Andrew who might be out somewhere disposing of Erica's body even now.

Or suppose they were in on it together—Robert and Andrew, accomplices somehow. Or . . .

Speculation. Useless. He pushed all such thoughts aside. In a calm voice he asked, "What did Mr. Stafford say?"

"He denied it. It sounded sincere. But I don't know. He's

good at that, you know. At sounding sincere." She looked at him. "He was a con man . . . before the marriage."

Another surprise. Connor hadn't expected Marie to know about that.

"A con man," he said evenly. "What makes you say so?"

"I heard them arguing about it. Mr. and Mrs. Stafford, I mean. A few months ago, around Christmas. She bought this little statue for her shop, then found out it was a fake. So she, like, traced it to where it came from originally, you know? I guess you can do that."

Connor knew it was possible. The dealer who'd sold the piece could supply the name of the previous owner, who, in turn, could explain where he'd bought it, and so on through the chain of custody.

He doubted Erica had done the detective work herself. There were experts who specialized in establishing the provenance of fine artworks.

"What did she find out?" he asked, already knowing the answer.

"The statue came from Mr. Stafford's shop. That's as far back as she could trace it. Some mail-order place he used to run. So she got worried, and she hired some private detective in Philadelphia to look a little further. And he told her . . ."

"Yes?"

"He told her this wasn't the only time Mr. Stafford had sold something phony. His whole business was a racket. He had people making these statues for him, just cheap knockoffs, you know? Like when they try to sell you a Rolex watch on a street corner, and it was really made in Hong Kong?"

Connor guessed she'd learned of that scam from one of her TV shows. He smiled. "I think I've heard of that."

"Oh, right. You used to be in New York. So you know all about this kind of stuff. Mr. Stafford was selling fakes, and he's nothing but a fake himself. A fake and a phony. She called him that. Well, not those words. She said he was a, uh, a charlatan."

She pronounced the word clumsily, putting stress on the last syllable. Connor only nodded.

"He just married her for money," Marie whispered. "That's what she said." She seemed to remember decorum, and added,

"It's not that I eavesdrop all the time or anything. They were shouting, is all."

"I understand."

"She was real upset, and Mr. Stafford was trying to explain, but she wouldn't listen. She said he was just a fraud like, uh, like Mr. Furnell. I don't know who Mr. Furnell is, do you?"

"No."

"Somebody who hurt her, I guess. Who used her. She's been hurt a lot . . . I felt so bad for her. She deserves better."

This last was stated with a peculiar emphasis, and Connor suddenly had an uneasy suspicion.

"What else did you hear?" he asked. "Tonight, I mean, when Mrs. Kellerman came over."

Marie hesitated, her expression almost demure. "Well . . . she said she thought Mr. Stafford had a motive."

"What motive?"

"He might've felt like he's lost his wife anyway. Like she's not really his anymore."

"Why would he feel that way?" Connor pressed, though part of him wasn't sure he wanted to know the answer.

"Because . . ." A gulp of breath, twitch of her mouth, and she said it. "Because Rachel had already told him you and Erica are . . . you know."

Connor stood unmoving, every part of him still.

"Told him," he whispered. "Rachel told him."

How could Rachel have known?

But that wasn't the issue. Of course it wasn't. In a small town people learned things. There were no secrets. He should have known as much.

"When?" he asked. "When did she tell him?"

Marie wrung her hands, chewing her lip, studying the floor. "I don't know. A while ago, it sounded like."

A while ago. So Andrew had been on to them all along. Had known for weeks, perhaps for months. Had known when Connor passed him in the street, sketching a wave, or when they discussed police charity events. Had known in the sunroom earlier today, and in the woods outside Robert's cabin. Had known, and had betrayed no hint of his knowledge, ever, at any time.

Connor felt heat in his face, as if he'd been slapped. The affair was the one shameful thing in his life. If it was shameful. Maybe it wasn't. He couldn't say, couldn't judge—he was too close to it.

But it *felt* shameful—and Andrew knew. Marie knew. Rachel knew. How many others?

Forget that. It didn't matter. Concentrate.

"What happened," he asked, guiding his voice along steel rails, "after Rachel accused him?"

"Mr. Stafford denied it. I don't know if she believed him. She left in a big sweat, and he went back in the guesthouse without supper. Stayed there till just before you showed up."

"The guesthouse. Does he go there often?"

"Now and then. Not a lot."

"What's in there? Anything special?"

"Well, it's kind of like an office. There's a desk and some other furniture and stuff, and an intercom, a phone—"

"Separate phone line?" She nodded. "His private line?"

"Yeah, I guess. Mrs. Stafford never uses it. Never goes in there at all."

Connor remembered Andrew's business card on the table in the cabin. The scribbled message: *We need to talk.* The handwritten phone number.

He'd been in the guesthouse awaiting Robert's call.

"Okay, Marie. Thanks."

Connor turned to go, but she stopped him. "You think Mrs. Kellerman was right?"

He tried to decide how to answer. He chose honesty.

"I don't know what to think," he said, "about any part of this."

Then he was running down the steps to the cruiser, sliding behind the wheel, transmitting on Tac One again.

"Paul, this is Ben. Come in. Come in."

No response for a worrisome fifteen seconds, and then Connor was relieved to hear Elder's voice. "Read you, Chief."

"You may be getting a visitor." He avoided specifics, aware that the press and others must be monitoring the frequency. "Somebody stopping by to chat with our friend."

"I don't think so, Chief. The birdie's flown the coop."

Connor's gut clenched like a fist. "Say again."

"He snuck away. I can't quite figure out how. Either I underestimated him or I overestimated myself. Probably a little of both. Anyway, his vehicle's still here, but he's vamoosed."

"On foot?"

"Looks like."

Fear hit Connor hard. *We lost him.* The words were a silent scream. *We lost him and Andrew too, God damn it, and they could be doing anything together, could be killing Erica right now—*

And it would be his fault for leaving Elder on stakeout, for not bringing Robert in for questioning. His fault, as Karen's death had been his fault. First Karen, now Erica—everyone he loved—

Stop it.

Connor caught his breath and tried to think. Robert had left the cabin. Why? Perhaps he was meeting Andrew someplace. The phone call had been their way of arranging a rendezvous. The phone call—

But Robert didn't own a telephone.

"Paul, are there any pay phones nearby?"

"Out on the main road," Elder said, "there's a filling station. Couple phones there. That's the closest place."

The main road. He meant Route 36.

Connor nodded, suddenly energized. "That's where he went. Where he still may be."

"I'm on my way."

"I'll join you there. And, Paul—watch yourself."

"Don't you fret, Chief. I won't misjudge this boy again."

After fifty paces Erica emerged into the labyrinth's main corridor. She passed the red arrow, marked in her lipstick, which pointed toward the distant exit.

Half of her stash of matches remained unused. She was going to make it. Unless Robert materialized like an apparition within the next few minutes, she was sure to reach the sinkhole. Then it was only a question of climbing out, a difficult feat, but with fear as a spur she would find the necessary agility and strength.

Stalactites teased her hair as she ducked under the corridor's sloping roof. Limestone walls wavered in a flicker of shadow-play. The damp chill seemed to trickle into the marrow of her bones.

This place had seemed magical once, when she was a child, glad to escape the world of adults. And after her father's death, when Great Hall became a prison, she and Robert had been happy to find refuge here, where their mother's scolding voice and alcoholic laughter couldn't reach them, where they could be alone to play their strange, obsessive games.

But there was nothing magical about Barrow Caves any longer. She saw them for what they were—the dank, leaky underbelly of the world, cold and clammy and claustrophobic, fit only for the outcast eyeless creatures that darted in its brackish pools or crawled among the rain-worn furrows of the walls.

The caves were a crypt, nothing more. But not her crypt. She was getting out. Please, God—she was getting out soon.

The lighted match in her hand was starting to sputter. It would expire before long. She moved faster, balancing speed and caution, watching the deep crevices in the floor and the puddles of ooze.

She didn't like to think about what would happen after her escape. Robert would be arrested, charged with murder and kidnapping. A shudder quivered through her as she thought of her brother put on display for the news cameras, caged like a beast.

And she had another, deeper fear, a fear she hated to admit even to herself. Once in custody, Robert might . . . he might . . .

Darkness.

The match had winked out. She had five left.

Standing in place, afraid to take even a single step without a flame to guide her, she removed another match from her shirt pocket and struck it on the side of her boot heel.

Light flared, pushing back the dark. Shadows wavered at the edge of the glow, tenebrous and hungry.

One shadow moved.

It came at her, a blur of speed, and crazily she thought it was Robert—he'd crept up on her, taken her by surprise—and then a furred darting shape brushed her cheek and she smelled something rank and flatulent. Instinctively she pivoted away, even as she registered its mouselike squeaking and knew the thing was only a bat, startled from its solitary roost.

The bat flitted down a narrow side passage, lost to sight, and Erica's foot slipped.

She went down on one knee with a hard crack. Pain blinded her. For a moment she was not a person anymore, only a bundled confusion of nerve endings all shrieking at once, and in place of conscious thought there was nothing but white light and a high humming monotone.

Then awareness jerked back into focus, and she shook herself alert.

The match was still in her hand. She had not released it even in her momentary fugue. But the other matches, stowed in the front pocket of her blouse . . .

They had flown free and lay scattered—one, two, three of them floating in a pool of scum, instantly waterlogged, useless.

"Damn," she muttered, tears clawing at her vision. "Oh, damn it, I'm so *close*."

The match she held was already sputtering. So soon? She must have been unconscious longer than she'd thought.

Scanning the floor, she saw a single dry match and groped for it, even as the match in her hand blinked out.

For a few frantic seconds she couldn't find the dry match. She might have inadvertently brushed it farther from her grasp, even knocked it into the puddle.

No, here it was. She retrieved the match stick with trembling care, terrified of dropping it or breaking it somehow.

Her last hope. But it would never burn long enough for her to reach the sinkhole.

Maybe it didn't have to. The main corridor ran straight. If she could orient herself, she might be able to grope her way to the exit, even if she had to crawl.

But it wouldn't be possible to see the final arrow, the one that pointed to the crevice leading to the sinkhole. Could she find that crevice in the dark? There were so many gaps in the wall, countless side passages and niches. She would have to feel her way past each one, relying on instinct or memory to avoid a fatal wrong turn.

"You can do it," she whispered, though she was not at all certain this was true.

Still in darkness, unwilling to light the last match until she had to, she tested her left knee. Though it throbbed with slow pulses of agony, it flexed freely enough. She was fairly certain the leg would take her weight. Whether or not she could chimney up the sinkhole in this condition was another question, but she would confront that challenge when she had to.

Clumsily she struggled upright, keeping her head low to avoid obstructions. Already the pain in her knee was diminishing to an ache. Later it would stiffen, but for now, as long as she stayed active, she would be mobile.

She bent double at the waist and struck the match head on her boot heel.

Nothing happened.

Oh, no.

The match couldn't be defective. That just would not be fair.

Her hand was shaking badly. She tightened her grip on the match stick and tried again, scraping the sulphur head along the side of her heel in a long, brisk swipe.

Light.

There was no time for relief or gratitude. She had to turn in the right direction and get moving, cover as much ground as possible before darkness closed over her again.

Yet inexplicably she hesitated, her gaze drawn down the side passageway used by the bat as an escape route. The passage was barely three feet wide, six feet high, hardly a tunnel at all, and there was no reason to be looking into its depths.

Except . . .

In the shadows of the tunnel, perhaps twenty feet away, something small and glassy and low to the floor caught the light of her match and cast it back in a pale reflective glint.

A lantern? One of the many she and Robert had dispersed throughout the labyrinth when they were children?

He'd gathered up the others, it seemed. Perhaps he had neglected this one. Or perhaps it wasn't a lantern at all, just a fleck of quartz imbedded in the rock wall.

Even if it was a lantern, there was no guarantee it contained any kerosene. Bone dry, it would be as useless to her as the soggy matches swimming in the pool of scum.

Still, with a lantern, a working lantern, she could reach the sinkhole in no time and even have light to guide her as she climbed out.

She hesitated, afraid to risk wasting her last match on a fool's errand, yet afraid to pass up what might be her best chance.

The mystery object winked at her from its shadowy niche. She was almost sure she saw a rectangle of glass, the pane of a kerosene lamp. Or had she merely willed herself to see it?

"Oh, hell," she muttered, and slipped into the passageway.

It had to be a lantern, and it had to be filled with fuel. She wouldn't permit the universe to frustrate her hopes again.

The tunnel was a tight fit. She crabbed forward, breathing hard, making difficult progress. Fear tickled her, and a strange beating pressure filled her skull.

The walls were so close. No space, no air. A squeeze of claustrophobic panic compressed her ribs, and abruptly she felt she was drowning—drowning in the black Aegean waters—sinking into oblivion as her lungs strained for breath.

She fought the urge to turn back.

No, come on, almost there.

And in truth, she was close now. Close enough to see that, yes, thank God, it *was* a lantern, identical to the one she'd smashed in the throne room.

It sat on the floor, forlorn and abandoned, caked in limestone dust. Behind it rose a flat white wall, a dead end.

Had Robert forgotten the lamp, or had he placed it there for a reason?

The answer didn't matter as long as there was kerosene inside.

Her match began to sputter.

"*No.*" The word was a sob.

If the match died now, she would have no way to light the lamp. She scrambled faster, praying for time.

The passage widened by a foot or so, and she was able to

cover the last stretch of ground in two strides. She could see the lamp clearly, the long wick feeding down into the lower chamber, where a pool of kerosene was visible through the glass.

Fuel, it had fuel in it, the damn thing would *work.*

She squatted, oblivious to the yell of protest from her knee, and thrust the match head at the wick.

The wick wouldn't light.

"Come on, *come on!*" Distantly she knew she was screaming, hysterical, riven by panic.

She tried again and again, jabbing the small flame at the wick, drawing no response.

"Come on!"

Her shout returned to her in a crowd of echoes.

The wick wouldn't light, and the match was guttering, flaring and nearly dying, flaring again . . .

It went out.

An instant of darkness and the death of all hope—but a sliver of flame traveled to the extra-long match stick itself, which blazed up in a last display of ruddy orange light.

She jammed it at the wick, willing the slender strawlike stem to ignite.

The wick smoldered damply. Water seepage had moistened it. Maybe the liquid in the lamp wasn't kerosene, after all. Maybe it was only rainwater, collected drop by drop over the years, mocking her like a mirage.

"Oh, come on, please come on . . ."

Though the match stick was long, the flame was consuming it quickly. Pieces of the stick fell away in a patter of char. Heat singed her fingers as the flame progressed inexorably downward.

The wick refused to burn.

She uttered a final plea, as useless as the others, and then the last of the match stick was shot through with red candescence, burning her fingertips, and involuntarily she dropped the match as it went out.

But she was not in darkness.

It took her a bewildered moment to understand that the wick, at the very last instant, had caught fire.

The lantern was lit. It cast a dull, unsteady glow over the passageway.

She'd succeeded. She had light, as much light as she would need.

"Thank you," she whispered. "Thank you, oh, thank you."

She had no idea whom she was addressing, whether God or the cosmos or a bronze Persephone on a fishing wharf.

For a moment she just huddled there, feeling only gratitude, an emotion she had known too little of. Finally, lifting the lantern, she rose to her feet and started to turn.

Then she paused, looking at the wall before her, the passageway's dead end.

It was too white and smooth to be limestone, and the faint irregularities in its surface were not made by the scouring action of water. They were trowel marks.

The wall was concrete. Robert had sealed up the passage, using lanterns to guide his work. And when done, he'd left one lantern here, half filled with kerosene, as a convenience in case he needed to return.

She raised the lantern higher, and in the circle of its glow, a small imperfection in the wall was thrown into harsh relief.

It was a hole, barely six inches wide, at the level of her chest. The only aperture in the wall, a peephole, an airway . . .

Shoulders hunched, she peered in.

The wall was a foot thick at least, and the hole was a miniature tunnel. In it lay a drift of white bones.

The remains of a rat, perhaps. That was what she thought at first.

Then she saw that the bones were finger joints, knuckles, the radius and ulna of a fleshless wrist.

A skeleton's hand and forearm. A human skeleton.

Shock punched her hard, and she gripped the handle of the lantern tight to be sure it wouldn't slip from her grasp.

Someone had been . . . walled up . . . sealed alive behind this barrier of troweled concrete. And left here, like the victim of some medieval torture. Imprisoned alone in these catacombs, to die of starvation and thirst.

She wanted to pull back, look away, but one detail held her.

Encircling the bony wrist was a silver Rolex, still shiny.

She knew that Rolex. In a terminal at Newark Airport, when

leaving on her first European trip, she had stood beside its owner as he cocked his wrist impatiently to check his watch.

It was the last time Erica had seen Mr. Furnell.

Until now.

17

Faith was not among Andrew Stafford's virtues. He had spent too many years betraying people who trusted him to ever place his trust in another.

Robert might be planning an ambush, or he might not. Andrew would assume the worst.

Half a mile from the turnoff to the drop site at Barrow Falls, he shifted the Ferrari into neutral and killed the engine. Guided by parking lights and the moon's ambient glow, he coasted downhill for a hundred yards, then pulled into the woods, parking in a copse of pines.

If Robert was here already, lying in wait, he would not have heard Andrew's arrival.

From the floor of the car on the passenger side, he retrieved a small carrying case he'd brought with him from the guest cottage at Great Hall. He hung the strap over his shoulder, then folded the oversized envelope from the safe-deposit box and stuffed it in a cargo pocket of his coat.

Leaving the car, he was careful to shut the door softly, making no sound.

A path led to the lookout, but he didn't take it. Instead he crept through the forest, pausing occasionally to listen for any sound of pursuit. He heard nothing but the endless hiss of the falls somewhere in the distance, beyond the trees.

When the hiss was loud enough to drown out most other noises, he knelt and unslung the carrying case.

Inside the case was a monocular Moonlight telescope, eight

inches long, featuring 4.3X magnification and a 10,000-power light amplifier that turned night to day. An illuminator affixed to the bottom of the scope could project an infrared beam over a distance of four hundred fifty feet, improving visibility under difficult conditions.

Andrew hadn't used the scope since that night in January when he'd staked out Robert's cabin, kneeling in the frigid brush. The thing felt clumsy and unfamiliar in his gloved hands, and he had some trouble focusing the lens and adjusting the brightness control.

The image in the eyepiece was a greenish blur, dim and indistinct because the dense evergreens filtered out most of the moonlight. But when he activated the illuminator, sending a ray of invisible light deep into the woods, he saw a sudden profusion of detail.

He smiled. His adversary was smart, perhaps even a genius in his twisted way, but he lacked technological sophistication. He would not own a toy like this, and so he would be blind in the night. Andrew, all-seeing, had the edge.

The carrying case was an encumbrance. He left it behind as he proceeded toward the falls, holding the scope in his left hand and his pistol, fully loaded, in his right. He moved slowly, counting paces. At regular intervals he stopped to scope out his surroundings, lifting the tube to his eye and turning in a full circle to pan the green-tinted world.

The hiss of the falls swelled to a dull roar. The trees thinned. He crouched low, advancing nearly on all fours. On the tennis court he had liked to summon the ferocious tenacity of the jaguar, and now he needed another of the jungle cat's qualities, its stealth, its liquid suppleness. He must be part of the night.

On the verge of the clearing that bordered the falls, he used the scope again. A fan of infrared passed slowly among the feathery boughs of pines and holly trees, the branches glowing bright green, shimmering like molten metal, forming intricate nets of pure light. It was oddly beautiful, a wholly different way of seeing the world. It—

There.

He pressed the eyepiece closer to his left eye.

Robert, a blob of brighter light in vaguely human outline, lay in the brush perhaps a hundred yards away, awaiting his quarry.

Carefully Andrew set down his pistol, then with his right hand dialed the focus knob, bringing the image into crisper relief against the dull green background.

He saw Robert clearly now, or at least his luminous silhouette. He rested prostrate amid the low shrubs near the clearing. From that vantage point he would have an unobstructed view of the path to the falls. He could fire from his hiding place, cut down anyone who approached.

Andrew lowered the Moonlight scope. The thing had come from The Sharper Image and had cost five hundred dollars. He figured it had just paid for itself.

He picked up the pistol.

Even from this distance he was probably a good enough marksman to make the shot, with the help of the night vision scope.

But he wouldn't do that, of course. Because Robert had lied about one other detail of their agreement. He had not brought Erica.

If he died now, she might never be found.

Andrew needed the bastard alive but disarmed. Needed to make Robert talk.

He licked his lips, chapped and creased in the dry cold air. Single combat was something new to him. He was meant for more civilized pursuits. Though he had risked jail in the course of his financial scams, he had never put his life on the line. To do so now—not for monetary gain, but for a woman who hated him, who'd cheated on him, who might even implicate him to the police when she learned of the blackmail plot—to risk everything for Erica seemed suddenly insane.

But he would do it anyway.

Silently he began to crawl forward, closing on his quarry by slow degrees.

En route to the gas station, Connor heard his cell phone buzz.

"Yes?" he snapped with the phone to his ear.

"Chief, it's McArthur." The desk sergeant, his voice rising over the incongruous sounds of laughter and celebration. "Got some good news for you."

"I can use it."

"Vicki's out of surgery, and they think she'll be okay."

Connor exhaled a long breath.

"Chief? Hello?"

"I'm here, Dave. I read you. That's . . . that's what I wanted to hear."

"She's still unconscious, so she hasn't I.D.'d her assailant—"

Connor already knew who'd wounded her. "Don't worry about that. Has Miller gotten hold of her family?"

"Finally tracked them down. They're on their way now. They'll be at Vicki's bedside when she wakes up."

"Sounds good." A new chorus of cheers rose in the background. "And, Dave—better tell the boys to turn down the volume on that party they're throwing. I'd hate to write them a citation for disturbing the peace."

McArthur laughed, a sound of giddy relief. "I'll pass on the word, Chief."

Connor switched off. He felt something unfamiliar on his face and realized it was a smile.

One thing, at least, had gone right.

After a moment's thought he activated the phone again and made a call.

"Maginnis," the voice at the other end squawked.

"Vicki's okay," Connor said without preamble.

There was a pause, and he knew it contained all the things she could never say to anyone.

When her voice reached him again, it was low and curiously childlike. "You're sure?"

"McArthur talked to someone at the hospital. She's going to make it. And her folks are on the way."

"Thank Christ . . ."

The quaver that rippled through the words was the strongest emotion Connor had ever heard from Marge Maginnis.

Then she spoke again, her tone almost businesslike except for hiccups of indrawn breath at irregular intervals. "Bloodhounds aren't here yet, but they're coming. Got Woodall, Hart, and Sergeant Larkin at the scene. We still need something that carries her scent."

He fingered the pocket of his jacket, where the headband was sealed in its plastic bag. "I'm bringing it. I'll be there soon."

"Understood. And, uh, thanks, Ben. For the update, I mean."

Update. Connor had to smile at that word, so coolly professional. "No problem, Lieutenant."

He turned off the phone. Ahead, the gas station was approaching. Connor came down from his temporary high and refocused on the job at hand.

Elder's empty Buick sat on the roadside. Conner steered past it, into the filling station, then parked and left the engine running.

As he swung out of the cruiser, he drew his Smith .38. The feel of the gun dismissed the last traces of the smile from his face. This was no time to get careless. Vicki was alive, but so was the man who'd nearly killed her.

Connor surveyed the shadows. The gas station was dark, the service court floodlights extinguished.

"He's not here, Chief."

The shout was Elder's. He stood near the service island, arm lifted in a wave.

Connor approached him, crossing yards of tarmac at a run. "You check around back?"

Elder nodded. "Checked everywhere. Place shuts down for the night at eight o'clock. They got the closing time posted on the door."

"Where are the phones?"

"That way." Elder pointed out two kiosks at the edge of the lot. "They've both got dial tones. Who'd he call, anyway?"

"Andrew Stafford." Connor flicked on his flashlight, a big steel model with a wide, brilliant beam. "They must've arranged a meeting. If Robert's on foot, the rendezvous has to be someplace close."

The oval of light played over the gas pumps on the service island, then slid across the tarmac toward the cashier's booth.

"Maybe Andrew picked him up here before I arrived," Elder said. "They could've gone somewhere together."

"It's possible. But . . . hold on." The flashlight beam came to rest on a dark, glossy smear not far from where Elder stood. "See that?"

Elder shrugged. "Oil stain."

"I don't think that's oil."

Connor moved closer, and the circle of the beam shrank and brightened. He could make out several long ragged smudges, each still wet.

He knelt by the nearest one, touched it with a fingertip. The stuff was tacky and thick, and up close it wore a telltale red sheen.

"Blood," he said. "A lot of it."

His heart began to pound. At first he didn't know why. Then he realized he was thinking of Erica. Could Robert have brought her here for some reason? Perhaps she attempted an escape, and he shot her with Vicki's gun or gutted her with a knife. Perhaps . . .

Get a grip, he ordered himself. Slowly he stood.

"So where's the victim?" Elder said. "He just walk off?"

"Not after losing that much blood. Besides, look at those stains."

Connor cast the flashlight beam over the tarmac again, highlighting the long smeared lines of red.

"The body was moved," he said. "Dragged."

Elder squinted at the ground. "Danvers was left where she dropped. Why'd Robert change his M.O. this time?"

Connor didn't know.

Andrew crept closer, approaching Robert from the rear. Even without the aid of the night vision scope, the man was plainly visible now. He lay on his belly, legs splayed, head tilted to peer along the long barrel of a rifle or shotgun.

Uncanny how Robert had not shifted position in all this time. But he was insane, of course. He must be able to focus his total concentration on the task of waiting, just as another psychopath could study a blank wall for hours on end.

The risky part would come next. Andrew had to jump his quarry and pin him down before he could swing the long gun around and fire.

But first he had to cross a dangerous stretch of ground largely empty of cover.

The falls were close, a hint of cold spray reaching him on icy drafts of wind. He could hear the raging sibilance of the white cascade as it plunged down a stepladder of rock outcrops to the creek two hundred feet below.

The hissing roar was loud, but not loud enough to drown out the throbbing heartbeat in his ears.

Andrew set aside the Moonlight scope, a hindrance now, then sank down, prostrate on the frozen earth. He began to crawl.

The distance was five yards. How quickly he could cover that much territory on a tennis court, his racket outstretched to meet the blur of the ball. He wondered what his many vanquished opponents at the club would say if they could see him now, inching his way forward through brittle weeds, advancing with pelvic thrusts and jerks of his elbows, a pistol trembling in his hand.

Three yards to go.

He thought of his argument with Erica after she discovered his secret past. Hot with rage, she had declared their marriage a lie and a sham. He'd insisted she was wrong. *How can I prove I really love you?* he shouted as she buried her face in her hands. *Do you want me to beg? To crawl?*

Well, he was crawling for her now.

One more yard. He could reach out and touch Robert's shoes if he wished. And still Robert hadn't altered his position, hadn't glanced over his shoulder, hadn't heard a thing.

Andrew tightened his grip on the pistol. Slowly, so slowly, he drew back on his haunches, poised to pounce.

He wished his heart weren't beating so furiously in his ears. He wished sweat would stop trickling into the corners of his eyes and fuzzing his vision.

The leap came before he even knew he was ready. It was as if his body simply propelled itself forward, and time shifted into surreal slow motion, his sensory perceptions sharpening with cinematic vividness, every detail fully clear, larger than life.

He saw the gun in Robert's hands—not a rifle, a shotgun, single-barrel—and a wedge of Robert's face in profile, the cheeks more sunken than he remembered, a rash of zits on his jaw.

His jaw. His clean-shaven jaw.

Robert wore a beard.

With a dizzying thump Andrew landed astride his quarry, and he knew.

This was not Robert. This was some kid. Pimples on his face. The dull glaze of death in his eyes.

A corpse. A decoy.

From somewhere in the surrounding dark Robert's voice called out, *"Drop the gun!"*

"Okay," Elder said thoughtfully, "so what've we got? Signs of foul play, but no corpse. Think the victim was Andrew Stafford, maybe? Him and Robert met here, got into a little spat?"

Connor shook his head. "I doubt there's been time." He concentrated, trying to conjure a scenario that did not involve Erica. "Maybe someone else pulled in to use the phone, and Robert killed him."

"I doubt this place gets many visitors after closing time. It's not exactly situated on an off-ramp of the interstate."

Connor looked around at the dark woods, the distant lights of a solitary farm, the highway empty of traffic. "Guess you're right."

"Charlie gets pretty lonely, he tells me."

"Who's Charlie?"

"The attendant. Works the second shift."

The two men looked at each other, sharing a thought.

Elder frowned. "I hope not," he said in answer to an unspoken suggestion.

"When did you say this place normally shuts down for the night?"

"Eight."

Connor glanced at his watch. "It's eight-forty-five now. If Charlie stayed late, he might've still been here when Robert showed up. Did you check the locks?"

"Didn't think of it."

Connor started walking, careful to sidestep the blood. "Let's go."

The door to the cashier's booth was at the side of the station. When Connor tested the knob, it turned easily.

"Charlie wouldn't leave without setting the deadbolt." Dull dread flattened Elder's voice. "He's a reliable kid. Not the brightest, but he does his job."

Connor went in first, his gun leading him. There was nothing in the booth—no Charlie, and no sign of a struggle. Some cash remained in the register drawer. Elder counted it while Connor glanced under the counter.

"Seventy-three bucks," Elder said. "Charlie's supposed to clean out the register before he locks up."

"You said you looked around back. Is a car parked there?"

"No cars. It's empty." Elder seemed puzzled by the question, then understood. "He stole Charlie's car. That's what you're saying. Killed him, and stole his damn car."

"I think so. You happen to know what he drives?"

"Can't say I do."

"Where's that portable I lent you?" Elder handed over the radio, and Connor thumbed the transmit button. "Central, this is Chief Connor. I need to know if there's an auto registered to a Charles, uh—"

"Whittaker," Elder prompted.

"Charles Whittaker, county resident."

The dispatcher ten-foured, and the frequency went silent while the request was processed.

At the rear of the booth was a door, unlocked. Connor opened it and flipped a wall switch. An overhead bulb cast pale light on a storage room.

Amid the clutter of mops and buckets and empty gas cans stood a rusty lawn chair and a card table. The chair had been pushed back, as if hurriedly abandoned. The table was piled high with automobile magazines, tented open in disarray.

"Charlie like cars?" Connor asked.

Elder nodded. "Only thing he's interested in. All day long he watches them go by."

"So after he's turned off the lights outside and in the booth, he comes in here. Sits for a while, thumbing through his magazines."

"Funny he wouldn't just go home."

"Does he live alone?"

"With his folks, still."

"Well, maybe he needed some time by himself. Then he hears footsteps outside, or someone talking on the pay phone. He goes to investigate. But before he leaves this room, he turns out the overhead light, so as not to alert the intruder."

He led Elder back into the booth. Despite the circumstances, he felt a cold, furtive thrill of relief, because it was not Erica's blood on the tarmac.

"Charlie stops here on the way out," Connor said, "and in the dark he takes his shotgun."

"Shotgun? That mama's boy never handled a firearm in his life."

"Look under the counter."

Elder bent low, ducking his head, and saw the empty mounting Connor had noted earlier. He swore. "Damn fool kid. Thinking he's ol' Clint Peckerwood just because he's toting iron." He measured the mounting with his hands. "Shotgun or a rifle, for sure."

"It was a shotgun. I saw a box of Federal shotshells in the utility room."

"Time was, I would've noticed a thing like that."

"Maybe I just got lucky."

Elder grunted. "Maybe I just got old."

The radio crackled with the dispatcher's voice, reporting the results of a database search. "Only one Charles Whittaker is listed as a resident of this county, and he owns a 1984 Honda Civic." She recited the license plate number and added, "No warrants, no priors."

"I want an APB on that vehicle. Countywide."

"Roger, Chief."

"Vehicle may be stolen, driver may be armed and dangerous, may have a hostage."

"Uh, roger that."

"Nobody takes any chances, all right? You pass that message along to all units, and to the sheriff and the highway patrol. We don't want any more incidents like . . . well, we want to play it safe. Got that?"

"Roger, Chief Connor. I hear you."

Connor switched off. He was shaking. The conversation had

brought it all back—Danvers on the radio, his judgment call, then her desperate Code 99, her bloodied body, the sharp thrust of guilt and self-accusation.

With effort he kicked free of those thoughts and resumed his reconstruction of the crime.

"Charlie went outside"—Conner exited through the side door, Elder following—"and slipped around the corner and approached the phones." He traced the boy's steps as far as the blood spatter, then pointed to the twin kiosks fifty feet away. "Then he confronted Robert."

"And the bastard shot him," Elder said, finishing the thought.

Something in the older man's voice made Connor look at him more closely. He saw pale anguish on the strong, lined face.

"What is it, Paul?" he asked gently.

"Now I know how you felt when you found Danvers."

It took Connor a minute to get the point. Elder was saying that if he'd done his job properly at the cabin, Robert would never have gotten this far.

Guilt, self-accusal. Connor had no monopoly on such feelings tonight.

"This isn't your fault," he whispered, but Elder only looked away.

For a long moment Andrew didn't move, couldn't react.

"Discard the gun," Robert said in a softer voice. "Throw it. Throw it far."

Gad damn him. The man sounded almost bored.

With mechanical obedience Andrew pitched the gun like a horseshoe, and it spiraled into the night and vanished with a thud.

"Wonderful. You're my puppet, Andrew, my marionette. I pull your strings and watch you perform. Quite a role reversal, given our recent history, wouldn't you say?"

"Robert," Andrew croaked, feeling a need to speak, negotiate, talk his way out, "we had a deal."

"I'm not much of a businessman, I'm afraid."

It hit Andrew then: a blind, reeling surge of panic, the worst terror of his life.

Shouldn't have come, shouldn't have tried to save Erica; he wasn't cut out for this, not him, he was no hero, he just wanted to crawl away and hide.

"Did you bring the envelope?" Robert asked from the concealing shadows.

If he was anywhere in the open, the Moonlight scope would have picked up his image. So he must be hiding behind some obstruction, a tree or a dense hedge, something.

"I asked, did you bring it?"

Andrew debated how to answer. Yes, and Robert could shoot him down and take his prize. No, and Robert might have to keep him alive a little longer. Even a few more seconds seemed crucially important, the most important thing in the world.

"No," he said.

"Liar."

The fatal shot was coming. Andrew could sense it. He had to do something, anything.

His reflexes were quick. If he snap-rolled away from the decoy, scrambled for cover in the closest trees . . .

Yes, right, that was what he must do.

But he couldn't seem to move. Fear had closed over him like a fist, squeezing him into a tight little huddle of immobility and shuddering helplessness.

"You brought it," Robert said.

He was close, so close, not more than twenty feet away. But where? The clearing was utterly dark, the moon now hidden behind a sheet of cumulus. Shadows swarmed everywhere.

"You love your wife," Robert went on softly, "and you'd do nothing to jeopardize her chances. Show it to me."

Andrew still couldn't move, couldn't think.

He'd thought he was tough. A criminal had to be tough, and he'd been a criminal for years, selling shares of nonexistent condominium developments, hawking forged artworks to pretentious dilettantes. He'd thought he was ruthless. Just look at the way he punished his hapless adversaries on the tennis court—hell, he had them begging for mercy by the end of the second set. He'd thought he was smart, smart enough to outthink a crazy son of a bitch like Robert Garrison, smart enough to cover every angle and anticipate every move and countermove.

Wrong. Wrong. Wrong. Game, set, match.

A gunshot, sudden and shocking, and the dead man beneath Andrew finally shifted his position as a bullet struck home with a sickening meaty *thwap*.

Andrew saw a new, ragged hole in the coat collar above the shoulder blades.

"Obey me!" Robert screamed.

Andrew, hating himself, started to cry.

His hands fumbled at the cargo pocket of his coat, struggling to pull out the bulky, folded envelope. Soundless sobs wrenched his shoulders. He had no dignity. He was a blubbering mess. Henry, the obsequious bank manager, would be amazed to see him like this. He could hear the man's sotto voce comment: *That's Mr. Stafford. One of our best customers. Also a damned cowardly weakling, wouldn't you say?*

"Hurry up," Robert said in his pitiless way.

Finally the envelope came free. Andrew unfolded it with spastic fingers. His world was a haze of tears. Strange noises bubbled and chirped at the back of his throat. He had never thought much about dying, but when he had, he'd invested the occasion with a certain solemnity. Nothing like this.

"Take out what's inside."

Robert wanted to be sure he'd really brought the blouse. Well, that made sense, didn't it? The man had used a decoy of his own. He had to consider at least the possibility that Andrew would prove equally crafty.

And once he saw the blouse, satisfied himself that it was genuine . . .

Then it would be over. Andrew would die here, straddling a corpse, unable to move or map a strategy or even summon an inspiring thought.

He had done all this for Erica, hadn't he? He wondered why. She meant nothing to him now. He couldn't even picture her face or recall her voice. Probably he did love her, but love was a distant concept, abstract and unreal.

Reality was each shaky breath, the booming of his heart over the hissing of the falls, the sheen of sweat that coated him like a second skin.

Clumsily he tore open the envelope, then reached in and pulled out a pink wad of fabric. It fell open to reveal itself as a woman's long-sleeved blouse, unbuttoned, patchy with dried bloodstains and red whorls of fingerprints.

"Very good, Andrew. First you dig it up like a sniffing dog, and now you bring it to your master. I am well pleased."

This was it. Endgame.

Andrew's lips moved, and he found speech. "Why didn't you burn it, burn all her things?"

The question was meaningless, a stalling tactic. Robert surprised him by answering.

"Because they are holy relics, sanctified by sacrifice. That blouse, for instance. Before that night, it had been only an insignificant scrap of cloth. Probably she bought it at Kmart, on sale for fourteen dollars. But once anointed by her blood, it became more sacred than the shroud of Turin or a splinter of the True Cross. Do you understand?"

"No."

"Of course not."

Then Robert rose, even closer than Andrew had thought, ten feet away, huge as a colossus, a revolver in his hand.

He had been hiding behind a low hillock of frozen earth, the embankment of a ravine. In the darkness Andrew hadn't even seen it. It made for ideal cover.

The revolver tilted down fractionally, targeting Andrew's chest.

"Now your blood will sanctify this relic in a new ablution," Robert whispered.

Andrew dropped the blouse and waited, facing death through a scrim of tears, wishing he had not died so poorly, sniveling and whimpering, a beaten dog.

Robert smiled. "Goodbye."

And a white stripe of moonlight graced the clearing in a sudden glittery fall.

The gun did not fire, not yet.

"Look, Andrew." Robert's smile had widened. His eyes shone

with beatific craziness. "Your cold mistress has removed her veil of cloud to watch you die."

For one moment Robert tilted his head, glancing up at the emerging crescent in the sky.

What Andrew did then was not planned, was not the product of conscious thought or calculation. It was instinct.

He pivoted at the hips, and in a single continuous motion he seized the shotgun, wrenched it free of the dead man's hands, and swung it toward the hillock.

His finger curled over the trigger. He had time to think that if the gun was unloaded, he was dead.

The world was ripped apart by a crash of noise.

He was knocked backward, sprawling on the ground, and he was sure he'd been shot, bloodied, his last chance wasted because Robert had fired first, and then he understood that the shotgun's recoil had blown him off balance.

Somewhere over the bright clamor of bells in his ears, there rose an anguished groan.

Robert—hit.

"Hear that?"

Connor nodded in reply. A single percussive crack, distant but clearly audible.

"Could've been a shotgun," he said.

"Like Charlie's."

"Let's go."

Connor slid behind the wheel of the squad car, Elder slipping in beside him as the motor caught.

A second blast fractured the night stillness.

"Coming from due east," Connor said.

He reached for the radio mike, but Elder had it already, and as the car screamed onto the highway, he heard the older man speaking with a practiced blend of urgency and calm, requesting backup.

Andrew pumped the shotgun again, fired a second time at the embankment, and then the gun was empty. He discarded it and rolled into the brush, his world a riot of pinwheeling shadows.

He needed another gun, and he knew roughly where to find one—the pistol he'd tossed away—if he could hunt it down . . .

Crawling through weeds. His face nicked by brambles. Blood on his cheeks. The hiss of the falls louder than before, impossibly loud, a consuming roar, but of course it wasn't the falls he heard, it was the buzzing static in his deafened ears.

Elder hung up the microphone, then seemed to remember that he wasn't the police chief anymore.

"Sorry, Chief," he said almost sheepishly. "Guess I stepped on your territory there."

"Forget about it. You thought quicker than I did. And no more of this crap about getting old."

"I feel plenty rejuvenated right now."

Backup was on the way, a pair of units speeding from downtown. They would intercept Connor and Elder on Route 36 in three or four minutes.

Connor slid down the side window, indifferent to the rush of winter air, listening for more gunfire but hearing none.

"About that file," he said as the highway poured under him in a blur of speed.

Elder grunted. "You read it, did you?"

"Skimmed through it. Kept the clipping." Connor yanked the folded sheet of newsprint out of his pocket and handed it over. "I take it you think they were responsible. The two of them."

Elder unfolded the page and glanced at it. Connor knew he was looking at the headline, GARRISON SCION DIES IN DROWNING ACCIDENT, and the large black-and-white photo above the fold. A photo of two grieving people who hugged each other before a body draped in white on the lake shore.

He remembered the caption: *Lenore Garrison, widow of Duncan Colin Garrison, is comforted by the family physician, Keith Wyatt, M.D.*

"Yes indeed, Chief," Elder said. "I believe it was them."

There. The pistol. A smear of shining metal in the newfallen moonlight.

Andrew snatched it with a snarl of pleasure and whipped toward the embankment.

Robert was silent now.

Dead?

If he wasn't, he soon would be.

"They killed Duncan Garrison," Connor said over the engine whine. "Lenore and Keith. His wife and the family doctor. That's what you think?"

"Sure."

"But it could never be proved."

"No, and what would be the point? They were both long dead by the time I wrote that fancy sawbones in Baltimore."

"Then why'd you bother to write to him at all?"

Elder lifted his bony shoulders. "Curiosity. Haven't you ever wanted to get to the bottom of a thing, no matter what?"

Connor thought of the rogue cops in New York. He nodded. "I know the feeling. But—"

In the near distance rose a flurry of staccato bangs, unmistakably handgun fire.

"Hell," Elder muttered. "Some kind of small war going on."

Connor accelerated to seventy-five.

Andrew thought he glimpsed movement along the embankment, and with reflexive savagery he thrust both arms out, the pistol leading him, and he fired three times, his shoulders jerking with each shot, plumes of dirt exploding from the hillock in a glittery mist.

Then a hectic scramble to new cover, closer to his target. Sprawling on his belly, he fired twice more.

Get closer still. Go.

He ran in a crouch to the shelter of a deadfall a yard from the ravine and emptied the pistol with two more shots.

The pistol's action was hot, the last two expended shells sparkling around him in stripes of moonlight.

Huddled behind the deadfall, he fumbled a spare magazine out of a cargo pocket and managed a clumsy reload.

Then he peered at the embankment again, half-expecting to

see Robert stalking toward him, and ready to cut the insane motherfucker to pieces with another seven rounds.

No one was there.

Was he dead? Was the goddamned bastard dead?

Andrew wanted him dead, wanted it so badly.

With a start he came back to himself.

No, Robert couldn't die, or the trail to Erica would be erased. If she was still alive, his captive someplace, she would die slowly, her whereabouts forever unknown.

Enthralled by fear, he'd forgotten her, forgotten everything.

Shame made him reckless. He left his hiding place and ran to the embankment, daring Robert to open fire.

At the edge of the ravine he looked down.

Empty.

Robert was gone.

Cutting speed, Connor approached a side road. "Should I take it?"

"Dead end," Elder said. "Nothing down that way but the Oldham farm."

Connor kept going. The shots had fallen silent after a trio of bursts. Six or seven rounds had been expended. He thought of the firefight in his apartment. Another battle was being waged tonight somewhere in these woods. And he knew who the combatants had to be: Robert and Andrew. Their rendezvous, it appeared, had not gone quite as planned.

With effort he refocused on another night of violence, many years ago. "Keith and Lenore killed each other in Great Hall," he said. "It was more than a lovers' quarrel."

Elder nodded grimly. "They were conspirators. Way I see it, they got to hating each other. Guilt'll do that. But they couldn't split up. They were bound together by a common secret and by a common greed."

Greed. Yes, that must have been the motive. Keith's motive, at least.

"Tell me about Keith Wyatt," Connor said as he slowed the car further, looking for another side route.

"Well, he was a handsome man, you know. Tall and limber,

and all the ladies liked him. He was Barrow's most eligible bachelor. Took over as local GP after Doc Braddock retired in '72. He was thirty-two, a year older than Lenore."

"And Duncan was fifty-three."

Nod. "Older husband, younger wife. Perhaps there'd been some love between them once, or perhaps not. Either way, after bearing two children, Lenore grew restless, I think. She wanted fun. She wanted to be a girl in love, not a housewife with a spreading middle and stretch marks on her tummy. And along came young Dr. Wyatt."

"They had an affair." Connor hated saying that last word, hated the ugly sense of a connection between him and Keith Wyatt, a shared sin.

"Must have, though they kept it quiet. My guess is, she wanted a handsome young beau, and he wanted money. The Garrison fortune. Together they worked out a way."

"Easy enough," Connor said. "A doctor would have access to pharmaceutical products."

"Including cyanide."

"The autopsy showed Duncan had eaten breakfast."

"Scrambled eggs." Elder released a brittle chuckle. "Seasoned with white powder by his loving wife."

"Wouldn't it have kicked in right away?"

"I asked Dr. Kondracke in Baltimore about that. He said the reaction time varies. In Duncan's case, he had time to walk to the pond and begin his morning swim. The attack must have come on in a wave of pain—terrible pain. He swallowed water and went down. They found him at the bottom of Turtle Pond with his face in the muck . . ."

Elder let his voice trail off, and Connor knew they were both picturing the sudden convulsive shudder, the panicky thrashing, the desperate effort to reach land, and then a final crash of pain and weakness. Death in the water, a man's body sinking into layers of sand like a forgotten toy left at the beach.

All that remained was for Lenore to put on an appropriate display of grief, and for Keith, summoned on an emergency call, to gravely report that there was nothing he could do. His initial diagnosis of a heart attack and subsequent drowning would only be confirmed by the unsuspecting coroner, who would never think of running the lab tests necessary to detect cyanide.

"After a barely decent interval," Elder said, "Keith moved in with Lenore. Later on, they announced their engagement. People talked, but the gossip didn't go very far or very deep. No one suspected murder."

"Except you."

"Well, I thought it was funny, how fast Keith Wyatt showed up. He got there before the ambulance. As if he was expecting the call. Or maybe he was even there already, waiting around in case of any last-minute complications. Besides, he was a strange one. I, well, I did a little asking around."

"And?"

"He might've been a family doctor, but he was no Marcus Welby. More like a hippie character, flower child. He'd been at that love fest in San Francisco, that Summer-of-Love thing, a few years earlier. He dressed nice in public, but around the house he put on silky robes or sometimes those jumpsuits like the Viet Cong wore. Went barefoot indoors all year long—some crazy notion he got in one of the mimeographed magazines he read. You know the type."

"Sure."

"Anyway, the whole situation just didn't sit right with me. But there was nothing to nail down. I couldn't pursue it in any official way."

"So you waited until you could go through unofficial channels, with no one looking over your shoulder."

"By then, Lenore and Keith were dead, and the way they died only increased my suspicions. Family fights can get vicious, but people of that social class don't usually pull guns on each other."

"Which of them fired first? Does anyone know?"

"Had to be Keith. I think I even know how it happened. Lenore, see, she'd become a drunk. Shambling around in her nightgown at all hours of the day and night, talking too much. Keith must have been afraid she'd give them both away. Probably took out the gun just to threaten her, make her shut up, but things got out of hand and it went off. That's the way I read it."

"He shot her at close range," Connor said, putting it together. "And she got the gun away from him."

"That's right. Funny how hate can keep you going, even with a mortal wound."

Connor knew about that. NYPD locker rooms were full of stories about perps who'd absorbed two, three, four hollow-points and kept on coming, pumped up by adrenalized rage.

"She staggered after him, into the living room," Elder went on, "and she put a round in his handsome face, and then she collapsed on him, and they died together in a heap."

"And the kids saw it. Robert . . . and Erica."

"They were covered in blood. They must've been right there. When I found them hunkered down in the upstairs closet, I wondered if they'd ever get over it. Wondered if they'd turn out normal, or . . ."

"Erica worked through it," Connor said. "But not her brother. It warped him. It's what drove him insane."

"That—and maybe something else."

"What else?"

"You have to wonder how much he and his sister heard that night. How much they learned about Lenore and Keith and the secret they'd been keeping. It's just a notion that's been troubling me since our visit to the cabin. That rant of his, the religious gobbledygook he was spouting. You see how it might tie in?"

Connor didn't see anything. "Tell me."

"This goddess he's so fired up about—he compared her to the black widow, as I recollect. The spider who kills her mate. He said she was the female principle, the true power in the world, the universal womb. And what name did he call her by?"

"Mother . . ." Connor whispered.

Elder nodded. "A psychiatrist could make some hay with that, don't you imagine? I'd guess—"

Headlights on a side road. A car veering around a bend.

Instinctively Connor swung toward it, pinning it in his high beams—a Honda Civic, charging hard.

Connor flipped a dashboard toggle, and from the roof the squad car's siren blared a long ululant scream.

18

Boots slapping on the limestone floor, breath bursting from her mouth in raw chuffs, the lantern's light bobbing like a will-o'-the-wisp as she staggered, nearly fell, caught herself, and ran on.

She was going too fast, had to slow down, couldn't.

Her injured knee throbbed with hot new protests. Out of the darkness a scum-flecked pool appeared before her, and she splashed through it, cold filth spattering her pants. A fetid stink reached her nostrils, the stink of decay, and she thought of him again—Mr. Furnell in his crypt.

Erica ran faster, heedless of risk.

A low stalactite brushed her hair as she ducked, gasping. The lantern swung wildly, printing blurred comet tails on the walls. She didn't even know where she was anymore. She might have missed the exit, might not have seen the final lipsticked arrow. Might have doomed herself to run and run and run until the kerosene was consumed and she was in the dark forever.

Stop this. *Stop.*

Shaking, she halted. She bent over, nausea climbing through her bowels. A dry retching noise scratched at the back of her throat. She thought she would be sick.

Walled him up alive, Robert walled him up alive . . .

The urge to run nearly propelled her into another pell-mell flight. She forced herself to stand motionless.

Mr. Furnell was dead. Dead for years. Nothing left of him but bones and a shiny wristwatch and tatters of rodent-chewed clothes she'd glimpsed in her last, horrified look into the peephole.

There was no point in running from him. He was no threat to her. No threat to anyone.

"How could you do it?" she whispered to the caves. "Robert . . . how could you?"

But she knew the answer. Robert had hated Mr. Furnell, hated him for years. It was Mr. Furnell who'd put Robert in the Maryland boarding school, where the other boys taunted him endlessly for his abnormal shyness, his wounded-animal help-lessness, his aversion to violence of any kind.

His years of social isolation had nourished the seed of insanity within him and brought it finally to full blossoming life.

She supposed Robert had every right to hate their strict, un-bending guardian. But to kill him—and so cruelly . . .

She pictured Mr. Furnell, alone in his tomb, beating on the concrete wall until his fists were red and raw, screaming until his voice was gone. Then the cramps of hunger, the itch of thirst. The despair that would curl him into a fetal pose, shiver-ing like a beaten dog.

Had Robert visited him? Taunted him with promises of food and water? Perhaps there really had been gifts of nourishment, intended merely to keep Mr. Furnell alive that much longer.

How long had he lasted? How many days or even weeks?

It was worse than what Robert had done to the Wilcott girl. Her death had been quick. A stroke of a knife, and she was gone—while Mr. Furnell had languished in terror and starva-tion, in loneliness and pain . . .

But Robert, too, had known loneliness, pain, terror. Robert had been starved of love and friendship. He must have found Mr. Furnell's incarceration a fitting punishment.

And, in a way, didn't she . . . didn't she . . . ?

She pushed the thought away, but it came back to her.

Didn't she find it fitting also?

"I hated him too," she breathed.

But she'd never wanted him to die. Had she? Well, all right, maybe she had, but it was childish spite, not a serious intent—and there was no part of her, not even the smallest remnant of the wounded child she'd been, no part whatsoever that was . . . glad.

Of course not.

Calmer now, she raised her head and looked around. She

didn't think she had passed the exit after all. This part of the corridor seemed familiar. She must be close to the crevice that led to the sinkhole. Close to escape and freedom.

Her breathing was deeper and more regular as she proceeded, the lantern's light leading her.

She remembered the day in Rome when she'd learned that Mr. Furnell had disappeared, leaving what appeared to be a suicide note. *Please forgive me for what I've done,* he had written.

Once his embezzlement was discovered, everyone assumed he was begging forgiveness for his betrayal of his clients' trust. But was he?

Robert must have made him write those words, and Robert would have neither known nor cared about the embezzlement. What he wanted was an apology for the nightmare of his adolescence, a public apology, but one so carefully ambiguous that nobody would discern its actual meaning.

Well, he'd gotten his apology, and his revenge. His awful, unspeakable revenge.

A new tremor of sickness pulsed through her, but she forgot it, forgot everything, as she stopped short.

Less than a yard ahead, a red arrow flickered in the oval glow of her lamp, marking the crevice that opened onto the sinkhole.

For a timeless interval all thought was suspended, and all breath, as she slipped through the gap. Then with startling abruptness she emerged into the shaft, and above her was the night sky, awash in stars, ornamented by a crescent moon.

Such beautiful things to see. She sagged, relief and happiness making her weak.

Her private celebration lasted only a moment. She wasn't out yet. She had to ascend the shaft.

The rope was gone, as she'd expected. She reached out, testing the wall of the sinkhole with one hand. The stone was rough and pitted. She could find handholds, toeholds. And her knee had not stiffened. She was limber enough. She could climb.

Climb twelve feet straight up? Climb, simply by wedging herself in the narrow shaft?

She had to. That was all. It was climb or die.

Unless . . .

The police had been here earlier. They might still be searching.

Carefully she set down the lantern, then cupped her mouth and drew a breath and put all the force of her lungs into a desperate shout.

"This is Erica Stafford, *can you hear me . . . ?*"

The cry traveled upward and escaped into the night. She awaited a reply, heard none.

They were gone, then. Or at least too far away to help.

She rubbed her hands together, wishing Robert hadn't removed her gloves. Limestone was rough, and her bare skin would be chafed raw before she reached the top of the shaft. But it was only pain, and pain didn't matter. Nothing mattered except starlight and moonlight and currents of crisp night air—deliverance from the underground, a return to the world of the living.

She was Persephone. And her sojourn in hell was nearly done.

She pulled in a series of shallow breaths, reminding her body of its training, the daily four-mile jogs that had strengthened her heart and lungs. Extending both arms, she ground her palms into the walls of the sinkhole. Slowly she lifted herself, braced by counterpressure, while her right boot sought a foothold.

And found one. There.

Trembling with strain, she inched farther up the shaft.

The Honda didn't even slow down. It came barreling forward at an insane speed, and for a second Conner was sure the hatchback was going to plow head-on into his cruiser.

Instinctively he spun the wheel, veering sideways, his siren still yodeling madly, naked trees dancing in the flashbar's staccato bursts.

The Honda blew past him, close enough to shear the side-view mirror from the doorframe, trailing a wake of sparks. With a howl of tires it bounded off the road into the woods.

Connor slewed the cruiser around, manhandling the wheel. His high beams sliced through a blur of shadows and illuminated a fire road. The Honda hadn't taken off into the trackless forest after all. Connor could see the receding glow of its taillights, already a mile away.

He gunned the engine, and the cruiser pounced on the fire road and clawed up distance. The road was rough and pitted, strewn with debris, and the car shook like fury.

Ahead, the Honda wiggled and shimmied on the uneven surface. The little hatchback was being driven hard, but its four cylinders were no match for Connor's eight. Even now the gap was closing.

"Get ready!" Connor's shout rose over a racket of rattles and engine roar.

He drew his revolver, then saw that Elder's gun was already unholstered.

The road twisted in a sudden turn, and Connor flung the cruiser to the left, bare branches raking the windshield and roof.

His high beams glinted on the Honda's rear fender. He could see Robert hunched over the wheel, a ragged outline of unkempt hair and bony shoulders.

The cruiser's speedometer was pegged at eighty-eight. The Honda's top speed on this road was probably ten miles lower. It wasn't a fair contest.

Elder was thinking the same thing. "Son of a bitch should've stolen a faster car," he yelled.

Less than a hundred yards separated the two vehicles now. The Honda weaved from side to side, Robert desperate, crazed, or maybe just trying to maintain control of the car as he pushed it beyond its limits of tolerance.

Connor shut off the siren and got on the P.A. system. "Pull over to the side of the road. Pull over—"

An arm swung out of the Honda's window on the driver's side, and Connor glimpsed a purple muzzle flash, heard a bullet sing past the cruiser.

Elder barked a nervous laugh. "Guess he's not much for following orders."

Connor gave up on the loudspeaker, reactivated the siren. Its blare unwound from the rooftop in spirals of earsplitting whine.

Robert fired again, the shot flying wide to the left.

"Fuck you," Connor said.

He refused to drop back, would not be intimidated. Recklessly he continued to narrow the gap with the hatchback, aware that he was risking Elder's life and his own.

Robert's driving had deteriorated. The Honda could hardly stay on the road. It jerked and fishtailed, glare from the cruiser's flashbar cycling in crazed pulses across the large rear window.

Then Robert started blasting his horn.

Connor didn't understand why. Maybe there was no intelligible reason. Robert was insane, after all, and in a panic.

He was dimly visible in the red and blue flashes, a shaggy figure in the front seat, banging with apelike ferocity on the wheel. The horn blatted feebly above the siren's scream.

Its scream . . .

A thought prodded the edge of Connor's awareness—the wax earplugs in Robert's cabin—the way he'd looked when Connor asked what noise a man would hear in the stillness of the woods.

Then the Honda darted to the left, quick as a hummingbird, and it took Connor a startled second to realize that the road had coiled in another treacherous curve.

He cranked the wheel counterclockwise—

Too late.

The Chevy floated in a skid, leaving the road, a swarm of leafless shrubs hammering the passenger side, fracturing glass, cracking one headlight, gravel spraying everywhere, Elder thrown hard against the door with a grunt of pain, and then miraculously the car found its footing and jumped back onto the road, but directly ahead the Honda had not been so lucky.

The sharp turn had spun the hatchback sideways, and now it spun crazily and came to rest straddling the road, exposing its flank to the cruiser.

Connor had time to see Robert drop down, and then the cruiser tolled with a clang of impact.

The front end accordioned. The windshield fell apart in a rain of gummed fragments. The radio, crackling idiotically all this time, burped up a blast of static and went dead.

Connor saw white, a world of white, the airbag ballooning to enfold him, then deflating an instant afterward. The back of his skull hit the headrest, and there was pain everywhere and, for a moment, darkness.

Robert clapped his hands to his ears and screamed.

It was behind him and above him and all around him, the noise, *their* noise, the terrible sound of their tormenting pursuit, and he couldn't stand it, he would do anything to make it stop, make it go away—

Some rational fragment of his mind understood that it was only a police siren he heard, unspooling mechanically, a meaningless distraction, but he couldn't make the thought real, not when *that noise* was in his head, bursting against the fragile walls of his skull, exploding like bombs, clawing like fingernails, making him *insane*.

The voices. *Their* voices. Screeching at him, his night visitors, his tormentors—and the things they said, the terrible things they said—

Look at him, crying again, pathetic child.

Like Niobe, all tears.

Loathsome he is, a bug of a man.

Not a bug. Excrement. Inhale the stink of his foulness.

Stink of pollution.

Of blood. He shits red, there's so much blood in him.

Ought to kill himself now, rid us of his disease.

He hasn't the nerve, he's a comb without a cock—do you know he's never been with a woman?

What woman would have him? He disgusts humanity, repels all living things.

As he should—outcast, pariah, scapegoat unpenned.

Oedipus blinded, Cain marked and exiled, a man of no nation, a suppliant turned from every altar.

The wind carries the smell of him, smell of ordure and piss.

He's nasty as a boil, soon to be popped.

Let him feel the sting of our scourges.

Let him scream.

Let him beg.

Let him die.

Let him die.

Let him die.

"Stop it!" he was howling, his hands pressed to his head as he writhed across the hatchback's front seats. "Stop it, just stop it, stop saying those things, just leave me alone!"

But they would never leave him alone, not for long, and his only chance, as always, was to outrun them.

Yes, run. This was the solution.

Get out of the car, the wrecked car, and flee.

But the door wouldn't open. It had been crushed like a can in the collision. He tugged on the handle, but the door was wedged in its misshapen frame.

And the screaming was louder, closer, a thousand bats disturbed from their roost and beating him with their wings and shrieking their ugly clamor.

Hurt him, he deserves pain, it's his inheritance.

Lash him, he's a whipped dog and his whimpering is good to hear.

Squeeze him like a pimple till the pus runs clear.

Drag your talons through his brain and groove the runnels deep.

Make him scream, scream for his mother and his lost childhood.

Scream, Robert! Scream like one accursed!

He hammered the steering wheel, the horn, howling in terror, but the horn's noise would not drown out the greater cacophony around him.

There was another door.

The thought came to him with perfect clarity, one lucid insight torn from the whirl of his terror.

Another door on the passenger side; he could exit that way, could escape, outdistance his enemies, do it, *do it now*.

He scrambled across the front seats on his belly, kicking, flailing, the terrible voices washing over him in wave after wave after wave, the riptide of their malice dragging him backward away from the door he so desperately needed to reach, but with a final frantic effort he thrust himself at the handle, and his fumbling fingers cranked it down, and the door swung ajar.

He had no perception of actually going through the doorway. There was only a blur of motion on all sides of him, indecipherable and frightening like a rush of free fall, then a sudden hard impact and a crunch of dirt and gravel under his skinned palms.

And by his right hand, jostled out of the car in his crazed escape—Vicki Danvers's gun.

Do it, worm, use the gun, use it now.

There's nothing for you to live for, nothing but pain.

Use the gun and you'll be free forever.

For a moment he thought how simple it would be—just lift the gun, put the muzzle to his forehead, and pull the trigger.

One bullet, and he would cut his tether to this earth, escape from torment. One bullet.

He'll do it now, the wretch.

See him lift the gun.

How light it is in his hand. He yearns for death.

Die, Robert.

Die and be free . . .

No.

Their words were lies. He would not be free. Death would not cleanse him of pollution. His corrupted soul would fly down into hell, pursued by his tormentors, who would hound him for eternity.

To be purified, he must live.

Must offer the final sacrifice.

Erica. Tonight.

With that thought he snapped back inside himself, and then he was on his feet and running, and though his enemies tried to pursue him through the colonnaded trees, Robert was faster, and as he covered yard after yard after yard, their voices faded as they fell behind.

The darkness cleared, and Connor came back to the world.

Beside him, Elder was groaning, unconscious, a lot of blood leaking out of his left coat sleeve. Broken arm maybe.

Connor couldn't think about that now. He shifted in his seat, felt no twinge of fractured bone. The big Smith was still in his hand.

Go.

He wrenched the door ajar, slid out of the cruiser. Something tore—his jacket, speared by a wedge of metal protruding from the warped doorframe. He pulled free of the obstruction, splitting his pocket, and dropped to his knees behind the open door, the revolver in both hands.

"Exit the vehicle!" His shout competed with the siren's idiot blare. "Exit with hands up!"

How long had it been since he'd said those words? He had not ridden patrol in a decade.

"Robert? Do you hear me? *Exit the vehicle now!*"

He was aware that Robert might be unconscious in the Honda, might even be dying or dead, but he was taking no chances.

"Exit right now!" he screamed.

The siren howled on. Around him the air was acrid with smoke rising in soft billows from under the cruiser's hood. The flashbar still cast its surreal dance-party glare over yards of dirt road and the two disabled cars locked in a snarl of steel.

Robert hadn't acknowledged the order or shown himself. The thing to do was wait here until the backup unit arrived. Surround the car, take no chances.

Oh, hell. There was no time.

Connor broke cover and approached the Honda, aware that Robert could cut him down easily if he were huddled inside.

Nothing happened. He examined the hatchback's interior in the light of the squad car's high beams and flashbar. The car was unoccupied.

The passenger door hung open. In the dirt road just beyond that door, Connor found a ragged trail of shoe prints, veering into the woods.

Connor sprinted off the road, but the tracks instantly disappeared in a dense ground cover of weeds.

"Shit," he hissed.

He returned to the squad car. Elder was stirring.

"Where . . . ?" Elder breathed. "Where is he?"

"Steady now, Paul." Connor shut off the siren, then tried the dashboard radio. It was dead. He rummaged on the floor for the portable. "He left the wreck, continued on foot. We were both out cold for a while."

"Can't have gotten too far." Elder tried to sit up, then winced. "Hang it. Think I busted a wing."

Connor recovered the portable. "You're lucky that's all you busted. We hit him at sixty miles an hour. Now rest, will you?"

Elder chuckled. "You sound like Corinne." But he let his eyes slide shut.

Connor thumbed the transmit button and told the dispatcher to patch him through to Lieutenant Maginnis on the tactical frequency. Maginnis's voice rasped over the cheap speaker a moment later.

"Chief, what the hell's happening? I've been monitoring the crosstalk—"

"Can't explain it all now. Who've you got with you?"

"Woodall and Hart, and Larkin just showed up."

"Okay, listen good." There was no way to phrase this indirectly to confound eavesdroppers, and no time to worry about it. "There's a suspect, armed and dangerous, on foot, probably headed right for you. It's Robert Garrison. Erica's brother. You copy that?"

A beat of surprised silence. "I copy, Chief."

"We had him in a high-speed pursuit on a fire road, but both vehicles got trashed, and he's on the run. I expect him to return to the area where the Mercedes was found. You and Hart and Woodall need to stay alert. You see him, get a weapon on him fast. No fooling around. This guy is out of control."

"Copy."

"Out."

Connor switched back to the main frequency and ordered an ambulance from the dispatcher. He was signing off when he glimpsed a flare of headlights in his rearview.

"Backup's here," he told Elder.

Elder didn't open his eyes. "Ain't backup. No Barrow P.D. rust bucket's got a motor that smooth."

He was right. The car was low slung, the tires wide-set. Not a sedan. A sports coupe. A Ferrari.

Andrew Stafford leaned out the window. "Need a lift?"

Robert kept to the shadows, staying clear of the moon's gaze. If she saw him, she might set her minions on his trail.

For now he'd outdistanced his pursuit. The voices had

diminished into silence, and there was only the great quiet of the woods at night.

He leaned against a tree, catching his breath, and listened.

Somewhere an owl questioned the darkness. Dry leaves crackled in a gust of wind. Bare branches scraped and groaned.

These soft sounds soothed him like a lullaby. He felt his racing heartbeat slow as his head cleared.

He'd escaped his nemeses, but not for long. They would track him down. They always did. Remorseless, they never gave up the chase. Next week or tomorrow or an hour from now, they would descend on him again, their catcalls bursting like bombs in his brain.

They were more than simply voices, of course. He had *seen* them—sometimes in dreams, sometimes in shadows or in ripples of reflection.

But what he'd seen . . . it was vague in memory, the images blurry and disjointed. He could call to mind pieces of what he'd glimpsed, parts of the whole, but somehow he could not integrate these isolated elements into a total picture. He'd tried. Just this morning he'd scrawled crude illustrations on sheets of writing paper, but as always he'd ended up with particular details, not a finished portrait.

Still, the details were bad enough.

Dog snouts. Bat wings. Nests of snakes. Hooked claws.

The snouts were for sniffing out his trail, and for barking and whining and raising their wild, ululant cries. Wings—so they could fly after him, or fly up to the heavens and scan the earth for his tracks. Snakes, writhing, sprouted from their scalps like hair, fanged snakes that unleashed a cascade of hisses, another noise that tormented him. And claws, yes, sharp and curved, claws that would sink into his skin and past it, into his very soul, when they dragged the immortal part of him into the underworld and fed like jackals on his pain, forever.

He knew all this—and more. He knew their names.

Alecto. Megaera. Tisiphone.

Three sisters. The Mother's unholy three. The Mother, who was whore-bitch-beast. The bloody Mother, whose screaming harridans had plagued his sleep and haunted his solitude and left him finally with no choice but purification through blood.

Purification. Yes.

He might not escape this world's justice—not after his failure to dispatch Andrew Stafford, his run-in with Connor on the road. Unless he could escape or hide, he was sure to be arrested. He would spend the rest of his life in prison or in an asylum. Perhaps he would be put to death—burned alive, like Joan of Arc, or crucified upside down, like Peter.

They, too, had heard voices, though of a different kind.

But what was done to his body was of no consequence once his soul was clean. Free from psychic torment, he could bear any indignity, could face even death without fear. Death meant only that he would be a shade among shades, wandering in Tartarus, and though it must be a drab existence, a pale shadow of life above ground, still his soul could bear it, so long as his affliction had finally ceased.

He lowered his head and exhaled a jet of frost, shivering. For the first time he noticed that the night was cold.

But the caves would be warmer.

There was something in his hand. He looked at it, mildly surprised to see that, by some reflexive wisdom, he'd snatched up the gun, Diana-of-the-forest's gun.

He opened the cylinder. While lying in wait for Andrew, he had reloaded. Since then, he had used three rounds. Three were left.

Three. A mystic numeral. The number of the Mother, who was virgin and wife and hag, birth and life and death, moon and earth and hell. He nodded, pleased by this hopeful omen.

In his pocket he found the extra ammo taken from Vicki Danvers's dump pouch. He loaded the revolver, tamping three cartridges into the empty charge holes, then snapped the cylinder shut.

When the gun was again wedged inside his waistband, he leaned out into the open and oriented himself by the stars.

He had run east, due east. He was close to the sinkhole. Without conscious intention, he had covered the ground he needed to cover, reached the spot he was fated to reach.

Erica was very near.

"I'm coming, Sissy," he whispered, and the distant owl hooted its approval. "It'll be over soon—for both of us."

* * *

Slowly, with concentrated effort, Erica climbed higher.

The floor receded, and the sky drew close. Up the shaft rose the cone of flickering light from the lantern, outlining hand-holds and footholds in sharp relief.

Climbing was hard, but curiously she experienced the difficulty as if it were someone else's body being pushed to its limits, another person's muscles burning with strain. Her fingers were split and bloody, her palms rubbed raw, her wrists achingly sore. The injured knee had begun to swell; stiffening was imminent. It was impossible for her to go on, when every joint and tendon cried out in distress. Yet none of this could reach her, touch her. Her body was only an instrument bending to her will, its protests of no significance.

She would reach the top or die. There was nothing else in the universe—no pain, no exhaustion—nothing but this single purpose and the will that drove her toward it.

Gasping, glazed in sweat, she raised herself another few inches, then braced her body in the shaft. She glanced up to gauge the distance to her goal, and suddenly she felt a surge of emotion, dizzying in its intensity.

For a baffled moment she thought she was having a panic attack, fear of heights, something like that. Then she realized it was exhilaration she felt—exhilaration, because the top of the shaft was almost within reach.

Less than a yard to go. Nothing could stop her now.

This end of the shaft, scoured smooth by rainwater, offered no handholds she could see. To traverse these last three feet, she must rely on counterpressure alone.

She ground her palms into the walls. Shaking all over, blowing chuffs of breath in explosive bursts, she pulled herself ten inches higher.

Agony raged in her shoulders, her hips. Bolts of pain ripped her neck. Her left knee flared like fire.

So close now. The warmth of the caves was gone, the frigid night air enveloping her. The cold was numbing, soothing. It gave her strength. She couldn't fail.

Another upward glance. The lip of the sinkhole was just within reach.

Knees bent, boots planted, she braced her back against one

wall, then lifted her arm, groping for the rim of the shaft. In the chalky wash of moonlight, her fingers were bleached and surreal, skeletal fingers like Mr. Furnell's, reaching forlornly for a desperate hope.

Then she grasped the fringe of crumbly limestone, scrabbled for a secure hold. Chips of stone split off and pattered down, the edge of the shaft eroding to her touch.

This wasn't working. She needed to get higher, just another six inches or so. Laboriously she slid upward, hating her boots with their slippery soles, terrified of losing her precarious purchase on the rock.

Then she reached out again, groping for something solid, sure she could make it now, and a hand closed over her wrist.

Robert's hand.

"Go with him," Elder said, eyes still shut against the pain. "I'll wait here."

Connor frowned. "I can't leave you."

"Oh, hell, the damn arm's nothing. I've gotten banged up before, Chief. Anyway, we got a backup unit and an R.A. on the way. One of them'll get here before long. Now scat."

Connor nodded and swung out of the squad car.

"Take the portable," Elder added.

"You may need it. The squawkbox is—"

"Busted. I know. Take the portable anyway. If I need help, I'll holler."

"Better yet, use this." Connor thrust the cell phone at him, then sprinted to the Ferrari before Elder could protest.

Sliding into the passenger seat, he felt Andrew's cool, appraising stare. "Had a close encounter with our friend?"

Connor nodded. "Both cars are totaled. He took off on foot. Still heading east. At least that was how it looked from his tracks before they disappeared."

"He's going back to her. He's got her hidden someplace, and he's on his way there now."

"That's how I've got it figured too."

"He'll kill her. That's what he told me, when we talked on the phone. He said he would cut her throat. Called it his destiny—and hers."

"I've never believed much in destiny," Connor said.

Andrew eased around the pile-up. Connor glimpsed Elder in the front seat of the squad car, huddled in the pulsing glare of the flashbar.

Then the wreckage receded in the sideview mirror, and there was only the lightless fire road ahead. Andrew pushed the car hard, punishing the suspension on a series of ruts and bumps.

"Guess you're wondering how I happened to be in the neighborhood," he said.

"Not really. You arranged to meet Robert near here. Something went wrong. Gunfire was exchanged. He fled, and you're following." Connor looked at him. "Right?"

A smile, tight and forced, briefly warped Andrew's face. "You know, there was a time when I thought you might not be smart enough to cut it as police chief."

"Now fill in the blanks. What was the meeting about?"

"Erica. He's got her, obviously. I suspected as much from the start." He skirted a fallen branch, veering briefly off the road, his tires grinding up a thicket of weeds.

"Why didn't you tell me?" Connor asked.

"I thought I could persuade him to give her back."

"How?"

Brief hesitation. "A pay-off. I offered to reimburse him for Erica's safe return."

This was plausible, but Connor suspected it was a lie. Still, he let the issue ride for now. "What went wrong?"

"I don't know. I walked into an ambush. He tried to shoot me. I returned fire."

"Hit him?"

"Think so. Not sure."

"Did he hit you?"

"I was lucky."

The road curved, and the Ferrari sliced through an arc of motion without slowing down.

"This is a dangerous game you've been playing, Mr. Stafford."

"I'm not the only one who plays games."

Connor saw the bitter twist of Andrew's mouth and knew the reason for it. He almost didn't answer. But silence, here and now, would be cowardice.

"What's been going on between Erica and me," Connor said quietly, "was never a game. Not for either of us."

Andrew flicked a glance at him. "Is this a confession?"

"You already know about it. I found tonight that you've known for some time. I . . . I'm sorry about that."

"Of course you are. You're terribly sorry to have been balling my wife."

"She thinks you don't love her. She thinks you just married her for money."

"I did. It was a con. A scam. That's all it ever was."

"Then why did you meet Robert in the woods tonight? If Erica dies, you'll inherit everything, won't you? So why not let it happen?"

Andrew didn't answer. Connor nodded slowly.

"I thought so," Connor said.

Robert squeezed Erica's wrist, the pressure of his fingertips shooting lines of pain down her forearm.

"Well," he said in what might have been amused appreciation. "Haven't *you* been a busy little bee?"

She stared into his bearded face, his glinting pinpoint eyes. He smelled of sweat and dirt and something else.

Blood. That was it. His left shoulder was a shiny hump. A red glaze coated his neck, his collarbone.

She remembered the last time she had seen him bloodied, when he clung to her in the bedroom closet, the circle of her arms confining him as his small body shook.

She wanted to say something, reach out in some way, perhaps still make contact even now—

"Robert," she whispered.

A smile cracked the mat of his beard. "Bitch."

Then he thrust her away, clear of the sinkhole, his hand releasing her wrist with contemptuous indifference, and she was falling.

Andrew thought he must be crazy, picking up Ben Connor.

He hadn't planned on it, of course. His intention had been to follow Robert, and when he saw tire tracks in the dirt road, he pursued at high speed. When the pile-up had appeared around a bend in the road, he'd barely had time to stop.

Even so, he might have executed a U-turn and gotten away clean. But then he would have forfeited any chance of finding Robert.

And Erica would die.

The woods blurred past on both sides, tree trunks flickering in the glare of the Ferrari's high beams. He slammed the coupe over ruts and humps and, once, a small deadfall of broken branches deposited in a rain gully. The car would never be the same.

Well, what would be the same, after tonight?

At a crossroads he braked his speed. A second fire road intersected with the one they'd been traveling.

"Which way?" he barked.

"I don't know. East."

"Which way's east?"

"I'm all turned around. Have you got a map?"

"In the glove compartment."

Connor struggled to unfold the map as Andrew snapped on the reading light.

"Go left," Connor said after a moment spent squinting at the section of the map marked Barrow Woods. "And in about two miles, make another left."

Andrew steered through the turn. "We're taking the long way around."

"Can't be helped. There's no direct route."

"There is for Robert. He's on foot."

Connor nodded. "And he's got a head start."

No more conversation after that. Andrew was glad. He preferred not to answer any further questions about his rendezvous. He was weary of half truths and lies.

At least Connor seemed to have bought his story. The only remaining risk was the envelope tucked under the driver's seat, containing Sherry Wilcott's blouse.

Andrew had retrieved the blouse before leaving the ambush site. He couldn't let the police find it when they scoured the woods for clues, as they surely would once the decoy's body was discovered. Both the envelope and the blouse itself bore

Andrew's smudged fingerprints now. He would have to burn the package as soon as possible.

Unless, by some mischance, Connor found it first.

"Turn here," Connor said.

The next crossroads. Andrew spun through a left turn, nursing the brake. A sapling's branches scraped the car on the passenger side, dead leaves slapping at the window, and then he slewed into the middle of the road and barreled ahead.

Inertia tugged the envelope halfway out from under his seat. He kicked it back out of sight.

Damn.

If Connor saw it, opened it . . .

Then Andrew, having no way to explain how the blouse had come into his possession, would face a prison sentence. Accessory to homicide, concealing evidence of a felony—what would he get for that? Ten years? Twenty?

He shook off his fear. Ridiculous. Connor had no valid reason to search the car. He would never find the envelope. Never. He—

"Slow down," Connor said suddenly.

Andrew cut the Ferrari's speed and saw two uniformed cops not far ahead, carrying flashlights and guns.

One was a woman, redhaired, long-boned. He knew her from police charity functions. Maginnis was her name. Her companion wore a sergeant's stripes, but Andrew didn't know him.

Connor held up a hand. "Stop here."

Andrew braked the Ferrari in a swirl of floating dirt. Connor got out even before the key had been extracted from the ignition slot.

By the time Andrew joined the three, they were deep in discussion. He gathered that Robert hadn't been spotted, that two other officers named Woodall and Hart were patrolling the area, and that this very stretch of road was where his wife's Mercedes had been found.

Disoriented, he thought he was in the middle of the woods, miles from any major thoroughfare, until the hum of traffic reached him from beyond a nearby hill. Highway traffic—he saw the streaking trails of headlights. Route 36 must run past this spot.

He had driven down that highway while returning from the

racquet club. He must have passed the place where Erica's Mercedes was parked. If he had looked past the guardrail into the woods, perhaps he would have seen the car. Perhaps . . .

But it did no good to think about that now.

"Erica's got to be here someplace," Connor was saying.

Maginnis looked fatigued and much older than she ever had before. "Search patrols covered every inch of this area."

"They overlooked her somehow. They must have." Connor slapped a fist against his palm, shifting his weight restlessly, anxious for action. "What about the dogs? They show up yet?"

The sergeant, whose nametag identified him as Larkin, waved toward the highway. "Just arrived."

Andrew made out a distant human figure standing on the hillside, and with him a trio of four-legged shapes, low to the ground.

"Bring them down here," Connor said.

Maginnis cupped her gloved hands to her mouth and raised a yodeling cry. "Hey, Earl—get those mutts in gear!"

From the hill a dog bayed as if in answer.

Bloodhounds. Andrew felt a chill pass over him at the thought of the dried blood on Sherry Wilcott's blouse. Surely the dogs wouldn't sniff it out?

Dread gathered in him. He felt heavy and tired. He wanted to rest.

Then he realized Maginnis was looking his way for the first time. "What's he doing here?" she asked, punctuating the question with an inquisitive finger stabbed in his direction.

Connor started to answer, but Andrew cut him off.

"She's my wife," he said simply. "Is that a sufficient reason?"

Maginnis, eyes narrowed, studied this response, then nodded once. "I suppose it is."

Erica threw out both arms, wedging herself in the narrow shaft, and for an instant she thought she'd arrested her fall—but no, she was still descending, not plunging but sliding down, the gritty limestone peeling away her shirtsleeves and the skin of her palms.

A soft sound of fear, part grunt, part gasp, pursued her down the shaft, and dimly she knew it as her own.

Then as she slid lower a rock outcrop glided into view, and with her right hand she grabbed hold.

Her fingers were bloody, knuckles and palm and the heel of her hand all scraped raw, but she held on.

Above her, Robert swung his legs into the hole.

She looked down. A drop of perhaps four feet. Too far.

A powdery skitter of limestone rained on her face, her hair. Robert was descending, moving fast despite his injury, his shoes finding footholds.

He would carry her back to the throne room, put her on the table, secure her with the straps . . .

No.

She wouldn't allow it. Never again would she lie on that table, in that room of death.

There was no time to climb down, not with Robert directly above her. She had to risk a jump, hope she didn't break an ankle.

A breath of courage, and she released her handhold, plunging into space.

This time the fall was so short as to consume no time at all. She experienced only a rush of vertigo, then a slam of impact as both boots hit the stone floor simultaneously.

Her ankles held, but her left knee, weakened by her earlier stumble, failed her. She collapsed, twisting on her belly, agony shooting waves of brightness across her field of vision.

More dusty rain on her face. Robert, hurrying down, limber as an ape.

Had to get up. Run.

The knee wouldn't work. It had stiffened.

She scrabbled at the floor, trying to push herself upright, but her skinned palms kept slipping on their own slick blood.

Robert—huge now, filling the shaft.

She turned on her right side, trying to take the weight off her injured leg, and something hard and sharp bit her hip.

And she remembered.

The knife.

The dogs arrived at the fire road in a confusion of slobbering and agitated whining. There were three of them, all purebred bloods—"not mutts," as their owner pointed out to Maginnis with a wounded air.

Andrew was worried by them. He watched them writhing like the Hydra's heads at the ends of three taut leashes, and he wished he'd thought to shut the Ferrari's doors.

Could the odor of old blood, blood that had dried months ago, still carry to the hounds' sensitive noses?

He tried on various explanations. Robert brought the package to the rendezvous. No, that was no good; why would he? Andrew found the blouse in Robert's cabin earlier today and . . . Equally bad; it raised more questions than it answered.

There was no hope of talking his way out of this. If the dogs caught the scent, he was finished.

Maginnis was making introductions. "Chief . . . Mr. Stafford . . . this is Earl Cashew, local dog handler."

Cashew was an old, splotchy, bandy-legged fellow with a toothpick planted between yellow stumps of teeth. He grinned a greeting, and his dogs sniffed the air and one another's rumps.

"Mr. Cashew," Connor said, "we've got a suspect on the run."

"Suspect?" The toothpick wobbled giddily. "Thought it was some missing woman you was after."

"It is. There are two people. They—"

Cashew waved off the explanation with an uncaring hand. "Don't matter none to me. I get paid a flat rate, see? Regardless."

"You'll be paid," Connor said impatiently.

One of the dogs was straining in the direction of the Ferrari. It had caught the scent, God damn it. But Cashew hadn't noticed.

"Then all we need," Cashew said, "is something for my gals to sniff. They got to work that scent into their noses, they do."

Connor reached for the pocket of his vinyl jacket—then swore.

Everyone looked at him. Even the dogs seemed suddenly intent on the drama of the moment.

"I brought something of Erica's," he said, tugging at the place where the pocket had been, the pocket that was now ripped nearly in half, dangling by a thread. "A headband—she used it when she went jogging—I put it in my . . . my . . ."

In his pocket, of course. The one that had been shredded, emptied.

Connor turned the pocket inside out, then reversed it again, his face looking shocked and drained.

"It's gone," he said unnecessarily. "I had it, but somehow—in the car wreck, I guess—somehow it got lost . . ."

Larkin unclipped his radio. "We can send someone to Great Hall—"

"There's no *time*!" Anguish lifted Connor's voice to a shout. "He got a head start on us, and he must've made a beeline through the woods. Damn it, he could be here already."

He looked around, as if expecting Robert to appear out of the maze of shadows. Maginnis and Larkin followed his gaze, and even Andrew found himself making a furtive survey of the surrounding hedges and trees.

Only Earl Cashew didn't look. He merely worked up a wad of spit and expectorated juicily on the ground.

"No way my gals can do the job without a scent to follow," Cashew said, sounding much too chipper under the circumstances.

Connor's eyes were darting as he cast about for some idea. "Can't they just sniff the ground," he asked, "find a recent trail?"

"Lots of scent trails around here, Chief. Squirrel and rabbit. People too. Cops like you. Lord, a stew of smells. My gals, they need to zero in on a particular scent, see? Like tuning in a certain radio station. Got to know the, whatchacallit, the frequency."

Connor turned to Maginnis, something like pleading in his face. "The Mercedes—it's been towed?"

Grimly she nodded. "Like I told you. All the way to the impound lot."

"You keep anything from it?" Desperation in his voice. "Her purse? Anything?"

"Forensics bagged it all. It's in the crime lab now."

Cashew made a token effort to be helpful. "You said there was two of 'em. Maybe you got something from this suspect on the lam. Something he's worn or handled. Don't have to be too recent, neither. Scent can linger for months."

Two dogs were snuffling in the direction of the Ferrari now.

Andrew watched them. He thought of Robert, ranting about the moon. He thought of Erica, soon to die at a madman's hands.

From a great distance he heard himself say, "For months?"

"Yessir, in some cases. Depends on the item, naturally. Fabric's best. Cloth'll hold a scent right good. The smell of a person just works itself into the weave and settles there."

"Cloth," Andrew said.

All three dogs were growling at the Ferrari now.

"Best if it's undergarments," Cashew went on conversationally, "or something else that would be close to the skin. Gets all sweaty, you know, and it's the sweat that really carries the odor, the real good stink my gals like."

Connor was looking at Andrew. "You have something of hers?"

Andrew took a long moment to answer. He cast a look around at the bare trees, the open sky. A prison cell was so small. Sometimes there was a window, but it would look out only on an exercise yard—dirt and stone. Nothing green flourished in a prison compound. There would be no buds to announce the spring, no scent of roses on a waft of summer air.

"Mr. Stafford?" Connor pressed.

The dogs pulled on their leashes, mesmerized by a scent they recognized, a scent of blood and sweat and death.

"I have something," Andrew said. "Not of hers. Of *his*."

He turned and stepped to the car, and it was the easiest thing in the world, really, no strain at all. He simply bent down and reached under the bucket seat and withdrew the soiled envelope, then walked back to Connor, the package held lightly between his palms.

The dogs barked. Cashew quieted them.

"This," Andrew said. "This is what you need."

His hands were not trembling as he gave Connor the package. He was glad about that.

Connor opened the flaps and took out the blouse, and his eyes narrowed.

"Sherry Wilcott's," Andrew said. "Robert handled it. Got his fingerprints all over it. Must've gotten his sweat on it too. The dogs can smell him, track him."

Larkin and Maginnis were staring at him. Slowly Connor raised his eyes from the blouse. "How long have you had this?"

Andrew met his gaze. "Long enough, Chief."

For a moment they simply looked at each other, and then with a jerk of his shoulders Connor turned away and gave the blouse to the eager, snuffling hounds.

19

The knife.

Erica gripped the handle and pulled it out of the belt loop of her jeans, marveling again at how long it was, how big and crude, and how unmistakably deadly.

She remembered wielding the packing knife in the hallway of her shop, not more than ten hours earlier. When she'd identified the intruder, she'd been sure she couldn't hurt him. Stab Robert? Wound her brother? Even in self-protection, it was unthinkable.

But that was before she knew for certain he was Sherry Wilcott's murderer—and Mr. Furnell's as well. It was before he'd strapped her to a table and left her to await a midnight execution. Before she had passed through hell and found a new reason to live.

She could hurt him now. To save herself, she could kill him.

Her grip tightened on the handle. The raw chuffs of her breath shook her body like gasps of pain.

Beside her, two shoes stamped on the floor. Robert, dropping down.

She kept her right hand tucked underneath her midsection, hidden from view. The bronze was cold against the light fabric of her blouse.

Robert stared at her, huge and hirsute, silhouetted against the glow of the crescent moon.

"So," he breathed. "You tried to escape. But that was never possible. This is *moira*. You know that word, don't you?"

She swallowed. She knew.

"Moira," Robert said. "Fate. Justice. And . . ."

"Death," Erica whispered.

"You do know." He seemed pleased. "You didn't forget."

How could I? she wanted to ask. *I taught it to you.*

Then he was reaching down for her, his fingers closing over her left hand, pulling her upright. Her knee flared but did not fold.

"Now," he said. "We'll do it now."

He would see the knife at any moment.

This was her last opportunity. Her choice was to do this or lie on the table again. Do this or die. And she would not die.

Her arm came up, and in a single sweep of motion she thrust the knife forward—then stopped, holding the blade a half inch from the hollow of his throat.

She looked into his eyes and thought of *moira* and the other things she'd taught him. Too many things. The wrong things.

The knife shook, spastic in her grip.

She lowered her arm.

Almost gently Robert took the knife from her.

"You couldn't do it," he said simply, no flutter of fear or relief in his steady intonation.

She moved her head from side to side, her vision blurring in an onset of tears. "Can't hurt you, Robert. Can't hurt you."

"Because you lost your nerve."

"No. Because I've hurt you too much already."

"You lost your nerve," he said again, pitilessly unmoved.

He tucked the knife handle under a rolled-up shirtsleeve, leaving the blade exposed, a triangle of bronze lying flat against his sinewy biceps. From his pocket he withdrew a coil of cloth and shook it smooth.

It was a scarf, bright red, and embroidered on it were the initials E.S., white and curlicued and festive.

Her scarf. Andrew's gift to her, stolen by the wind this afternoon. She had no idea how Robert had obtained it, and no strength to ask.

He stretched the scarf, drawing it taut, and she realized he meant to bind her wrists with it—bind her like a trussed calf.

Once bound, she would be helpless, and the future she'd fought so hard to win would be erased forever.

She spun toward the crevice. She would squeeze through, slip away, hide in the caves. Help might come. Anything was possible.

But Robert was too quick.

His fist closed over her shoulder from behind, and he jerked her up against his body, into the musky cloud of his rank sweat, and she was twisting, pivoting at the hips, trying to break free, and he laughed.

"No use, Sissy." His voice, soft as thought, rained down on her in a patter of ghost echoes from the walls. "I'm all grown up now, and hide-and-seek is a game I just don't play."

He yanked her arms behind her back, and there was a sudden burning pressure on her wrists, then numbness in her hands as he tied her with the scarf.

"Let me go," she breathed, the plea senseless.

His only answer was to twist the scarf still tighter, knotting it like a tourniquet.

Then he picked up the lantern, enclosing them both in a wobbly bubble of light.

"Move," he ordered, no kindness in his voice.

He pushed her through the crevice and into the main corridor, and although she struggled, she could not pull free of him or slow his steps as he marched her forward, relentlessly forward, to the throne room, where death and destiny waited for them both.

"That's enough," Earl Cashew said. "They got it in their noses now."

Connor nodded, some remote part of him amazed that a mere whiff of soiled cloth could stamp an impress in the dogs' olfactory sense. Carefully he replaced the blouse in the envelope and gave it to Tim Larkin.

"Find, gals," Cashew cried. "Find the bastard for me!"

The three hounds sniffed wetly, their sensitive snouts leading them instantly to Andrew Stafford. One dog bayed, and another tried to stand on Andrew as he backed away.

Cashew yanked the leashes, pulling the dogs clear. "Not him! No, gals, no!" He glanced at Andrew. "Some of you was on that blouse too."

"I handled it briefly," Andrew said, and then his face darkened, overcast with sudden anguish. "Does that mean the blouse is no good? They . . . they can't use it?"

"Nah, it'll do." Cashew spat again, and shifted the toothpick adroitly from one side of his mouth to the other. "A purebred blood like my gals can follow two, three scent trails at once. Can pick out your smell from another man's, even when they've mixed together." One dog was inching toward Andrew again. "Not him, I said! Find! *Find!*"

The hounds were briefly confused. Then the largest dog seemed to understand that the desired scent was another of the mingled smells imbedded in the cloth. She lowered her snout, snuffling and snorting with new eagerness, and her two companions followed suit.

Cashew followed the pack as they led him off the fire road into thickets of weeds. Connor watched them for a moment, then turned to Andrew. Curiously he was reluctant to face the man.

"You've incriminated yourself, Mr. Stafford."

Andrew's answer was only the slow incline of his head.

"Unless," Connor added, almost hoping Andrew had a way out, "you can explain how that blouse came into your hands—"

"I can't."

Connor let a moment pass. He hated what he was about to do. Of course Andrew Stafford deserved punishment. He'd concealed evidence crucial to a homicide investigation. There was no reason to feel sympathy for him. He was shallow, deceitful, opportunistic, and a criminal. He was everything Connor ought to hate.

But he hadn't been forced to give up the blouse. He'd done it of his own volition. He'd done it to save Erica—Erica, who was so very sure her husband didn't love her.

Connor almost wished he could hand back the envelope, pretend he'd never seen it. But there were witnesses. Besides, he played by the rules, didn't he? Always, by the rules.

"In that case, Mr. Stafford," he said with slow formality, "I'm placing you under arrest. You probably don't want to say anything further until you've spoken to a lawyer."

Andrew surprised him with a sly, subtly ironic smile. "Now you tell me."

By the roadside, the dogs had caught a new drift of scent and were loping in half-circles, trying to pick up the trail. Then one of them bounded off the road, and the others followed, all three scrambling to a dead oak tree.

Briefly they paused amid the lap of gnarled roots, whining and snorting, then ran on, deeper into the woods. Earl Cashew, playing out slack on the long leashes, panted to catch up.

Connor nodded to Larkin and exhaled a shaky breath. "Better take Mr. Stafford to your car." Larkin began to pull out his handcuffs, but Connor stopped him. "That's not necessary."

Andrew nodded his appreciation for the gesture. "Thanks, Chief. I suppose I won't be needing this."

From his coat he withdrew a Colt .45, the Combat Commander model. He held it daintily by two fingers.

"It's unlicensed, of course. A little souvenir of my salad days." That wispy, ironic smile returned. "I could've pegged you with it this afternoon, nice and easy."

Connor took the gun, remembering how Andrew had surprised him from behind while he was glassing the cabin.

"Maybe you wish you had," he said quietly.

Andrew only shrugged. "It wouldn't have helped me get her back."

The words were ambiguous enough to register only one meaning with Maginnis and Larkin, and Connor was grateful for that.

Then Larkin took Andrew by the shoulder in a firm but gentle grip. "Let's get going, Mr. Stafford."

Connor watched the two men begin the long walk up the hill toward the highway, Andrew holding his shoulders straight and his head high, like a victim climbing the steps of a scaffold.

"Hell of a thing," Maginnis said softly. "It's that house, you know. Great Hall. Nothing good ever came out of it."

"I didn't know you were superstitious, Lieutenant." Connor

managed a smile. "We'd better move. Those dogs are making tracks."

Maginnis nodded and jogged in pursuit of Earl Cashew and his bloods. Connor slipped the .45 into his jacket's inside pocket, then followed.

Cold wind raked his face. He ran through billows of his own breath.

At the oak he paused, wondering why the dogs had halted here. His pocket flashlight cast a spill of yellow light over the mossy bark. Carved initials jumped out at him, bold letters notched deep in the dead wood.

E.G.

R.G.

Erica and Robert Garrison. Sister and brother had played in this section of woods.

He ran on, trailing Maginnis, the two of them pursuing the noise of Cashew's footsteps and the eager tramping of the hounds. The woods folded over him. Bare branches clattered in restless currents of air. He thought of bones clinking.

Overhead the stars were sharp and brilliant as cut diamonds, the Pole Star brightest among them. The crescent moon, riding a band of dissipating cirrus, cast its blue glow on drifts of dry leaves.

Near a copse of pines two blue uniforms surprised Connor in the dark—Hart and Woodall, who'd heard the dogs and were joining the chase.

"Who're they tracking?" Woodall asked, jogging alongside him. "Mrs. Stafford?"

Connor shook his head. "Robert."

Hart swore. "Knew he was the one. We should've taken him in." Then he remembered whose decision it had been to leave Robert in his cabin. "Uh, sorry, Chief."

"Don't be. You're right. I've made some bad mistakes today." Connor was thinking of Vicki Danvers, wounded because he'd rushed her into a dangerous place without backup, and the gas station attendant, Charlie Whittaker, surely dead because Robert had been left free to roam and kill.

He ducked under a low branch, feeling a sweep of pine needles across the top of his head. In his path some small animal, apparent only as a skittering blur of shadow, darted into the concealing brush. He sucked air and tasted the bitter cold. His cheeks stung. His lips were chapped and raw.

The dogs came into view, shambling along at the ends of taut twenty-foot leashes, Cashew running hard behind his team.

"My ladies got a good scent!" Cashew called in a stage whisper without looking back. "They're on your boy's ass now!"

Connor wanted no more mistakes. "Slow down and keep quiet. This man's armed."

Cashew reined in the hounds. "Christ on an oyster, why didn't you say so?"

Progress was more deliberate after that. The hounds, alerted to the need for stealth by some telepathic connection with their owner, quit their whining and mewling. There was no sound but the crackle of snapping twigs and the rasp of frozen breath from five human beings and three dogs.

Then the trees thinned, and a low, rocky hill rose in the moonlight. Boulders were scattered before it, interlaced with brown weeds.

Was Robert huddled here? Hunkered down in the rocks?

Connor touched Cashew's arm, held him back. "Sit, gals," Cashew ordered with a quick pull on the leashes. The dogs dropped to their haunches, panting hard.

On the verge of the clearing Connor splashed his flashlight beam over a litter of ground cover and the mosaic of fragmented stone. Nothing stirred except the hounds, eerily quiet but quivering all over in their instinctive need to pursue the scent.

"Cashew," Connor hissed, "unleash your dogs."

"You want 'em to take a bullet? Is that it?"

"Better them than us."

"My ladies here—"

"That flat rate you mentioned—whatever it is, I'll double it."

"Even double won't cover the loss of a purebred blood."

"I'll cover the loss out of my own pocket if I have to. Now unleash your goddamned dogs."

Cashew fumbled at their harnesses. The dogs, though shaking with frenzy, were well trained, and they stayed put even after the collars had come off. Then Cashew patted the biggest dog on her twitching rump—"Find!"—and instantly the three bloods sprang forward, thirsting after the scent, wild with exuberance as they closed on their quarry.

Connor watched them scramble nimbly over the strewn boulders, nosing among the rocks before converging on a point.

They stopped, staring, panting, and somehow managed to convey the impression of both triumph and disappointment in their ragged stance.

No gunfire sounded. If Robert was there, he was dead or unconscious.

Connor brushed past Cashew, who lingered in the safety of the trees. He crossed the clearing, with Maginnis, Hart, and Woodall close behind.

The rocks were slippery and loose, and Connor lost his footing several times as he worked his way forward to the patient dogs.

Then he stopped, his flashlight beam bisecting the circle of hounds and showing him a narrow hole in the earth.

He eased closer, risked a look. It was a limestone shaft, angled in a vertical descent.

Robert was down there. Erica too. He'd hidden her below the ground.

The other three cops reached his side. "What the hell?" Maginnis breathed.

A restless hound, perhaps encouraged to break the silence by the sound of a whispered voice, let out a soft, anxious whine.

"It's the entrance to a cave," Connor said, "or a whole cave system."

"Sure." Hart's eyes were wide and bright. "The Barrow Caves. My granddad used to talk about 'em. They were sealed by a rockslide sometime way back when. At least that's what he said. I never knew whether to believe him or not."

"Well, you know now," Connor said, and thumbed his portable. "Tim? You read me?"

"Copy, Chief."

"We found what we were looking for. It's a network of sub-terranean caves. Repeat, underground caves. To get in, we need to execute a vertical drop of ten or fifteen feet. You got any rope in your cruiser?"

"Hell, Ben, I don't think so."

He glanced at Maginnis. "You?"

"Rope? No."

Hart and Woodall shook their heads also.

Connor thought hard. He needed rope or something similar—belts tied together or blankets in a knotted line or . . .

"Cashew," he called into the dark, summoning the man out of a pool of shadow. "Get over here. And bring those leashes."

She was fighting him, resisting with every step, but her efforts failed even to slow him down. Robert hustled her down the side passageway, toward the throne room, the lantern in his right hand swaying giddily, painting the limestone walls in swirls of light.

The glow limned the doorway of the grotto just ahead. Erica struggled harder. If she could break free of his grip . . .

But the scarf that bound her wrists was clutched tight in his fist, and he would not let go.

Through the doorway, into the room, the lamplight falling on the table, and she saw the loose straps that hung down like drooling tongues, and the blood-spatter pattern on the wood and the floor, and with a wild cry of rage she rebelled against his hold on her, every living part of her refusing to lie on that table again, refusing to accept the fate he had ordained.

Pivoting at the hips, she caught him off balance, and for an instant his grip on the scarf loosened, and she sensed her chance and pulled free.

The doorway was close, but she couldn't reach it, because he was there, tiger-quick, blocking her path, the lantern still in one hand, and the other hand coming up fast in a blur of speed that connected with her jaw.

The sting of his knuckles drove her sideways, her bad knee nearly buckling, and as she staggered he thrust her at the table.

She fell across the slanted tabletop, her bound hands pinned beneath her, and lay there gasping as ribbons of vertigo unspooled in her head.

"Stupid *bitch*!"

He pulled the knife from under his shirtsleeve, bronze flashing, the tip diving at her face and hovering an inch from the bridge of her nose. Past the blur of the blade loomed his face, bearded, flushed, framed in shaggy brown hair, and his lips skinned back from yellow teeth in a snarl.

"Stop fighting me. It's over. Can't you see that? It's *over*!"

And with a sensation of sinking numbness she knew he was right.

It was over. Yes.

There was no escape. If she ran, he would catch her. If she fought, he would win. If she hid, he would track her down.

Nothing was left for her, no option, no way out.

Her future was the knife in his hand. That was all.

"All right, Robert," she whispered in a voice so low and empty that it might have been a stranger's. "All right."

He studied her for a long moment, then nodded, plainly satisfied that she would pose no further threat. Slowly he backed away, setting down the lantern on the stone pillar where the other one had been, and crossed the room.

There was an interval when she couldn't think, couldn't move. Then she twisted onto her side, looking for Robert through a bleary haze.

He knelt by the cabinet, his head bent low over something on the floor, something hidden from her sight by his bulk and a slanting fall of shadow. The knife, she noticed vaguely, was not in his hand any longer. But he was not unarmed. A gun—a handgun of some kind—was wedged in the waistband of his pants, near his hip. She hadn't even seen it before.

He could have shot her at any time. But of course he wouldn't do that. She was an offering to whatever strange god he wanted to appease. She could not be blemished. She must be pure. Pure . . .

"It won't work Robert," she said softly, the words sticky in her mouth, like paste. "I'm not the one you want."

"Yes, you are. Hush now."

He was fumbling with the item in the shadows.

"No." It was difficult to speak. Her tongue felt swollen and numb. "I'm not . . . not *parthenos* anymore."

"Don't talk nonsense."

"It's true. You said I could never give myself to another. You said I was . . . poured metal. Cold stone. But not now. I've changed. I've grown. You need someone unattached to the world. That's not me, Robert, not any longer."

He stood, turned, and he was wearing the mask, the one she'd identified by touch in the darkness earlier, a stylized mask in the ancient tradition.

A bull's face. Angular and strange, its proportions exaggerated, the eyes too large under huge brows, the mouth a painted line.

From the corners of the mask twin horns protruded, carved not from wood but from antler, the rack of some buck Robert must have tracked and killed. The horns were narrow, tapered, curving, their polished smoothness shimmering in an orange gloss of lamplight.

Robert the bull-man. The Minotaur. An image weirdly appropriate here, in this stone labyrinth.

"You haven't changed," Robert said from behind the mask, his voice muffled and unreal. "You can't."

"Look at me. Take a good look. You'll see."

Almost unwillingly he took a step forward, then another, and leaned over her, peering down, and she stared up into the eye holes of the mask and met the glimmer of his gaze.

And he did see. She caught the flicker of recognition in his eyes, the sudden awareness that she was not the person she had been.

"I'm an initiate in the Mysteries, Robert," she whispered, choosing a reference he was sure to understand. "Like the novices in Eleusis, I've run the labyrinth in the dark. I've been reborn."

He didn't move or speak. For a moment she was certain she'd reached him.

Then with a jerk of his shoulders, a reflexive tremor of denial, he turned away.

"No," he said.

"Robert—"

"*No!*"

He returned to the cabinet, pulled out the chalice, set it on the floor by the table.

The chalice that would collect her cataract of blood, when her throat was opened in a sweep of bronze.

"It won't work," she insisted. "Not this way. You'll only make things worse."

"Worse?" He released a bull-snort of laughter. "How can things be worse? Worse than what they do to me every night and day? Worse than *that*?"

He seized her shoulders, bending close, the mask filling her world.

"You should hear them, Sissy. You should hear the words they say, the awful words—taunts and threats and jeers and curses—and it never stops, not for long, because no matter where I run, they find me, and they won't leave me alone . . ."

In her mind she was twelve years old again, at a boarding school in New Hampshire, holding a telephone receiver to her ear and listening as her brother sobbed at the other end of a long-distance connection—sobbed about the bullies who teased and harassed him, called him faggot and weakling, beat him up, played cruel pranks, *and they never leave me alone, Sissy, not for one minute, not ever!*

"Who, Robert?" she asked now, as she stared up at the bull mask and glimpsed the boy behind it. "Who is it you hear?"

"*You* know. Bitch. They're yours—and *hers*. Yours and the Mother's."

"Mother . . . ?" She couldn't follow this.

The mask jerked closer, the carved wood brushing her face. "Don't play innocent with me, you lying cunt!"

He was enraged now. She could hear the harsh rasp of his breathing, see the lurid glint in his eyes.

"Robert." Her voice soft and soothing, the voice of reason, which couldn't reach him now. "Whatever you hear . . . it isn't real."

"But it is. It's the only reality. The deepest reality. The oldest truth."

He pulled back suddenly, giving her space and air, and she drew a ragged breath as he stepped away.

"Others call it myth. But *we* know better." He spoke softly, a man in an animal mask, and for a moment she saw him as he must want to be seen: a priest, a shaman, the last holy man to follow the oldest path. "Myth is only the mind's best conception of the inconceivable, the finite expression of the infinite unknown. Myth is real. And *they*—they are real, all too real— the ones who torment me. I know them, and they know me."

"Then who are they?" she whispered.

The mask tilted, and again she saw the gleam of his eyes below the painted horns.

"Why, they're the Furies, Erica," he said, as if it were the most obvious thing in the world. "And they want blood."

Connor knotted the three leashes together. Their combined length was sufficient to stretch from the bottom of the sinkhole to a tree at the clearing's edge. Though the quarter-inch nylon lines were frayed and soiled, he thought they would take a person's weight.

An update from the dispatcher had informed him that a rescue ambulance had found Paul Elder and was transporting him to the medical center. A state trooper and two sheriff's deputies were en route to Connor's location, but the ETA was at least ten minutes from now.

Connor didn't want to wait that long, not when he was so close. But he worried that he was rushing again, making the same mistake he'd made with Vicki Danvers when his personal feelings had capsized his professional judgment.

His own life was his to risk. But the lives of those with him were another story.

He reached his decision. "Those knots secure?" he asked Woodall, who had lashed one end of the line to the tree trunk.

Woodall nodded, and Hart, kneeling by him, said, "Ray's a regular Boy Scout, Chief."

"Okay, then." Connor took a breath. "I'm going in. Alone."

"What the hell?" Woodall blurted out, and Hart swore.

"You two stand post with Lieutenant Maginnis, guard the entrance in case Robert doubles back and attempts to escape. Don't go down the hole till you've got reinforcements."

"Chief," Woodall said, "this is a really bad idea."

Hart concurred. "You need backup. This son of a bitch is a friggin' psycho. You go down there alone, and—"

"I'm not soliciting your opinions, Officers. Stand post."

Connor moved away before they could protest further. They might be right, of course. He really might be crazy to risk entering a warren of dark caverns with no one to cover his back. But he didn't care.

If there were to be any more casualties, he would be the one carted to the hospital—or the morgue. He, and nobody else.

"Ben."

Maginnis's voice. He turned and saw her standing just behind him, an unreadable expression on her face.

"I don't want an argument," he said curtly.

"Ben. This isn't New York. And it's not Cortez and Lomax you're up against this time."

He opened his mouth and shut it, baffled. Cortez, Lomax—how could she know about them? How could she . . .

"You don't have to tackle this alone," Maginnis added in the first gentle tone she'd ever used with him. "We're with you. All the way."

"Even after what happened to Danvers?"

A shadow passed over her face and was gone, and with a shrug Maginnis said simply, "It was a judgment call."

"You were going to file a complaint."

"Consider it dropped. Now do you want to be a hero, or do you want company down in that goddamned hole?"

Connor felt some of the night's tension easing out of him. "Come to think of it, a little company might be nice."

"Then let's do it." Maginnis clapped her gloved hands once. "Ray, Todd, get over here."

Woodall and Hart joined them instantly.

"All right," Connor said. "Lieutenant Maginnis has convinced me there should be a change of plans. Hart, you'll stand post alone. We need somebody guarding the entrance. Woodall, you'll accompany me and the lieutenant into the caves."

"Shit," Hart said, "Ray gets all the fun."

"Pipe down. And stay alert."

At the lip of the sinkhole Connor paused to tuck his flashlight into his belt, the beam aiming downward. Earl Cashew, squatting nearby, steadied his restless dogs.

"My ladies want to go down there with you," he said with a crooked, curiously impish smile.

Connor summoned a smile of his own. "They've done a good night's work as it is."

Then in one easy motion he grasped the nylon line in both hands and swung his legs into the shaft.

Hand over hand he descended. The line, pulled taut, shivered with the strain of his weight, but the nylon didn't tear, and the knots held.

Lower, lower. His heart working hard as he left the moonlit world behind.

Looking down, he saw pale dust floating in the cone of light from the flash. Limestone dust, a chalky cloud. He tasted grit in his mouth.

The floor was close. He released his grip on the line and dropped down, then instantly drew his gun, wary of an attack. His flash panned the limestone chamber.

It was empty, the walls scrubbed smooth by rain, except for one vertical crease that revealed itself as a narrow crevice offering access to a wider chamber or perhaps a tunnel.

Maginnis was already shimmying in pursuit. When Woodall reached the bottom, the shaft felt suddenly crowded.

Connor pinpointed the crevice with his flash. "That way. Keep your voices low."

He went in first, the flashlight leading him.

Erica, he thought, we're coming.

Maginnis and Woodall followed, and above them the hounds lifted their heads, baying in unison, a chorus of primal wails rising through the frosty air to the moon's white smile.

"Listen."

Robert hissed the word. Lamplight threw a flickering play of shadows across the bull mask, but no light reached his eyes.

Over her beating heart Erica heard a faint high-pitched howling, wolfish and strange.

"It's *them,*" Robert said. "The three."

The Furies. That was what he meant.

Erica knew about them, of course—the trio of hideous sisters who stalked the guilty, drove them mad. Winged like bats, hissing like snakes, dog-faced, shrieking and barking in a lunatic clamor. Though they had coexisted with the gods of classical Greece, the Furies had been bred from older stock. They were an offshoot of a primordial faith predating civilization— an aspect of the earth–moon goddess in her darkest phase, when she reigned as a deity of death and blood.

And to Robert, they were real.

"Have to hurry," he whispered. "They're on my trail."

The naked terror in his voice was awful to hear. His whole body was racked with shivers, shoulders jerking, hands twitching, and seeing him this way, Erica felt a sprinkle of moisture at the corners of her eyes.

"They never give up. They found me—even here." He took a sudden step toward her. "*You* led them to me, didn't you? Witch. Sorceress. Enchantress. You did it, of course you did."

She wanted to deny it but couldn't find the words, and it didn't matter, because he had already turned away.

He crouched by the cabinet, rummaged frantically in its shelves, removed the wreath of leaves. "They're out to stop me, your devil dogs. They know if I make a proper sacrifice, I'll be cleansed, absolved. They'll be cheated of their prize."

Hands shaking, he placed the wreath on her head, a crown of dried weeds. Royal adornment for the sacrificial victim.

Erica looked into the slits in the mask, where his eyes dimly glinted, and tried one last time to reach him.

"Robert, I'm not what you think I am. Please. I'm not."

But she knew he couldn't hear her. He heard only the maddening voices within his own skull, the voices that had driven him to kill Sherry Wilcott—and now, to kill again.

Connor squeezed through the crevice and found himself in a limestone corridor stretching in two directions. He'd never been inside a cave before. He was a city boy, always had been. Subways and stairwells he knew, but not a place like this.

The twin emotions of awe and dread competed for priority

within him. The corridor was weirdly beautiful: limestone columns like melting ice sculptures, masses of stalactites dripping from the roof like heavy strands of moss, intricate patterns of rust in shades of red and orange. For a moment he was a boy again, reading about Tom Sawyer in the cave with Injun Joe.

But there was fear too, the body's instinctive recoil against a sunless, airless world. Close walls, no light but the flashlight's feeble, wavering glow, and the dank taste of decay. He'd once been present at the exhumation of a body, and the smell from the opened coffin was the same one that lingered here.

A fifty-pound weight of claustrophobia pressed hard on his chest. He had to force his lungs to work.

Then Maginnis and Woodall were at his side, and he turned to them, grateful he did not have to face the caves alone.

"Which way?" Woodall breathed.

That was the question, all right. All three scanned the area with their flashlights, the beams panning and intersecting, widening and narrowing.

Hart saw it first. "There."

An arrow, red and glossy, was drawn on the wall near the crevice, pointing to Connor's right.

Connor touched the arrow, and it smeared under his fingertip. "Lipstick," he whispered. He didn't add that it was Erica's shade.

Woodall turned to the right, anxious to get started, but Maginnis stopped him.

"It could be pointing the way she went," Maginnis said softly, "or the way she intended to return."

Connor nodded. The same dilemma had presented itself to him. The lone arrow was too ambiguous a signpost.

"We need to find another one," he said. "Then we'll know if we're on the right track. For now . . ." He hesitated for only a moment. "We've got to split up. You two go to the right. I'll go left. If you find anything, raise me on Tac One. I'll do the same."

Maginnis frowned. "I don't like it, Ben. You'll be alone."

Connor wasn't crazy about the idea either, especially with fear of close, dark places tugging at his every nerve ending, but there was no time to hash it out. "Just go," he ordered.

She almost said something further, but stifled it with a visible effort. Motioning with her flash, she led Woodall in the direction indicated by the arrow.

Connor headed off the opposite way, moving fast into a tunnel of shadows.

From the cabinet Robert withdrew the small clay jar filled with liquid, and the woven basket. Violent tremors shook his hands, and he spilled some of the jar's contents even before he reached the table.

"They won't stop me," he was muttering in an urgent, breathless undertone. "Won't stop me, won't stop me, I'll be free of them soon, be free."

Erica felt a cool splash on her blouse, then another, and more. Robert was emptying the jar, sprinkling her with lustral water, pristine water doubtless drawn from a forest spring. Purifying her before the kill.

Mixed with the liquid drizzle was a patter of dry kernels. Barley grains from the basket.

They were the symbols of an ancient religion—grain and water, the flesh and blood of the living earth. She stared up at her brother, and for a moment she was not a woman of the late twentieth century, riding the millennial cusp; she was a virgin girl of Agamemnon's day, prostrate on an altar, rigid in expectation of death—and bending over her was a priest in his ritual mask, lit in a fireglow under a limestone roof.

The last grains dribbled from the basket. The last droplets spilled from the jar.

Robert tried to set the jar aside, but in his haste he dropped it. The jar hit the floor and burst in a spray of ceramic shards, like flower petals. He didn't seem to notice.

"Won't stop me," he whined.

He thrust his hand into the basket and brought it out, and in the lamplight Erica saw the bronze gleam of the knife.

She tried to speak, but her mouth was too dry, her throat too tight, and no words would come.

The knife flicked at her, and she was sure this was it, her last moment, the death stroke—but the blade merely snipped a few strands of her hair, which Robert collected in his open palm.

Breathing hard, sweat trickling from under the mask, he touched the shorn hairs to the lantern's wick.

Distantly Erica remembered that this, too, was part of the ancient ceremonies, this offering of the victim's locks to the fire, though she couldn't recall its meaning.

She knew only that it was the penultimate stage of the ritual. Death would come next.

Her wrists twisted slowly beneath her, rubbing against the knotted scarf. She squirmed on the table. She ought to fight, do something, buy time, even another few seconds. But curiously she couldn't find the strength.

Robert turned to her. She saw the bull's face, the crowning horns.

She waited, her last bit of willpower spent.

His left hand reached for her. Rough fingertips, hard as knobs, gripped her face. Erica moaned.

And slowly, with trembling care, Robert forced her head back to expose her throat.

The corridor was long and straight, and Connor made fast progress, pausing only to sidestep stalagmites and filmy pools swimming with impossible life. The caves were warmer than the outside world, and he was working up a good sweat under his jacket.

At each intersecting passage he played his flashlight beam over the walls, looking for another arrow, finding none.

He was ready to conclude that Erica had gone the other way and he was wasting his time, and then he saw a splotch of red, brighter than rust, on a wall a few yards ahead.

It was an arrow, drawn at the corner of another side passageway, pointing in the same direction as the first.

He peered into the long horizontal shaft and dimly made out a glow of lamplight many yards away. It spilled from another passage or from a grotto of some kind.

Instantly the walkie-talkie was in his hand, the volume dialed low. "Maginnis? You read me?" His voice was a whisper. "Marge?"

Only static answered.

The radio was useless, its signal blocked by thick walls of stone.

There was no time to double back and find Maginnis and Woodall. He would have to go in alone.

Do you want to be a hero, Maginnis had asked him, *or do you want company down in that goddamned hole?*

He didn't want to be a hero. But it looked as if he had no choice.

Connor switched off the flash and pocketed it, trusting to the ambient glow of lamplight to guide his steps. With his .38 in a two-hand grip he moved down the side passageway, praying he was not too late.

This was it, the final moment, climax of the ceremony, and abruptly Robert felt no more fear.

He had won. The vengeful ones, his persecutors, the Erinnyes, the Mother's Furies—they could not stop him now.

He would be released from the curse of their ugly torment at last. They had wanted blood, and now they would have it, Erica's blood in substitution for his own.

And when her hot arterial spray fountained into the chalice under the sting of his knife, then he would dip his hands in the bowl and receive absolution.

He would be cleansed—body and soul, disinfected of disease, purified of *miasma,* and there would be no fog of pollution enclosing him in its stifling cocoon.

A humming euphoria overtook him. Triumph sang in his heart. Behind the mask, he breathed one word.

"Moira."

He had spent his life in thrall to that word and to its meaning. He knew it well. He neither loved nor hated it. What *logos,* the universal order, had been to St. John—what karma was to those who dared its mysteries—this was what *moira* meant to him.

The Greeks had coined the word and the concept it named. They had seen the tight weave intertwining fate and justice, justice and death. Like Ahab, they had punched through the pasteboard mask of the obvious, and glimpsed the cosmic underlying theme.

Necessity. That was what *moira* really was. No more and no

less. The universe was bound up in a net of necessity, all existence contained within that taut, impenetrable skein.

There was no freedom ultimately. There was no choice. Fate could not be challenged. Justice could not be escaped. And death . . .

No avoiding death, either. For anyone.

Even gods surrendered to necessity. No human being could resist it. Mr. Furnell could not. Sherry Wilcott could not. Erica could not. Robert himself could not.

None of this—here, now—had been chosen. The knife and the lustral water, the barley and the grass crown, and Erica rigid on the table . . . all of it was ordained, and he had been merely wise enough to know what must be done, and to do it without complaint.

Through slits in the mask he looked down at Erica, helpless before him.

What must be, must be.

It was time.

The knife rose up, bronze blade gleaming, a polished shaft, smooth as lacquer—and reflected in its mirror shine, a man.

A blurred figure in the doorway of the cave.

Connor.

With a howl of rage and despair, Robert released Erica and turned, the huntress's revolver plucked from his waistband and coming up fast in his left hand, and he fired six times, emptying the gun.

Connor heard Robert scream and saw him turn, saw the revolver appear out of nowhere, and instantly he calculated the odds of hitting his target while missing Erica.

Not good. She was too close to Robert, and even if Connor fired with perfect accuracy, the bullet could still ricochet off bone.

And he knew only too well what a deflected bullet could do.

These thoughts lived and died in the time it took the man in the mask to finish turning and point the gun.

Muzzle flash, boom of a report, chips of limestone spraying Connor's face as he pivoted out of the doorway to hug the tunnel wall, then another shot, a third, a fourth, a fifth, a sixth, the caverns echoing with multiple detonations, miniature rock-slides launching feathery combs of grit into the air.

For a flash of time he was in his New York apartment again, caught in a firefight with Lomax and Cortez, hot rounds racing past him in the dark.

The gun was Danvers's duty weapon, had to be, the department-issue Smith .38 that Robert had taken from her in the woods. Six-round capacity, and Connor had counted six shots, so the gun must be empty now.

Move then—fast—before Robert could reload.

Connor swung into the doorway, scanning the cavern over the sights of his own Smith & Wesson, ready to shoot the bas-tard, shoot to kill—

"I wouldn't," Robert said, his voice loud enough to be audi-ble over the ringing in Connor's ears.

He stood against the far wall, holding Erica tight against him.

The gun was gone, discarded on the floor, but the knife was in his right hand, the blade testing the taut skin of Erica's throat.

Connor froze.

"Drop the weapon, Chief." Robert had swept the bull mask from his face, and it hung across his shoulder, the horns throw-ing huge distorted shadows on the wall. "Drop it, or she dies."

"Ben," Erica whispered with the faintest shake of her head, "he'll kill me anyway."

It was her face that was now a mask, immobile and expres-sionless. Only her eyes were alive, and they stared past Con-nor, past this room, their gaze focused on death.

Connor asked himself if there was any chance of dropping Robert fast enough to prevent the fatal stroke of the knife.

He knew there wasn't. A SWAT sharpshooter might pull off the direct hit to the brain that would be necessary. But he was only a patrol cop who'd spent too many years behind a desk.

He relaxed his hand and let the gun fall. It clattered on the stone floor.

Erica groaned, and behind her back she wrung her bound wrists.

"Now kick it to me," Robert said.

Connor gave the gun a gentle kick, and it skated across the floor and spun to rest midway between the two men.

Robert frowned. He'd wanted the gun closer, of course.

Connor watched his face, red with an insane fever, shiny with sweat, and he knew Robert was thinking that he could kill Erica now—sure, easy, one slash of the knife—but then there was a chance Connor would dive for the gun and reach it first.

As long as he had Erica as a shield and a hostage, he could hold Connor at bay.

Robert took a step forward, his gaze locked on Connor, the knife never wavering from the tender hollow beneath Erica's chin. Connor searched Robert's eyes, looking for a spark of reason, finding only a lightless abyss.

"It's all over," he heard himself say, and he was distantly surprised that his voice was steady, his speech lucid. "There are other officers searching these caverns. They must have heard the shots. They're on their way here right now. Even if you could get past them, the exit from the caves is guarded. And you've been ID'd. We have the Wilcott girl's blouse. We know everything. You can't get away."

The empty caverns of Robert's eyes lit up for a moment, but only with a merry glow of madness.

"Don't be so sure," he said, and his tongue swept his lips, darting like a lizard from between his yellow teeth. "These caverns are a maze. Your fellow officers won't find this room too soon. By the time they do, I'll be safely hidden. There are a thousand passageways. Other exits too. I can hide, and no one will find me. I can escape, and not be caught." He took another step. "Anyway, I'm smarter than your friends. Smarter than all of you."

This wasn't working. Robert interpreted the threat of arrest as an intellectual challenge.

"I know you're smart," Connor said, trying a new approach. "But you're scared too, aren't you?"

Robert snorted. "Of you?"

He advanced again, pulling Erica forward. Her face floated at the edge of Connor's awareness, a pale and beautiful face, but he couldn't look at her, couldn't shift his gaze from Robert's empty eyes.

One more step would bring the madman within reach of the gun, and then it would be the end.

"No," Connor said. "Not of me. You're scared all the time. Scared because part of you is still the little boy who watched his mother die."

"Ben," Erica whispered, "don't."

Connor barely heard her. His attention was fixed on the radar screen of Robert's face, scanning for any blip of a reaction. "You've never gotten over it, have you? It's *her* screams you hear at night, and it's *her* face you see when you think of the goddess you worship—"

"Shut up," Robert snapped.

His grip on the knife tightened dangerously. Connor gentled his voice.

"I'm not trying to accuse you of anything. That's what you need to understand, Robert. Listen to me." The next words came hard, and Connor's voice surrendered its steadiness to the pull of painful emotion. "I lost someone I loved once. I blamed myself for it. I still do. I think . . . I think you're doing the same thing."

Robert didn't answer, didn't move. Connor allowed himself to hope he was getting through.

"You tell yourself it's your fault," he went on, his speech sinking to a whisper. "Your guilt. It tears you up inside. I know about that. I know how it is." Hear me, he begged the man before him, hear what I'm telling you, please. "The sleepless nights, the dreams—all of it. I know."

Still no response, no expression.

"But it's not your fault, Robert. You were only a child. You don't have to take the blame."

Robert stared at him for a long moment, and then he smiled, a tight, unhappy smile of hidden meanings. "Don't I?" His gaze flicked to Erica. "Tell him, Sissy."

Erica hesitated. Her face belonged to a ghost, someone lovely and dead, and for a moment it was Karen's face as he'd seen it when he sat on the bed with her, holding her reddened hand.

Then the knife pressed closer, raising a thin line of blood, and Robert breathed, *"Tell him."*

She shut her eyes. Her voice was low and faraway, a sleep-walker's voice.

"You've got it wrong, Ben. All wrong. Keith and Lenore—they didn't kill each other. *We* killed them. We did it, the two of us, together. Robert and I."

20

Erica hadn't wanted to say it, hadn't wanted anyone to know, ever, and least of all Ben Connor.

In his face she saw bewilderment, then the dull, ugly shock of comprehension.

"You . . . ?" he whispered, the question trailing into silence.

"Yes, Ben." Her voice was hoarse and strained, a feeble rasp raising dusty echoes from the corners of the room. "We killed them both, and . . ." She couldn't say this, but she had to. "And it was me, really—I'm to blame, I'm responsible. Not Robert. It was me."

Connor didn't answer. She knew she'd betrayed him. In the last moments of their lives, she had made a mockery of his trust, his love, and she could see it in the blank astonishment in his eyes.

Then Robert released a single snort of laughter, harsh as a gunshot in the stillness.

"Oh, that's a fine *mea culpa*." His breath was hot on her ear, the knife teasing her throat. "Just lovely. But if you're so much at fault, why am I the one who's suffered?"

Turning her head, she glimpsed his profile, the hollow of his cheek, the matted filth of his beard, and she smelled the musk rising from him in nauseous waves. The fool on the hill—that was what he'd said the townspeople called him, and the knowledge twisted her heart.

"I know you suffered, Robert. I know. But . . ." She thought of the Greek wharf, the black water of the Aegean, the bottomless emptiness in her soul. "But I did too."

"Did you? Well—not enough."

He took the final step.

Connor's gun was within reach.

And she saw it, saw the future, saw exactly how it would happen.

Robert would pick up the gun, would fire, and Connor would go down in a spray of blood—

Saw it so clearly, because she'd seen it before, seen it on that night twenty-four years ago—the booming gun, the crimson splash, Robert with no expression on his face . . .

The shriek was torn out of her, breathless and wild.

"No, Robert, no, not this time, *no*!"

With a wrench of her shoulders she sprang free of his grasp, the knife nicking her chin as she jerked her head aside, Robert snarling an oath, and in desperation she launched a kick at the gun on the floor, trying to send it skidding back to Connor—

She missed.

Robert seized her.

A muscular contortion of his upper body, and he threw her down.

Hands bound, she couldn't break her fall, and she landed hard on the unforgiving limestone, all her breath expelled in a wheezing rush.

Looked up, eyes bleary, and now it was happening just as she'd feared—Robert bending, reaching for the gun.

A replay of the night at Great Hall, but worse this time, because Connor would be the victim, and Erica couldn't stop it, couldn't do anything at all.

There was one second—just one—when Robert was distracted as he shoved Erica away and stooped for the revolver.

One second when he broke eye contact with Connor.

One second, and one chance.

Connor threw himself sideways, twisting into a graceless dive, sliding under the wooden table in the center of the room.

Hand in his jacket, thrust deep into the inside pocket, and his fingers closed over Andrew's Colt .45.

He pulled out the gun, thumbed the safety off, snapped into a crouch, Robert pivoting toward him, Erica sprawled on the floor between them but lying low.

Connor aimed high and fired once.

Robert had time to see the pistol in Connor's hand, time for one startled question—*Where did that come from?*—and then he staggered, and the floor tilted, the cave liquefying in a rush of heat and strangeness.

He shook his head. Couldn't think. Unreal sensations flooded him and washed away, leaving him numb and disoriented, the way he felt when inhaling the incense that brought the spirit of Delphi's pythoness to the throne room.

Blood glazed him. Hot froth bubbled in his mouth.

Shot.

That was it. Connor had shot him.

And the revolver—the revolver he'd picked up only a moment earlier . . .

He looked for it, studying his right hand, which was empty.

He'd dropped the gun. It must be lying near him somewhere, but he had no more chance of finding it than if it lay at the bottom of an abyss.

So he'd lost after all. He would die uncleansed, his soul stained and polluted by the murder of his mother, the mother who was all mothers, the universal Mother of earth and moon and sky, the world her womb, her womb his tomb . . .

Nonsense thoughts. His mind a whirlpool, a raging blur.

But spinning in the vortex—one clear thought—one certainty.

They would have him.

In death there would be no escape. No hidey-hole for him to huddle in, no solitude, no promise of relief.

His tormentors would chase him into hell, their screams mingling finally with his own.

Or perhaps not.

Perhaps there was still a chance.

He had the knife.

Light waves bent and wavered all around him. Through a

fog of distortion he saw Erica prone at his feet, sprawled on the stone floor.

Iphigenia in the sacred grove. Andromeda atop the towering cliff.

A bound sacrifice on a rock altar. His sacrifice.

He had performed each step of the ritual properly. He need only finish it.

Finish it now.

Robert raised the knife in both hands.

And fell forward, lunging at his sister, the blade driving at her throat.

In a tight crouch under the table, holding the .45 in a two-handed grip, Connor watched Robert stagger, a red hole in his chest.

He didn't want to shoot again. Erica was too close, the risk too great.

Then Robert turned and the knife flashed, and Connor had no choice.

He fired, the pistol steady in his hands as he prayed for accuracy.

Robert plunging forward, Erica beneath him, the knife descending.

And searing agony in his neck—a second bullet—eyesight lost in a sudden fall of darkness.

He heard the dull crack of metal on stone and knew the blade had missed its target.

There was no strength in him. He slumped on something warm and living, which was Erica's body, and he tugged at the knife.

It wouldn't move. It was imbedded in the limestone floor.

Sword in the stone, he thought. Test of virtue. Who can untie the Gordian knot?

He had unraveled it. He, and he alone in the modern world, had seen past mere appearance to the essence of things.

And he saw so much more now—now, when he was dying—a kaleidoscope of images, a rush of patterns, intricate webs, dazzling in their complexity—everything interconnected—

truth revealing itself in a million metaphors, and though they were all different, they were all the same, and it was . . . beautiful . . .

A high angry whine rose within him and around him, but he didn't hear it, he was transfixed by worlds of revelation appearing and vanishing, prolific as soap bubbles, each perfect and self-contained, yet combining with others in an endless chain.

The whine became voices, keening and triumphant.

Their voices.

No.

He strained for the insights he'd been granted, clutching at his visions of truth, but they fell away and were gone, and only the voices remained.

Louder now.

Close.

"Go away," he muttered. "Leave me alone . . ."

Screeching voices.

Watch him, sisters, watch him wriggle, a snake with a broken back.

Struggling for life and failing, and soon he'll be ours.

Ours for vengeance and retribution.

An eternity of reprisals, payment for his mother's blood.

An offense against all mothers, against the Mother who is all.

Did the poor worm think she would ever consent to leave him unpunished?

He thinks he's suffered, but a thousand years of pain will not be suffering enough.

Agony forever, our claws in him, our wicked fangs.

And our screaming voices—hear them, wretch—hear them now and for all time . . .

He heard them. He heard nothing else.

And sometimes they sounded like his mother Lenore, when she would snap at him in a drunken rage. And sometimes like Sherry Wilcott, calling him a freak and a thing of shame as she ran from the pond where his father had drowned. And sometimes like the boys at boarding school, who thought he was a coward because he would not fight—a coward, because he alone, of them all, knew what real violence was, and feared it.

But in the end the voices were none of those things.

They were only the Furies, the Great Mother's bloody body-guard, descending in a hectic, shrieking swarm to capture their long-sought prize.

Connor scrambled out from beneath the table and lurched upright, his ears ringing from the two shots, bands of chalky dust weaving through stripes of lamplight.

Walking was difficult. He must have hurt something in his dive to the floor, pulled a muscle, strained his back. But it didn't matter.

Nothing mattered except Karen—not Karen—Erica.

It was Erica now. Erica, who had to be alive, though she wasn't moving or speaking.

The second bullet could have ricocheted off bone. Could have . . .

But it would be too unfair. There couldn't be so much injustice in the world, so much needless pain and loss.

He clung to this faith as he staggered forward, limping, the gun in his hand.

They lay together, Robert and Erica, their two bodies entwined and motionless before a limestone gour in the shape of a giant throne.

And on the floor there was blood, a spreading lake of red.

Robert's blood. Or was it Erica's also?

Karen flashed at him, bloodied, and he felt again her warm lifeless hand . . .

Then Connor reached the spot where they lay, and he looked down.

Relief and fear hit him together as a single shock.

Erica's eyes were shut, her face twisted by pain.

She was alive—but in agony.

Wincing, he knelt beside her. "Are you hit? Erica, *are you hit?*"

Her eyes opened, and he saw a sparkle of tears.

"No, Ben. I'm not hurt. Not that way."

All the color had left her face. She might have been a bust of polished marble, if not for the bright, brittle light in her eyes. He thought he'd never noticed just how beautiful she was— more beautiful than Karen, though it felt like heresy to think it.

Then she shifted her position, and Robert, slumped across her, groaned suddenly, his hands brushing feebly at something that was not there.

"He's dying," Erica said, not asking a question.

Connor looked at Robert. The second bullet had punched through his neck, inflicting mortal damage. The dense mat of his beard was stained deep red, and a dull cast of blueness was overshadowing his face. His eyes were shut; the lids twitched as if with dreams.

Slowly Connor nodded.

Erica turned on her side, showing her hands, bound with a scarf. Her red scarf.

"Cut me loose," she whispered.

Connor searched his pockets before remembering the bronze knife imbedded in the floor. With a grunt of effort, he wrenched the blade free and sliced the scarf.

In the circle of her arms, Erica hugged her brother, holding him close to her chest.

"It's all right, Robert. It's all right now."

She spoke to him as if he were a child frightened by a nightmare.

Robert whimpered, his eyes still closed, his lips pursed in a pouting line.

"All right now, everything's all right."

Low under his breath Robert murmured: "They'll *get* me . . ."

"No, they won't. I'm here. I'll look out for you. I'll always look out for you." Weeping, rocking him in her embrace, her voice a gentle whisper. "I won't let them get you, I swear I won't."

Abruptly Robert lifted his head, eyes open and huge, and in his directionless gaze Connor saw pure terror, and he knew that whatever Robert heard at night, whatever made him stuff his ears with wax and hide in solitude, was visiting him now, for the last time.

"They won't get you," Erica said, but Robert didn't hear.

His mouth widened in a silent scream. A shudder racked him.

Then slowly he lowered his head to Erica's bosom and expelled a final, rasping breath, and he was gone.

Erica held him for a long moment, then reached out and clasped Connor's hand.

He sat on the cold stone floor, his fingers laced in hers, and neither of them moved or spoke until Maginnis and Woodall arrived with guns drawn, too late.

21

Black water.

Its depths beckoned. Mysterious darkness. Cold silence.

A single step, a plunge, a frigid shock of immersion chasing consciousness away, and after that, nothing more.

Escape from pain, from grief, from guilt.

A single step.

Erica stood at the scenic lookout at Barrow Falls, her head lowered, gazing down the steep foaming cascade toward the creek two hundred feet below.

She found it odd, how little had changed in eighteen years. As a teenager she'd stood on the wharf of an Aegean fishing village, contemplating death in dark water. Now here she was again, facing the same swirl of foam, thinking the same cold thoughts, and only the external circumstances had changed.

It had been past midnight then; it was late afternoon now. Instead of a warm Mediterranean summer, there was Pennsylvania's winter landscape, crisp in the pale light. On the wharf she had been naked, and here she was tucked in a heavy coat, protection against the chill gusts shaking the trees.

And last time, most important, she had been young, still a girl. Now her youth was gone, and with it the naive hope that she could outrun the past and leave it forever behind her.

Black water. A single step.

She wouldn't take that step, of course. She had fought too hard for life to surrender it. Her hands were still creased with pencil-thin scars from the cuts and abrasions suffered in her climb up the sinkhole. There was another small scar, not more than a dimple of puckered flesh, on her neck where Robert's knife had nicked her. Bruises tattooed her legs and arms, and the dark crescents under her eyes had yet to fade.

Battle scars. Reminders of all the pain she'd endured, just for the chance to stand in sunlight and watch the flow of water over stone.

No, she would not die. But at times she wished she could. Because what she had fought for was more than mere survival. She'd fought for a chance at intimacy with the only man she had ever loved.

And now he knew the worst part of her past, the one secret she'd hoped never to share, and she didn't think he would want her, or could even face her again.

So she would go on alone. It was hard, but she could bear it. But without him, without anyone, her life would be as cold as the winter air, as desolate as the denuded woods.

And the meaning of her life? Its purpose?

She didn't know. On the wharf, Persephone had saved her. At least she liked to think so. But now . . .

There was no Persephone here. Was there?

Erica glanced over her shoulder, feeling foolish as she looked almost superstitiously for a gleam of bronze.

She saw it.

Not a statue. A badge.

Ben Connor stood watching her from the edge of the woods.

Surprise jostled a gasp out of her, and involuntarily she stepped away from the precipice. "Ben—you startled me."

"Sorry. I should have said something. But I didn't want to disturb you."

He came forward along the path that led through the forest from the road. She noticed he was still limping slightly, his left leg hampered by a strained hamstring that would require weeks to heal.

"I stopped by Great Hall," he said as he reached her. "Marie told me you might have come here."

He stood at her side, and for a moment they said nothing further, just watched the plummeting water as it surged over the limestone cliff and burst into rainbows of spray on descending tiers of rock.

She hadn't seen him in the week since Robert's death. He had not been present when she gave her statement to detectives from the sheriff's department. He had not visited her at home.

He'd been avoiding her, and she knew why, of course. And why he was here now.

There were so many ways to begin. But all she said was, "How are things?"

He didn't look at her. "Paul Elder's up and around. Arm's in a sling, but he'll be fine. He made me sign the cast."

"What about Vicki Danvers?" Erica had visited her several times at the medical center. "Is she out of the hospital yet?"

"Going home tomorrow. Her mom will stay with her. Used to be an Army nurse, apparently."

"Vicki told me there'd be a long rehabilitation period."

"Doctors say six months. But she'll be all right, in time. She may have to live with some lingering numbness, but she'll have full mobility."

Erica lowered her head. "Thank God."

The unspoken topic hovered between them. Still she refused to acknowledge it.

"They denied Andrew bail," she said after a moment.

"I know."

"I would have posted it for him. Any amount."

"The judge thought he was a flight risk."

Erica didn't respond. Of course Andrew was a flight risk. Given any opportunity, he would run from trouble. He had never been brave, never in his life . . . except once. For her sake.

"At the trial," she said, "I want to testify on his behalf. Will that help, do you think?"

"Sure it will."

"How about you?" She allowed herself to slide closer to the forbidden subject that had brought him here. "How are you doing?"

His shoulders lifted. "Still employed."

On the day after the nightmare in the caves, Connor had submitted his resignation to the town council. No one had requested that he do it. The gesture was prompted only by his feeling that he'd shown poor judgment in his handling of the case. His sole comment had been: *I made mistakes.*

The council had rejected his resignation. Lieutenant Maginnis had spoken in Connor's defense; perhaps it was her statement that had saved him. More likely, Paul Elder had engaged in a few discussions behind the scenes.

"I know you are," Erica said. "And I'm glad."

"Not sure I am."

"Nobody blames you, Ben. Vicki got hurt doing her job. And that young man, the one at the gas station—he was in the wrong place at the wrong time."

"It was fate, you mean?"

"Maybe. Maybe it was."

He shook his head. "If I'd held Robert for questioning . . ."

"Then why didn't you?"

"I thought . . . if I left him free to roam . . . he might lead us to you."

"And he did."

Reluctantly he accepted this. "I guess that's right. But at a price."

"Everything has a price," Erica said, her voice so low it was all but swallowed by the falls, roaring like surf.

The wind kicked up, colder as the sun westered, bare branches rattling in the dusky woods.

She was sure it would come now, the inevitable question, and the answer she dreaded.

Instead he said, "It was the Furies, wasn't it?"

For a moment she couldn't respond. She had told no one what Robert thought he heard. She had left that part of the story out of her official statement.

"How did you know?" she asked softly.

"I've had some talks with Officer Woodall." A shrug. "He's sort of our resident scholar. You met him . . . that night."

"I remember. Nice young man."

"Vicki seems to think so too. He's been spending a lot of time with her." A play smiled at the corners of Connor's mouth, then faded. "Anyway, Woodall told me an interesting story. From mythology. The Greeks."

Connor still didn't look at her. He stared down into the beating violence of the water on the rocks.

"It seems there was this king," he went on quietly. "His name was Agamemnon. He was powerful and rich. He thought no one could challenge his reign. But what he didn't know was that his wife had taken a lover. And together they conspired to kill him. They drowned him in a bath."

This was another thing she hadn't expected him to know. A chill caressed her, and she shivered inside her coat.

"They got his throne, his palace, his treasure. They got everything. They might have ruled the kingdom for a lifetime. Except for one thing."

She waited, watching his face in profile against the dying sun.

"The children," he said. "Brother and sister. They knew what had happened to their father. And they wanted revenge."

Connor turned to her at last, his gaze cool and alert.

"Have you heard this story?" he asked.

She stared at him for a long moment. Then she took Connor's hand, squeezed it, felt the rhythm of a pulse in her fingertips pressed to his palm—whether her heartbeat or his, she didn't know.

"I've read it," she said. "Robert and I—we used to read to each other all the time. The library at Great Hall is full of books. Classics, old, musty—ancient history, mythology, drama. We would take a book and hide out in the caves, reading aloud. If it was a play, we'd act it out. Talk loudly, hear the echoes."

"Hide out—why?"

"Because we didn't want them finding us—Lenore and Keith. That's all she was to us after our father died. Just Lenore. Not our mother. She had no time for us, no interest. We'd been a burden our father had expected her to carry, and now that he was gone— an unwelcome burden. She hated us. And we . . . we hated her."

Connor said nothing, his silence inviting her to continue, to tell the story at her own pace, in her own way.

"She was drunk all the time," Erica said. "She talked too much and too loudly. Keith told her to be quiet, but she wouldn't listen. She never listened to him. He was nothing to her, just a tool she'd needed. Needed . . . You know why."

He watched the foaming descent, his face impassive as a priest's in a confessional. "Tell me."

"Because they killed our father, of course. They killed Duncan Garrison. Drowned him—not in a bath—in a lake."

"And you knew."

"I told you, she talked too much. Revealed too much. Though we were only children, we understood. I did, anyway. Robert was too young, only nine. I was twelve, and I heard her mock our father's memory and laugh about the breakfast she'd served him on his last morning . . . and I knew."

The wind stirred, cold eddies swirling under the hem of her coat. She shivered.

"But what could I do? The police wouldn't believe me. I was sure of that. No one takes a kid seriously. And all the while the day was coming—the day I feared more than anything—the day Keith would marry her, and he would replace our father, officially and legally and forever. He would get away with it. They both would. They would have won, then, won everything they wanted—and there was nothing I could do."

"Except there was," Connor said gently. "There was one thing. The only thing."

"Yes."

"Tell me, Erica."

She swallowed a draft of frigid air, and the wind bit harder, launching flurries of dead leaves.

"First, you need to know that it was all my idea. My plan. I thought of it. I'm responsible. Regardless of what Robert may have thought or felt—it was entirely my fault."

Connor waited.

"I'd found a gun. It was in the storage shed, where the lanterns were kept—the ones we used to light the caves. A gun and bullets, boxes of them. Keith and Lenore probably didn't even know it was there. And I thought . . . I thought all it would take to be rid of them forever . . . to avenge our father . . . all it would take . . ."

Tears blurred her sight. She tightened her grip on Connor's hand.

"All it would take was for me to shoot them both and make it look like they'd shot each other. They fought all the time. It wouldn't be so hard to believe they'd turned violent. I thought I could do it—but for the plan to work, Robert had to vouch for me. Had to back up my story to the police when the time came."

"You said he didn't know the truth about your father."

"He didn't. I had to tell him. More than tell him—I had to make him see and believe. He was smart, of course. Brilliant, even, and so grave and serious, but he didn't think in concrete terms, practical terms. Even at that age, nine years old, he saw things as images, metaphors . . ."

"Myths."

"Myths. Like the ones we read, the ancient plays we acted out. The story Woodall told you—it was one of those plays, almost the oldest, as old as the Parthenon. Aeschylus wrote it, but the story goes back long before him. The story of Orestes and Electra, avenging Agamemnon, their father. That's how I explained it. That's how I got him to understand. Duncan was Agamemnon, murdered by Clytemnestra and her lover Aegisthus, you see. And I was Electra, of course, and Robert . . . Robert was Orestes. We had played the roles before. Only, this time we would act them out in real life . . ."

In real life. A rush of shame enveloped her, and for a moment she just stood there trembling until she was ready to go on.

"I practiced firing the gun in the woods every day that summer. Finally I thought I was ready. And one night in September, when the housekeeper was out and Robert and I were in our p.j.'s, I took the gun from my closet and I went down the staircase to the ground floor."

Eyes shut, she saw it again, her hand on the bannister, her bare feet on the cold steps, and before her the sweep of the main hall, the hearth blazing and the windows shut against the autumn chill, and from the library, raised voices—another argument, Lenore slurring her words and coughing up laughter, toasting Duncan's memory, and Keith wearily saying he was sick of her, sick to death.

So leave me then, Lenore said with a bitter chuckle.

You know I can't. I didn't get involved in this to walk away empty-handed.

Maybe I want you to go.

I don't give a damn what you want. You're stuck with me, you bitch. God help us, we're stuck with each other.

Till death do us part, Lenore said, and there was a gurgle of pouring liquid and a musical splash.

Erica crossed the living room, her toes sinking into the deep carpet, the gun heavy, so heavy, in her hands.

Near the door to the library she waited, trying to breathe, drawing no air into her lungs.

She'd been sure she could do this. She had rehearsed it in her mind a million times. But the act itself, the reality of it, was so much larger and more overwhelming than any fantasy.

To enter the room—to raise the gun and shoot—and the chaos of blood and screams—

"I couldn't go through with it," she whispered now, her voice all but lost in the crash of Barrow Falls. "I just stood there, out of sight, and I tried to make myself do it, but . . ." She shook free of the memory. "I decided we would go to the police after all. Maybe if Robert and I went together, they would listen."

Connor nodded. "Paul Elder would have."

"I think so. But back then, I didn't know him. It seemed like such a risk—but not as bad a risk as doing what I'd planned to do. So I started to back away . . . and Lenore saw me."

She'd come out of the library, an empty glass in her hand, heading for the liquor cabinet in the dining room, then had frozen, staring down at her twelve-year-old daughter.

The revolver was in plain view. Lenore saw it and knew everything.

Her lip curled. *You little bitch.*

She showed no fear, only a gigantic wrath, regal and dizzying, and Erica backed away, forgetting the gun she held and how to use it, feeling suddenly defenseless.

Bitch! Lenore screamed, and hurled the glass at her.

Erica stumbled backward, tripped, fell on the floor and dropped the gun, then lay there, staring up at her mother, huge as a nightmare, her mother advancing in a rage, face red with alcohol and anger, and abruptly Erica was sure her mother would seize the gun and use it.

With surreal clarity she thought: I'm going to die.

"She would have killed me," Erica said. "Literally killed me, I know she would. But she never got the chance. Robert saved me. Robert saved my life."

He'd been listening on the staircase, huddled behind the bannister, and when he saw things go wrong, he descended in a rush, and before Lenore could react, he grabbed the gun—snatched it off the floor and lifted it in his two hands—no time to aim or think, just a squeeze of the trigger, a crash of sound, waves of percussive shock vibrating in the room—

"He shot her," Erica said. "He looked very calm. He just pulled the trigger, and there was blood, arterial spray. It splashed him. He didn't seem to notice."

But Erica had noticed, Erica who lay frozen in terror as she stared at the gash in Lenore's chest, the spurting wound, and then she heard her mother's scream—an animal wail torn from her throat—a sound from a nightmare, and the seed of nightmares to come.

And somewhere a voice, her own voice, whimpering in childish futility, *No, Robert, don't, it's wrong, please don't.*

Too late, of course. Much too late.

"Then Keith was there," she whispered. "He'd left the library, and he saw Lenore go down on her knees, saw Robert turn and point the gun at him. He ran."

Her heart was beating fast and loud, and in her ears it sounded like the hammer blows of Keith Wyatt's footfalls pounding through the kitchen in desperate flight.

If he'd gone out the back way, he might have made it, and everything afterward would have been different. But . . .

"He panicked and charged the front door, and Robert shot him on the threshold of the foyer. Shot him dead at point-blank range."

She could still see him, a small boy in Superman pajamas, the gun huge in his hands, and no expression on his face, nothing in his eyes, only a terrible blankness, the dead calm of a void.

He turned to her, and she thought he might kill her also, might kill and go on killing until there was nothing left.

But he only frowned. *You lost your nerve,* he said. *You didn't want to get all bloody, did you?*

He dropped the gun, held out his hands splashed with gore. *All bloody like me,* he said.

I'm sorry, she whispered, knowing she had failed him somehow, failed them both. *Robert . . . I'm sorry.*

He didn't answer. She wasn't sure he heard. He just stood there, swaying slowly, eyes unblinking, a boy bathed in blood.

"Robert went into shock," Erica said. "I had to . . . finish things. Cover up for us. On my own I managed to drag Lenore to where Keith lay. I draped her over him, put the gun in her hand. By that time, Robert was gone. I found him in an upstairs closet, shivering, and I hugged him, and we both stayed there for what seemed like hours."

The police found them, and she told the story she'd invented. Robert never vouched for it, never spoke of it at all.

"And no one ever suspected," she said in a hushed voice, and smiled. "How could they? We were children." The smile faded, leaving her empty and tired. "Children don't do such things."

She stared at the white water on the mountainside, the falls bursting into sparkles of spray. She thought how clean the water looked, how pure. She had not felt that clean in years.

"So," she whispered finally, "what happens now?"

"What do you mean?"

"Well—do you arrest me?" She heard a lilt of hysteria in her voice. "After all, I was an accessory to murder. I covered up two homicides. There's no statute of limitations on a thing like that, is there? Is there?"

"Don't be ridiculous."

"No, really. Maybe you should. Maybe it would be for the best. I told you, it was my fault—what happened that night, and everything since. I put the idea in Robert's head. I made him Orestes. Only, I never thought he'd play the part so well. Never thought he'd hear the Furies, as Orestes did. Never thought they'd drive him mad, like Orestes, or that . . . that he would . . ."

She couldn't say it, even now.

"Until I heard about the Wilcott girl. That's when I suspected. I knew Robert had never gotten over the trauma of that night . . . the trauma, and the guilt. He felt dirty, polluted by sin—the worst sin of all, matricide. A sin that, in the old myths, can be wiped clean only by ritual sacrifice. Blood for blood. Innocent blood . . . I ought to pay for that, shouldn't I? I ought to pay."

"I think you have," Connor said, his voice as low as hers.

"Not enough."

"I'm not going to arrest you, Erica."

She nodded and kept on nodding, as if she couldn't stop. "All right. Then we'll just say goodbye. I don't want to be in Barrow after this. Rome . . . I might go back to Rome. I had some good years there, at the university—"

"You're not leaving for Rome or anywhere else. This is where you belong. Here, with me."

The words were so unexpected, she needed a moment just to make them real.

"With you?" she breathed. "Even . . . now? Even when you know what I did?"

Distantly it occurred to her that she'd conserved her secret for so long, she had lost the ability to imagine that anyone could ever understand it or forgive.

"You were a child," Connor said gently. "You took on too big a burden, and it overwhelmed you. It's time to stop hating yourself for that. Your brother—he never stopped. You can."

Erica looked at him, and in his face she saw compassion and a sadness that seemed old, somehow, and strangely wise.

"It's gone on too long," he told her. "There's been enough punishment, enough pain. Let it end now. Let it end."

"You're sure?" She heard the tremor in her voice, the suppressed tears. "I mean, I know you, Ben. You don't believe in cutting corners. You always play by the rules. Always."

Connor smiled. "Sometimes the rules don't apply."

She sagged against him, relief draining her last strength. He hugged her, and she held him in her arms and thought of a small boy she'd hugged this way on a night of death so many years ago.

The wind whipped up, fiercer than before. On the horizon the sun was ashes, the western sky a fading memory of light.

"We'd better get going," Connor said. "It'll be dark soon."

Erica thought of the caves, the wharf, the winding course of her life. "I'm used to being in the dark," she whispered.

"Not anymore."

They went up the path, Connor limping, Erica with head bowed, the two of them huddled close together against the chill twilight and all the howling fury of the wind.